THE UNSEEN

IRINA SHAPIRO

Storm
PUBLISHING

Ebook ISBN: 978-1-83700-238-2
Paperback ISBN: 978-1-83700-239-9

Cover design: Debbie Clement
Cover images: Shutterstock

Published by Storm Publishing.
For further information, visit:
www.stormpublishing.co

AUTHOR'S NOTE

In this installment of the *Echoes from the Past* series, you will meet several new characters, most of whom are Russian. Unlike in English, in the Russian language, surnames change based on the person's gender. For instance, the Tsar would be called Nikolai Romanov, whereas his wife would be referred to as Alexandra Romanova. Their collective children would be Romanovi. The first names change as well, based on the relationship between the characters. There are formal names, followed by the father's name (meaning *son/daughter of*), and there are familiar names, which can be numerous for each name. Below is a list of the most common variations of the characters' names, which will make the conversations and relationships easier to follow.

Valentina Kalinina—Valya, Valenka
Tatiana Kalinina –Tanya
Nikolai Kalinin—Kolya
Ivan Kalinin—Vanya
Elena Kalinina—Lena, Lenochka
Dmitri Ostrov—Dima
Alexei Petrov—Alyosha
Svetlana Petrova—Sveta
Stanislav Bistritzky—Slava

Michael Ostrov—Misha

I'd also like to point out that St. Petersburg, where my story takes place, changed names several times during the twentieth century. The original name, Sankt-Peterburg, was changed to Petrograd in 1914. In 1924, it was renamed Leningrad, and then, in 1991, the city became St. Petersburg, a name which is still in use today.

PROLOGUE

Silence settled over the house like a downy blanket over a sleeping child. Everyone within was warm and snug—even the body submerged in the tub, its skin still flushed from the heat of the bathwater. Wide-open eyes stared from beneath the soapy water in an expression of shock and disbelief.

A woman sat on the bathroom floor, sure if she managed to get up and dared to look at herself, her expression would mirror that of the corpse. Shock and disbelief. Shock at what she'd done. Disbelief at the chain of events that had led her to this moment, this inevitable act of savagery. How was it possible to fall so far so quickly?

Within the coming weeks she would find out if she'd swing for her crime or be granted a reprieve in the form of a life of constant fear. She'd always be looking over her shoulder, wondering if someone would come to take her away and make her answer for what she'd done. But even if no one came and she never felt the rough hemp of the rope against the tender skin of her neck, life would never be the same. She knew what she'd done, and she'd have to live with it always, praying that her true nature would remain unseen.

ONE

DECEMBER 2014

London, England

The day dawned gray and cold, a miserable drizzle coating everything in a slick film of moisture. By the time Quinn left the flat, a steady rain was coming down, the kind that tended to last for hours. She stopped beneath the awning of the building, gave a cursory glance to her shoes, which would be soaked in minutes, and made an executive decision to take a taxi. It'd cost a bomb in this weather, since the journey would take twice as long, but it was a legitimate business expense, so she wouldn't worry about it. It took a few minutes to actually flag down an unoccupied taxi but was well worth the effort, since she got to stay warm and dry while the taxi crept toward its destination inch by inch. Quinn fished her mobile out of her handbag and dialed Jill. Her cousin had left several messages, but Quinn hadn't had a chance to ring her back. Judging by the amount of traffic, they'd have time for a proper conversation.

Jill answered on the second ring. "Hey, Quinny. What are you up to on this dreary morning?"

"Actually, I'm on my way to examine human remains. You?" Quinn could almost hear Jill smiling on the other end.

"Only you can make that sound like a treat. I'm marking down merchandise for the Pre-Christmas Sale I'm planning to start next week. After Christmas, it will be labeled a Going-Out-Of-Business Sale."

"So, this is it?" Quinn asked. Jill had decided to close down her clothing shop in Soho and return to a career in forensic accounting. Her shop had never been a success, but for the last few months, the business had been in the red, which for an accountant was tantamount to death.

"Yes, I've decided. I gave it my all, Quinn, but it simply didn't work out as I'd hoped. To be honest, I'm sort of looking forward to working for someone else again. It'll be nice to go to bed at night and not worry myself sick about my overhead, cost of stock, and lack of sales. There's something to be said for being an employee. Stop by the shop when you have a chance. I have some items I've set aside for you. I think you'll like them."

"Oh, thank you, Jill. I'll be sure to stop in. I could use some new clothes since I still haven't lost all the baby weight."

"You look amazing," Jill said. "How's my favorite baby?"

"Alex is wonderful. He's beginning to sleep through the night, which is a blessing since I don't think I can take many more sleepless nights. By the time he's finished nursing, I'm wide awake and can't get back to sleep. And sometimes he wakes Emma. She's a very light sleeper."

"You need a bigger place."

"We've started looking for a house now that Seth has gone home," Quinn replied. She'd met her biological father only seven months ago, and the road to a father-daughter relationship had not been a smooth one, given what had happened when Quinn visited New Orleans last spring. It would take time for them to find their footing, but they were well on their way, especially after Seth's visit.

"How was his visit?"

"It was great, actually. I was a little worried about having him here for ten days, but the time just flew by. He loved spending time with Alex, and he was very attentive and kind to Emma. He brought her an American Girl doll with several changes of clothes. Emma is in heaven. That doll goes with her everywhere. She's even neglected Mr. Rabbit, who's been a hands-down favorite since she was a baby."

"Well, she is growing up. That doll is more age-appropriate. Did Seth's and Sylvia's paths ever cross?"

Quinn winced at the mention of her mother. Their relationship was complicated at best, disastrous at worst. Having abandoned Quinn at birth, Sylvia had only come into Quinn's life a year ago, and had done nothing but wreak havoc since. Quinn had done her best to make allowances and try to be understanding of the woman who'd walked away from her without a backward glance, not even bothering to go through the proper adoption channels, but then more revelations had rocked their already fragile bond. Quinn had discovered that Sylvia had given birth to twins that day and had left Quinn's sister, Quentin, at a hospital, since the infant had difficulty breathing. Sylvia had never gone back, so she'd had no inkling of what became of either of her daughters—an outcome she'd been satisfied with until she found Quinn, quite by chance, just over a year ago.

"Thankfully, no. Sylvia rang when Alex was born, and she came to Emma's birthday party, but we haven't properly spoken since I confronted her about Quentin. To tell you the truth, being with Seth is a lot easier than spending time with Sylvia. He says what he means and means what he says, something you could never accuse Sylvia of. I don't think she ever allows anything to leave her mouth without first considering if she can disclaim it later."

"Have you completely given up on the idea of having a relationship with her?" Jill asked. Jill, of all people, knew what it meant to Quinn to have finally found her birth mother after decades of wondering where she'd come from and why she had been abandoned.

"I don't know, Jilly. I don't think I want to cut ties with her forever, but I need some time to adjust my expectations and figure out what I hope to gain from my relationship with her. Sylvia will never be the mother I want, so I have to decide whether I can live with the mother she is."

"And Seth?"

"I miss him now that he's gone back to the States. It was fun having him here. He made us an American Thanksgiving. It was lovely. Perhaps next year we can have Thanksgiving in New Orleans, with him and Kathy. I think they might be cohabitating again by then."

"Losing a child either tears people apart or brings them together. How is Brett?"

"Brett is still serving his sentence and Seth visits him in prison once a week. We didn't talk about him much, but Seth has made peace with the situation. He brought me a letter from Brett."

"Did you read it?"

"No, I couldn't bring myself to. Regardless of what it says, Brett intended to kill me and my baby. Even if he's remorseful, I could never forgive him for leaving me to die in that tomb in New Orleans. Perhaps I'll read the letter someday, when I'm ready."

"I don't blame you. I probably wouldn't read it either."

"Well, looks like I'm almost there."

"Are you meeting Rhys?" Jill asked, referring to Rhys Morgan, producer of the BBC series *Echoes from the Past*.

"Yes, Rhys is already on-site with a camera crew. He's practically crowing with delight at this new find."

"I can't picture Rhys Morgan crowing about anything," Jill said. "He's always so intimidating."

"Hardly. Rhys does have a softer side, and now that his girl-friend is expecting, he's fuzzier than ever. Being around him is almost a joy." Quinn laughed.

She had liked Rhys since the day they met. He was a consummate professional and a master of his trade, and now, a year on, a good friend, despite the fact that she'd once suspected him of being her biological father. These days, Rhys was like a cuddly teddy bear, coddling his pregnant girlfriend and baking treats she refused to eat for fear of gaining too much weight. He was genuinely happy, and Quinn was happy for him, especially since he was no longer seeing Sylvia. That situation had been rife with complications, and given Quinn's professional relationship with Rhys and her toxic personal relationship with Sylvia, it was for the best that those two had parted ways. Sylvia was still seething with anger, believing Quinn had had a hand in Rhys's change of heart, but Quinn was innocent of any interference.

Rhys had decided to break things off with Sylvia all on his own, finally realizing their relationship was based on nothing more than guilt over past events on his side and loneliness on Sylvia's end. Rhys had shared with Quinn, swearing her to secrecy first, that he intended to propose to Haley after the baby was born. He had no wish to overwhelm her with the prospect of planning a wedding when she should be focusing on her fast-approaching motherhood.

"Have you had any news of your sister?" Jill asked. It was a sore subject, but Quinn didn't mind discussing it with Jill. Jill was the closest thing she'd ever had to a sister, and that would never change, even if Quinn finally found her long-lost twin.

"No, nothing. I rang her solicitor several times, and he assured me he sent my letter on to Quentin but has heard nothing back. Seth and I discussed it at length while he was here, and he believes we need to start searching for Quentin on our own. He's not here to do it in person, but he's offered to finance whatever steps I wish to take."

"Actually, Brian has an idea he'd like to discuss with you."

"Really? I can't wait to hear it. Oh, Jill, I've arrived. Give my love to Brian. We'd like to have you over for dinner soon."

"Great. Let's put something on the calendar."

Quinn paid the driver and climbed out of the taxi. She'd loved being at home with Alex these past few months, but it was nice to be back at work. She tingled with anticipation at the prospect of examining the remains.

TWO

Rhys opened the door before Quinn had a chance to ring the doorbell. "What time do you call this?" he bristled as he stepped aside to allow her to come in out of the rain.

"Sorry, but there was a lot of traffic."

"Come in. Melissa and Paul are expecting you."

Rhys led the way into the front room, which looked like something from a museum. Life might have gone on outside the walls of this house, but the parlor looked frozen in time at the turn of the last century. It wasn't just the old-fashioned furniture and heavy velvet window hangings, but the lack of anything modern, like a television, a telephone, or a stereo system. The décor predated the First World War, but was still in remarkably good condition. Several lamps were lit against the gloom of the rainy morning, and Quinn almost expected them to be fed by gas rather than electricity.

A couple in their forties sat on a butter-yellow settee, a porcelain tea service in front of them. The woman jumped to her feet and came forward to greet Quinn. She was dressed in jeans and a dusky purple knit top, and her short dark hair had streaks of blue and pink. Her husband, whose light brown hair brushed his shoulders, wore paint-splattered trousers and a stretched-out Led

Zeppelin T-shirt. The couple looked grossly out of place in this Edwardian parlor, which seemed to be the centerpiece of their home.

"Dr. Allenby, it's a pleasure to meet you. We've seen you on television. Haven't we, Paul?" Melissa asked, eager to bring her husband into the conversation. "I do love archeology. The episode about 'the Lovers' nearly tore my heart out. What a gruesome end. I do wonder what happened to their little boy, but I suppose we'll never know. Will we?" she prattled on as she motioned for Quinn to take a seat on the settee facing the one where Paul Glover sat in amused silence. "And that duplicitous priest," she exclaimed, referring to the second episode of *Echoes from the Past* that had just aired the previous week. "I never knew much about Dunwich, but now I want to go see it for myself. 'The Atlantis of Britain.' Such a romantic name for such a tragic place."

"Thank you, Mrs. Glover. I'm so glad you're enjoying the program." *Maybe they have a TV in the bedroom*, Quinn thought as she took a seat on the uncomfortable settee. Rhys wisely remained standing, his hands clasped behind his back as he stared out over the rain-soaked street.

"Please, call me Melissa. Can I offer you a cup of tea? Mr. Morgan, will you have a cup?"

"Thank you," Rhys replied and came to join Quinn on the settee, his brows knitted with impatience. If Quinn knew Rhys, he was eager to get started and had no desire to spend a quarter of an hour on idle chitchat, but he graciously took a seat and smiled pleasantly at Melissa.

Quinn accepted a cup of steaming tea and took a restorative sip. The tea was good, and it was nice to be out of the biting cold and rain. Besides, before examining the site, she wanted to hear the story of how Melissa and Paul had come to find the remains. The details were often as important as the find itself.

Melissa poured a cup for herself last, like a proper Edwardian hostess, then leaned back, ready to tell her tale. "You are probably wondering what Paul and I are doing in this old relic," she began.

"Well, yes," Quinn admitted with a smile. "It doesn't seem to suit your image."

"We had a flat in London but moved to Dorset five years ago. We love it there. Don't we, Paul?"

"We do. The light is perfect in the mornings," he added, confirming Quinn's suspicion that he might be an artist.

"I inherited this house when my uncle died three months ago. Prostate cancer. He went rather quickly, poor dear, but he said he preferred it that way. Didn't want to linger and cause any more suffering than was strictly necessary. Uncle Michael was very unassuming."

"Did he live here?" Quinn asked. The house was not one an unassuming man would choose to live in.

"Lord, no," Melissa exclaimed. "He inherited it from my grandmother on her death in 1977, but he never lived here. He was a musician, a violinist. He toured nine months out of the year with the orchestra, and when he returned to London, he stayed at his girlfriend's flat. She is a cellist, and they had been together for three decades but never made it legal. Too Bohemian for such nonsense, he liked to say. Anyway, he never liked this place and rarely set foot in it. He never did anything to modernize it. He never had any children of his own, so I, being his only niece, inherited the lot." She looked toward the window, her eyes sparkling with unshed tears. "He was a lovely man, Uncle Michael. I miss him."

"I'm very sorry for your loss," Quinn said softly.

Melissa nodded and went on. "Once Paul and I took possession of the house, we agreed that we'd use some of the money my uncle left to completely revamp the place. Modern, light, and minimalist. That's what we like. And we were going to make a studio for Paul—he's an artist—and a study for me. I'm a graphic designer. I have my own firm but work from home. It would be convenient for us to have a London base again, although we're not at all sure we're ready to leave Dorset."

Darren, a cameraman who worked on the program, appeared

in the doorway. He must have been filming upstairs. It was just like Rhys not to waste time. Darren positioned himself in such a way that he could film both Quinn and Melissa without any difficulty. The interview would be made to look like an informal chat. Paul excused himself and moved away, leaving Melissa alone on the settee.

"How did you come to find the remains, Melissa?" Quinn asked, putting on her professional persona.

"We brought in an architect to remodel the house, since we planned to do considerably more than give the walls a lick of paint and buy new appliances. We intended to knock down walls and combine some of the rooms. Anyway, I digress," Melissa said with an impish smile. "This project is something of a dream come true for me."

"I would enjoy a project like that as well," Quinn replied, wishing she had her own house to remodel, or at least decorate.

"When Grady—that's the architect—looked at the blueprints we found in the library, he pointed out that the measurements of one of the bedrooms didn't match the original scale. It seemed there should have been a dressing room or a bathroom attached to the bedroom, but the wall was smooth, and there was no doorway where one should have been. Grady found it, of course. The door had been cut directly into the wall and was operated by a spring mechanism, so there was no doorframe or a handle. The panel had been blocked by a heavy wardrobe. Once he and Paul moved the wardrobe, the panel was easy enough to open. And that's when we found the remains."

"Can you describe what you saw?" Quinn asked as Darren panned to Melissa, who seemed to enjoy the prospect of being on television and ran a hand through her hair playfully.

"The room was an old-fashioned bathroom. Of course, everything in this house is old-fashioned, so it wasn't any different than the rest, except that it didn't have electricity. Electricity had been installed at some point in the 1920s, I believe."

"Can you describe the room?"

"There were no toiletries or even a dressing gown. Several towels hung on a rack. They must have been white once but were now yellowed with age. The tub was tightly covered with a sort of tarpaulin tied down with twine. Paul and Grady removed the tarp to see what was underneath. The skeleton was there in the tub, positioned as if the person had been taking a bath."

"Was there anything in the tub? Traces of blood, perhaps?"

"No, but there was a white powder beneath the tub and on the rim."

"A white powder?" Quinn asked, leaning forward. Now this was interesting.

"Yes. I thought it might have been soap powder, or tooth powder, the type they used before the invention of toothpaste, but I didn't touch it."

"Was there any moisture?"

"No. I suspect it had evaporated over the years."

"Did you find anything that belonged to the person? Clothes, jewelry, purse?"

"No, nothing. There wasn't a scrap of evidence to the person's identity. The police checked. The coroner certified this wasn't a recent crime, which was when we rang the hotline."

"Hotline?" Quinn asked, perplexed.

"Yes, the *Echoes from the Past* hotline," Melissa answered. "There was a number to call at the end of each episode."

"You created a hotline?" Quinn turned to Rhys, who was hovering just behind Darren. Darren stopped filming and glanced at Rhys, smirking. Seemed he didn't know about the hotline either.

"I certainly did. What better way to get the viewers involved and find new subjects for our program?" Rhys replied, looking pleased with himself.

"Right. May I see the remains now?" Quinn asked.

"Of course. The room is upstairs."

Melissa set down her cup and invited Quinn to follow her toward the staircase. Paul Glover remained where he was, by the window, looking out at the dreary day.

Melissa led Quinn up the stairs and toward a large bedroom at the end of the corridor. It was a masculine bedroom with maroon bed hangings adorning the heavily carved four-poster bed, and a maroon and navy-blue carpet that matched the heavy drapes at the window. The furniture was made of walnut, and old-world gas lamps with glass lampshades stood on bedside tables. One almost expected a valet to come striding into the room, ready to help his master dress for the day or for an evening out on the town. Quinn noted that there was no light switch in the room. It wasn't wired for electricity, unlike the rest of the house.

"It's through here," Melissa said as she pointed toward a massive wardrobe that had been pushed away from the wall, revealing the doorway to an adjacent chamber. Rhys handed Quinn a torch that he'd brought along, since the room beyond was lost in shadow, having neither a window nor a light fixture.

Quinn entered the room and trained the torch on the back wall, where there was a large porcelain tub with clawed feet. It was wider and deeper than the newer tubs designed for smaller modern bathrooms. The skeleton lay in the tub, its skull resting against the back and its leg bones strewn haphazardly on the bottom, having collapsed after the tendons holding them together decomposed. The arms might have been folded across the belly, but now lay below the ribcage, the fingers splayed against the column of the spine. Quinn approached slowly, mindful of the white powder on the tile floor around the tub.

"What do you think that is?" Rhys asked, peering over her shoulder.

"I'll have to send a sample to the lab."

"Do you think the person died in the tub or was placed there after the fact?" he asked, his head tilted to the side as he considered the scene.

"I don't see any dried blood in the tub, or any hair, so it's possible the person died elsewhere and the body was placed in the tub to contain the decomposition process."

"So you think it was murder?" Melissa asked, coming up beside Quinn and staring at the skeleton with undisguised curiosity.

"Of course, it's possible the person drowned in the tub by accident, but I think it unlikely. Had that been the case, I strongly doubt the remains would still be here. They would have been properly buried. I would venture to guess that someone killed this individual, placed the corpse in the tub, got rid of all their personal belongings, then closed up the room and moved the wardrobe in front of the door to prevent discovery. Seems like an awfully impractical way of getting rid of a corpse, but it clearly worked, since the body wasn't discovered until now."

"Do you think the victim was poisoned with that powder?" Melissa asked.

"I really couldn't say, but I mean to find out," Quinn replied. "I don't want to touch this until I know what I'm dealing with. I'll ring Dr. Colin Scott, our bones expert, and ask him to come give us a hand."

"Excellent idea. I'll have Darren film you two packing up the skelly and taking samples of the powder," Rhys said. "Think Colin will come now?"

"He might. He loves a good mystery."

"I'll ring him right now."

Quinn turned to Melissa. "Do you have any inkling as to who this person might have been? Any family legends of someone going missing or leaving unexpectedly, never to be heard from again?"

"Not that I can think of."

"Do you know whose room this was?"

Melissa shook her head. "No one ever used it, at least not that I can recall. My grandmother kept it locked."

"Has this house been in the family for generations?" Quinn asked. She needed something to go on, a starting point, but Melissa was giving her nothing to work with.

"No. I believe my grandparents were the first of our family to live here."

"Would you have anything that belonged to your grandmother? A piece of jewelry, or an object that meant a lot to her?"

"Everything here belonged to my grandmother," Melissa replied, making an expansive gesture.

"I mean something more personal. Something that was special to her."

"There's this." Melissa pulled a gold chain from beneath her top, exposing an egg-shaped pendant. The egg was covered with blue enamel and decorated with a delicate pattern of gold and diamonds.

"That's beautiful. Is that...?"

"Yes. It's Fabergé. This necklace was my grandmother's prized possession. She never took it off, according to my mum. Mum wanted to take it for herself, but my grandmother left specific instructions to pass the necklace to me after her death."

"It truly is stunning. Would you allow me to borrow it for a little while? It will help me piece together something of your grandmother's past. Is there anything you can tell me about her?"

Melissa shook her head again. "She died before I was born. My mother didn't like to talk about her mother. They didn't have an easy relationship. Grandmother was born in Russia; that much I do know. She came to England when she was a teenager."

"What was her name?"

"Tina Swift."

"That doesn't sound very Russian," Quinn replied as she extracted a plastic baggie from her handbag and held it open for Melissa, who carefully removed the necklace and allowed it to pool at the bottom.

"Her full name was Valentina, and Swift was my grandfather's surname. I don't know what her maiden name was. My grandfather was her second husband. He's my mother's father. Uncle Michael was my grandmother's son from her first marriage, but he took his stepfather's name when his mother remarried. He preferred it because it didn't sound ethnic."

"Are there any photographs of your grandparents?" Rhys asked as they returned to the parlor. "The viewers love to see what the real people looked like, and compare them to the actors in the episode."

"My mum has some old photos. I can give you her phone number. She'll be happy to talk to you."

"That would be great," Rhys said. "Please don't touch anything until we return. It seems Dr. Scott is in the middle of an autopsy and won't be finished for several hours. We'll return tomorrow to box up the skeleton and collect samples, if that's all right with you."

"Yes, of course," Melissa rushed to reassure them. "Whatever you need. Honestly, I just want it gone. I've had trouble sleeping since we discovered the remains. They creep me out."

"One more night, and you'll be rid of your tenant, Mrs. Glover."

They said their goodbyes and left the Glovers' house. Darren walked off to his van with strict instructions to return at ten o'clock tomorrow morning.

"Can I give you a lift home?" Rhys asked Quinn once they were in the street. His Range Rover was parked in front of the house, its black exterior slick with rain. The air had cooled and a brisk wind had picked up.

"Yes, please."

Quinn closed her umbrella and climbed into the car, glad not to have to take the tube or hunt for a taxi. Her feet were damp and she was cold. She should have worn a warmer jumper.

"Are you hungry? I have time for lunch," Rhys said as he pulled out of the parking space.

"Sorry, I have to get back. I only left enough breastmilk for one feeding."

Ordinarily that type of confession would send Rhys running for the hills, but today he smiled and nodded in approval. "I hope Haley will decide to breastfeed. It's so much better for the baby. And it's kind of sexy too. I love seeing a woman nurse her infant."

"Too much information, Rhys."

"Right. Sorry."

"Do you know if you're having a girl or a boy?" Quinn asked. Normally, she'd refrain from asking too many personal questions, but Rhys liked nothing more than to talk about the coming baby.

"They couldn't tell from the last scan. The baby had its legs crossed, but I'll be happy with either."

"No preference?" Quinn asked. Didn't men always want sons, even these days when it wasn't a question of inheriting titles and estates and carrying on the family name?

"Well, if I had to choose, I'd like a girl. I've always wanted to have a daughter."

"Perhaps you will."

"As long as the baby is healthy, I don't care. I know people say that all the time, but it's true. So many things can go wrong."

"Yes," Quinn agreed, thinking of Quentin and the heart murmur that had led to their separation at birth. Had Quentin been born healthy, perhaps Social Services would have kept the girls together and they'd have been adopted by the same couple. How different life might have been had Quinn grown up with her twin.

"So, what did you make of Melissa?" Rhys asked as he stopped at a red light.

"Seems nice. A bit flighty, I suppose."

"I can't stand people who know nothing of their own history," Rhys vented. "If my grandmother came from Russia and had a genuine Fabergé necklace, I'd want to know how she came by it. Clearly, she was no peasant. There's history there. Interesting history. And I can't wait for you to fill me in on it."

"And I will, but don't rush me. First, I'd like to find out more about the skeleton and that white powder. Once we know more about the victim, genetically speaking, we can start to try to piece together what led to the murder."

Rhys nodded. "I won't rush you, I promise. I know you have your own process; I'm just fascinated by it. By the way, the first two episodes got excellent ratings."

"I'm glad. I know how happy good ratings make you."

"They should make you happy too. With the second series already in production and the popularity of the hotline, this program can go on for years."

"Have you had many calls?" Quinn asked, amazed that anyone had called in at all. "I can't imagine that people routinely trip over centuries-old skeletons."

"This is England, my dear. You'd be surprised what you can trip over."

"I'm an archeologist, Rhys. I trip over things for a living."

"Precisely. We've had three calls, to be exact. One woman claimed she'd found the remains of a child in her garden. Turned out to be a dog. Another old biddy claimed there is a Saxon burial mound on her land. Turned out to be just a hill. And then there was Melissa Glover. Very odd, that."

"It is odd. Why would anyone keep a body in their house all these years? Surely, they could have disposed of the remains at some point, instead of sealing off the room. Someone was bound to come across the skelly sooner or later."

"Definitely later, in this case. I wonder how long that poor tosser's been lying there."

"You think it's a man?"

"Don't you?" Rhys challenged her.

"I do. Too tall and narrow-hipped to be a woman, but given its position, I could be wrong in my assessment. Perhaps once it's laid out on the slab, it'll look different."

"Well, we know it isn't Grandma Tina. Perhaps it's her first husband," Rhys mused as he pulled up to Quinn's building.

"Never mess with a Russian woman," Quinn quipped. "It can end badly."

"If you only knew," Rhys replied cryptically, possibly referring to a previous relationship. "Regards to Gabe and the children," he said as Quinn opened the passenger door. "I expect to hear from you tomorrow."

"You will."

THREE

Gabe was sitting cross-legged on the floor, Alex in his lap, when Quinn came home. Emma was in her room, probably playing with her new favorite doll. Seth had made sure to select a doll that resembled her, and she called it Emme, in honor of herself.

Gabe looked up, a happy grin on his face. "Alex smiled at me."

"Did he? And I missed it?"

"I'll make him do it again." Gabe gently tickled Alex's tummy, making the baby gurgle. He kicked his legs and his mouth stretched into a toothless grin. "There."

Quinn grabbed her mobile and snapped a photo. "Got it."

"I smile all the time and no one takes photos of me," Emma grumbled as she came into the room. She alternated between doting on her brother and seething with jealousy.

"We take photos of you all the time, even when you're not smiling," Gabe replied. "Would you like to hold him?"

"Not now. When's lunch? I'm hungry."

"After I nurse Alex. Maybe Daddy can make us some sandwiches in the meantime," Quinn suggested.

Gabe handed over the baby and headed into the kitchen to prepare lunch while Emma sat down on the sofa next to Quinn, her doll momentarily forgotten. She watched in fascination as Alex began to suck greedily, his cheeks puffing out and making her laugh.

"Did I do that?" Emma asked.

"I am sure you did." Quinn had no idea if Jenna had nursed Emma or bottle-fed her, but it seemed a harmless enough lie.

"Did I like it?"

"I think all babies like it. It's their only source of food, and it's comforting to be held."

"But it's kind of gross."

"It's no worse than sucking on a bottle with a rubber nipple," Quinn replied patiently. It was only natural that Emma was curious, and Quinn was glad she felt comfortable enough to ask.

"Does your belly still hurt?"

"At times. The incision is still healing, but it feels much better now."

"Does this mean you'll have another baby soon?" Emma pinned Quinn with an accusing stare.

"No, darling, it doesn't mean that. Why do you ask?"

"Because Aidan at school said that you and Daddy will start shagging again and you'll get up the duff."

"Well, Aidan needs to mind his own business."

"*Will* you start shagging again?" Emma persisted.

"Do you know what that means?"

Emma looked shamefaced for a moment. "No. But it sounds like something that would be fun."

"It is fun, darling, at the right time and with the right person, but you're only five years old, so you have years and years to go until you have to concern yourself with that."

"Will you explain it to me when I grow up?"

"Of course. I will answer any questions you have, as I always do. Now, how about you go wash your hands before lunch?"

"All right," Emma conceded as Gabe came back into the room. "Daddy, do you like shagging?" she promptly asked. "Mum said it's fun."

"Well, I'm glad she thinks so," Gabe replied.

"Do *you* like it?"

"Very much. Now, go wash your hands." Gabe looked at Quinn, who was doing her best not to dissolve in a fit of giggles. "What was that all about?"

"Evidently, Aidan from school has been putting ideas in her head."

"Ah, Aidan. That child is very well informed for a five-year-old."

"He certainly is. Shame they're in the same class again this year."

"There's always going to be an Aidan," Gabe replied. "In my primary school, there was Billy Bacchus. He was a fount of useful information. I think my father would have loved to box Billy's ears if such a thing were still acceptable. We'll just have to answer her questions as honestly as we can without volunteering too much unnecessary information. It's only natural that she should be curious with a new baby in the house."

"Yes, that's about the age they start wondering where babies come from. I remember asking my mum after Jill's baby brother was born. I wanted a sibling so desperately. I thought maybe I could nudge my parents into having another baby. That was before I knew I was adopted."

"Any word on Quentin's whereabouts?" Gabe asked.

"None. Logan tried reaching out to Mr. Richards again, but he's not even taking our calls at this stage. I spoke to Jill earlier and she mentioned that Brian has an idea."

"What kind of idea?"

"I didn't get a chance to find out. I'd like to have them round for dinner next week."

"Sounds great. Shall I cook?"

"I would like them to survive the evening," Quinn joked as she fastened the buttons of her top. Alex was fast asleep, a small satisfied smile tugging at his lips.

"Takeaway then?"

"No, I'll cook. It's been a while since I practiced the culinary arts, and Jill and Brian are not finicky eaters. Pasta and salad will do." Quinn laid Alex carefully in his cot and followed Gabe into the kitchen.

Emma was already seated at the table, eyeing the sandwiches. "I want that one," she said, pointing to a ham and tomato sandwich.

"Made it just for you," Gabe replied cheekily. "How do you both feel about spending Christmas in Berwick this year? My mum is ready to sell the house, so it will be our last Christmas in the family home."

"Of course. And I'm glad she's finally come to a decision. Odd timing, though."

"Not really. She's already signed with an estate agent and the property has been listed. There probably won't be much activity before the New Year, but hopefully after the holidays, things will pick up."

"There'll be much to do. You'll need to decide what to do with the contents of the house. Your mum will only be able to take a few pieces with her once she moves into the retirement community. Is there anything you might want to hold on to?" Quinn asked.

"I think Mum's already decided what she wants to take with her. She'd like to move as soon as possible."

"I can't say I blame her. After learning about Catherine de Rosel, I can't say I look forward to returning to that house either. What a sad story." Quinn sighed. "I'm glad you've arranged to have her buried properly after all this time. It's the least we could do for her."

"She'll be interred as soon as Rhys releases the remains and the artefacts."

Catherine de Rosel would be buried at the parish church, next to her husband, Hugh de Rosel, and her lover, Guy de Rosel, who had fallen at the Battle of Bosworth Field. She'd be interred with her amber rosary and Guy's sword, his most prized possession, which he had laid to rest with Kate and what he'd assumed were the remains of his unborn child in an unmarked grave in the family chapel.

"They're almost done filming the episode. We'll be able to take Kate with us when we drive up to Berwick for Christmas," Quinn said as she reached for an egg and watercress sandwich.

"Who's Kate?" Emma piped in as she reached for another sandwich.

"She was someone who died a long time ago," Gabe replied, not wishing to get into the details of Kate's murder.

"I'm glad we'll be having Christmas in Berwick. I miss Buster. And Grandma Phoebe. When are we going to see Grandma Sylvia? And Jude?" Emma asked.

Quinn and Gabe exchanged glances over Emma's head. How could they explain to a five-year-old that her uncle Jude was now in a rehab facility, battling his heroin addiction, while Quinn and Sylvia hadn't seen each other since the day of Emma's birthday party in August when Jude had dropped a heroin fold that Emma picked up, mistaking it for a sticker?

"We'll see Grandma Sylvia soon," Gabe replied vaguely.

"Can I bring Emme when we go to Berwick?"

"If you like," Quinn replied. She secretly felt sad for Mr. Rabbit, who'd been ruthlessly replaced in Emma's affections. "What about Mr. Rabbit?"

"He can stay at home. Stuffed rabbits are for babies. Alex can have him," Emma replied.

"I'm sure he'll love him as much as you did," Gabe said.

"Yeah. Whatever."

FOUR

Quinn pushed Alex's pram down the corridor of the mortuary, disregarding people's curious glances. Alex was asleep after their walk, and she saw no harm in bringing him along to her meeting with Dr. Colin Scott. The door to his office stood wide open, making it easier for her to maneuver the pram inside.

"It is Bring Your Child to Work Day?" Colin joked. He sat behind his desk, a surgical mask hanging around his neck and his sandy hair twisted into an artful man-bun.

"I don't have a child minder," Quinn explained. She'd have to find someone eventually if she planned to keep working, but she wasn't ready to leave Alex just yet. He was only ten weeks old, not nearly old enough to entrust to a stranger, and her hours were flexible enough that she could work around Gabe's schedule, making sure that one of them was always there to look after the baby.

"Well, if he doesn't mind, I don't mind," Colin replied. "Come through."

Quinn followed Colin into the lab where the skeleton was laid out on a slab. Now that it was lying flat, Quinn was sure it had been a man, and a powerfully built one at that. Colin's assistant, Dr. Sarita Dhawan, stood bent over the skelly as she worked on extracting a tooth.

"Good morning, Dr. Allenby," Sarita called out as she dropped the tooth into a plastic container. "Congratulations. May I take a peek?" she asked, smiling at Alex.

"Of course."

Sarita pulled off her latex gloves and came to peer into the pram. Alex was still sleeping peacefully. His face looked as round as a full moon and his mouth was slightly ajar. His lashes brushed his rosy cheeks and several dark strands of hair had escaped from his knitted hat.

"Oh, he's lovely. He looks just like your husband."

"Don't I know it? Not a trace of me in there," Quinn said, shaking her head in mock dismay.

"You'll just have to have another one," Colin quipped as he smiled at the sleeping child.

"Have you been spending time with Aidan?"

"Who's Aidan?" Colin queried.

"Never mind. Tell me about the skelly." Quinn left the pram in a quiet corner and came to stand next to Colin by the well-lit slab.

"All I can tell you with any certainty is that what we have here is a male in his late thirties or early forties who lived approximately one hundred years ago."

"Is that all?"

"I'm afraid so. The white powder on the tub and on the floor was lye. Whoever killed him used the lye to erase any shred of genetic information. Believe it or not, lye is making a comeback as a means of disposing of corpses. Mostly animal carcasses, of course, not human. When submerged in a vat of lye and water and heated for several hours, the carcass liquefies and boils down to a few ounces of brown sludge. Had our perpetrator heated that tub, there'd be nothing left of Mr. X, not even bone fragments."

"Do you think the killer might have been a scientist?"

"I doubt it. People have used lye to accelerate decomposition for centuries. Traces of lye can be found in most plague pits from the sixteenth and seventeenth centuries. This person was most likely well educated, but not a scientist."

"Is there nothing we can learn from him?" Quinn asked, nodding toward the skeleton. "Can you tell how he died?"

Colin shook his head. "There are no signs of obvious violence, and I found no traces of blood in the tub. The skull is intact and there are no nicks or scratches on the bones, which might have been there had he been shot or stabbed. Of course, that's not conclusive. The bullet might have lodged in soft tissue, but then we probably would have found it at the bottom of the tub after the tissue decomposed. Likewise, he might have been stabbed. The knife doesn't always graze the bone. He might also have been poisoned or asphyxiated."

"Do you think he was killed in the tub?" Quinn asked, desperate for something to go on.

"Possibly. Or he was murdered elsewhere and placed in the tub after the fact, which was actually very clever on the part of the killer. The porcelain tub was the perfect receptacle. As the body decomposed, the fluids simply drained away. This left behind a skeleton that's as clean as a plastic skelly used in biology class."

"They really knew what they were doing, didn't they?"

"Yes, I think so."

"Do you think the killer was deranged?" Quinn asked.

"What makes you ask that?"

"Who, in their right mind, would leave a body to decompose in their own home and not eventually get rid of the remains?"

"Who is to say the killer left the body in their own house? Perhaps the house belonged to the victim."

"Would no one have found him then? And what about the blocked panel? Surely, someone who had access to the house knew there was a bathroom connected to that particular bedroom."

"You'd be amazed how many human remains are found entombed behind walls and beneath floorboards. People think that burying someone within the confines of the house gives them control over the situation. It's entirely possible that whoever killed Mr. X sealed off the room then sold the house to some unsuspecting individual who never bothered to study the blueprints very carefully. Had the Glovers not hired an architect and decided to renovate, they'd never have discovered our man. He'd have remained in that room for another hundred years."

"Yes, you're right. Mrs. Glover's grandparents might have had nothing to do with this man's death. They might have bought the house never suspecting that human remains were hidden behind the bedroom wall."

"Rhys will not be pleased with the results," Colin mused. "Not enough information to build an episode around."

"What about the tooth Sarita extracted?" Quinn asked.

"We'll use the tooth to perform isotope analysis, but it's a lengthy process, not to mention costly, and the BBC might not wish to foot the bill, since, in the end, all it might tell us is that the person enjoyed a plentiful diet, consisting of foods readily available on the British Isles. Judging by the man's height, I'd say he got plenty of nutrients during his formative years. Proving he wasn't a pauper will do little to advance your hypothesis."

"So, it's of no help to us whatsoever," Quinn concluded.

"Precisely."

"Rhys is a master storyteller. He'll think of something," Quinn replied. Colin had no idea that she could see into the past when holding an object that had once belonged to the dead. If there was something to see, she would see it, and Rhys would take the facts and turn them into supposition, which would make for a riveting episode of *Echoes from the Past*.

Quinn thanked Drs. Scott and Dhawan, said her goodbyes, and wheeled Alex's pram out of the mortuary. Now that she knew for certain she had no facts to go on, it was time to see what the Fabergé egg had to tell her.

FIVE

MARCH 1917

Petrograd, Russia

The sun shone brightly, making the ice glimmer and adding a playful sparkle to the mounds of snow lining the riverbank. Whoops of laughter and gasps of delight followed Valentina as she carefully walked off the ice and made her way to the nearest bench. She removed her fur muff and began to unbuckle the skates attached to her boots. She loved skating, but next week might be the last time she took to the ice this winter. Despite the bitter cold, spring was on its way, and in a few weeks, the Neva wouldn't be safe to skate on anymore. The thaw would set in and the thick crust would begin to thin and crack, leaving great chunks of ice floating on the surface of the river and crashing into each other with surprising force, groaning and creaking like living things. Still, no one could be sad about the approach of spring, not even dedicated skaters.

Valentina gave a jaunty wave to her sister and brother, who were still skating. Tanya navigated the rink with confidence and finesse, but Kolya was too timid to go faster than a crawl or try a spin or a pirouette. At seven, he still longed for someone to hold his hand and catch him should he fall, and called out to Tanya every time he wobbled on the ice.

"You'll catch your death out here, Valentina Ivanovna," Nyanushka grumbled as she sat down next to Valentina on the bench. She was bundled up as if she were on her way to Siberia, wearing a knee-length sheepskin coat and matching hat. A finely woven down shawl peeked from beneath the hat. The ends were wrapped around her neck and tied at the back to keep them in place. Nyanushka had been the nanny in the Kalinin household since Valentina was born, but she still called all the children by their formal names as a sign of respect. Her parents and friends called Valentina "Valya," the diminutive form of her name. Formality was reserved for staff, strangers, and social functions.

"They're almost done, Nyanushka," Valentina replied. "Just give them a few more minutes. They're having such fun."

"In my day, no one was concerned with having fun," she grumbled, rubbing her mitten-clad hands together to warm them. "We had more important things to think about."

"And it shows. It's all right to enjoy yourself from time to time."

"Don't be impertinent, young lady."

"Why don't you go get a cup of tea? We'll meet you there in a few minutes."

During the winter months, a table was set up on the riverbank, complete with a pot-bellied samovar and platters of poppy seed rolls, raisin loaves, and spiced gingerbread *pryaniki*. The tea was hot and sweet. Valentina liked hers with a slice of lemon that gave it a slightly tangy flavor. At home, they drank tea from tall crystal glasses set in silver-plated holders, but here on the riverbank it was served in tin mugs. She always brought enough money to buy everyone a treat after their exertions. Nyanushka got a treat just for being such a trouper and chaperoning them every week despite the cold and boredom she had to endure while they skated. Their parents would never permit them to come alone, even though Valentina was nearly eighteen and old enough to look after her siblings. It wasn't proper for persons of their station.

Valentina walked toward the ice and gave Kolya a hand as he shuffled toward her. "Come, let's get your skates off. Where are your mittens?"

"I dropped them on the ice," Kolya whined as he sat down on the bench and stuck his feet out, ready to be assisted. "I want tea. I'm cold."

"We'll all have tea as soon as Tanya graces us with her presence. Who's that she's skating with?"

"I don't know," the boy replied. He wasn't interested in socializing, only skating.

Tanya finally said goodbye to her companion and left the ice, joining her brother and sister on the bench. "You dropped these, Kolya," she chided as she handed him his red mittens. They were covered with ice shavings, but Kolya still pulled them on to warm his reddening hands.

"Who was that you were skating with?" Valentina asked as she stowed Kolya's skates in a leather satchel that already contained her own skates.

"Sergei Mironov. He's a friend of Alexei. We met him last summer, remember?"

"Vaguely. Come, get your skates off. Nyanushka is fuming."

"What's there to fume about? She has as much fun as we do, gossiping with all the other nannies and drinking liters of tea."

"Perhaps that's the problem," Valentina said with a smile. "She's probably ready to burst."

"I'm not ready to go. I want my tea and cake," Kolya complained.

"You'll get your tea, you crybaby. Here, take twenty kopeks and go get yourself tea and a seed roll. We're right behind you."

"I want a pryanik."

"So, get a pryanik."

The boy took the coins and happily ran off toward the tea table.

"Children are so annoying," Tanya said as she removed her

skates, tied them together, and dropped them into the open satchel. "Always complaining."

"He's not so bad. Come on. I'm cold now that I'm not skating." Valentina stuck her hands into her fox muff to keep them warm until she could wrap them around a hot mug of tea. Their mother didn't like them having tea in public, proclaiming the mugs to be unsanitary, but tea and cake after skating was tradition, and Valentina wasn't about to give it up. Besides, it was a long time till supper, and she needed sustenance.

After their treat, they walked the seven blocks home, followed by a disgruntled Nyanushka. She was getting on in years and couldn't walk as quickly as her charges. "I miss the days when you took naps after lunch," she complained. "I got to rest after you ran me off my feet."

"You can still rest. We're not babies anymore. We don't need to be minded round the clock," Tanya snapped.

"You're young ladies. You need to be minded more than ever. Your reputations are your only protection against evil tongues and unsavory suitors."

"I don't have a suitor, and Valentina is nearly engaged. Alexei would never believe any mean-spirited talk about Valya."

"Nearly engaged is not the same as married, my girl," the nanny replied. "She's my responsibility till then."

"Tanya, stop aggravating the poor woman," Valentina admonished her sister. "She's doing her best for us. Always has."

"I know. I just don't like being treated like a child. I'm fourteen—nearly a grown woman."

"You're hardly a grown woman. You still have several years in the schoolroom before you are presented to society. Be patient."

"Easy for you to say. You're on the verge of something wonderful, while I have to molder in that schoolroom with that fusty governess. God, she bores me to tears."

"She's only doing what she's paid to do."

"Don't I know it," Tanya complained. "She should focus on Kolya. He needs all the help he can get."

"Father will get him a different tutor this year. Kolya's education will be quite different from ours, him being a boy."

"You mean he won't have to spend countless hours playing excruciatingly dull minuets on the pianoforte and memorizing poetry? She won't even let me play a waltz, that miserable cow. Boys get to have all the fun," Tanya grumbled as they reached their door and knocked, eager to be admitted into the warmth of the house.

"Oh, I don't know about that. I have plenty of fun," Valentina replied. She enjoyed teasing her sister.

"That's because you have Alexei."

Valentina handed her fur-trimmed coat, muff, and fur hat to a footman before heading into the parlor where her mother was reclining on a chaise, reading. She was a great fan of Alexander Pushkin and knew many of his poems by heart, but at the moment she was enjoying a volume by Mikhail Lermontov, her second favorite.

"Did you have a nice time, Valya?"

"It was splendid, Mama. How was your afternoon?"

"Lazy," her mother replied, smiling guiltily. She was still beautiful at thirty-eight, with blond ringlets that framed her heart-shaped face and large blue eyes, just like Valentina's, fringed with thick lashes. "Your father tried to entice me with a sleigh ride, but I was so comfortable here by the fire with my book."

"You need fresh air, Mama."

"And I'll get some tomorrow. You know how I dislike the cold. And the bright sun reflecting on the snow makes me squint, and you know what that means."

"That you'll get wrinkles around the eyes. A definite no-no." Valentina gave her mother a peck on the cheek and settled in the chair closest to the fire.

"Don't get too comfortable, Valya. Go and make yourself presentable. Countess Petrova sent word that Alexei will be stopping by. He wishes to speak to you." Elena Kalinina looked like a cat that had got at the cream, her eyes sparkling with mischief and her mouth twitching as she tried to suppress a smile.

"Really?" Valentina gasped.

"Really."

"What should I wear?"

"Why don't you put on that light blue frock I like so much? It brings out your eyes."

"All right."

Valentina exploded out of the chair in a most unladylike way and hurried to her room. If this was "The Talk," she meant to be ready for it.

"You're so lucky," Tanya grumbled as Valentina dashed past her. "I wish it was my turn."

"It soon will be."

Valentina stripped off her warm woolen gown and put on the blue silk her mother had recommended. The dress was feminine and frilly, adorned with Belgian lace and tiny cloth-covered buttons. It was lovely. She ran a brush through her thick blond hair, tied it with a matching blue ribbon, and examined her reflection in the mirror. She looked happy and excited, a girl on the cusp of womanhood, and if her mother was right, on the threshold of marriage.

Valentina had known Alexei all her life. Their fathers had become great friends during their time in the Imperial Army when they were young Hussars. The two families were close, and it had always been assumed that Valentina would marry Alexei, Count Petrov's oldest son. Valentina couldn't think of anything more wonderful than marrying Alexei. He was handsome, charming, and fun, and always made her feel like she was the most beautiful girl in the world. It was agreed that their relationship wouldn't be formalized until Valentina turned eighteen, but she would be eighteen the following week, and a supper party was planned to celebrate her birthday. Her parents assumed there'd be an announcement to make. And now Alexei was on his way.

"Count Petrov is here," a footman announced after knocking on Valentina's door. "He's waiting in the music room."

"I'll be down presently."

Valentina threw one last look at herself in the mirror. Everything would be different by the time she returned to her room. Her adult life was about to begin.

SIX

Alexei sprang to his feet when Valentina glided into the music room, floating on a cloud of happiness. Even if Alexei did not propose today, she was still the luckiest girl in the world. Her life was perfect, and she was astute enough to realize that. Her father worried incessantly about the political situation and rising tensions in the country, but Valentina paid little attention to his concerns. There would always be tensions and people who were dissatisfied with their lot in life. Many of them were probably even justified in their complaints, but they had nothing to do with her or her immediate future. Her life went on much as it had before, even after the war broke out, and as long as Alexei wasn't sent to the front, she had no reason to think about it.

Alexei was in uniform, having probably come directly from the barracks. To Valentina, he always looked splendid. Even the drab gray of his uniform couldn't dull the gleam of his honey-blond hair or the sparkle in his dark blue eyes. He'd recently grown a moustache. Valentina hadn't liked it at first, but it was beginning to appeal to her. It made him look older and more commanding, which was fitting for an officer of the cavalry.

Alexei came forward to greet her, his hands outstretched. He took her hands in his and brought them to his lips, one after the other, brushing his lips against her skin.

"Valya, you look beautiful. But then, you always look beautiful," Alexei added with a knowing smile, "even after I tried to dunk you in the river and you crawled out looking like a drowned rat. You flipped back your hair, flashed me a look of contempt, and stomped off in nothing but your underthings."

"That was ten years ago," Valentina exclaimed. "I was seven."

"It's a sight I'll never forget."

Valentina swatted Alexei playfully on the arm and invited him to resume his seat on the apple-green settee. "Would you like some tea?"

"No, thank you."

"Then shall we get down to business? Are you here to ask me?" she demanded. "It's not my birthday yet, but I think it's all right if you're a bit early."

"Valya, for the love of God, let me do this properly. I know it's not exactly a surprise, but for once, allow me to take charge of the situation." He grinned, as though well aware that wasn't likely to happen. He knew her too well, and miraculously, he still liked her.

"Well, go on then. I won't say a word until you've finished."

"Promise?"

"Promise. So, are you going to sit there all day?"

Alexei laughed at her impatience, but took the hint and dispensed with the preliminaries. He got down on one knee and took her hand in his, his eyes searching her face as he waited for her to give him her full attention. "Valentina Ivanovna Kalinina, will you do me the honor of becoming my wife?" he asked solemnly.

"Of course I will, you silly. As if I'd say no."

"With you, I never know," Alexei replied with an indulgent grin. He extracted a thin gold band from his front pocket and slid it onto Valentina's right hand, as was the custom. She had her ring ready as well and put it on Alexei's finger. They were officially engaged, and the rings would become their wedding bands once the church ceremony took place.

Alexei kissed her cheek and resumed his seat on the settee, looking relieved that the difficult part was over, but he wasn't finished. "Valya, our parents have planned our union since we were children, but I think you know me well enough to realize that if I didn't love you, I wouldn't agree to the match. I don't ever want you to think that I married you out of obligation or duty. I can't imagine sharing my life with anyone but you. I know it won't be easy, since you probably won't let me get a word in edgewise, and will question my every decision and try to win every argument, but I love you, and I am prepared to embrace a lifetime of suffering."

Valentina sputtered with laughter. "And I love you, Alyosha, because you're the only man in my life who allows me to be myself. Yes, I will drive you mad, most likely, but I promise, you'll never be bored."

"Heaven forbid," Alexei replied, rolling his eyes. He grew serious as his gaze met hers. "May I kiss you now that we're engaged?"

"You don't need to ask for permission."

Alexei leaned toward her and slid his arm around her waist, pulling her closer. His eyes were closed as he captured her mouth with his own, and she gave herself up to the sensation, eager to experience her first grown-up kiss. It was different than she'd expected, sweet and romantic, but it was also so much more than that. It made her want to move closer and wrap her arms around Alexei's neck as she pressed her body to his. The buttons of his tunic were hard and cold against her breasts and his moustache tickled a little, but she pulled him even closer, eager for something she couldn't quite name. They'd touched each other playfully in the past, especially at the Petrov *dacha* where they went swimming in the river and spent hours traipsing through the countryside, but this was different. This was a bit frightening, but exciting at the same time, and she didn't want it to end.

As though sensing her eagerness, Alexei deepened the kiss,

sliding his tongue into her open mouth and exploring it in a surprisingly intimate manner before finally pulling away from her abruptly. His pupils were dilated and his breathing uneven as he studied her features, as if seeing her for the first time. Valentina was breathless.

"What's the matter?" she asked him, wondering if she'd done something wrong.

Alexei shook his head and smiled in a way that made her heart flutter. "Absolutely nothing, my darling Valya. Now that I've had a taste of what's to come, it'll be that much harder to wait for our wedding night."

Valentina blushed. She had a general idea of what took place in the marriage bed, but she'd assumed it was awkward and embarrassing, especially the first time. After that kiss, she wasn't so sure. The only thing she was sure of was that she wanted to be kissed that way again, and again. "Do your parents ever kiss like that?" she asked Alexei. His eyes widened in surprise.

"No. My father gives my mother a perfunctory peck on the cheek at breakfast and then another one in the evening before she retires to her own bedroom. Theirs was never a love match, but they have great affection and respect for each other."

"Promise me you'll never stop kissing me this way."

"I promise. We're going to be wonderfully happy, you and I," he said, and she was reassured to see that he looked entirely serious.

"Valya, I have something for you. It's an engagement gift. I have a birthday gift for you as well, but you'll have to wait for that one. It's bad luck to give a birthday gift early." Alexei withdrew a long velvet box from the pocket of his uniform and handed it to her. "I chose it myself," he added, clearly worried that she wouldn't like it.

Valentina opened the box. Inside, nestled on folds of deep blue velvet, was a gold necklace with a little egg pendant. The egg was crafted of blue enamel and worked in a pattern of gold and diamonds. She breathed a sigh of delight. "It's exquisite, Alyosha."

"Open the egg."

She carefully opened the egg to reveal a tiny golden chick sitting in the center. "It's charming," Valentina exclaimed.

"It's for all the chicks we're going to have," Alexei clarified.

"I don't want to raise chickens, I want babies." She laughed at her own wit and threw her arms around him. "I love you, you know. I've loved you since I was a little girl."

"Well, now that you're no longer a little girl, I hope you love me still. Let me help you put that on."

Alexei closed the delicate clasp behind her neck and smiled. He looked relieved, his mission accomplished.

"How soon can we be married?" Valentina demanded. "I wish we could do it tomorrow."

Alexei laughed at her naiveté. "Oh, darling, if our mamas have anything to say about it, and they do, this will be the wedding of the year, and those take ages to plan. Besides, we need to find a house and furnish it to our liking. Surely you'll enjoy that. Imagine, our own home."

Valentina sucked in a happy breath. The notion of being mistress of her own house was too exciting to even contemplate, even if choosing the house would be a group project. Alexei's parents, as well as her own, would be involved in every aspect of choosing and decorating their home, given that they'd be the ones paying for it, but Valentina didn't mind. Her mother had exquisite taste, and Alexei's mother wasn't too bad, as far as future mothers-in-law went. She was older than Valentina's own mama, and a bit stodgier, but still a good sort.

"Well, I won't stand for the wedding being any later than the beginning of September. I want fine weather on our special day. Once the autumn comes, it's nothing but wind and rain," Valentina said.

"Surely you don't want to marry during the summer. Everyone is away from the city, enjoying their country estates. There'll be no one to attend."

"No, I suppose not. And I don't want to be married during the white nights. I want hundreds of candles glowing in the ballroom and reflecting in the mirrors while we dance, and that's a lot more dramatic when it's fully dark outside."

"Well, I'll leave the planning to you, dearest. I'm sure you and the mamas will do what's best. I must return to my duties."

"Alyosha, you won't be sent to the front, will you?" Valentina asked, suddenly worried. The war felt very far away, here in Petrograd, but Alexei was a soldier, and soldiers went where they were sent. Valentina paid little attention to her father's daily tirades when he read his morning newspaper, but she knew the war wasn't going well.

Alexei shook his head. "Not at this time. You've no reason to worry."

"Papa says this war will bring shame upon Russia."

"All will be well."

"Alyosha, I'm no longer a child, and as the fiancé of a soldier, I deserve to know the truth of what's going on. I want to be prepared."

They didn't normally discuss politics, but current events would impact their future, and if their relationship was to evolve it was imperative that they be able to speak freely to one another. Valentina was grateful Alexei didn't ignore her request.

"The war is a disaster. There's mutiny in the ranks. The men are being subjected to harsh disciplinary action, but morale is low and desertion is rife. There's been a change of command, and the Tsar put himself in charge of the Russian Army in the hope of inspiring the men and earning their loyalty, but the troops have no taste for the fighting and want to go home. They have nothing against the Germans and see no compelling reason for Russia's involvement in the war."

"Doesn't that mean additional troops might be sent to the front?" Valentina asked, fearful for Alexei.

"We're needed to protect the capital. There's too much unrest to leave the city undefended."

"What kind of unrest?"

"The common people are unhappy with the current situation. There's great resentment festering among the working classes. They want food, land, and opportunities for advancement, and they feel that the Tsar is indifferent to their plight."

"Is he? Does he not love all his people and see to their welfare?"

"No, Valya, he doesn't. He's deaf to their pleas. A small percentage of the population controls all the land and industry in this country. The peasants are starving, especially since so much capital is being funneled into the military. The army needs food, horses, arms, and vehicles if they are to continue to fight this war against Germany. The common people see very little in the way of government aid."

"You sound as if you sympathize with them."

"I can understand their grievances, and think they should be addressed before this simmering cauldron of discontent boils over."

"Could that really happen?"

"I would like to think not, but if it does, there aren't enough regiments stationed in Petrograd to hold off a full-scale revolution."

"You're scaring me, Alyosha. If the situation is so dire, why is everyone pretending nothing is wrong?"

"Because that's what they do best. They bury their heads in the sand, host balls and musical evenings, and spend a fortune on gowns and jewels. The Romanovs have been ruling Russia for three hundred years, so everyone believes everything will just go on as before. There have been periods of discontent and uprisings before now. Several attempts were made on the life of Alexander III, and even on our current Tsar, but the demonstrations were put down, the leaders executed, and opposition squashed. Life for the ruling classes went on largely undisturbed, much like right now. But this time things might be different."

"Why?"

"Because they have numbers on their side, and they're organizing and arming themselves. These are no longer ignorant serfs with axes and pitchforks, Valya. They have educated men to lead them and given the current situation, they don't have much left to lose."

"You could be arrested for such talk." Valentina gasped. She'd never heard Alexei speak this way before, and the depth of his disillusionment shocked and frightened her.

"Yes, I could, but I trust you, and you asked me to be honest."

Valentina nodded. She had asked him to be honest, but this wary, bitter side of Alexei made her see him in a whole new light. It was disturbing, but also reassuring. She didn't want to be lied to or pacified with half-truths and false promises. She'd rather know the truth.

"Have you ever killed anyone?" Valentina asked. She suddenly realized that Alexei's smart uniform wasn't worn only to make him look handsome and dashing. He was an officer in the Imperial Army, trained to kill and sworn to defend Russia's interests.

"This conversation has turned awfully grim, and I really must go. Please, don't concern yourself, Valya. Hopefully, the war will end soon. Once it does, the situation will change for the better."

"Take care of yourself, Alyosha. For me."

"For you," he replied and kissed the tip of her nose. "I will see you at your birthday celebration, Valya."

"Thank you for my present. I will wear it always."

"I'll buy you many necklaces once we are married," Alexei promised as he bowed formally and took his leave.

"But I'll still wear this one," Valya whispered to his retreating back. She sat down on the settee and sighed miserably. Alexei was right, the conversation had turned grim. This was supposed to be a happy day in her life, and it was, but the revelations he'd shared with her left her feeling frightened and depressed. She'd been blithely going about her business, completely oblivious to what was happening right under her nose. In her defense, she clearly wasn't the only one, but the reality was a lot scarier than she dared to admit. The Romanovs had ruled for three hundred years, and might rule for three hundred more, but what if this time, they couldn't neutralize the threat?

Valentina got to her feet and headed for the door. Her parents would be waiting for her to report on her meeting with Alexei, and she was more than ready to share her happy news and shed this mantle of melancholy. She'd set aside the worrisome information he'd shared with her. There'd be plenty of time to think about it later. But as she crossed the silent corridor, an odd thought flashed through her mind. *It's not getting engaged that makes you a grown-up; it's having the blinders removed from your eyes, allowing you to finally see the things that were hidden from you before.*

SEVEN
DECEMBER 2014

London, England

Quinn set aside the necklace with a sigh of sadness. Russian history wasn't her forte, but any historian worth their salt knew what had happened in Russia in 1917. At the time of Valentina's engagement, Russia had been days away from the February Revolution—a name that caused some confusion for history novices, since it took place in February according the old Julian calendar used in Imperial Russia, but fell in March on the newer Gregorian calendar used in western nations. It was the first of two revolutions that changed the face of Russia forever, overthrowing the monarchy and installing a proletariat government headed by Vladimir Ilyich Lenin, a beloved revolutionary leader whose embalmed remains were still on display in a mausoleum in Red Square in Moscow to this day.

"Why so pensive?" Gabe asked as he came into the bedroom with a basket of clean laundry.

"I just met Valentina," Quinn replied, pointing to the necklace lying on her nightstand.

"And?"

"And her life is about to be blown apart in ways she can't even begin to imagine. She's in Petrograd, on the eve of the Russian Revolution."

"I gather she was an aristocrat?" No peasant or factory worker would own a Fabergé necklace, so Valentina's status was obvious.

"Yes. She was a countess, or would have been had the monarchy not been toppled."

"She came to England." Gabe sat down next to Quinn and picked up the necklace. He held it in front of his face, letting it swing like a pendulum. "And she owned a house in Belgravia, which is one of the poshest neighborhoods in London. Things couldn't have gone too badly for her."

"Yes, you're right, but I find it strange that she wound up in England. Most Russian émigrés fleeing the Revolution flocked to France. There was a large Russian community of ex-pats living in Paris."

"I suppose the fact that French was the official language of the Russian court made it easier for them to find their feet."

"Yes, that might have been a factor," Quinn said. "Why did they prefer French?"

"The Russian aristocracy considered their native tongue to be coarse, the language of the peasants. To speak French was a mark of sophistication attainable only by those of elevated station. Did Valentina speak English?"

"I don't know. It's possible. I suppose I'll find out in due course."

"Will Rhys be interested in doing an episode on Imperial Russia, do you think?" Gabe asked.

"I don't see why not. Viewers still tune in for adaptations of the Russian classics. I hear *War and Peace* is getting a remake, and *Anna Karenina* is always a hit. I loved the 1997 adaption with Sean Bean. He made a very handsome Count Vronsky. And there was a new version only two years ago, with Keira Knightley. So there's definitely a market."

"But this is a later time period, and a more volatile one."

"Later, yes; more volatile, not really. *War and Peace* is all about the Napoleonic Wars. Hardly a peaceful time in history. And *Doctor Zhivago* takes place around the time of the Russian Revolution. One of the most popular films of the twentieth century."

"True," Gabe conceded. "I can't wait to hear more. I've always been fascinated with Russian history."

"And this time, it's not one of your ancestors."

"Thank God for that. I'll never look at my family tree the same way again. Seems my ancestors weren't as noble and heroic as I liked to believe when I was a boy."

"Few people are truly noble and heroic in real life. Self-interest is the driving force of mankind, and self-interest doesn't usually translate into selflessness."

"No, it doesn't. Still, we all need our heroes, don't we?" Gabe glanced at the digital alarm clock on the bedside table. "Jill and Brian will be here in less than two hours."

"Bollocks," Quinn exclaimed. "I got so caught up in Valentina's story, I nearly forgot. Can you pop into the off-license and get a bottle of Malbec? Or two. I'll start on dinner."

"I'll take Alex with me. He can use a bit of fresh air. Is there anything else you need from the shops?"

"Get me some grated Parmesan and fresh basil."

"Yes, ma'am."

"Thanks." Quinn stowed the necklace in a drawer. She'd spend more time with Valentina later, but for now, she had dinner to prepare.

EIGHT

Brian leaned back in his chair and patted his ridiculously flat abs. "That was lovely, Quinn. Truly. I wish Jill was a better cook." His eyes twinkled with merriment as his gaze slid sideways to take in Jill's reaction to that inflammatory statement.

Jill promptly elbowed him in the ribs, making him gasp dramatically. "I make a mean bangers and mash," she said. "And excellent roast beef, in case you forgot."

"That you do," Brian agreed. "And I'm a very content man on those semiannual occasions."

Jill opened her mouth in outrage, but Brian quickly leaned in and kissed her. "I'm only joking, love. You're a great cook. You're a great everything."

"That's better," Jill replied with a triumphant smile.

Quinn was happy to see Jill and Brian so at ease with each other. Their relationship seemed to have blossomed over the past few months, since Jill had come to terms with the inevitable, and stopped worrying so much about the future of her business and making Brian feel as if he wasn't as important to her as her shop. They had gone through a rough patch a few months back when Jill discovered that Brian was still in contact with his ex-girlfriend, but seemed to have come back stronger. Quinn hoped the relationship would last. With Jill's business going under, she needed something solid in her life, something that made her happy.

"Brian, Jill mentioned you have an idea regarding finding my sister," Quinn said. She'd hoped he would bring up the subject on his own, but she was growing impatient. Anything was better than the limbo they found themselves in, unable to extract any information from Quentin's lawyer and failing to find a trace of Quentin online.

"I do, actually. I hope you don't mind me sticking my nose into your private business," Brian added, looking a bit embarrassed.

"Not at all. We need all the help we can get."

"Well, it's my cousin, you see. Drew was a detective in the Met before he got hurt on the job. Shot in the leg while pursuing a perp. The bullet shattered his knee, so he was forced to retire prematurely. Drew is not the type of person to take his retirement package and spend the rest of his days growing pansies. He started his own security firm and does some private investigating on the side. He only takes the cases that interest him."

"Do you think he'll be able to help?"

"I'm sure he will. He still has contacts on the force, and those can be very helpful in certain situations."

"You mean he has access to information other private investigators wouldn't be privy to?" Gabe asked.

"Exactly. Drew can help you trace your sister."

"Would he be interested in taking the case?"

"I took the liberty of mentioning the situation to him, and he's eager to help. He's a good bloke, Drew, and honest. Not like some, who'll charge you by the hour and pad the bill to fleece you in your desperation. Here's his card."

"Thank you," Quinn replied. She liked the man's card. It was stark and professional, the card of a man who didn't waste time on frivolities. "I'll ring him tomorrow. I hope he'll be able to make some headway. Logan and I weren't able to get very far on our own."

"I'm sure he will," Brian replied. "Drew actually invited me to join his security firm as a partner. There's an ever-growing demand for private security."

"You mean you'd be a bodyguard? I thought you work in IT," Quinn said.

"I would still be doing IT. Many of Drew's clients are interested in sophisticated alarm systems for their homes and a high level of encryption for their data," Brian replied. "I can certainly provide that. And it would be nice to be my own boss for a change."

"It's not as glamorous as you might imagine," Jill said, a trifle bitterly.

"I know it didn't work out for you, love, but this is different. It's not retail."

"You're still dealing with clients, and people can be fickle and unreasonable."

It seemed they'd had this particular argument before, and Jill wasn't in favor of Brian joining his cousin's business, probably because he'd no longer work set hours and would have to shoulder more responsibility, possibly making him more reluctant to commit to a future with her anytime soon.

"Jill, what are your plans?" Gabe asked as he poured her more wine. "Have you started looking for a job?"

"No. The lease on my shop doesn't expire until February first, so I will have a pre-holiday sale followed by a Christmas sale, and then a post-holiday sale that will flow into a going-out-of-business sale. Hopefully, I'll be able to dispose of most of my remaining stock. I'll have to take a loss, but it's still better than nothing. Once I close the shop, I will go on holiday," Jill announced. "I'm calling it the 'Demise of a Dream' holiday. Perhaps I'll go to Belize or the Maldives. I'm hoping Brian will come with me," she added, smiling at him coyly.

"I might be persuaded," he replied with a smile. "Do my dreams have to be shattered as well to join in?"

"No, you may hold on to your fantasies."

"You must be devastated," Gabe said. Jill had dreamed of

opening up a vintage clothing shop for years before finally taking the plunge.

"Yes and no. Having my own business is a lot harder than I imagined. It truly is a twenty-four seven commitment, which is what I keep telling Brian. If the business is successful, the effort is well worth it, but if it isn't, then every day becomes a struggle to keep one's head above water, and frankly, I'm tired of kicking. I'm ready to come ashore."

"I'm glad you're taking a philosophical approach," Quinn said, teasing her cousin.

"What other approach is there? I can throw myself a pity party, get royally drunk, make a fool of myself, and wake up with a huge headache come morning, or I can learn from this experience and move forward. I'm a professional who has the education and skills to earn a comfortable living. I'm better off than most."

"Where can a man find a woman that doesn't complain? For her price is well above rubies," Brian joked, bastardizing a Biblical proverb to suit his own purposes.

"Quinn never complains either," Gabe said with a straight face, earning himself a filthy look.

"You two really are cruising for a bruising, you know that?" Jill said as she drained her glass and held it out for a refill. "I think we need a girls' night out to get a break from you lot."

"Perhaps we should wait until I can actually have a drink. A girls' night is never as fun when sipping orange juice. I'll be nursing Alex for a few more months at least."

"Oh, right, you're nursing. I forgot," Jill said, her shoulders drooping. "Shall we put something on the calendar for June, then?" She probably didn't mean to sound petty, but couldn't seem to disguise the bitterness in her voice. "Baby comes first."

"Come on, Jill. That's not fair," Quinn snapped.

"I know. I'm sorry. I'm just green with envy. I want one of those," she said, jutting her chin toward Alex, who was happily lying in his playpen. Jill's eyes grew misty, possibly because her biological clock was banging away inside her, or more likely because she'd had too much wine.

"Well, I think it's time we were going," Brian announced, folding his napkin and moving his chair away from the table. "Come, Jilly. Time for bed."

"But we haven't even had coffee and dessert," Quinn protested.

"I think princess here drank too much. She gets maudlin when she drinks," Brian explained as he helped Jill on with her coat.

"Sorry, Quinn," Jill said. "Brian is right. I did drink too much. I'm just a little emotional these days, you know, given the situation."

"I completely understand. Ring me tomorrow." Quinn walked Jill and Brian to the door and waited until they got in the lift.

"Well, that went well," Gabe said as he began to clear the table. "Brian clearly knows when it's time for an emergency exit."

"Jill's more upset than she's letting on. That shop meant the world to her."

"I know. It's never easy to let go of a dream."

"Did you ever have a dream you had to let go of?" Quinn asked as she wrapped her arms around Gabe's waist and pressed her cheek to his chest, listening to the steady beat of his heart.

"I tried to let go of my dream of you for eight years. I didn't succeed." Gabe drew her close and kissed the top of her head.

"Thank God," Quinn murmured.

NINE

Quinn lifted the baby onto her shoulder and paced the room, rubbing his back gently. He'd been fussy since she fed him just after Jill and Brian left, and cried as soon as she tried to put him down in his cot. "What is it, little man?" Quinn asked softly. "What's troubling you?"

She continued to pace, hoping the baby would drop off to sleep, but he began to whimper every time she stopped. Gabe came into the bedroom, having finished clearing up in the kitchen. "Still fussing?"

"He won't let me put him down. I'm exhausted."

"Here, let me have him," Gabe said as he held out his arms for the miserable baby. "I'll get him down. Go to bed. You look knackered."

"Are you sure?"

"Of course. You've got to be up in a few hours for the next feeding."

"Thank you."

Gabe held the child against his chest and cradled his head in his palm. Alex rested his cheek against Gabe. "I think he's listening to my heartbeat."

"He seems to find it soothing," Quinn replied as she got ready for bed. "He likes it when you sing to him."

"I don't think I'm up for singing right now, but I'll ring my mum. The sound of my voice might lull him to sleep."

"It's certainly worth a try."

Gabe walked through to the other room and picked up his mobile. "What do you say we lie down for a bit?" he asked the baby as he settled on the sofa with the child lying on him. "There you go. Isn't that comfortable?" Gabe pulled an afghan over them both. Alex began to fuss again, but seemed to settle down once Gabe began to speak.

"Hi, Mum," he said softly. "How are you?"

"Why are you whispering?"

"I have Alex with me. He's having a hard time falling asleep."

"I see. Have you tried singing?"

"I don't want to give the child nightmares."

"You have a lovely voice," Phoebe protested. "I always took you caroling with me when you were a boy."

"Yes, I remember cringing with embarrassment when you made me do a solo of 'Silent Night.'"

"It was lovely. Your sweet young voice ringing out in the darkness of the winter night." Phoebe sighed. "Anyway, how is Emma? Is she in bed?"

"She just fell asleep."

"And Quinn? How's she feeling?"

"Physically, she seems fine. Emotionally, I'm not so sure."

"You must keep an eye on her, Gabriel. Postnatal depression can be a very serious thing."

"She's not depressed."

"Are you sure?"

Gabe thought about that for a moment. He'd been sure up until a second ago, but now he couldn't say with any certainty that Quinn wasn't going through something other than the normal recovery from a caesarean section. She'd been tense and a little distant, and shrank from him the few times he'd reached for her over the past few weeks. Dr. Malik had given her the all clear, but Quinn had been reluctant to resume intimate relations. Whenever she allowed Gabe to hold her or kiss her, she seemed miles away, clearly eager for him to release her so she could go to sleep.

"No, I'm not sure," Gabe finally replied truthfully. "Is it common?"

"Unfortunately, it's all too common, and most women are too ashamed to admit to it."

"Why?"

"I suppose they're afraid of being judged. People think having a baby is the most natural thing in the world. You'd think so, wouldn't you, but there's nothing further from the truth."

"How do you mean, Mum?"

Gabe heard his mother sigh, probably thinking he was too obtuse to work things out for himself. "Gabe, you became a parent to Alex at the same time as Quinn, but your body hasn't changed, and neither has your routine, for the most part. You still get up in the morning, go to work, come home, have dinner with your family, and go to bed. The only real difference is that now your evenings are filled with children rather than watching a program on TV or reading a novel. Quinn's life has changed inside out. She'd gone through months of feeling unwell, to the point of having to be confined to bed rest, then having her body cut open to extract the baby. She's not the same as she was before the pregnancy, and might never return to the same physical condition. And I'm not talking about losing the weight she gained during her pregnancy. Everything is different, even her ability to feel desire."

"Really? That changes too?"

"Of course. Has that been a problem?" Phoebe asked carefully. She didn't shrink away from asking difficult questions. Gabe was her only son, and she felt it her duty to help him in any way she could, so he might avoid making some of the mistakes his own father had made when Gabe was born.

"She doesn't seem very interested."

"Give her time."

"How much time? Alex is nearly three months old."

"As long as it takes."

"I miss her, Mum."

"And she misses herself."

"What?"

"Gabe, up until a few months ago, Quinn was a working woman who could come and go as she pleased. Since Alex's birth, she's been tethered to him, her breasts his only source of nutrition. She can't even take a walk by herself without taking his feeding schedule into account or asking someone to mind him. That baby is her priority twenty-four hours a day. That's not an easy transition from being in charge of your own time. It's a difficult adjustment, especially for a woman who's worked steadily, and often traveled for her job, for the past decade."

"Did you have difficulty adjusting when I was born?" Gabe asked, genuinely curious. It was only since he and Quinn got together that he'd begun to learn more about his own mother. She'd never talked about herself much, probably because after years of her needs being overlooked, she hadn't seen the point.

"In my day, no one had postnatal depression." Phoebe scoffed. "At last no one ever admitted to it. I was besotted with you, but I have to admit there were times when I felt angry, weepy, and trapped. Your father wasn't much help, God rest his soul. He'd sooner go to his study and smoke a pipe while reading a fishing magazine than give me an hour to myself. Those first few weeks, I barely bathed. I was terrified to leave you unattended. Eventually, I developed a routine and used those precious hours when you napped to see to my own needs. I wasn't a working woman though. I didn't have to balance my career accomplishments with taking care of a newborn."

"Are you saying that Quinn might resent the baby?"

"It's not unnatural to experience moments of resentment."

"Does she resent me?"

"She might. It doesn't mean she doesn't love you, son. What she's going through is natural and will all work itself out in time."

"Now I feel like an insensitive clod." Gabe carefully shifted as Alex's little body grew heavier in sleep.

"Gabe, you're a wonderful husband. You're so much more understanding and helpful than your father ever was. Just don't take it for granted that Quinn is all right. Talk to her. Help her. She's going through a lot, especially now."

"You mean Quentin? Quinn spent decades fantasizing about finding her family, and now that she has, she's had nothing but heartache and disappointment," Gabe said, angry on Quinn's behalf.

"I don't know if I agree with that."

"No?"

"Gabe, no family is perfect. Of course, Quinn imagined the best possible version of her parents and possible siblings. Reality takes some getting used to, especially since she was blessed enough to grow up in a family where she was loved and cared for. Seth is a good man. He's straightforward, solid, and seems to genuinely care for Quinn. I see a long-lasting relationship blossoming between those two. And Logan has been wonderful. He's a good boy."

"What about the rest of them?" Gabe asked snidely. "It's not every day your brother locks you in a cemetery vault and leaves you to die."

"What happened in New Orleans was regrettable, and I'm sure Quinn will carry the emotional scars of that betrayal for the rest of her days, but her relationship with the others can still improve."

"Mum, Sylvia is emotionally unavailable at best, a compulsive liar at worst, and Jude is a tragedy waiting to happen."

"Maybe so, but tragedies happen in all families. And as for Sylvia, well, you have to try to understand where she's coming from."

"And where is that?"

"Her mother left her at a time when she needed her most. The teenage years are difficult for a girl. Sylvia must have felt abandoned and emotionally adrift, and likely tried to find what she was missing in other ways. Instead, she wound up getting pregnant and having twins, one of them seriously ill, without the support of her family or the children's father. She was seventeen, Gabe. Only twelve years older than Emma."

"Mum, how can you compare?"

"Do you think Emma might not have gone off the rails had Jenna died when Emma was older? She was very lucky to have you and Quinn to love her and look after her, but things might have been very different. She might have ended up in foster care, or with someone who couldn't cope with her emotional needs."

"How is it that you see all these things and I don't?" Gabe asked, smiling in the dark. "You're incredibly astute."

"When you look at things from the perspective of old age, you see many things you might have missed when you were a young person. There's no substitute for life experience, and the ability to listen. Besides, it's always easier when you're not the one going through the harrowing experiences life throws at you."

"I love you, Mum."

"And I love you. Now, go put that baby in his cot and go to bed. You sound tired, and you mustn't allow your performance at work to suffer. Few people make allowances for new fathers."

"Good night."

"Good night, son. I can't wait to see you all at Christmas."

Gabe disconnected the call and set aside the phone. Alex was sound asleep, his breathing even. He was warm and soft, his downy head damp against Gabe's chest. Gabe kissed the top of the baby's head and carefully sat up, so as not to disturb him. He carried him to the other room and laid him in his cot. Alex lifted his arms, as if declaring surrender, and turned his head to the side, his mouth slightly open. Gabe had never seen anything as perfect as his tiny son, and he felt a pang of regret at missing the first four years of Emma's life. Phoebe's words still rang in his ears. Perhaps he'd been too hard on Sylvia and Jude. The most important things in life took time and effort.

TEN

MARCH 1917

Petrograd, Russia

The house was shrouded in darkness and veiled in silence. The servants were in their quarters, cowering in fright, no doubt, and Nyanushka and Olga Alexandrovna, the governess, had elected to stay in the nursery with Kolya, believing themselves safer in a room on the top floor that faced the back of the house. No lamps were lit anywhere besides the front parlor, where the family had gathered. The heavy drapes had been pulled closed, and only one oil lamp burned, adding its light to the glow from the fire.

Elena Kalinina reclined dramatically on a chaise, a cool compress on her head, while Ivan Kalinin stood before the fireplace, staring into the flames, his hands clasped behind his back. Valya and Tanya sat on the settee furthest from the window. The room wasn't cold, but they huddled together, their shawls wrapped tightly around their shoulders. Normally, they'd be full of questions, but tonight, neither girl wished to know more. It was all too distressing already.

"What will happen, Vanya?" Elena moaned, addressing her husband by his pet name. "What will become of us?"

"Please calm down, Lenochka," Ivan replied, his tone even and measured. "This rebellion will be put down. There's not a doubt in my mind."

"But the city is overrun with rabble. They're armed and dangerous."

"Lena," Ivan replied patiently, "this is nothing more than a disorganized, clumsy attempt by ill-trained and poorly armed peasants and factory workers to seize control of the city. They've enjoyed a measure of success, but it will be short-lived, I tell you. The rabble-rousers will be put down, their leaders executed like mad dogs. They cannot succeed. It's impossible. Think of it, Lena; they are nothing more than an ignorant, unwashed mob with scythes and axes. They have a few rifles among them, and perhaps a dozen horses. How can they stand up to the might that is the Imperial Russian Army?"

"Where is the Imperial Russian Army?" Elena screeched. "Where were they when the government buildings were seized and the Imperial Guard easily disarmed?"

"My darling, I know you're frightened, but you are overreacting. Petrograd wasn't prepared for an armed revolt, not with our troops fighting the Germans, but His Imperial Highness will not tolerate such a blatant attack on his monarchy. Troops will be diverted from the front, and this unfortunate episode will be erased from our nation's history, washed away like a drop of blood from a pricked finger."

Elena seemed momentarily mollified by her husband's certainty. "I hope you're right, Vanya," she said petulantly. "I hope His Imperial Highness will not be lenient with these thugs. Hang them all, I say. There are plenty more where they came from."

"I'm sure he will do whatever it takes to restore order. Our only responsibility during this time is to look to our safety and to the safety of those employed by us. Kindly inform the servants tomorrow that they are not to leave the house. We have enough provisions and firewood to last several weeks at the very least, so they need not go out."

"But what of Valya's birthday supper next Saturday?" Elena demanded, her mind already turning to more practical matters.

"The supper will go on as planned. We will not allow a bunch of filthy peasants to impact our daily life. Besides, Valentina's birthday is ten days away. By that time, this will all be an unpleasant memory. Go to bed, girls," Ivan said. "You are safe in this house, and will remain so. Tomorrow, life will go on as before."

"Yes, Papa." Valya was only too happy to escape the gloomy atmosphere of the parlor. Her mother's vapors was not what frightened her; it was her father's uncharacteristic gruffness. Beneath the calm exterior, she could tell he was frightened.

"What will happen, Valya?" Tanya asked as they prepared for bed. "Do you think Papa is right and the rebellion will be put down quickly?"

"I expect so, but they might rise up again."

"Why do you say that? Will they not be deterred if their leaders are captured and executed? I can't imagine anything worse than death by hanging." Tanya shuddered at the thought. "To suffocate slowly..."

"Perhaps they'll lie low for a time, but they won't stay quiet forever. Alexei said their grievances are legitimate."

"Did he? But that kind of talk is treasonous. Does he support their cause?" Tanya sat down on the bed and stared at her sister, clearly shocked that Alexei might have sympathy for the people they'd been taught to think of as irrelevant. To imagine that they had just cause wasn't something that ever entered anyone's mind, least of all the narrow scope of a teenage girl's understanding.

"He wasn't advocating revolt, Tanya, he was only pointing out that life can be very difficult for the poor. They want to earn enough to feed their families and keep their sons from being conscripted into the army. Millions have been killed. They want an end to this war."

"Conscripted?" Tanya asked, her mouth forming an "O" of surprise.

"Yes, of course. They don't join voluntarily; that's reserved for sons of the nobility, like Alexei. And highborn young men come in as officers, not foot soldiers."

"I'm scared, Valya. Did you hear all the shouting in the street? It sounded like there were thousands of them, all intent on killing us in our beds."

"They have no interest in us, Tanya. They are after the army and the government. They want reform."

"I hope you're right. May I sleep in your bed tonight?" Tanya asked, her voice small and frightened.

"Of course. But you'll see, by this time next week, this will all be forgotten, like Papa said," Valya announced with more confidence than she felt. She tried to be brave for Tanya, but she was scared, especially for Alexei. No one had mentioned that he was out there with his regiment, defending the city from the mob. Valentina cowered at the thought. Alexei was a cavalry officer, and they were armed with swords. What good were swords against guns? Alexei had joined the cavalry because he loved horses, but at this moment, a horse could be his undoing. Valentina's vision blurred with unshed tears as she imagined an angry peasant stabbing a horse with a pitchfork or cutting it off at the legs with a scythe. The rider would be pulled down into the crowd, defenseless against a mob that was enraged enough to hack him to pieces.

"He'll be all right, Valya," Tanya said, accurately discerning her thoughts. "He's strong and brave, but most of all, he's smart. He'll keep out of harm's way."

"Soldiers are not meant to stay out of harm's way. He'll do his duty, not slink away like a coward," Valya snapped.

"I didn't mean to imply that Alexei is a coward, Valya."

"I know. I'm sorry. I'm just frightened for him."

"Thank God Kolya is not old enough to fight," Tanya mused as she slipped on her nightdress. "You know how he can't wait to join the army when he comes of age. He hero-worships Alexei."

"He's seven," Valentina replied. "It's only natural he should look up to Alexei. Perhaps he'll change his mind once he's older. He can go to the university instead."

"They don't give out gorgeous uniforms at the university, nor do women swoon at the sight of students."

Valya smiled. That was true. There was nothing like the sight of a cavalry regiment on parade, their backs erect, their sabers slapping at their thighs. Even the most unattractive young man looked heroic and handsome in his uniform, his boots gleaming and his cap set at a jaunty angle as he stole discreet peeks at the ladies, who weren't shy in their admiration.

Tanya climbed into bed and snuggled next to her sister. "It will all be right. Won't it, Valya?"

"Of course. Now go to sleep."

ELEVEN
MARCH 15, 1917

Petrograd, Russia

The news came just after lunch, in the form of Petr, the coachman, who told his wife the cook, who in turn told Nyanushka, who came running down the corridor, as fast as her arthritic knees would allow, in search of her employer. Her wails could be heard throughout the house, high-pitched and mournful, and all the more frightening because Anna Sergeevna Portnaya was not a woman who gave vent to her emotions, especially in front of her betters.

It had been only a week since what was now being called the February Revolution had rocked Petrograd. The rebels were in charge of the city, and a provisional government had been established to preside over the country during this uncertain time. No one was quite sure what would happen next, but Ivan Kalinin fervently believed the situation would be resolved as soon as His Imperial Majesty got wind of it and send in troops to quash the rebellion. Ivan had little information to go on, as the newspapers were instructed what to print by the insurgents, and members of the family hadn't left the house for fear of being harassed in the street by the rebels.

Valya and Tanya were in the music room, practicing their duet on the pianoforte, when they heard the commotion.

"Dear God, what now?" Tanya cried as her hands dropped away from the instrument.

"Let's go find out."

"Perhaps we should stay here and allow Papa to deal with it," Tanya suggested.

"You can stay here. I'm going. I refuse to live in ignorance," Valya countered and hurried toward the door.

The screams grew louder as Valya approached the library, where her father liked to spend an hour or two after luncheon. He read the paper, smoked his pipe, and occasionally took a well-deserved nap, safely away from the constant prattling of his wife. Kolya was allowed to join his papa for a game of chess now and again, but the girls never went into the library while their father was there, having been taught to respect his need for solitude. Living in a household consisting primarily of women wasn't easy for any man, particularly Ivan Kalinin, who was intelligent and decisive, and couldn't abide being argued with, something he had to deal with on a daily basis as a husband and a father of two teenaged daughters.

"Papa, what's happened?" Valentina cried as she erupted into the library. Nyanushka was sitting in Papa's chair, her apron pressed to her streaming eyes as Ivan tried to cajole her into accepting a snifter of cognac.

"Come now, Anna Sergeevna. You must calm down, for the sake of the children."

She just shook her head, wailing even louder. Elena walked into the library, her hand held to her breast, her face the color of fresh snow. She'd been resting in her room after lunch, as was her custom.

"Vanya, what's happened?" she cried, her eyes huge with fear.

Tanya came up behind Valentina, unable to keep away from the drama playing out in the library. She reached out and took

Valya's hand. Their father was pale, his eyes wide with a look of shock and uncertainty, and his movements unusually clumsy.

"It is being said that His Imperial Highness, Tsar Nikolai II, has abdicated the throne on behalf of himself and his son," Ivan Kalinin announced. "Get the smelling salts," he cried as Elena went down in a heap on the parquet floor. "Lenochka, darling, can you hear me?" he pleaded with his wife. He lifted her into his arms and carried her into the next room, where he set her down on a satin settee. "Elena," he called to her. "Elena."

Elena's eyelids began to flutter as she woke up, but she instantly blanched and cried out in alarm, recalling what her husband had said just before she fainted. "What's happening? What will become of us, Vanya? How could the Tsar abandon us this way?"

"I'm sure he felt he had no choice, darling."

"How can you say that? He's the Tsar of all the Russians, not some middling bureaucrat. Of course he had a choice."

"Elena, I will go out and try to discover all I can, but you must believe that all will be well."

"How can anything ever be well again? Who will rule this country?"

"I expect the provisional government will continue to govern, as they have done for the past week. I'll know more once I've spoken to—"

"No!" Elena bellowed. "You are not to go out there. Do you hear me? If it's indeed true that the Tsar has abdicated, then the news will be in tomorrow's paper. That's not the sort of information those cretins would wish to suppress. And if it isn't true, we'll find out soon enough, hopefully once the Imperial Army sweeps in and slaughters those traitors once and for all. I won't have you out there on your own, braving the streets when they're overrun with those... those..." Elena gave up as words failed her.

"All right. I won't go anywhere. I will remain right here where you can keep an eye on me," Ivan answered softly to pacify his near-hysterical wife. "You are right. Tomorrow's papers will carry the story. This is the sort of news the rebels will want to crow about from every rooftop."

"We'll have to cancel the party. And on such short notice. That's terrible manners, Ivan. What will everyone think?" Elena moaned.

"Elena, this is not the time to concern yourself with parties, and no one will think ill of us. I wager most of our friends are too frightened to go out, much less attend parties. The important thing is that we are all well. The banks are still operating, the provisional government is maintaining control, and the streets are relatively safe. That's all we can ask for at the moment. We'll find out more in due course. Now, everyone, please return to what you were doing."

Valentina and Tanya shuffled back to the music room, their spirits in tatters. "I'm sorry about your birthday, Valya."

"So am I. I was really looking forward to the party, and the announcement of the engagement. Telling everyone makes it more real somehow, more tangible."

"It is real. You need never doubt that."

"I know. It's just that this was supposed to be such a happy occasion. I've dreamed of it for months, imagining exactly how it would happen."

Valentina sighed and allowed herself to momentarily revisit the fantasy. In her mind she could see the dining room, lit with countless candles. The oil lamps were reserved for everyday use, but it would be candles for the party, long and white, glowing in the crystal chandelier suspended above the table and from the silver candelabras positioned around the room. The table would be covered with her mother's best damask tablecloth and decorated with a gorgeous centerpiece contrived of flowers and vines. The footmen would bring out one dish after another, tempting the guests with delicious food and keeping their glasses full with champagne. A music quartet would play discreetly in the background during the meal, setting the mood, but not distracting the guests from their conversations.

The crystal and silver would glow in the candlelight and ladies' jewels would glitter and sparkle, making even the plainest of women appear beautiful. Everyone would be talking and laughing, and having a wonderful time. Papa, ever the showman, would wait until dessert was ready to be brought out before getting to his feet, raising his champagne flute, and tapping his knife against the crystal until everyone was silent and paying attention. And then, he would announce Valentina and Alexei's engagement and all the guests would cheer them and chant "Gorko." Valentina had always liked that particular custom. It was reserved mostly for weddings, but the betrothed couple would be allowed one kiss. She wasn't sure how the tradition had begun, but it was customary for the guests to cry out 'Bitter, bitter' and encourage the couple to kiss and make it sweet.

"I suppose we'll be eating well for the next week. Mama ordered smoked sturgeon, beluga caviar, pheasant, and other delicacies for the supper. She won't allow them to go to waste. You love blini with caviar," Tanya said in an effort to lift Valentina's spirits.

"The way I feel right now, I don't think I'll ever be hungry again. My stomach is in knots. The Tsar is the head of the Imperial Army. If he has abdicated, then what becomes of the regiments stationed in Petrograd? They're outnumbered and without proper command."

"If they are without command, then there's no one to order them to fight against the rebels," Tanya pointed out wisely.

"Yes, that's true, but they still have their immediate commanding officers who might decide to act on their own. Imagine how celebrated they would be if they managed to put down the rebellion from within."

"That would be rather heroic."

"Heroic and suicidal."

"Come, Valya, let's practice our duet. It will take our minds off things," Tanya suggested and took her seat at the piano, but Valentina eschewed the piano and curled up in a high-backed armchair instead. The chair was upholstered in butter yellow and the sunny color normally lifted her spirits, but not today.

Until last week, the most dramatic thing to ever happen to Valentina had been the death of their puppy, Dimok. They'd named him "Smoky" because of his fur, which was the bluish-gray color of chimney smoke rising into a winter sky. He'd been less than one year old when he'd foolishly run beneath the wheels of a carriage while the family strolled through the Summer Garden last spring. Kolya had been holding his leash but let go when Dimok suddenly bolted, having spotted something that interested him. Kolya had been inconsolable for weeks and refused the offer of a new puppy as a way of punishing himself for his negligence.

And now they were in the midst of a revolution that seemed to be happening right on their doorstep. Valentina wondered if the people in other large cities, such as Moscow, were affected by the revolt. They must be if the Tsar had abdicated. This revolution must be affecting the entire country.

Valentina wrapped her arms around her legs and rested her forehead on her knees. She couldn't quite grasp the implications of the situation. What did it all really mean? What would happen to the royal family? Who would take the Tsar's place? Who'd be in charge? And what would happen to everything the royal family owned: their palaces, carriages, jewels, and automobiles? What would become of the aristocracy without a tsar? What would become of her?

This should have been the most exciting time of her life. She was newly engaged, about to begin planning her wedding and her future with the man she'd loved since she was a little girl, but instead she had to worry about matters of state, and the war that raged somewhere out there, beyond the scope of her imagination, a war that had caused such discontent among the common people that it had finally tipped them over the edge of reason. Would the troops be recalled from the front or would they go on fighting? It was all too confusing to even contemplate.

Valentina abandoned her refuge and returned to her room. She rummaged under her pillow until she extracted a folded piece of paper, the note hastily written in graphite. It had been delivered four days ago by a young boy who had stood awkwardly before her, hand outstretched, until she gave him a few kopeks for his trouble. Valentina had breathed a sigh of relief when she recognized Alexei's handwriting, and she'd retreated to her room to read the note in peace.

Dearest Valya,

I'm all right. Please don't worry about me. Stay indoors and well away from the windows. I'll come by as soon as I'm able.

Love,

Alexei (your future husband)

Valentina refolded the note and pressed it to her lips. Alyosha was all right, and that was all that mattered at this moment. As long as they'd be together in the future, they'd survive anything that life had to throw at them.

TWELVE
DECEMBER 2014

London, England

Quinn checked on Emma, tucked in Alex, who was sleeping peacefully, and climbed into bed, grateful to be off her feet at last. It had been a long day and she was tired. Gabe was already in bed, reading a book about Richard III. He marked his place, set the book aside, and switched off the bedside lamp. He turned to Quinn, watching as she settled in, leaving a wide gap between them.

She wanted to reach for him, but she felt tense as a spring, her body rigid and unyielding. Jill's accusing words about Alex being her first priority and Emma's earlier queries about sex had left her feeling hollow and weepy. Jill was right—it was all about the baby. His needs eclipsed everything, especially her need for intimacy. She and Gabe had made love twice since she'd recovered from the cesarean, but it wasn't the same. Something was missing, and she knew it was on her end. She hadn't felt a twinge of desire since the baby was born and had pretended to enjoy Gabe's caresses to spare his feelings, but she was sure he knew, probably tipped off by the fact that she had lain there like roadkill, waiting for him to finish.

The thought of being touched upset her and made her want to curl into herself like a shrimp. Her body was no longer her own.

Her breasts were engorged with milk, her nipples sore from nursing every three hours, and her belly marred by angry red stretch marks that flowed across her milky skin like rivers on a map. The incision had healed, but the scar was ropy and sensitive to the touch. She didn't feel attractive and couldn't see how Gabe could find her desirable. He was just going through the motions, taking care of his physical needs.

"Have you completely gone off me?" Gabe suddenly asked, as if reading her thoughts.

"No."

"Then why do you shrink away from me every time I reach for you? You always used to snuggle up against me when you came to bed, but now you're all the way over there, rigid as a plank, hoping I'll turn over and go to sleep without bothering you."

"Because I think you're reaching for me out of a sense of obligation rather than desire. I'm afraid you find me repellent," she muttered, wondering if it was a mistake to admit to her insecurity.

"Repellent?" Gabe gaped at her, clearly stunned by her words.

"Don't you? I see how your eyes slide away whenever I'm nursing Alex. My breasts are huge and swollen, and you find them repugnant."

Gabe let out a frustrated sigh and rolled onto his side, his head supported by his hand so he could look down at her. "Quinn, that's not the reason I look away."

"Then what is?"

"I look away because I am ashamed of myself."

"Why would you feel ashamed? You're not the one lactating like a cow."

"Because watching you nurse our son brings out some primal, uncontrollable urge in me. I want to push you down, force your legs apart, and go at you until you hurtle over the edge of your restraint and give yourself to me without reservation. I don't want to be gentle or considerate, I want to be selfish and forceful, and pound you like a madman until you remember that you are mine, and that I have the power to make you scream as you straddle the knife edge between pleasure and pain, your body at my mercy as I show you what it means to be desired and well loved."

"Is that really how you feel?" Quinn asked, stunned by how far off the mark she had been in her understanding of Gabe's feelings.

"Yes, and it's awful, I know. I'm not that man. I'm not some thug who wants to hurt his woman and force her into sexual submission. I'm a civilized human being who's been taught to take his partner's needs into consideration and never do anything that might cause pain or discomfort, but the desire is too strong to master, so I look away, terrified that you'll see it in my eyes and despise me."

Quinn felt a white-hot bolt of desire strike her lower belly as her nether regions began to throb with need. Gabe's words had unleashed something in her, pushing past her apathy, fatigue, and lack of confidence. She wanted him, and she wanted him this minute. She didn't want him to kiss or caress her. She wanted him to just take her. "Do it," she ordered him.

"Do what?"

"What you just said. Be selfish and forceful."

"Are you sure that's what you want?'

"Yes. I want you to give in to that urge and show me what it feels like."

"I don't think I'll be able to stop once I get going."

"Then don't. Don't stop until you get what you need."

Gabe rolled on top of her and pinned her wrists to the mattress. His eyes were like dark pools of desire, his pupils dilated in the darkness of the room. His face was set in harsh lines, the familiar features suddenly foreign and frightening. He yanked her knickers off and pried her legs open with his knee before taking possession with one hard stroke.

Quinn cried out and arched her back, desperate to take him in deeper as he went at her, again and again, hard and fast. There were no words of love or tender kisses, just raw unbridled lust that made her insides quake as she slammed her hips against his. She raked her nails over Gabe's back and cried out with every thrust, breathless with ecstasy and completely oblivious to the baby sleeping just a few feet away. Gabe grabbed her legs and draped them over his shoulders, penetrating her deeper and harder until something inside her snapped and she tumbled over the threshold, her body shuddering with the type of release she hadn't experienced since the night she conceived Alex.

Gabe had been furious with her that night for putting herself in danger and lying to him about her intention to confront the man she believed to be her biological father, and he'd been aggressive and unyielding when they came together, as much in anger as in love. Perhaps that was what she wanted. She needed to allow herself to surrender to his passion, to give up control for just a little while. She was always an equal partner, but sometimes she had no wish to be. Sometimes she wanted to be mastered, possessed, and reminded that she had the power to drive him mad with desire and jealousy until the veneer of civility fell away, allowing her a glimpse of the man he might have been had he not been brought up in the twentieth century. For one brief moment, she had a vision of Guy de Rosel, and the two merged, the academic and the knight, so different, yet so alike.

Quinn went limp beneath Gabe, her body weightless as she floated on a cloud of pure blissful pleasure. Her insides were quivering, like aftershocks after a volcanic eruption. Gabe collapsed on top of her, damp with perspiration. He was still inside her, their bodies joined in the age-old dance of possession and love. He kissed her temple, then bent down and captured her lips in a sweet kiss. The storm of passion had passed, leaving them both utterly spent.

"All right?" he whispered into her ear.

"More than all right. It was earth-shattering," Quinn confessed, a sated smile tugging at her lips.

"So, you don't mind a bit of rough now and then?" Gabe asked, only half-joking.

"No, I don't. You never have to feel like you can't tell me what you want, Gabe. As a matter of fact, you're not the only one who appreciates the breastfeeding experience."

"Meaning?"

"Rhys was just waxing poetic about its power to arouse," Quinn explained.

"Did he now? And is it you he was aroused by?"

"Of course not. Are you seriously jealous of Rhys?"

"Rhys's feelings for you are complicated, to say the least."

"You've got nothing to worry about on that score."

"Go to sleep, love, unless you're up for another round." Gabe's voice was soft but full of promise, making her shiver. It was only as she began to drift off to sleep that she realized they hadn't used any birth control.

THIRTEEN

Quinn settled Alex into a baby carrier and set off for her appointment. She would have preferred to take the pram, but the tables in FreeState Coffee were too closely set up to bring it indoors and she didn't want to leave it outside since it had begun to snow. Logan had chosen the place for the meeting, since he could only pop in during his work break. Quinn strode along purposefully, her arms around the baby, whose cheek was pressed to her arm. He was wide awake, looking around with interest. If she walked long enough, he'd drift off and hopefully sleep through the meeting with Drew Camden, private investigator. Quinn had called him that morning, thinking they could chat over the phone, but Drew had wanted to meet in person, probably to get a sense of her as a client.

The coffee shop was half-empty, which was a blessing. Quinn took a table in the corner and ordered herself a decaffeinated cappuccino. She would have loved a blast of caffeine but felt too guilty to indulge while nursing. As soon as she weaned Alex, she'd have a bucket of coffee followed by several bottles of chilled white wine and a night out on the town. She might even stay up past nine o'clock and wear something besides her elastic waistband leggings.

Quinn's cheeks grew uncomfortably warm as she thought of

Gabe and his hungry hands on her body. Last night had been frantic and primitive, but this morning their lovemaking had been slow, drowsy, and decadent, reminding her of what their life had been like before the children came along. She had been barely awake when Gabe pulled her against him, his hand cupping her overflowing breast as he entered her from behind, his movements leisurely and deliberate, and so delicious. It wasn't just the sex that made Quinn happy, it was the physical intimacy between them that had been sorely missing for the past few months. It felt so natural and so right, like two halves of a whole coming together and locking firmly into place. Gabe still loved and desired her, and she'd rediscovered her hunger for him and realized that she was ravenous. They were parents to two children, but they were still a couple, still Quinn and Gabe, and they had to hold on to that no matter what. So many couples lost their bond as the responsibilities of family took over. She wouldn't allow that to happen to them.

Quinn tore her thoughts away from the boudoir and turned her attention to the baby. She removed Alex's fuzzy brown hat with monkey ears, pulled off his coat so he wouldn't get too warm, and settled him in her lap. He was wide awake, smacking his lips in that way he did when he was hungry.

"Oh no, you don't. I'm not nursing you here," Quinn crooned to him. "I have a lovely bottle for you, young sir." She extracted the bottle from her baby bag and adjusted the baby's position for easier feeding before allowing him to latch on. "There you go. Enjoy! Same product, different packaging."

"May I join you?" a gravelly voice inquired, nearly making Quinn jump out of her skin. "I'm Drew."

"Ah, yes, of course. Sorry, I was a bit distracted."

"I can see that. Sweet little lad. What's his name?"

"Alex."

Quinn took in Drew Camden. He was in his late forties or early fifties, with a head of thick, silver-streaked dark curls and light blue eyes that seemed to miss little. He was a bear of a man, and a little intimidating, if she were honest. Drew extended his left leg into the space between the tables as he sat down.

"Can't bend it all the way," he explained. "Gunshot wound."

"I'm sorry. Brian did mention you were shot in the line of duty."

"No need to be sorry. What happened, happened. Now, shall we wait for your brother, or would you like to give me the backstory?"

"I can fill you in while we wait. Logan should be here any minute. He's coming from work. He's a nurse at the London."

"A noble profession. There were some wonderful nurses looking after me after my injury. One of them was so sweet, I married her," he added as a charming blush stained his cheeks. "Every cloud and all that..."

Quinn smiled. Drew Camden suddenly seemed a lot less intimidating, and vastly more likable. "That's a great story. Logan met his partner, Colin, at the hospital as well. He's a lovely man, intelligent and kind."

"And where did you meet your husband?" Drew asked, smiling at Alex, whose eyelids were fluttering as he stopped sucking and began to drift off to sleep.

"We met on an archeological dig in Ireland. He was the dig supervisor and I was one of the students. It took us eight years to actually get together."

"Life has its own plan, doesn't it, and its own timeline."

"I don't know about that. Was it life's plan to separate me from my sister at birth? Seems awfully unfair."

"No one said it was fair, but maybe this is the way it was meant to be."

"Well, I mean to change that. I have to find her. I must."

"Tell me everything you know," Drew invited.

Logan came rushing into the coffee shop just as Quinn finished her summary, which was pitifully short. "Sorry I'm late. What did I miss?"

"Nothing yet," Drew replied calmly. "So, Quentin is not actually missing, just not in contact?"

"There's no trace of her anywhere," Logan reiterated what Quinn had already explained. "She doesn't come up in any search. Even if she were dead, her obituary would pop up."

"I think we need to work under the assumption that Quentin changed her name after leaving her parents' home. Since we don't know what she changed it to, that avenue of enquiry is closed to us. However, there are other ways to get to her."

"Such as? We've learned next to nothing from her siblings or the attorney who manages her trust fund," Logan said.

"Perhaps you didn't ask the right questions, or pose them to the right people."

"What other people are there? Her parents are dead, and the only people we can connect to her are her siblings and the lawyer," Quinn pointed out.

"There are others. No man is an island, as someone great whose name I can't quite recall once said."

"John Donne," Quinn supplied with a smile.

"Right. Look, I normally require a retainer of a thousand quid and then charge an hourly rate, but since you're Jill's cousin, I'll forgo the retainer. If I find Quentin, I'll bill you. If not, you'll only have to reimburse me for my time and expenses."

"Fair enough," Logan said. "But don't say 'if,' say 'when.'"

"Oh, I will find her," Drew promised. "Regardless of how long it takes."

"Where will you start?" Quinn asked, curious about his process.

"I'll start where it all began and work my way out from there. Leicester will be my first port of call. Don't expect a report from me every day. I'll only ring you if I have something to tell you, but just because you don't hear from me doesn't mean I'm not working on your behalf. Do you have a photo of Quentin?" Drew asked, looking from Logan to Quinn.

"No, we don't. Karen Crawford said all her parents' possessions had been placed in storage, including family albums. She didn't volunteer to obtain a photograph, and even if she had, it'd have been decades old," Logan pointed out.

"Shame, that. It would have been helpful."

"What if Quentin doesn't want to be found?" Quinn asked. The fear had been gnawing at her since she first learned of Quentin's existence. What if her sister had no desire to meet her twin and wasn't responding intentionally?

"If she doesn't want to have any dealings with you, then she can tell you so herself, to your face. Until then, we work under the assumption that she doesn't know you exist," Drew replied.

"How can she not? Wouldn't it be unethical for her attorney not to have told her or passed on the letter I sent?" Quinn asked.

"Yes, it would, but people do things for the oddest reasons. We won't know for sure until we find her and ask her outright. Sound like a plan?"

"Yes," Quinn and Logan replied in unison.

"I'll be off then. I have a train to Leicester to catch," Drew said as he heaved himself out of the chair. "I'll be in touch."

"What'd you think of him?"

"He seems confident that he can find Quentin, and I want to believe him."

"Mum keeps asking if we've heard anything," Logan said. "I hope you don't mind if I keep her up-to-date on our search."

"Of course I don't mind. If and when we find Quentin, it will be up to her whether she wants to meet Sylvia," Quinn said as she began to maneuver the sleeping baby into his coat. "I certainly won't try to discourage her."

"Would you want to meet Mum if you were her?" Logan peered at Quinn from beneath his lashes, like a little boy who feared being reprimanded by a teacher.

"Logan, you don't have to feel guilty about loving your mother. Sylvia raised you and loved you, and it's only natural that you feel loyal to her. I don't expect you to take sides. As far as Quentin goes, I honestly have no idea how she'll feel. She might be eager to meet the woman who gave birth to her, or choose to have nothing to do with her."

"It's just that she seems to have completely rejected her adoptive family," Logan replied. "Some people like to hold grudges."

"And you think she's one of them?"

"Could be."

"Sometimes people have a very good reason," Quinn replied as she carefully placed Alex in the baby carrier and pulled on her gloves. "I'm reserving judgement."

"I've always dreamed of having a worldly and wise older sister," Logan joked. He held the door for Quinn as she stepped out into the street.

"See? Dreams do come true." Quinn giggled and turned her face up to receive his brotherly kiss. She wasn't exactly sure when it had happened, but she suddenly realized she loved him and she recognized an answering tenderness in his gaze.

"See ya, sis."

"See ya, little brother," Quinn replied, smiling happily to herself.

FOURTEEN
APRIL 1917

Petrograd, Russia

Valentina's eighteenth birthday came and went without much fanfare. As Tanya had predicted, they ate well that week, and the one after that, but no one particularly enjoyed the food. Elena and Ivan presented Valentina with an exquisite choker crafted of three strands of pearls and adorned at the front with a diamond-encrusted lily. Tiny diamonds were evenly spaced throughout the necklace, their shine bringing out the luminescence of the pearls. On any other birthday, Valentina would have been speechless with awe. The choker was a present for a woman, not a girl, and her parents' acknowledgement that she was now an adult, a woman about to be married, but Valentina felt nothing but sadness. The weeks since the Revolution had been tense and frightening. No one really knew what to expect, and as the days wore on, they tried to regain some sort of normalcy.

Petr went out every morning and brought back every newspaper he could find for the master. As soon as he returned, Ivan locked himself in his study for the remainder of the morning, reading every word until he finally emerged in time for luncheon. He assured everyone daily that the situation was under control and all would be well, but Valentina expected nothing less of her father. He was surrounded by women, and like most men of his time, believed the womenfolk should be spared any unpleasantness. Elena rarely asked, preferring to focus on domestic issues and her sparse social calendar. People were slowly beginning to resume their lives, going about their business and even holding small gatherings to bolster their spirits. Elena insisted on attending a musical evening and a small dinner party, but Ivan drew the line at going to the theater.

"Elena, it's out of the question," he said, his tone firm, as if speaking to a wayward child.

"But why? The performances have resumed and I see no reason we have to hide here and give those beasts the satisfaction of knowing we're scared."

"Darling, think about it," Ivan reasoned with her, softening his tone. "Should anything happen, we'll be trapped in a building with hundreds of other people and few exits. There will be panic and a stampede, with everyone trying to get out. It's not safe."

"Princess Kuragina attended an opera at the Mariinsky Theater last Saturday. She is not afraid of a stampede," Elena argued.

"Princess Kuragina is eighty-six years old. Her children are grown and her husband's been in the ground these past thirty years. She doesn't have much left to lose. You, on the other hand, have our children to think about. An evening at the opera is not worth the risk."

Elena scoffed, but didn't argue further. Instead, she took a different tack. "How about we host a small supper then? We were forced to cancel Valya's birthday party, but we could make up for that. Perhaps I can convince Angelika Mironova to come and sing for us. She has the voice of an angel, and her brother might make a good match for Tanya one day."

Ivan sighed. "Lena, please. I know you're anxious and want nothing more than for normal life to resume, but these are uncertain times. We can't continue as if nothing's happened."

"You really are becoming quite stodgy, Vanya."

"If that's the worst you can say about me, I can live with that," Ivan grumbled.

The morning after her parents' argument, Valentina knocked on the door of her father's study. Not knowing what was really happening was much more frightening than knowing the truth, no matter how dire, and she meant to talk her father into explaining things to her. If he believed that going to the theater wasn't safe, then clearly, he wasn't telling them the whole truth of the situation.

"Come," Ivan called.

She entered and shut the door behind her. "I'd like to talk to you, Papa."

"Are you going to demand an outing to the theater as well? I already told your mother it's out of the question."

"That's not why I'm here. I need to understand what's happening. You burn the newspapers after you read them, and I've hardly been anywhere since the uprising. I haven't even seen Alexei, and his notes are about as informative as your daily reports. Please, Papa, I'm a grown woman now, and I deserve to know what's happening."

Ivan leaned back in his chair and studied Valentina, as if seeing her for the first time. His brown eyes softened as he looked at her and he nodded, decision made. "I suppose you're right, Valya. You are a grown woman, and you're different from your mother. I tend to forget that."

"In what way am I different?" Valentina asked as she took a seat across from her father.

"Your mother was hardly more than a girl when I met her. I was charmed. She was beautiful, vivacious, and childlike, in a most endearing sort of way. Trouble is, she never really grew up. I saw to everything from the day we were married, and shielded her from anything that might distress her. I only wanted her to be happy, you see, but she's not strong or decisive. She never had to be. You will make a good wife to Alexei. You'll be a true partner to him."

"Are you saying Mama is not a true partner?" Valentina asked.

Her father had never said a negative word about Elena in the presence of the children, and the revelation that he had doubts about her ability to handle hardship came as a shock.

"She's my partner in all the ways that count, Valya, but she's not strong-willed like you. She's happy to let someone else make the important decisions, which has worked well for us over the years."

"Papa, tell me what's happening. I want to know the truth."

Ivan sighed and leaned back in his chair. He suddenly looked older than his forty-five years. Valentina hadn't noticed the strands of gray at his temples or the deepening lines bracketing his mouth. To her, he was still her handsome Papa, but the past few weeks had taken their toll and the cracks were beginning to show.

"The truth is that no one really knows, dochenka."

Valentina almost teared up at the endearment. Her father rarely used the diminutive version of "daughter" to address her, not since she was little. He still called Kolya *sinok*, but Kolya was seven, not really old enough to be called "son," as an older boy would. Her father was feeling more emotional than she'd realized.

"There are several factions vying for power, and I really don't think the provisional government will last long."

"Do you think it will be replaced by a new tsar?"

"That would be the ideal solution, but right now that doesn't seem likely. Grand Duke Michael has been named successor, since he's next in line for the throne, but he hasn't accepted. He's asked for ratification of his claim by an elected assembly."

Valentina gaped at her father. She'd always been taught to believe that the Romanovs had divine right to rule. They'd been emperors of Russia for three hundred years. To ask an elected assembly to sanction a tsar was like asking your groom whether you might have permission to ride your own horse. She'd never taken Grand Duke Michael for a coward, but he clearly feared the revolutionaries and had no desire to put himself in harm's way.

"Will they ratify his claim?"

Ivan shook his head. "I don't think so. At this stage, no elected assembly will agree on anything. Do you remember that Krylov fable I used to read to you when you were little, about the swan, pike, and crab? You loved that story."

"You mean the one where the swan, pike, and crab were harnessed together to a wagon, but couldn't move forward because they were all pulling in different directions?"

"That's the one."

"Are you saying that's what's happening in this country, Papa?"

"In simple terms—yes."

"So, what would have to happen for this situation to resolve itself?" Valentina asked, but she already knew the answer. One of the factions would have to break free of the others and seize control.

"I don't know, Valya. I really don't know. Come summer, I will be sending you all to Pulkovo, to the Petrov dacha. You will be safer there, away from the city."

"What about you, Papa?"

"Count Petrov and I will remain here in Petrograd. We will come to visit you, but we must protect our interests and our investments. Your mother will try to argue with me and demand that we go to our own dacha at Tsarskoye Selo, but it's not safe right now."

"I will back you up, Papa. Don't worry. I like the Petrov dacha better anyway. It's more private and we're not constantly under the watchful eye of other summering families."

"I just don't want you near the Alexander Palace."

"Why?"

"Because that's where the royal family is being kept under house arrest."

"Do you think they're in danger, Papa?" Valentina asked. She hadn't given the royal family much thought over the past few weeks, but she suddenly wondered what became of a dethroned tsar. What would be his role in this new Russia, and how long would the revolutionaries keep the family under arrest? Surely they had to release them at some point. Perhaps they would seek asylum in Europe until things settled down, and maybe, in time, Tsar Nikolai would be invited to take the throne once again.

"I don't think they're in any immediate danger, Valya, but their situation is certainly unique, to say the least."

"Will you keep me up-to-date, Papa?" Valentina asked.

"I will do better than that. I will save the newspapers for you so you can read the articles for yourself, but please, do it while Tanya and Kolya are at their lessons and your mother is otherwise engaged."

"It will be our secret."

"Our secret," Ivan agreed and came from behind his desk to kiss Valentina on the forehead. "You're a good girl, Valya. May God keep you safe. Now and always."

FIFTEEN
DECEMBER 2014

London, England

Quinn set aside the necklace once Alex began to fuss. He'd been asleep for over two hours and would now need a clean nappy and a feeding. She enjoyed the hours of peace and quiet while he slept, but was always happy to spend time with him when he woke. Alex was a happy baby. As long as he was dry and fed, the world was his oyster. Quinn deftly changed the baby and put him to her breast, happy to see him suck greedily. He had a good appetite and was putting on weight: signs of a healthy baby. She loved seeing his little hand splayed on her breast, as if he were holding on to her, afraid she'd take the breast away before he was truly full.

"Don't worry, sweetheart, I'll never leave you hungry," she said to him, her voice brimming with tenderness. "You take as much as you need."

Alex continued to suck happily, oblivious to the doorbell that buzzed unexpectedly and startled Quinn out of her reverie. She wasn't expecting anyone. Perhaps it was a parcel delivery. Gabe might have ordered something online. Quinn carefully got up without disturbing the nursing baby and went to check the little screen by the door. Sylvia. For one brief moment, Quinn considered not allowing her to come up, but then she dismissed the idea. Sylvia had come all this way. It'd be rude not to let her in. Quinn buzzed her up.

"Oh," Sylvia said as she came in and saw the infant at Quinn's breast. "I didn't realize you'd decided to nurse."

"It's better for the baby."

"I bottle-fed the boys and they turned out just fine," Sylvia commented as she shrugged off her coat and hung up her scarf. She refrained from mentioning that Quinn had been bottle-fed as well, since her adoptive mother hadn't had the option to nurse her, although Susan Allenby would have liked nothing more.

Sylvia came into the living room and held out a prettily wrapped package decorated with a sparkly blue bow. "This is for my grandson. The toy is store-bought, but the blanket I knitted myself. It's machine washable and won't shrink," she added.

"Thank you. That's very kind. Eh, why are you here, Sylvia?" Quinn asked. She had no wish to be rude, but she didn't have the type of relationship with Sylvia where they just dropped in on each other. She doubted they ever would.

"I wanted to talk to you, Quinn, if that's all right."

"Give me a moment to finish nursing and then I'll make us a cup of tea."

"I can make the tea; you concentrate on the baby. Looks like he's full," she added. Alex had stopped sucking and was watching Sylvia with interest.

Quinn hoisted the baby onto her shoulder and held him upright as she patted his back lightly. Alex let out a belch worthy of a sailor and smiled happily. "What do you say to a little time on your play mat?" Quinn asked. "You like playing there, don't you?"

She lowered Alex to the floor and laid him down on his back, so he could look up at the colorful plastic shapes suspended from the overhead arches and reach for the lower-hanging toys. He was in heaven. "Let's have tea in here, so I can keep an eye on him."

"I'll get it. Milk, no sugar. Right?"

"Right."

Sylvia brought out two mugs of tea and set them on the coffee table before getting settled in an armchair across from the sofa. She looked tired and not as elegantly turned out as she usually was. She wore an oversized navy jumper over a pair of leggings and short boots, not her normal chic style at all. Sylvia's face looked puffy, and her mouth was downturned at the corners.

"Are you all right, Sylvia?"

"I've been better, if you must know. I miss Rhys."

"I'm sorry it didn't work out for you two."

"It might have, but let's not rehash that again." Sylvia reached for her mug and took a long swallow of tea, as if bracing herself for a difficult conversation. "Look, Quinn, I need you to stop punishing me for something I did when I was seventeen. It's not fair. I could have handled things better, I know that now, but I will not keep apologizing for the choices I made."

"I'm not punishing you for something you did when you were seventeen. I'm punishing you for something you did last year. You should have told me about Quentin."

"Yes, in retrospect, I should have probably told you, but I was afraid."

"Of what?"

"Of this. Of your unyielding moral superiority. You don't know what you might have done in my place. It's easy to judge when you have a loving husband and a well-paying career. I only just found you, and I didn't want to destroy our relationship before it had a chance to begin. I wanted to get to know you, and I hoped that once you got to know me, maybe you'd be more understanding when I finally told you the truth."

"Let's face it, Sylvia, I don't think you were ever going to tell me the truth. You wrote Quentin off the moment you left her at the hospital, just as you wrote me off. Had you not stumbled on that article about me, you'd never have tried to find me. You were content enough living without me for thirty years."

"Quinn, I know you're angry, but can you not find it in your heart to give me the benefit of the doubt?"

"I was so happy to have met you, and so excited to learn something of where I came from, especially once I got to know Seth, but now that I have my own baby, I find it even more difficult to comprehend how you could have just left a child that was gasping for breath and walked away without a backward glance."

"I'm not proud of what I did, but I was young and foolish. I wanted my life back. I wanted a future. You two were better off without me."

"And better off without our father? Seth is a good man, Sylvia. I like him. He's kind, caring, and most of all, he's direct."

"Well, he is American, isn't he?" Sylvia retorted.

"He loves me, Sylvia. I can feel it every time I speak to him, and every time I see him. I've never felt that from you."

"I do love you," Sylvia snapped.

"Do you?"

"Quinn, I'm not an overly demonstrative person, but the thought of losing you again devastates me. Please, give me another chance."

Quinn tilted her head and looked at Sylvia. This was her chance to find out the answer to a question that had been bothering her since the day she'd met her birth mother. It wasn't fair to use Sylvia's desire to have a relationship with her as leverage, but she needed to know, especially if she hoped to maintain her relationship with Seth.

"All right, but I will ask you a question and I need an honest answer. I won't judge you or hold what you said in the past against you, but I need to know for the sake of my relationship with my father. Did Seth rape you? Did any of them?"

Sylvia hung her head. Her hands were folded in her lap, her fingers intertwined in a way that had to be painful. When she finally answered, her voice shook with emotion. "I couldn't tell you the truth, Quinn. I just couldn't. I was too ashamed."

"Go on."

"We were all quite drunk. It was the most fun I'd had since my mother walked out on us and I didn't want the night to end. I didn't want to go home to my dour father and my lonely room. It was Christmas Eve, but we didn't have so much as a wreath, much less a tree. My father had just given up and made no pretense of even trying, not even for my sake. I had no idea where my mother had gone, and even though I hoped she'd ring me on Christmas, deep down I knew she wouldn't. She'd abandoned me, in every way it was possible to abandon a child. At least I never really knew you and your sister, but my mother had raised me. We'd had a relationship, a bond. I missed her," Sylvia whispered.

She looked up at Quinn, her eyes searching for understanding, and Quinn nodded, acknowledging Sylvia's pain. She could understand how bewildered Sylvia must have felt, how bereft, especially if her father had shut down after his wife left and paid little attention to his daughter's feelings.

"The other two girls went home, seeing which way things were headed, but I stayed. Willingly. Robert was the first to make his move. I resisted a bit at first, but he was an aggressive bloke, sure of himself and his appeal. He was used to getting his way. He began to kiss me and slid his hands beneath my jumper and cupped my breasts. It felt good. He made me feel sexy and desirable. We just snogged for a while, and then he pulled me down to the floor. The room was dim, with only the light from the fireplace casting a glow over the scene, and the carpet beneath me was thick and soft. It was surreal, in a way. I should have stopped him. I knew what he would try to do, but I just lay there, warmed by the fire and drowsy from the champagne.

"I allowed him to pull off my jeans and knickers. Seth and Rhys watched, and it turned me on to see the hunger in their eyes. They wanted me too. I felt no fear, no shame. Robert had me right there and then. He didn't rape me. I allowed him to do it. He was drunk, and it only lasted a minute or so. He wasn't up to much. When he was done, I reached out for Seth. He was so good-looking, so strong, and his American accent and confidence were like an aphrodisiac. I hadn't really enjoyed it with Robert, but Seth took his time. He cared about my pleasure."

"And Rhys?" Quinn asked.

"Rhys just stood there, rooted to the spot. He was shocked, but couldn't force himself to look away. I guessed he was still a virgin and I felt sorry for him. 'Have a turn,' I told him. 'You might as well. Your mates have had their fun.'

"He was reluctant, probably too embarrassed to lose his virginity in front of his friends, but they egged him on, as men do. He was the youngest, and his shyness amused them. He finally gave in. By that time he was so aroused, he could barely breathe. It was quick with him, but in some booze-soaked part of my brain, I was happy to have given him something to remember. I was so drunk, I could barely keep my eyes open after that. The next thing I knew, Robert had me in his car and he was taking me home. He brought me to my door, wished me a happy Christmas, and left, like nothing out of the ordinary had happened."

"So you led me to believe that my father was a rapist when the whole time you knew that to be a lie."

"Quinn, how do you tell a daughter you've just found after thirty years that you had sex with three men you barely knew and enjoyed it? You would have thought me a world-class slag and wouldn't have given me the time of day."

"Why did Rhys feel so guilty then? Why did he not dispute the accusation?"

"He'd been drunk and had a hazy recollection of events, at best. When you told him I'd accused them of rape, he believed it."

"Would they have allowed you to leave had you wanted to, or would things have still gone the same way?" Quinn asked, needing to be sure of what had really happened that night.

"Robert offered to take me home after the other girls left. He didn't force me, but he did manhandle me a bit, which I actually enjoyed. His persistence made it easier for me to give in."

"Does Rhys know?"

"Yes. I told him the truth after both Robert and Seth denied the accusation."

"Is that what drove him away?"

"No, I don't think so. It was never truly right between us, not in that way. Rhys has never been married or had children of his own. He's on the verge of a fresh start, a whole new phase of life. Nothing will ever be fresh for me again. I was married for more than two decades and gave birth to four children. I've lived with my secrets since I was seventeen, and the lying took its toll. I never told my husband about that night, or about the children that came from it. It was a heavy burden to bear even though he never questioned my past. He was a good man. He deserved better than the likes of me."

"Was that the only time you went that far—sexually, I mean?" Quinn asked, in equal parts fascinated and repulsed by Sylvia's admission. Sylvia was certainly a lot more uninhibited than her daughter, and that knowledge came as something of a surprise.

"Getting pregnant and giving birth to twins does wonders for your perspective. I was afraid after that, spooked. I remained celibate for two years and then it was all monogamous relationships until I met my Grant." Sylvia leaned forward, her desperate gaze fixed on Quinn's face. "Do you despise me now that I told you?"

"No. I wish you'd told me the truth before. You'd have spared me a lot of anguish. I'm glad to know my father is not a violent man."

"No, he isn't." Sylvia set the mug down on the coffee table and slowly got to her feet. She'd said her piece and now it was up to Quinn to decide how to proceed. "Is there a chance for us?" Sylvia asked as she prepared to leave. "Can we start again?"

"Sylvia, I would like you in my life, and in the lives of my children, but it'll take time for me to learn to trust you. You've lied to me too many times. I can understand why you did it, but that doesn't make it any easier for me to excuse. Please, give me time."

"I want to see her," Sylvia pleaded. "I want to see my girl. She'll reject me out of hand if you tell her the truth right away."

"I won't do anything to turn her against you. She can meet you and decide for herself," Quinn promised.

"I would appreciate that."

"I will let you know when we find Quentin, but until then, I'd appreciate a little space. Can you give me that?"

"Yes. Ring me?"

"Yes, I'll call you when I'm ready. Give my regards to Jude. I hope he's well."

"As well as can be expected. He's signed on with a methadone program, but it's very easy to revert to old habits, especially in the music business, where drugs are a way of life."

"I'm sorry, Sylvia. It must be difficult for you to see your baby try to self-destruct and not be able to stop him."

"You've no idea. Enjoy him while he's tiny," Sylvia said, smiling down at Alex. "Motherhood can be the most heartbreaking thing to ever happen to you."

Quinn walked Sylvia to the door and allowed her mother to kiss her cheek.

"I'm really proud of you, Quinn, for what it's worth. You're everything I never was or ever will be. You're a star."

"Thank you. That's high praise."

"It's how I feel. I will love you always, no matter what happens."

Quinn closed the door behind Sylvia and returned to the living room, where she scooped Alex up off the play mat and held him close. "I love you so much," she whispered into the baby's downy curls. "I will never let you down, I promise, and I will stand by you no matter what. You hear? No matter what."

She held the baby so tight, he let out a whimper of protest, alerting her that she was hurting him. Quinn kissed him again and returned him to the play mat, her eyes full of tears.

SIXTEEN

Quinn felt a flurry of excitement as she headed toward FreeState Coffee. This time Alex had remained at home with Gabe, sleeping peacefully when she left. It felt good to be out on her own, and she walked along at a brisk pace in an effort to keep the winter chill at bay. London was glittering in the afternoon sunshine, its urban sophistication softened by the magical touch of Christmas decorations. Christmas was just two weeks away, and everyone seemed happier, more excited, and more purposeful as they went about their day. Several women carrying colorful shopping bags passed Quinn, laughing and talking, their cheeks rosy with cold. The pubs were full, still serving the lunch crowd, and several people smiled at her for no reason other than they were in a festive mood.

Quinn was filled with anticipation as she approached the coffee shop. Drew had said he had something to share with her and Logan, and regardless of what news he had to impart, she planned to take a few hours after their meeting and go Christmas shopping. She'd already ordered several things online, but she wanted to experience the pleasure of buying gifts for the people she loved in person, and she wouldn't be filling their gift boxes with pajamas and socks. The gifts would be personal and special, something to really put smiles on their faces. And this year, she'd be buying more than ever. There'd be presents for Logan and Jude, a little something for Colin, gifts for Seth and Kathy, a present for Rhys, and even a gift for Sylvia. And of course, there'd be gifts for her parents, Phoebe, and Jill. She'd feel like a right old Father Christmas.

Quinn pushed open the door and entered the warm, fragrant café. There were few empty tables, but she managed to snag one and ordered herself a decaffeinated cappuccino and a chocolate croissant. She felt the urge to indulge. The baby weight was far from gone, but she had a craving for something decadent.

Logan arrived a few minutes after Quinn. His normally spiky hair was nicely combed and he sported what he referred to as "designer stubble." "Sorry, was running late this morning and didn't have time for the beauty routine," he explained. "Overslept."

"Right. Did Colin oversleep as well?" Quinn asked, grinning at Logan. She knew only too well what usually led to Gabe "oversleeping."

"He did, rather," Logan admitted. "But his patients don't mind waiting, being dead and all."

"Always an advantage."

"Do you think Drew's found Quentin?" Logan asked as he unwound his scarf and settled into a chair.

"He'd have told us, I think. This is more of a status report."

"Better than nothing, I suppose."

"We're about to find out," Quinn replied as she spotted Drew Camden passing the café window and opening the door.

Drew lumbered into the café and headed straight for their table. He wore a plaid scarf in green and red and a charcoal-gray wool coat that made him look more like a corporate executive than an ex-copper.

"Good afternoon," he said as he took the outside chair and sat down, stretching his damaged leg before him. "I love this weather. Very bracing."

"Indeed," Logan replied with a smile. "Love freezing my bollocks off. There's nothing like it."

"Dress warmer," Drew suggested, glancing at the short black leather jacket slung over Logan's chair.

"Have you been able to discover anything?" Quinn asked, eager to get to the point. She'd waited a long time to learn something about Quentin, and she didn't want to waste time on pointless banter.

"Not much, but I thought I'd give you a progress report nonetheless. I know how anxious you two are."

"Go on then," Logan invited.

"I had a relatively productive day in Leicester. I began with Karen Crawford."

"We've spoken to her already. She didn't give us much," Logan interjected.

"Well, I hit a brick wall with her as well, although I believe she knows much more than she's letting on. She might not have stayed in touch with her sister, but their father was in contact with his adopted daughter and would have mentioned her from time to time. The brother was equally tight-lipped."

"Why are they so reluctant to help us?" Quinn exclaimed. "What do they have to lose?"

"I don't know, but I'd like to find out," Drew replied.

"So was that all?"

"No, there's more." Drew leaned back in his chair, confident and relaxed. He seemed satisfied with the progress of the investigation. "After interviewing Karen and Michael Crawford, I stopped into Quentin's old school. Few teachers who taught there when Quentin was in sixth form were still there, but there were two old biddies who were happy to talk to me. One was Miss Mackie, an art teacher, and the other a Mrs. McComb, who helped Quentin prepare for her A-levels. Mrs. McComb didn't have much to impart other than recalling that Quentin struggled with math but worked hard to pass her exams. She never got to know her on a personal level but was quick to reassure me that Quentin was a pleasant, well-mannered young lady."

"Helpful, that," Logan snorted.

"Patience, Logan," Drew drawled.

"Sorry, please go on," Logan said, looking contrite.

"Miss Mackie was vastly more helpful. She taught art to Quentin for two years and knew her quite well. She said Quentin was very artistic, and extremely imaginative. She loved art and excelled in it. Miss Mackie said Quentin often stayed after class, since it was her last of the day, to chat."

"What did they talk about?" Quinn asked.

"This and that. Miss Mackie didn't recall the actual conversations, but she was able to remember the name of Quentin's best friend—Sarah Denton, who just happens to live at the same address she resided at during her school years."

"Did you speak to her?" Logan demanded.

"I did. Lovely woman. Looked after her sick mum until the mum died two years back and left Sarah the house. She lives there with her five-year-old son. Single mum."

Quinn kicked Logan under the table before he had a chance to blurt something out once again. Drew had his own way of getting to the important bits, so they had to be patient. Perhaps the details weren't that important to her and Logan, but they helped form a more comprehensive picture for Drew.

"Sarah and Quentin were inseparable in the sixth form. Quentin came to the house often, and slept over once or twice a month at the weekends. Sarah went to the Crawford house only once and got the impression that Quentin wasn't comfortable having a friend over. She preferred to come to Sarah's house, where she felt more at ease."

"Did Quentin ever confide in Sarah?" Quinn asked.

"She said they spoke mostly of music, fashion, and boys. Quentin didn't like to talk about her family, especially her siblings."

"Well, Karen said they never really got on," Logan chimed in.

"Was she able to shed any light on where Quentin might have gone after her mother's death?" Quinn asked.

"She was, actually. Quentin met a man in her final year of

school. He was a local photographer who came to do the school portraits. They began a relationship and she moved in with him after she left home."

"Did you get his name?" Logan asked.

"Jesse Holt. He has a studio in High Street and I have an appointment with him tomorrow. I'd have stopped in while I was in Leicester, but the studio was closed and Mr. Holt only sees people by appointment."

"Can I come with you?" Quinn asked. She hadn't meant to interfere with Drew's investigation, but she desperately wanted to speak to someone who'd known Quentin and hopefully loved her.

"If you like. I'll be at St. Pancras tomorrow at ten. Meet me on platform three."

"I'll be there," Quinn promised.

"I wish I could come, but I have an early morning shift at the hospital. Fill me in after?" Logan asked.

"Of course. I only hope there will be something to tell."

"Don't get your hopes up, Quinn," Drew warned.

"I can't help it. You've already discovered four new leads, which is a lot more than we were able to accomplish. Perhaps this Jesse Holt will point us in the right direction."

"See you tomorrow then," Drew said as he laboriously got to his feet. "Enjoy your Christmas shopping."

"How did you know I was going Christmas shopping?" Quinn asked, astounded by Drew's skills of deduction.

"The list fell out of your pocket, probably when you put your gloves away and withdrew your hand after."

Quinn looked down at the floor. Sure enough, her shopping list lay beneath the table, with Gabe's name at the top. "And there I thought you were clairvoyant," she joked.

"I am. I can tell you with almost one-hundred percent accuracy that you're about to spend a lot more than you're planning to." Drew's laugh was rich and velvety, and Quinn and Logan joined in. Drew was spot-on.

SEVENTEEN

Quinn arrived at the station early, eager to get going. It being Saturday, she didn't have to rush back. She'd left Gabe with several bottles of expressed milk and a supply of nappies. He planned to spend the morning at home, then take the children for a walk, and stop in at Emma's favorite pizza restaurant on the way back.

"Don't worry about us. We'll be fine," he'd assured Quinn.

"You've never been alone with both children for such a long stretch before."

"I can handle it."

"I know you can. I'm just being neurotic," Quinn had explained.

"You're a new mum. You're allowed to be neurotic."

"Ring me if you have any problems."

"I won't have any problems."

Quinn knew that, but she still worried. Gabe was accustomed to being alone with Emma, but spending hours with an infant was new to him. She hoped he wouldn't forget to burp Alex after feeding or wait too long to change his nappy. Alex hated being wet.

Stop fussing, she told herself as she waited for Drew. *Gabe is perfectly capable of handling one little boy for a few hours. Give him some credit.* But she was still worried. She took out her mobile and sent him an exploratory text, to which he promptly replied that all was well. Quinn breathed out a sigh of relief and walked toward Drew when she saw him coming down the platform.

"Are you always early?" Drew asked with a friendly smile.

"No, you're just always late."

"That's what my wife says. We have a few minutes to spare before the train leaves, so I'm exactly on time. Are you going to fret the whole time?" Drew asked as he settled into his aisle seat.

"How do you know I'm fretting? Did something fall out of my pocket?" Quinn joked.

"No, it's written all over your face and you keep checking your mobile."

"You know, I'm glad Gabe is not a detective. Living with him would be pretty hard if I couldn't hide a single emotion."

"My wife says that too, although I'm not nearly as observant as she thinks."

"I see we're in agreement on a number of things, your wife and I. Wise woman."

"That's why I married her," Drew replied, smiling lazily. "Now, sit back, relax, and enjoy the ride. Nothing you can do from here anyway."

"You don't have children, do you?" Quinn asked, thinking Drew was too laid back to be a father.

"I do, as it happens. From my previous marriage. Two teenage girls. I think I have more reason to worry, wouldn't you say?"

"Can't argue with you there. Teenagers are terrifying," Quinn said.

"You have no idea."

The ride passed quickly and then they took a taxi to the studio. Drew was more than willing to walk from the station, but Quinn could barely contain her excitement and didn't want to waste time. The taxi dropped them off in front of the studio, called Picture Perfect. Portraits of varying sizes were displayed in the window, most of them of smiling families and adorable children. There was even a portrait of a poodle, groomed and adorned with a pink bow.

"Quinn, let me do the talking, all right?" Drew said as they approached the door.

"Absolutely. I'm just here to observe."

"Of course you are," Drew joked.

Jesse Holt was in his mid-forties. He wasn't very tall but looked fit, and his lanky frame showed no ill effects of middle age. His sandy hair fell almost to his shoulders, and his light blue eyes exuded friendliness and charm. Quinn could easily imagine how appealing he would have been to a seventeen-year-old girl fourteen years ago. He must have been very attractive; he still was.

"Good morning. You must be Mr. Camden," Jesse Holt said as he came forward to greet them. He probably assumed they were a couple, Quinn mused, as she smiled in response to his greeting.

"Yes. And this is Quinn Russell. We'd like to ask you a few questions, if you don't mind."

"Oh? What about?" A wary look passed across Jesse's eyes.

"Quentin Crawford."

"God, that's a name I haven't heard in a long time," Jesse remarked as he invited them to sit down on twin sofas in the waiting area. "What's the reason for your interest?"

"Quentin is my twin sister," Quinn explained.

"Really? I didn't know she had one."

"We were separated at birth and adopted separately. I've only just found out about her."

"Right. I see. How can I help?"

"Quinn is trying to get in contact with Quentin, but it's proving rather difficult, as no one seems to know where she is or how to reach her, except her attorney, who is not being overly cooperative."

"I'm sorry, but I have no idea where she is. I haven't seen Quentin in over a decade."

"But she used to live with you. Correct?" Drew asked.

"Yes, Quentin and I were involved for nearly four years. We didn't keep in contact after the relationship ended."

"She left you?" Quinn asked, ignoring the sharp look from Drew. Any tidbit about her sister was fascinating to her.

"Yes, she left me. The parting of the ways wasn't mutual." Jesse ran a hand through his hair, his relaxed demeanor gone.

"Would you mind telling us something about the relationship?" Drew asked softly. He was prying into the man's personal life, and Jesse had every right to ask them to leave. Thankfully, he didn't.

"There isn't much to tell, really. I met Quentin at her school. It was a lucrative arrangement for me. I took photos of the graduating class and various school clubs and teams toward the end of every school year. She was one of the students I photographed. To be honest, I didn't want to have anything to do with her at first. A romantic involvement with a student could have cost me the job, and I was just starting out then. I didn't want to risk my reputation."

"So, how did it begin?" Quinn asked.

"I saw her watching me while I worked. She smiled and asked if I needed any help. I politely refused. After I took her photo, she hung around for a while instead of returning to class. I didn't encourage any banter or flirtation. I had a job to do. Once I finished for the day, there'd be no reason for us to meet again, so I wasn't overly worried. A few days later, Quentin showed up at my studio. I was at a different location then, in a less desirable area. I used to live above the shop."

"What did she want?" Drew asked.

"She asked for a job. She said she was interested in photography and wanted to learn from a professional. She wanted to be my assistant."

"Did you give her a job?" Quinn asked, impressed with Quentin's forwardness at such a young age. At seventeen, Quinn had been shy and self-conscious. Luke had been her first serious boyfriend, and she'd been twenty-two when they got involved.

"Not right away. She came back again a few weeks later and left her information with me, but I didn't call her until she finished the school year."

"Did you hire her then?" Quinn asked.

"I did. I needed an assistant and she was willing to work for free in exchange for lessons. She was actually very helpful. She was great with the children. She could always cajole a smile out of them, especially the toddlers. She just had a way about her."

"What was she like?" Quinn asked. She had a hard time keeping the desperation out of her voice. She needed to know.

"Fun, beautiful, spirited. She was mad for art and history. She read every historical novel she could get her hands on at the local library."

"She loved history?" Quinn gasped. "Really?"

"Loved it. Why?"

"I'm a historian—an archeologist. We have something in common, then."

"You have the look of her too. I didn't notice right away, not having seen her in donkey's years, but now that I look at you, I see it."

"When did you become romantically involved?" Drew asked, giving Quinn a gimlet stare meant to remind her not to interrupt.

"We got involved that summer. It was a natural progression, I think. I always knew we'd end up in bed together."

"Were you happy?" Quinn piped in.

"Yes, we were. I loved her and was excited about the future when she moved in after her mum passed, but I always got the feeling she had another agenda."

"What kind of agenda?"

"Quentin wasn't happy at home, but she'd led a sheltered, comfortable life and wasn't ready to strike out on her own. I was a stepping stone, a safety net, if you will."

"You don't think she loved you?" Quinn asked.

"She liked me, but not enough to make a life with me."

"Were you hoping for a future with her?" Drew asked.

"Yes. I was thirty-two when Quentin and I met, nearly twice her age. I'd had several long relationships and was ready for something more serious. I was ready for a family. But, of course, Quentin was only eighteen by the time we got together. I proposed to her when she turned twenty-one, but she refused me. She said she wasn't ready to settle down. She wanted to travel and experience life, not spend her days working in a portrait studio and playing house with me."

"Were you angry?" Drew asked.

"I was hurt and disappointed, but I wasn't angry. I'd have said the same thing at that age. We were simply at different stages in our lives."

"So you let her go?"

"Of course. We agreed not to stay in touch."

"Are you married, Mr. Holt?" Drew inquired.

"How is that relevant?" Jesse bristled.

"It isn't. Just curious."

"Yes, I'm married. I have two children, aged ten and eight. Surely you don't think I did something to hurt Quentin."

"No, not at all. Do you know where she went after she left you?"

"I believe she went to London. That's really all I know."

"Would you have any photos of Quentin?" Drew asked.

"I'm afraid I don't. I got rid of them after a time. My wife wouldn't appreciate me keeping photographs of my old girlfriends. Now, if you will excuse me, I have another appointment in five minutes."

"Thank you for your time, Mr. Holt. Oh, may I ask you one more question?" Drew asked as he turned to leave.

"Of course."

"Was Quentin a virgin when you got together?"

"No, Mr. Camden, she wasn't, not that it's any of your business."

"Thank you. Have a good day. And please, ring me if you think of anything that might be important." Drew handed Jesse Holt his card and held the door open for Quinn. They stepped out into the street.

"Why did you ask him if Quentin was a virgin?" Quinn demanded as they strolled toward the train station.

"I just wanted to get a clearer picture of your sister at that age."

"Many girls are sexually active by seventeen, so what does that tell you about her?"

"Nothing, but the information might prove useful later on in the investigation."

"In what way?"

"I'll tell you when I figure it out."

EIGHTEEN
AUGUST 1917

Pulkovo, Russia

Valentina threw off the covers and stretched luxuriously. She'd slept deliciously well, despite the heat. All the windows were wide open to capture even the slightest breeze and the cool caress of a country morning felt wonderful on her face. A rooster crowed in the distance, and she heard the hushed voices of Masha and Polina as they went about preparing breakfast. Tanya was still asleep next to Valentina, her mouth slightly open as she made funny noises. Tanya's arms and legs were covered in mosquito bites, but Valentina's skin was unblemished. For some reason, the bloodsuckers weren't drawn to her. Elena said mosquitoes were only attracted to people who had sweet blood. *I guess I'm sour then*, Valentina thought gratefully, amused by the fact that in this instance it was a blessing.

She slid out of bed and went to stand by the window. She wore only a thin cotton nightgown, but there was no danger of anyone seeing her. The house was situated well outside the village, so there was no chance of anyone walking past. The morning was perfect, the sky a salmon pink as the sun began to rise into the cloudless sky. The grass sparkled with dew, the green of the stalks lush and vibrant. Valentina wished she could go outside barefoot and run through the meadow in her nightclothes. What a fuss her mother would kick up if she were caught. She'd done that once when she was about eleven, and it had been glorious. What wonderful, carefree days she'd enjoyed then. But now everything was different.

After nearly six months of living with daily uncertainty, Valentina had stopped believing life could ever be normal again. The Tsar and his family had recently been transferred from their apartments at Alexander Palace to Tobolsk, a move that didn't bode well for the royal family. The provisional government was still in place, but a new political party had gained power over the past few months. They were known as the Bolsheviks, the moniker literally meaning "the Majority," and there were also the Mensheviks—"the Minority." The Bolsheviks were calling for an immediate end to the war with Germany and demanding bread for the workers and land for the peasants. Their ultimate goal was to do away with the nobility and completely eradicate the ruling class. The Bolsheviks wanted class equality and state-controlled distribution of assets. Her father said this absurd and impractical system was called socialism. It all sounded far-fetched and frightening. What would happen to the aristocracy if the Bolsheviks seized control and instituted their ideas? How would her family live, and what would happen to all their possessions? Would they be taken away and given to the poor?

Already things were changing, even within the household. Several servants had deserted them in the past few months, refusing to work for the bourgeoisie, and even the governess, Olga Alexandrovna, had started behaving in a less respectful manner, having suddenly realized that the Kalinins weren't her betters. They were wealthy and titled, to be sure, but not in any way morally or intellectually superior. The family hadn't visited Tsarskoye Selo even once this summer. The Royal Village was virtually deserted, most nobles choosing to either remain in Petrograd to keep an eye on their homes and possessions, or retreating to smaller and less ostentatious country estates to bide the summer months. There was a general feeling of oppression and doom in the city, and when Count Petrov and Ivan came to visit their families, they looked gray and tense.

Valentina got dressed in a simple cotton dress and let herself out of the room. She didn't bother to put on stockings, since no one could see her legs beneath the long skirt. It was too hot to bother with such social constraints. Vera Konstantinovna Petrova, her future mother-in-law, was already in the dining room, sipping a cup of tea. She was flawlessly dressed, as usual, and her silver-streaked hair was pinned atop her head, but the sophisticated hair-style and fashionable gown didn't distract from her recent weight loss or the new lines etched on her face. There were deep grooves alongside her pursed mouth, and a trio of parallel lines marring her forehead.

"Good morning, Aunt Vera," Valentina said as she took a seat at the table. "You're up early."

"I couldn't sleep. Too hot, I suppose."

Valentina knew the reason Vera Konstantinovna couldn't sleep was because she was worried about Alexei. No one had seen him since June, when he'd managed to get a two-day furlough and come see his parents and Valentina's family. Alexei had appeared to be physically well, but like everyone else, he was tense and irritable. He'd looked leaner and older, Valentina had thought as she'd studied him across the supper table while he filled them in on the latest news. He'd eaten more than usual during those two days and had chewed his food quickly, as if he feared someone would take it away from him if he didn't eat fast enough. He hadn't said so outright, but it was evident that the rations had been cut and the men weren't getting enough food or rest. Everyone was on guard and in a constant state of preparedness for whatever might come. Vera Konstantinovna had cried when Alexei said his goodbyes before returning to town. She was terrified she'd never see her son again, so Alexei sent a brief note whenever he could, reassuring everyone that he was alive and well.

Valentina accepted a boiled egg from Masha, buttered a slice of bread, and poured herself a glass of fresh milk. They ate simply when they were in the country, not standing on ceremony as they did at home. She preferred it this way. It was easier to get up early, have her breakfast, and sneak off for a long walk before anyone else woke up. She was tired of the inevitable discussions, her mother's tearful laments, her father's dogged reassurances, and the Petrovs' tight-lipped stoicism. Even the children were subdued, reading and playing card games instead of playing outside all day long and going swimming.

Tanya and Svetlana, Alexei's sister, spent much time sitting beneath a tree out back, their heads bent over a book, while Kolya kept close to Petr. He enjoyed being around the horses and preferred to keep out of the way of the adults, who were constantly reprimanding him and urging him to read a book instead of skulking in the stable.

Valentina finished her breakfast, bid Vera Konstantinovna a good morning, and slipped out of the house. She didn't dare go far, but it was nice to be alone. She took off her shoes and walked through the meadow, enjoying the cool dampness of the grass. Had things been different, she would be in the midst of planning her wedding, but no one had even mentioned the possibility of her and Alexei getting married this autumn, as they'd initially planned. Perhaps they'd get married next year, once things settled down a bit.

She wiped an angry tear from her cheek. Who was she kidding? Nothing was about to settle down. This was the new normal, and their lives would never be what they once were. There'd be no more balls or evenings at the theater. There'd be no more sleigh rides through the endless white expanse of freshly fallen snow, and no more peals of carefree laughter as the bells jingled on the horses' harnesses and made music of their own. They hardly went out anymore, keeping close to home for fear of being set upon by angry revolutionaries. They'd suddenly become an object of resentment and hatred—a target.

Valentina drew up short when she saw a figure in the distance. The man was walking along the road, a small satchel in his hand. He wore simple brown trousers, boots, and a collarless linen shirt. He looked like a peasant, but Valentina's heart gave a leap of joy and she took off running toward the man in a very unladylike manner.

"Alyosha!" she cried as she hurled herself into his arms. He'd dropped his satchel when he saw her, and it remained in the dirt of the road as he held her close for just a moment before propriety demanded they pull apart. "What are you doing here?"

"I got two days, Valya. I caught a ride on a farm wagon leaving Petrograd. The farmer dropped me off just down the road. I'm so glad to see you. You look well."

"You look like a peasant."

"Best not to draw attention to oneself these days. My uniform is at the barracks. Is there any food? I'm famished."

Valentina grabbed Alexei by the hand and pulled him along. "There are eggs, freshly baked bread, and milk. And of course tea. We've been eating simply this summer. Lots of herring and boiled potatoes, and cold borscht with sour cream."

"My mother must be in a state. She never allowed 'peasant food' at the table at home."

"Neither did my mother, but times have changed, haven't they? It's prudent to economize and do with what we have. We did have roasted chicken the other day, and Petr caught a few trout last week."

"I don't care what I eat as long as I fill my belly. The rations are pitiful. We're getting less and less meat. It's all potatoes with bits of gristle."

"We'll feed you around the clock while you are here," Valentina said as they approached the house. Vera Konstantinovna had seen them from the window and came flying out the door, her arms outstretched as she pulled Alexei into an embrace.

"Sinok, thank the Lord you're safe. I was so worried. How long can you stay?"

"Two days, Mama."

"Come inside. You must eat. I'll tell Masha to bring fresh tea."

Alexei buttered a thick slice of bread and ate a boiled egg in two bites. "Is there any bacon?" he asked. "I haven't had svenina in months."

"Yes. Masha, bring some bacon," Aunt Vera called out. "And more butter."

The servant came rushing out of the kitchen, bearing several more boiled eggs, a plate of sliced cured pork, and a dish of butter. She set everything in front of Alexei, who was gulping down a glass of milk.

"Are they not feeding you?" Aunt Vera exclaimed. "You're thin as a reed."

"Keeping us fed is not a priority right now. The foot soldiers are close to mutiny, and several officers of my acquaintance have deserted and switched sides."

"They've gone over to the Bolsheviks?" His mother gasped. "That's treason."

"Let's not speak of it, Mama. I need a break."

"Of course, son. Whatever you need. I'll have Polina make up a bed for you. Would you like to sleep for a while? You look tired."

"No, actually I'd like to take a walk with Valya, if she'll join me."

"Of course. We can walk in the woods, if you like," Valentina suggested. The woods were dense and private, a place where they could talk without interruptions and maybe even steal a few kisses. She'd missed Alexei desperately, and having had a taste of his passion, she longed for more intimacy.

"A walk in the woods sounds heavenly."

Alexei finished his breakfast and pushed his chair away from the table. "I feel truly full for the first time in weeks. I hope I don't get sick as a result of my greediness."

"Walk it off," his mother suggested. "That's just the thing for a full belly."

Valentina and Alexei walked in near-silence until they reached the edge of the woods. The dew had burned off and now the sun was beating down, the heat building as the hour grew closer to midday. The woods were cool and fragrant, the thick green canopy overhead dappled with sunlight.

Alexei scooped up Valentina into his arms and kissed her hungrily. "I've been dying to do that since the last time I kissed you."

"I missed you so much, Alyosha. I hate not knowing when I'll see you again."

"Valya, I might be able to get another furlough next month. They'll give me a few days off if I tell them I'm getting married."

"You'd lie to get time off?"

"I wouldn't be lying. I want us to get married. There's no sense in waiting."

"But our parents would never agree. They still want a proper wedding, with a church service and a wedding feast."

"Valya, we can still have a church service, but the celebration might have to wait. Things are very uncertain at the moment. There are many who believe there'll be another armed rebellion. The Bolsheviks are gaining power and military support. If they succeed, the Imperial Army will most likely be disbanded, or worse."

"Worse?"

"The highest-ranking officers might be executed to prevent the army from reforming. I want out, Valya."

"You'd desert?"

"I'd rather be a live deserter than a dead soldier who did his duty to the end." Alexei sounded defensive, as if she were accusing him of cowardice, and partially turned away from her.

Valentina laid her hand over his arm to reassure him that she wasn't judging him. She was more surprised than upset. She hadn't expected this, but she certainly didn't think him a coward.

"Alyosha, you must do what you think is right. I would never fault you for leaving the army. But what would you do if you deserted?"

Alexei turned back to her, mollified by her response. "I want us to get married and go to Paris. I have an aunt there. She's a bit of a recluse, but she's comfortably off, and she'd help us get settled."

"But what about your parents, and your sister?"

"My parents wouldn't leave, and neither would yours. They're too set in their ways and too stubborn to see what's right in front of their noses. They still want to believe that all this will blow over, the monarchy will be reinstated, and the rebels will be shot like dogs. The Tsar is not coming back, Valya. He'll be lucky if he's allowed to live out his life in exile, and his brother is too much of a coward to fight for the throne. Life will never go back to what it once was. We need to think of our future, Valya, of our children."

"And what would we do in Paris?"

"We'd make a life for ourselves. We'd work."

"Work? At what? We have no skills to speak of."

"We're more skilled than you imagine. You can be a governess, and I can work as a chauffeur. They have many more private automobiles in France than they do in Russia."

"But you don't know how to drive."

"I've learned. There are several trucks where I'm stationed, and I asked one of the drivers to teach me. Oh, it's wonderful, Valya. So different from riding a horse. Automobiles are the way of the future. "

"Alyosha, that's mad. Our life is here. Our families are here. I don't want to be all alone in Paris."

"You'd be with me."

"But I'd miss my parents, and Tanya and Kolya, and even Nyanushka. And your mother would be heartbroken if you left. We can't. We simply can't. We must wait. Please, until next year."

Alexei hung his head in disappointment. "I won't pressure you, but please, think about what I said. Valya, it's not safe for us here."

"Then we should all go."

"Our parents will never leave; you know that," Alexei replied.

"They would have to abandon their homes, their possessions, and their entire way of life. They're not ready to make such a sacrifice. Do you understand that?"

"Yes, I do."

"Promise me you'll consider my proposal."

"I promise."

NINETEEN

Valentina did consider Alexei's proposal, but by the time he was ready to leave on Thursday evening, she was no closer to committing to his plan. Seeing his mother fuss over him, and his sister shyly ask him questions and blush when he complimented her on her budding beauty, made Valentina keenly aware of the heartbreak they'd be causing. She wanted nothing more than to stand before a priest and make her vows with Alexei, but she wanted to do so with the support of both their families. She was afraid to stay, but she was even more afraid to run away, to an unknown place and an unknown future. She'd never envisioned herself as a working woman. She'd been bred to be a lady, a countess, a woman of leisure and wealth. She knew what it was like to be a subordinate in someone's home. Olga Alexandrovna was like a mouse, always scurrying down corridors and out of sight, terrified to bring on her employer's displeasure. She was an unmarried woman from an impoverished family. She needed the work, and needed a roof over her head. Valentina couldn't imagine such a future.

And Alexei. Driving a cab. Ferrying paying customers like a lowly coachman when he was a count, a man who'd have wealth and influence in his own right. No, she couldn't agree to that. Things were difficult, but they could still change. Perhaps if the war finally came to an end, the people wouldn't be so angry, so desperate. They'd see the error of their ways and invite the Tsar back to take his rightful place. The Bolsheviks would disband and go back to their lives, perhaps with higher pay and better prospects, their livelihood improved by the changes instituted by the government and sanctioned by the Tsar. All this unrest and fear would pass, and a new day would dawn in which they could all reclaim their place in society and resume their lives.

"Valya, if you have a change of heart, send a message to me at the barracks once you return to the city," Alexei said when she walked him to the gate.

"Alyosha, I want to wait. Just a few more months. Let's see how things are by Christmas."

"It'll be more difficult to travel during the winter months."

"I know, but I'm just not ready. I'm afraid."

Alexei leaned down and kissed her gently. "I'm afraid too, dorogaya Valya. More afraid than I've ever been. But I will bide my time. I'll wait. But there's something I want you to do."

"What?"

"When you return to Petrograd, pack a small valise with a change of clothes, a winter coat and boots, and some undergarments. And sew a false pocket into one of your gowns."

"Whatever for?"

"To hide valuables."

"Why do I need a valise and a gown with a secret pocket?"

"Valya, there might come a time when you'll have to flee. There'll be no time to think clearly or make preparations."

"That will never happen." Valentina shook her head stubbornly as if she could chase away the terrifying thought.

"It's better to be ready and have no need of your supplies than to need your supplies and not be ready should the worst come to pass."

"You're frightening me, Alyosha."

"I'm only trying to impress the seriousness of the situation upon you. Should you need to leave, go to my aunt in Paris. Her name is Elizaveta Petrova and she lives at seventeen Rue Lafayette. I will meet you there as soon as I'm able. Will you remember the address?"

"Yes. Seventeen Rue Lafayette. Elizaveta Petrova."

"Good girl."

"We'd best get going, Alexei Vladimirovich," Petr said. He was waiting by the gate, sitting on the bench of the simple trap he'd use to deliver Alexei back to the city.

"Of course, Petr. I'm coming." Alexei kissed Valentina and looked deep into her eyes. "Do as I ask. Please."

She nodded and watched miserably as he climbed into the cart.

After Alexei left, everyone seemed listless and melancholy, but none as much as Valentina. Perhaps she should have agreed to his plan, she thought, as she moped about the house and garden. Perhaps he was right and the situation was a lot more desperate than she allowed herself to believe. She decided that if nothing changed by Christmas, she'd agree to his plan.

TWENTY
OCTOBER 1917

Petrograd, Russia

Once they returned to the city in the first week of September, life settled into an uneasy routine. Tanya and Kolya resumed their studies with Olga Alexandrovna, while Elena and Ivan Kalinin spent most of their time at home but occasionally went out to call on their friends and had some close associates come for tea or supper. The gatherings were small and much more modest than they'd been in pre-revolutionary days, but they could hardly stop living altogether. Valentina spent most of her days reading or pacing the back garden. She was too frightened to go far, but the lack of fresh air and exercise was driving her mad. Olga Alexandrovna invited her to sit in on the lessons if she was bored, but she had no desire to return to the schoolroom. She wanted to live her life, and to be trapped in a state of constant fear and uncertainty was unbearable.

She saw Alexei only once in September. He managed to stop in for a few minutes to reassure her that he was well, although he didn't look it, and to see how she was getting on.

"Did you pack the valise, like I asked you?" he said as soon as they were alone.

"No," she admitted. She'd considered doing it, but once they'd returned to the city, the idea of preparing for flight had put her off so much that she'd pushed her promise to Alexei to the back of her mind, to be dealt with later, like after Christmas.

"Valya, please, just do it, and ask everyone in the household to do the same."

"They'll never do it, especially Papa."

"He might. My parents have begun to prepare. My mother has sewn her most valuable jewels into the hem of her winter coat. And she's done the same for Svetlana."

"Really?" Valentina gasped. She'd never expected Vera Konstantinovna to take such drastic measures, but the fact that she had made Valentina question her own stubbornness.

"Yes. Valya, please. You might never have need of these precautions, but it's best to be prepared, just in case."

"All right. I'll do it."

"Do you remember my aunt's name and address?"

"I do."

Alexei pulled her into an embrace and held her tight. The wool of his coat felt scratchy against her face, but the karakul fur of the collar was soft and curly against her forehead. Such contrast, such inconsistency. "I love you, Valya," he said softly.

"I love you too, Alyosha."

He kissed her and let himself out the door, disappearing into the twilight of the September evening.

Valentina spent the next few days planning her getaway wardrobe. What would she need? What should she take? She'd pack her coat and boots, as Alexei had suggested, a change of undergarments, and a blue woolen gown with white piping. It was demure and serviceable, the type of garment that could be worn by a governess or even a shop girl. She considered sewing pockets into the skirt, but changed her mind. They would be too visible beneath the fabric, especially once she sat down. Instead, she unpicked the hem of her coat and added two pockets, one of each side. Valentina inserted the pearl choker her parents had given her for her eighteenth birthday, a pair of diamond earrings, and a diamond-and-emerald bracelet that had belonged to her grandmother. Grandmother had left the bracelet to Valentina, and she valued it greatly, not only because it was truly stunning, but because it reminded her of a grandmother she'd loved. She continued to wear Alexei's engagement necklace, but instead of displaying it proudly, she wore it inside her dress, close to her heart. She did manage to talk Tanya into making preparations, but neither her mother nor her father would listen to reason.

"We're not going to desert our home like rats fleeing a sinking ship," Ivan raged. "We are going to stay and defend what's ours. We're going to survive. I don't ever want to hear you talking such defeatist propaganda again, Valya."

"But Alexei said we should do it. His family is ready, should anything happen," she argued in vain.

"Nothing is going to happen. There will be a period of uncertainty—a long period—but in time, things will begin to settle down. We must keep our heads down and our spirits up. By this time next year, you'll be married, and hopefully expecting your first child. All will be well."

"And if it isn't?"

"Don't you dare second-guess me, Valentina. I won't have it. I'm your father and I know best, and until such time as you have a husband and must defer to his judgement, you will listen to me. Don't ever bring this up again. You hear?"

"Yes, Papa. I hear and I understand."

That night, Valentina sewed another bracelet and ring into her spare corset. She'd taken them from her mother's jewelry box. If her parents weren't going to listen to reason, she'd do it for them. She only hoped her mother wouldn't blame one of the servants for stealing the trinkets, but given that she hardly wore jewelry these days, she had little reason to go through her box. Besides, she had so many pieces of jewelry, she probably wouldn't notice if an item or two had gone missing.

Valentina hid the packed valise at the back of her wardrobe, behind several hat boxes. She hoped she'd never have need of it, but knowing it was there eased her anxiety somewhat. Currency could be devalued, but gold and diamonds would always be worth something and were a form of security against whatever was to come.

The rest of September and the first half of October passed in melancholy gloom. It was a rainy autumn with cool, damp days that turned into cold, rainy nights. Soon, she'd have to take her coat out of her valise and begin wearing it. Winter didn't officially arrive until the first of December, but the temperature began to plummet by the end of October and the first snow of the year usually fell by the beginning of November. The Neva would be frozen solid by mid-November, but there'd be no skating this year. She felt too fearful to walk to the river and draw attention to herself. She'd become a frightened little mouse, hiding behind the walls of her house and waiting for something to happen to put an end to the political stalemate that had the country in its grip.

Every day she hoped Alexei would stop by, and every day he didn't. He sent a note whenever he could, but the regiment was permanently on alert, all furloughs canceled until further notice. At night, Valentina lay in bed, imagining their wedding ceremony. She focused on every detail, losing herself in the minutiae of planning an event that might never take place. But it was a beautiful fantasy, and the only thing that lifted her spirits at a time when nothing was lighthearted or gay. She would be happy enough with an intimate wedding, with only a few dozen guests in attendance. The grandiose affairs of the past now seemed incongruous and pretentious, the lavish parties meant to showcase the wealth and influence of the families and show up their social rivals. She had no desire to impress anyone or be the talk of the town. She only wanted to marry her love and try to snatch that small bit of certainty from an uncertain situation.

Valentina hoped to get married at the Church of the Vladimir Icon of the Mother of God, where her own parents had been married twenty years ago. A May wedding would be lovely, when everything was in bloom. Spring was a time of rebirth and renewal, and starting her life with Alexei would be a form of rebirth. There were those that said marrying in May was bad luck, and preached doom for the newly married couple. "Budesh mayetza," they said. What nonsense. Why would they suffer just because they married in May? Valentina was a modern woman who didn't subscribe to these old-fashioned superstitions, but her mother and Aunt Vera might object. No matter, she'd be just as happy to marry in April or June.

Valentina closed her eyes and pictured her wedding dress. It would be a delicious confection of silk and lace, with a magnificent train that would trail behind her as she made her way down the aisle toward Alexei, who would be dashing in his uniform, his golden head uncovered, as he prepared to take his vows. The priest would invite them to stand in the middle of the church on a square of rose-colored fabric that symbolized their new life together, and ask them if they were entering into the union willingly and had not promised themselves to anyone else. That part always made Valentina smile. They'd been promised to each other since they were children, and neither one had ever questioned the decision of their parents. They were meant for each other, their union written in the stars. No, they weren't promised to anyone else, and yes, they would enter into their marriage of their own free will, to live together as husband and wife until death tore them asunder.

After the priest recited the *ektenia* and several other prayers blessing the couple, the members of the wedding party would hold gold crowns over the heads of the bride and groom while the priest wrapped his stole around their intertwined hands to symbolize their joining as man and wife. He would then lead them three times around the analogian on which the Book of Gospel had been placed. After the crowning, they would finally be pronounced man and wife, and Alexei would lift her veil and kiss her for the first time as her husband. The wedding party would then be dismissed by the priest with his blessings, free to return home and start celebrating in earnest.

Customarily, the wedding celebration lasted for at least two days. Dish after dish of heavenly food was brought out, starting with hot and cold appetizers and moving on to pies, roasted meats, baked fish, and all manner of potatoes and pickled vegetables. There was music and dancing throughout. When Alexei had visited them over the summer, he'd said he'd like to have a band of Gypsies perform at their wedding feast. No one got the guests going like the Gypsies, whose colorful costumes and exquisite music roused even the oldest and most decrepit guests, their feet tapping in time to the tune as the violinists played louder and louder, the tempo increasing until the dancers were breathless, laughing and clutching their sides, blood pounding in their ears.

Ivan didn't think having Gypsies at the feast would be appropriate, but Count Petrov dismissed his old friend's stodgy ideas with a wave of the hand. "Calm down, Vanya. The Gypsies are all the rage. They can come on for an hour or so, once the party starts to die down. Nothing like a bit of wild Gypsy music to get the inebriated masses going again."

"All right, but only if the wives don't object." Ivan looked at his wife, who pretended not to notice. She never argued in public, even when she vehemently disagreed. She'd share her views with Ivan later, once they were alone in their bedroom.

"Once the children are married, the wives will object to nothing. Their part in the planning will be over and done with, and as long as Elena did a competent job of explaining to Valya what's expected of her after the celebration, all will go according to plan, and you and I might become grandfathers in nine months. Nothing like a wedding night baby, eh?"

Valentina blushed scarlet, surprised that her future father-in-law would be so indelicate in mixed company. Her mother looked uncomfortable, and Vera Konstantinovna's gaze slid toward the window. She was clearly displeased by her husband's reference to the wedding night, but no one said anything and the conversation naturally flowed into other aspects of the wedding planning.

The talk came to nothing, of course. The date was never set, the celebration was never planned, and the dress was never ordered. But Valentina could dream, and hope. No matter what happened, they would still marry. Perhaps there'd be no glorious gown and no band of Gypsies, but there would be a marriage, and a wedding night, and hopefully, a baby.

TWENTY-ONE

DECEMBER 2014

London, England

"Tell me what you see when you hold the necklace," Gabe asked as he paced the bedroom, Alex in his arms. The baby had been fussing all evening, kicking his legs and crying pitifully. He'd quieted down when Gabe finally picked him up and began to walk, lulling the baby into drowsiness that had yet to translate into sleep. "The sound of your voice will help him sleep. Tell him a story."

"I don't think he wants to hear about the Russian Revolution," Quinn replied. She was tired after hours of trying to comfort the fretting child and had no desire to revisit what she'd seen. "It doesn't have a happy ending."

"Go on. Try."

Quinn pitched her voice low and began to speak, filling Gabe in on everything she'd seen to date. She described Valentina's dreams of her wedding to Alexei and the preparations for a hasty departure despite them.

"So she was open to leaving?" Gabe continued to walk from one end of the room to the other, rocking Alex gently.

"I think she finally began to see the sense of being prepared. Alexei frightened her enough to reconsider."

"But her parents wouldn't listen?"

"No, of course not. When do people ever listen? They wanted to believe life would return to normal if they waited long enough, and clung to their way of doing things."

"Did Valentina not chafe against an arranged marriage?" Gabe asked. "Seems rather archaic."

"I don't think their future was ever set in stone. There was no formal contract, more a hope that the children's friendship would grow into love. Had either one of them wished to marry someone else, they would have been permitted to do so. But they did love each other fiercely."

"How do you know there was no formal arrangement?"

"It was never mentioned, and there didn't seem to be one in place for Valentina's sister Tatiana, or for her little brother."

"So, if Alexei instructed Valentina to go to France, how did she end up here in London? And who was the man found in the tub? Could it have been Alexei?" Gabe asked. Alex grew quiet, his cheek pressed against Gabe's shoulder. Gabe tenderly kissed the baby's head but didn't attempt to put him down just yet.

"I've no idea. I believe Valentina was connected to him somehow, but I have no way of finding out who he was or why he died. At least not yet. I will need to provide Rhys with some sort of feasible story for the episode. He needs enough near-facts to be able to weave them into a narrative."

"Perhaps you should speak to Monty."

"Monty Ashworth?"

"Imperial Russia is a passion of his. He's written several books on the subject. I doubt he's sold more than a hundred copies, but he is very knowledgeable. He might be able to help put things in perspective."

"Hmm, that's not a bad idea. What days is he at the institute?"

"He lectures on Tuesday and Thursday mornings."

"I'll ring him tomorrow, if Alex is feeling better. I think he has a tummy ache."

"He's asleep," Gabe whispered as he lowered the baby from his shoulder and cradled him in his arms. Alex put his hand on Gabe's chest, his little fingers splayed like a starfish. "Poor mite, he's exhausted himself."

"I'll take him to the clinic tomorrow if he's still fussing. Can he be teething already?" Quinn asked.

"Isn't it too early? He's not even three months old yet."

"My mum said I had two teeth by the time I was four months," Quinn said proudly.

"You always were an overachiever," Gabe joked.

"I wonder if Quentin's teeth came in early as well."

"And I can guess what else you wonder," Gabe replied. "You wonder if she is able to see into the past, like you and Brett."

"Yes, I do. Would the fact that we are twins not practically guarantee psychic ability?"

"You're not identical."

"No, but Brett is only my half-brother and he's possessed of the same gift. And she was mad for history, Jesse Holt said," Quinn said wistfully.

"That doesn't mean she can see it."

"No, I don't suppose it does. Oh, Gabe, what I wouldn't give to meet her. It's been months since I found out about Quentin and we are no closer to finding out where she is," Quinn lamented.

"That's not strictly true. Several months ago, all you knew was that you had a twin sister. As of this week, you know you are fraternal twins and you can account for her whereabouts up to the age of twenty-one. I'd say that's progress."

"But there are no new leads."

"Leave it to Drew Camden; he's the detective."

"He hasn't phoned."

"He will." Gabe carefully lowered the sleeping child into his cot and covered him with the fleecy yellow blanket. "He's out for the count."

"Let's go to sleep. I'm knackered."

"You go to bed. I'm not ready. I think I'll watch something on television. I just need a little time to decompress."

"Gabe, did something happen at work?"

"I had a bit of a run-in with Luke this afternoon. Nothing worth talking about."

"What sort of run-in?" Quinn asked, instantly alert. Luke had returned from the U.S. and was now teaching at the institute. He'd applied for several grants, but none had come through yet, according to Gabe, so it seemed he'd be a permanent fixture at the institute for the foreseeable future. Quinn hadn't seen Luke since his aborted attempt at winning her back in New Orleans, but Luke had emailed her when Alex was born, offering his congratulations. Their history was still fairly fresh, and Luke's email had smacked of regret and resentment against Gabe. Quinn had deleted it without replying.

"There'd been several complaints from female staff regarding Luke's behavior. I had to give him an official warning."

"What has he done exactly?" Quinn asked, curious. Luke had always been easygoing and charming, which had attracted her twenty-two-year-old self to him instead of to Gabe, who'd been serious and intense, and not remotely interested in playing games. Luke knew how to make a woman feel attractive and desired, but he could also be a bit cruel and demeaning when he didn't get his way.

"He's made several inappropriate comments. Of course, it's his word against that of his accusers, and I must admit that Inga Sorenson can be a tad oversensitive at times. She nearly bit Monty's head off when he called her 'dear.' Called it sexual harassment."

"Monty calls everyone 'dear.' He doesn't mean anything by it."

"I know, but Inga sees an insult behind every bush."

"What exactly did Luke say to her?"

"He told her she'd make one hell of a sexy Viking, had she been born a few centuries earlier."

"Some would see that as a compliment, but I can understand why Inga would find it offensive. Luke has no business speaking to her that way in a professional setting."

"She felt insulted by the comment."

"Who's the other woman?"

"Monica Fielding," Gabe replied with a sigh of frustration. Things with Monica were never easy. Monica and Quinn had never got on, and Monica had done her best to discredit Quinn's findings due to professional jealousy and a desire to publicly humiliate her. Quinn strongly suspected that she'd even trolled her online. Since Quinn was no longer teaching at the institute, Monica seemed to have turned her resentment to Gabe, who had inadvertently tipped her off that her husband was having an affair, a development that had led to their separation.

"Monica? But Monica and Luke are great friends. What could he have said to her to cause offense?"

Gabe leaned against the doorjamb, hands in the pockets of his jeans. "Monica and her husband have started couples counselling in an effort to save their marriage. Monica is convinced a reconciliation is imminent because Mark is a changed man."

"Where does Luke come into this?" Quinn asked. She actually missed office gossip sometimes. It made for much better drama than anything on the telly.

"Luke, being the good friend that he is, told her that had she been a better lover, her husband wouldn't have strayed, and that unless she learned some new tricks, Mark would wander off again in pursuit of something more exciting than their Saturday night missionary."

"What a wanker!"

"Monica filed a formal sexual harassment complaint."

"What did Luke have to say for himself?"

"He laughed it off. Said it was a joke between friends and he never expected her to take offense. He'd offered to teach her the aforementioned 'new tricks' out of the goodness of his heart to help her save her marriage."

"Well, I would think she's feeling a bit insecure at the moment, given her husband's infidelity. Luke's comments must have hit a sore spot."

"Men rarely stray because their wives are not satisfying them in bed. They stray for other reasons," Gabe said with a shrug.

"Such as?" Quinn asked, eyebrows raised. "Do enlighten me, so that I know what to look out for."

She tried to keep her tone light, afraid that Gabe would see how the conversation affected her. Luke had cheated on her repeatedly, and she'd been none the wiser. It wasn't until he left her for a beautiful American student, Ashley Gallagher, that Quinn had realized their relationship wasn't nearly as solid as she'd believed it to be. Had she been a boring shag? Did Gabe think so too? Was that why he felt the urge to change things up? Quinn's belly twisted with worry at the possibility.

"They just fall out of love. They want freedom, excitement, and the thrill of the chase. It's not that the sex is better with someone else, it's just newer." Gabe walked over to the bed and leaned down to give Quinn a lingering kiss. His gaze was soft and reassuring. He wasn't as oblivious to her feelings as she sometimes imagined. "I love you, Quinn. I have always loved you, and I will love you till the day I die. You never have to worry about me straying. I'm a one-woman man, unlike Luke, who's always on the prowl."

Quinn wrapped her arms around Gabe's neck and kissed him back. She'd thought she loved Luke once, but having been with Gabe taught her the true meaning of love and partnership. Losing him would be like losing herself. She'd never survive.

"Come to bed," she whispered as she began to unbuckle his belt. "I'm up for anything you like."

Gabe's immediate reaction was answer enough.

TWENTY-TWO

The next morning dawned bright and sunny, but bitterly cold. Frost sparkled on the windowpanes and a stealthy wind moved through the trees. Gabe was already up, getting ready for work. He scooped Alex out of his cot and handed him to Quinn, who took him into bed with her. The baby looked at her with wide-eyed recognition and smacked his lips meaningfully.

"Are you feeling better today, little man?" Quinn cooed to him. Alex tried to smile, baring his toothless gums at her instead. "Hungry?"

Quinn watched him carefully as he nursed, but the discomfort of last night seemed to have been forgotten. He sucked greedily, eager to fill his little belly. "What do you say we go for a walk today? I know, it's cold outside, but I'll bundle you up. We can go visit Daddy at work and talk to a nice man called Monty. How does that sound?"

Alex gurgled happily in response.

"Is he eating again?" Emma asked as she came into the room, dressed for school. "Doesn't he ever do anything else?"

"He's a baby, Emma. What do you expect him to do?" Quinn asked.

"I want to play with him. I thought he'd be more fun. I still want a puppy, you know."

"I certainly do. You'll see Buster in less than a fortnight. He'll be so happy to have someone to chase, besides Grandma Phoebe."

"He doesn't chase Grandma Phoebe. He sits at her feet as she reads her romance novels. It's no fun for him."

"No, I don't imagine it is. Make sure you wear your hat and scarf," Quinn called after Emma as she retreated to the kitchen to have her breakfast.

"I know. I know," she called back.

"How's he this morning?" Gabe asked when he returned to the bedroom, having given Emma her breakfast.

"He's better. He ate well and now he's turning all shades of crimson, and you know what that means."

"I'd better make a run for it then. You're on nappy duty this morning. Quinn, perhaps you should take him to the clinic. He seemed to be really suffering last night."

Quinn nodded. "I'll go this morning. I wish my mum were here. It'd be nice to have someone to talk to about these things."

"Why don't you ring Brenda? She's been helpful in the past."

"I don't want to keep bothering her every time I have a question. She's busy with her own life, and it's been ages since her boys were little."

"Then why not join some sort of a mum-and-baby group?" Gabe asked carefully.

"I rang Alison several times—that's the woman I met at the antenatal yoga class—but her husband's been offered a job in Glasgow and they're moving right after the New Year. Shame, I really like her. I'll look into joining a group after the holidays."

"Okay. Ring me after the clinic."

"I will. Gabe, what would you say to buying Emma one more Christmas gift?"

"I thought you've already shopped for her."

"I have, but I want to do something special to make her happy. She's feeling displaced by the new baby."

"I'm listening."

Quinn quickly outlined her plan. "What do you think?"

"I think it sounds like a lovely idea. I'll take care of it," Gabe promised.

"You are a very good daddy."

"It's your idea. I can't take credit for it."

"No, you can't, but you're still a good daddy," Quinn replied, blowing him a kiss.

After Gabe and Emma left, Quinn changed Alex's nappy, deposited him on his activity blanket, and made herself some breakfast. She'd put off the walk for another day, as it was too cold anyway, and take Alex to the clinic instead before stopping by the institute to talk to Monty. And if she timed her visit right, Gabe might take her out to lunch. She wasn't the type of person who needed round-the-clock company, but she did get lonely, spending nearly every day by herself. Alex was amazing, but not a very skilled conversationalist just yet. She missed the bustle of the city and the comforting din of conversation as people enjoyed a good meal and a drink before returning to the business of the day.

The clinic was busy when Quinn came in, but luckily, there weren't too many people in front of her to see the pediatrician. Dr. Rankin was in his forties. He reminded Quinn of a large, cuddly teddy bear. His soft brown eyes, dark hair, and thick neat beard only served to reinforce the comparison. He had a gentle manner with both babies and mothers.

Quinn waited patiently while the doctor examined Alex. The baby didn't like having his stomach palpated and kicked his legs in outrage, his face warning Quinn that he was preparing to howl for help. Dr. Rankin finished his examination and tickled him, getting a happy snort instead. He allowed Alex to grab the stethoscope and study the shiny surface before carefully removing it from his hands and turning to Quinn.

"Is he all right, Dr. Rankin? He often cries and seems uncomfortable in the evenings."

Dr. Rankin gave her a reassuring smile. "I don't see anything wrong, Mrs. Russell. Alex is thriving and developing normally. What did you have for dinner last night?"

"Me?"

"Yes, you."

"I made pasta primavera. It's the easiest way to get vegetables into a five-year-old," Quinn replied proudly, having figured out how to outsmart Emma.

"What type of vegetables did you add to the pasta?"

"Broccoli, carrots, peas, and red and green peppers."

"Garlic?"

"Yes, I added some to the sauce."

Dr. Rankin nodded as if Quinn had just confirmed his suspicions. "Some babies can handle anything, but others have a more sensitive digestive system. Perhaps the garlic, broccoli, and peppers were too much for him. He doesn't ingest them directly, but everything you eat is in your breast milk. If you plan to continue nursing, you might want to try eating things that are easier for Alex to process."

Quinn shook her head in dismay. "I didn't realize the vegetables might upset his stomach. I've been avoiding harsh spices and processed foods. I thought I was giving him nutrients by eating more vegetables."

"And you thought correctly, but certain vegetables can be hard on his system, and garlic in particular."

"Thank you, Doctor. I will certainly keep that in mind."

"You can begin to wean him if you'd rather not continue nursing. Are you returning to work?"

"Yes, but my hours are flexible for the time being. I'd like to nurse him until he's six months old. I will do whatever is necessary."

"I'm glad to hear it. I'll see you next month for Alex's checkup."

Quinn dressed Alex and settled him in his pram. She was immensely relieved there was nothing wrong with him, but guilt gnawed at her gut. She'd been thoughtless and had caused her baby pain. And the worst of it was that she was desperately craving things she couldn't have, like curry and kebobs, and wine. It seemed even salad had to be avoided for fear of causing Alex suffering. Quinn sighed and rolled the pram out of the clinic. Being a mother was a lot different than she'd expected.

TWENTY-THREE

"Well, hello there, my dear," Monty gushed when Quinn pushed Alex's pram into his office. "You're looking radiant, if I may say so without causing offense." Monty winked at Quinn in a conspiratorial manner and peered into the pram. "And aren't you a lovely little lad. Daddy has shown me photos, of course, but they don't do you justice. Spitting image of Gabe, this one," Monty added as he beamed at Quinn.

"I know," Quinn replied with a sigh of resignation. If she didn't have a caesarean scar and leaking breasts, she could claim she'd never had anything to do with this baby.

"Could be worse. My sister looks just like my dad, and lovely man though he might have been, no woman should have that cross to bear. Gabe is a beautiful man, and I know beautiful men," Monty purred. For a short, round, bespectacled man who favored yellow polka-dot bowties, he attracted an inordinate number of attractive young men who were only too happy to be squired around town by the aging historian.

"Got a new boy toy, have you?" Quinn asked.

"Oh, darling, he's divine. Simply divine. Twenty-seven years old and looks like Colin Firth in *Pride and Prejudice*."

"Lucky you."

"Luck has nothing to do with it. They know a catch when they see one," he joked and winked at her happily. "So Gabe tells me you have some questions about Imperial Russia. Well, pull up a chair and let me put the kettle on because no conversation about Imperial Russia can be rushed. And if I drone on long enough, your little one will fall asleep out of sheer boredom. You can thank me later."

Quinn made Alex comfortable, got settled in Monty's guest chair, and waited patiently until Monty's electric kettle boiled. He made two mugs of strong, sweet tea and pushed a tin of chocolate biscuits toward her before sitting down at his cluttered desk. He leaned back in his chair and tilted his head to the side, looking remarkably like a wise owl.

"What do you want to know, my lovely?"

"I'm working on a storyline for a new episode of *Echoes from the Past*," Quinn began.

"I saw the first episode last week. Riveting. Absolutely riveting. I even shed a tear, I must admit."

"Thank you. I'm glad you enjoyed it. Monty, I need to know about the Russian Revolution and its impact on the inhabitants of Petrograd."

"Do you have a few hours to spare?" Monty chuckled.

"Just give me a comprehensive summary," Quinn suggested, knowing that if given free rein, Monty would indeed go on for a few hours.

"Well, that city has seen its share of tragedy, I'll tell you that. It started out as Sankt-Peterburg, of course, named by Peter the Great after himself. If you build a beautiful city, you should have every right to name it after yourself, I always say," Monty joked. "It was renamed Petrograd in 1914."

"Why?"

"Because the original name sounded too German, and given what was going on at the time, with World War I raging all around and wiping out thousands of beautiful young men, it seemed prudent to cut all associations with anything German, especially given the opposition to the war by the Russian people. The city was renamed again, to Leningrad in 1924, after Vladimir Lenin, who was one of the most important Bolshevik leaders of the Russian Revolution. You've heard of the Leningrad Blockade, of course, or the Siege of Leningrad, as it's referred to in the West. It lasted two and a half years. Thousands of civilians slowly starved to death. They say there wasn't a rat left alive by the time the blockade finally came to an end. Anyway, it remained Leningrad until 1991, when it returned to its original name and is now known as St. Petersburg."

"And during the Revolution?" Quinn prompted.

"On November seventh, 1917, which was actually October twenty-fifth by the Gregorian calendar, the Bolsheviks stormed the Winter Palace and ousted the provisional government, which had been in place since the February Revolution. They proclaimed Russia to be the first communist state."

"Was it a very violent rebellion?" Quinn asked.

"Darling, no revolution is without bloodshed. Of course, there were many casualties, before, during, and after, including the royal family, which was shot in July of 1918, along with four servants in a cellar of the house where they were kept under house arrest. Their remains were thrown down mineshafts to erase any proof of the crime, and discovered decades later. It was a brutal way to deal with the Romanovs, especially the children, but Nicholas II was not a popular tsar. He was known as 'Bloody Nick' among the common people."

"What earned him such a flattering nickname?"

"Nicholas's father, Alexander III, died quite suddenly at the age of forty-nine, leaving his twenty-six-year-old son to rule the vast empire. Alexander III was very distressed, as he lay dying, since he didn't believe Nicholas, who was spoiled and immature, was up to the task, and made Nicholas promise to heed his ministers before making any important decisions. Alexander had been correct, of course. Nicholas was a weak and ineffectual ruler whose ill-informed decisions led to the deaths of millions, but worse than that, he was unsympathetic and often cruel. He was blamed for the Khodynka Tragedy, where over a thousand people got trampled to death, anti-Semitic pogroms against poor, defenseless people who posed no threat to him whatsoever, a brutal and disproportionate response to the 1905 revolution, and Bloody Sunday, where soldiers of the Imperial Guard opened fire on a crowd of peaceful protesters as they marched toward the Winter Palace to present a petition to the Tsar."

Monty took a noisy slurp of tea and continued. "His wife, Alexandra, was no better, by all accounts. She wasn't a sympathetic woman and was often heard saying that Russians needed to feel the sting of the whip in order to remember their place. She formed an unsavory relationship with a self-proclaimed mystic named Grigori Rasputin, who she believed had the power to heal her son, Alexei. The Tsarevich was afflicted by hemophilia, which was passed on to him by his mother, the granddaughter of Queen Victoria, who herself carried the defective gene. Rasputin was able to worm his way into the family and began to exert undue influence on Empress Alexandra, which didn't go unnoticed. Alexandra urged her husband to listen to the advice of the man many believed to be a clever charlatan. She became increasingly unpopular, especially once rumors of an affair with Rasputin began to circulate among the highest levels of society. With her reputation in tatters, Alexandra's credibility came into question at a time when Russia was already teetering on the brink of an armed rebellion."

"Rasputin was murdered, wasn't he?" Quinn asked.

"He was, indeed. Rasputin was assassinated in December of 1916 by a band of noblemen who feared his influence on the royal family, but the damage had already been done. The Empress Alexandra was viewed with suspicion and contempt, and her refusal to curtail her spending at a time when the country was grossly in debt didn't help her image. Historical accounts report that she spent thousands of rubles on fresh flowers for the palace every week when the common people were starving. Compassion was not something the Romanovs were ever known for, so no compassion was shown to them at a time when it might have made all the difference."

"Do you think they knew what was about to befall them?" Quinn asked, shuddering at the thought of five children being gunned down in cold blood, especially the sickly Alexei, whose short life had been plagued by near-death bouts of hemophilia that left him hovering on the brink of death.

"Oh, I think Nicky had an inkling. It is said that in March of 1901, he went to Gatchina, accompanied by Baron Fredrichs and several other courtiers. The journey was undertaken in order to fulfill the wish of Tsar Paul I, who decreed that a chest he left behind for future generations be opened on the one-hundredth anniversary of his death. The chest contained a prophecy by a monk called Abel, the Russian Nostradamus, as he was nicknamed, that foretold the fate of the Tsar and the house of Romanov. No copies of the original prophecy or books written by Abel have survived, but the prophecy was pieced together from journal entries and personal letters, and went something like this:

"'A royal crown he shall exchange for a crown of thorns, and his people shall betray him, just as God's Son was. There shall be a great war, a world war... People shall fly through the air, like birds, and swim under water like fishes; they shall begin to destroy each other with evil-smelling Sulphur. The betrayal of the Tsar shall increase and grow in scale. On the eve of victory in the war the Royal throne will collapse. Blood and tears will soak the wet earth. Crazed common folk will seize power, and truly, an Egyptian sentence will dawn.' It's said that after that fateful trip, the Tsar became obsessed with the year 1918, believing it to be a crucial year for himself and the future of Russia."

"What became of the aristocracy after the Revolution?"

"Some remained but didn't fare very well. Many fled, mostly to France, where they lived in obscurity and often poverty. The forty-seven surviving members of the Romanov family lived in exile for the rest of their lives."

"Are there any living descendants?"

"Of course, but they are smart enough to keep a low profile. There was nothing to be gained by proclaiming their heritage during the communist years except a bullet between the eyes."

"And after?"

"In 1998, the royal family was buried with all the pomp and circumstance due them at the Cathedral of Saints Peter and Paul in St. Petersburg. I believe several of their descendants attended the funeral, but that was the last anyone has seen of them. The Romanovs were canonized by the Russian Orthodox Church and declared martyrs in 2000, so that's something, I suppose."

"Did many aristocrats flee to England?" Quinn asked, wondering about what might have led Valentina to Britain rather than France.

"Darling, Britain was having its own problems at the time, and the Russian Revolution was a very jarring wake-up call for the royal family. George VI, who was Nicholas II's cousin and could be mistaken for his twin, first offered asylum to the Romanovs after the Revolution, but then the invitation was discreetly rescinded. Any association with the Russian royal family would not have been looked upon favorably by the British people. The unprecedented slaughter of World War I reminded British subjects that the royal house of England was, in fact, of German descent, and responsible for Britain's involvement in the war. The strong anti-German feeling could very easily be redirected against the British monarchy if preventative measures weren't taken. It was at that time that the royal family changed their name from the House of Saxe-Coburg and Gotha to the House of Windsor. It was a calculated public relations move meant to disassociate the royal family from their German roots."

"Thanks, Monty. That's very helpful. I'm familiar with most of the events you mentioned, of course, but not in detail. Russia has never been a particular interest of mine. I've always been a lover of British history at heart, and now I'm developing more of an interest in American history as well."

"No! Say it isn't so," Monty sputtered.

"Turns out my biological dad is American. From Louisiana."

"Dear God, preserve us from the Americans!" Monty joked.

"Come, Monty, you and I will always have a *special relationship*," Quinn said with a huge grin.

"There'll always be a place in my heart for you. And Gabe. Because he's hot," Monty replied as he walked Quinn to the door.

"Monty, quit lusting after my husband. He has enough to deal with at the moment."

"Just window shopping, darling." Monty gave Quinn a peck on the cheek and waved cheerfully to Alex, who was looking at him with undisguised interest.

Quinn was still chuckling as she pushed Alex's pram down the corridor toward Gabe's office. It was nearly noon, and she had every intention of talking him into a pub lunch.

"Well, if it isn't Dr. Allenby, in the flesh," a familiar voice drawled as Luke stepped into her path. He'd emerged from one of the offices, no doubt lured from his lair by the sound of her voice.

"Hello, Luke," Quinn said. She'd have preferred to keep walking, but Luke effectively blocked her way, and she didn't fancy ramming Alex's pram into his legs.

"Hello, yourself. How've you been? Motherhood suits you. I've never seen you look so... wholesome," he said, a sarcastic smile tugging at his mouth. "You're positively Rubenesque."

"Thank you. I'll take that as a compliment," Quinn said, although, of course, it wasn't meant as one. He was implying that she was overweight and matronly, nothing like the girl who'd caught his eye nearly ten years ago.

"And how's the little moppet? I hear he looks just like Gabe. Well, at least that's one thing Gabe doesn't have to worry about."

"Meaning?"

Luke shrugged off the question, allowing her to draw her own conclusions. She'd never been unfaithful to Luke when they were together, so his insinuation was completely unfounded. Even if Alex hadn't resembled Gabe, there had never been any doubt that he was his son.

"How's your American daddy?" Luke asked, his mouth twisting with dislike. Seth had threatened to kick Luke into the middle of next week when he came upon Luke harassing her in New Orleans, and it clearly still rankled.

"He's very well. Thank you. He was just here in London. We had a nice visit."

"I bet."

"Look, Luke, I'd like to say it's been a pleasure to see you, but it really hasn't been, so I'll just get going, shall I? Please step out of my way."

"Don't get too comfortable, Quinny. Gabe is not the saint you believe him to be."

"Thanks for the warning," Quinn replied in response to his childish parting shot.

Quinn maneuvered the pram around Luke and walked off toward Gabe's office, head held high. She wasn't going to allow Luke to rattle her, which was exactly what he was trying to do. He'd implied that she was fat and undesirable, and then tried to make her doubt Gabe's loyalty to her. *What a wanker!* Quinn thought angrily as she rounded a corner. *What a bloody wanker!*

"You look murderous. I hope it's not toward me," Gabe said as she sailed past his PA and into his office, where she parked the pram alongside Gabe's desk and slumped into a chair.

"I just saw Luke in the corridor."

"I take it the reunion didn't go well."

"It was like exchanging pleasantries with Voldemort."

Gabe laughed, reached out to pick up Alex, and made a funny face at him. The baby smiled happily. "I think you deserve a treat. The Grafton Arms, or would you prefer the Marquis Cornwallis?"

"He implied I'm fat," Quinn muttered, ignoring the question.

"And you believed him?"

"No. Should I have?" she demanded, angry with herself for allowing Luke to get to her.

"I'm not even going to dignify that with an answer. Come on.

There's a glass of mineral water with your name on it and a pint with mine."

"Drinking on the job?"

"If you had to keep a bunch of self-important, mind-blowingly competitive, sex-starved historians from tearing each other to bits before lunchtime, you'd be drinking on the job too. And don't even get me started on the students."

"Your need is clearly greater than mine. Lead the way."

TWENTY-FOUR
DECEMBER 1917

London, England

Valentina woke early. The sheets were unpleasantly damp from the moisture that seemed to seep into every crevice and crack of the house. She shivered with cold and tried to burrow deeper beneath the inadequate woolen blanket. Her breath came out in puffy clouds in the chilly air of the dingy room, which was just beginning to emerge from the shadows as the first gray light of dawn crept stealthily through the window. Tanya was still asleep, her slight form pressed against Valentina's side. Kolya and Elena slept in the other bed, huddled beneath Elena's fur coat. Valentina would have loved a cup of hot tea, but going out to get water would wake the rest of the family, and she didn't want to disturb them. Instead, she slid out of bed and pulled on her coat and boots, desperate to get warm.

She kept a tight rein on her emotions during the day for the sake of the others, but at moments like this, when no one was awake to witness her pain, her resolve weakened and she often gave in to despair. The past two months had been surreal. Valentina moved from one task to the next like an automaton, steeling her mind against the pain that threatened to eviscerate her if she gave in to it. She had to remain strong for her mother, brother, and sister.

Elena Kalinina had virtually shut down since arriving in London, leaving all the decision-making to her daughter. She spent her days in a haze of confusion, alternating between sudden hysterics and periods of impenetrable silence, when she remained immobile for hours, staring out the window, her hands folded in her lap. Valentina was the one who purchased provisions, prepared the meals, and tried to comfort her brother and sister, who were bewildered and frightened.

Kolya still woke in the night, screaming for their father and shaking with terror, and Tanya carried on stoically, helping Valentina without a word of protest. They found satisfaction in mastering everyday tasks, since at the moment that was all they could aspire to. Making soup that didn't taste like slops was a triumph and washing their own garments brought a sense of quiet satisfaction. Neither Valentina nor Tanya had ever had to fend for themselves before. They'd never made a meal, mended a stocking, or laundered a garment. In those first days in London, they'd been paralyzed with uncertainty, unsure how to go about the simplest tasks. Now, after more than a month, they were finally learning how to get from day to day without going hungry or wearing soiled undergarments.

Valentina angrily brushed the tears from her cheeks. She was ashamed of her weakness, but at times, the tears flowed unchecked, no matter how hard she tried not to give in to her misery. Tanya and Kolya became upset when she cried, but Elena hardly noticed, so lost was she in her own impenetrable grief. She'd never been on her own, having gone from the home of her supportive parents to the loving embrace of her husband. The foundation of her life, which had always been solid and secure, had suddenly given way, a chasm opening beneath her feet and swallowing her whole in a matter of minutes. Valentina wasn't sure if her mother would ever recover from the shock and fear of the past few months.

She tried not to think of the day everything had changed, but sometimes she dreamed of those awful moments, and lost in her nightmare she screamed and screamed when she saw armed men breaking into their home, their faces distorted by hatred and blood-lust. That day, the day that was now known as the October Revolution, had begun quietly enough, but by afternoon, the Kalinins could no longer ignore the shouting in the street or the ominous sounds of gunfire and the roar of engines. The Bolsheviks were on the move, marching through the streets, armed and dangerous, on their way to the Winter Palace. Their numbers had swelled since the February Revolution, more and more workers and soldiers flocking to what was now the leading political party. The people were fed up with a war they didn't support, crippling poverty that brought them to their knees, and the lies and feeble excuses of a provisional government that tried to appease the upper classes while still ignoring the needs of the common people.

The city churned and heaved, the streets thronged with armed men and pulsing with the camaraderie of the insurgents. Many still brandished axes and scythes, but the majority now had firearms, horses, and even trucks and automobiles. They were no longer an angry mob, but an army of workers and peasants, intent on bringing down the provisional government and seizing power for the people. Valentina heard several names shouted over the din. Lenin. Trotsky. Those names alone seemed to be enough to inspire a manic loyalty among the men, driving them on to victory.

The Kalinins were too afraid to go to sleep that night, so they huddled together in a back room that faced the garden, wide awake and terrified. The noise seemed to die down toward the small hours and they managed a few hours of fitful sleep, but once the sun was up, it all began anew. And as with any armed rebellion, there was bloodshed and looting. The thugs came in the late afternoon on the second day; there were six of them. They broke down the door and surged into the foyer, looking around with a mixture of wonder and resentment. The men were armed with rifles and knives and dressed in homespun trousers, cotton-stuffed vatniki coats and hand-me-down army greatcoats. They overturned furniture, slashed several portraits, and ransacked the kitchen, searching for food. The servants hid in their rooms, correctly assuming that no one would bother burglarizing the bare, cold rooms of the lower classes. It was valuables and provisions they were after.

Things might have turned out differently had Ivan Kalinin simply allowed the men to take what they wanted and leave. They hadn't searched the back rooms, nor had they been interested in the members of the household, but fearful for his family and outraged by the insolence of the rebels, Ivan came charging out of the back room, intent on confronting the intruders.

"Stop this minute!" he bellowed. "What do you think you're doing? Does your esteemed Lenin approve of such barbarism? Does he encourage his men to loot and destroy other people's property?"

"Get out of our way, old man," a blond youth with a rifle replied. "Go hide like the rat that you are. Your kind is finished. It all belongs to us now. It's for the good of the people, and we are the people," he added, winking at his companions.

"You'd best leave while you can, high and mighty sir," an older man said to Ivan, poking him in the chest with meaty finger. "The new government will not tolerate freeloaders like you, who do nothing to earn their daily bread. They'll send you down the mines, or to muck out after the horses. You'll soon learn what it means to work for a living, you imperialist bastard."

"Get out of my house, you worthless miscreants!" Ivan roared. "You'll all be shot once this is over, or better yet, hanged like the criminals you are. You can't disguise petty thievery with talk of your shining ideals. Let go of that!" Ivan cried when he saw one of the men emerging from the master bedroom upstairs with Elena's lacquered jewelry box. He took the steps two at a time to get to the man. "Thief!" Ivan bellowed as he tried to wrestle the box from the man's grasp.

"Vanya, please, let them take it," Elena cried from the ground floor. "Please, come back here."

"I'll do no such thing. I will not allow this filthy vermin to intimidate me. I was in the military, and I can still put up a fight."

"You want to fight?" a swarthy middle-aged man asked, baring his rotten teeth. He brandished a lethal-looking knife in his right hand. "Come. Come at me, you pathetic maggot. I'll show you what it's like to fight a real man and not a trained baboon, used to obeying orders. I give the orders now."

Ivan charged the man, who held up Ivan's father's gold pocket watch in his left hand and let it swing like a pendulum. "Come and get it, your worship," he sang, mocking Ivan.

Valentina clapped her hand over her mouth as she watched the scene unfold. She recognized the man. He'd delivered coal to them for the past two winters. He'd always been dressed in layers, bundled into a threadbare coat to battle the cold wind blowing off the Neva, his hands reddened and chapped beneath his moth-eaten mittens. He knew exactly who they were, and she could see the hatred in his narrowed eyes.

"Papa, please, forget the watch," Valentina cried. "It's not worth it."

"That watch belonged to your grandfather Count Vasiliy Kalinin, and this dirty, flea-ridden peasant will not have it," Ivan cried, incensed.

The "dirty, flea-ridden peasant" went puce in the face and charged Ivan, grabbing him by the throat and forcing him against the polished banister until the wood gave and Ivan plunged downward, head first. Elena screamed in terror as her husband's head hit the black-and-white tiles below, cracking open like a ripe melon. A pool of blood spread around his head, forming a crimson halo.

Elena swooned, Tanya screamed, and Kolya buried his face in Valentina's side, shaking like a leaf.

"Please, take whatever you want," Valentina cried out. "We won't try to stop you. Just don't hurt us. There are only women and children here."

"And that makes you special, does it?" the blond youth exclaimed. "My family is also made up of women and children, who nearly starved to death this past winter because I was at the front, fighting a losing war while my elderly father tried to eke out enough to feed his family. He died trying. One of these trinkets would have kept them fed and warm for a year or more."

"Stop explaining yourself, Evgeni," the swarthy man rumbled. "Just get on with it. There are several more houses we can hit on this street before they try to rein us in. Take what you can and let's go."

The men continued to plunder, turning their backs on the terrified family. Valentina grabbed her mother, who'd come to, around the waist and tried to maneuver her into the back room where she'd be out of harm's way, but her eyes were glued to the body of her husband as an animal-like wail filled the foyer.

"Mama, come away. There's nothing you can do for him now."

"Vanya!" Elena cried. "Not my Vanya."

Tanya pulled Kolya away from Valentina and wrapped him in her arms. "Let's go, Kolya. Let's get away from here." She pushed him into the room, leaving Valentina with her mother, who knelt at her husband's side, refusing to be led away. The skirt of her dress was soaked with blood, and her eyes were wild, as if she didn't quite understand what had happened. "Vanya, it will be all right," Elena kept repeating. "I'll have Petr summon the doctor."

It was too late for a doctor, but the reality hadn't yet penetrated Elena's befuddled brain.

"Mama, please," Valentina pleaded. "Come away."

"Your father needs me," Elena protested. "Get Petr."

Valentina sighed in exasperation. She had no idea where Petr was, nor would finding him make any difference. Her father was gone, and her only concern was keeping the rest of them out of harm's way. The men were now trooping down the staircase, their arms laden with loot. She saw her silver-backed hairbrush sticking out of the blond youth's pocket, and her mother's pearls around one man's neck. They'd emptied the jewelry box and discarded it, having no need for the bulky container. Her mother's valuables had been distributed between pockets, which were now bulging with gold and gems.

Another few moments and the men would have left, but the front door, which was hanging off its hinges, swung open as Alexei and a fellow officer rushed in, sabers drawn. Alexei froze with shock when he saw Ivan's body, his head reminiscent of a crushed watermelon.

"Valya, are you all right?" Alexei cried.

"Alyosha, go, get out!" Valentina screamed, but it was too late. The men had reached the foyer and were advancing on Alexei, weapons drawn.

"Don't you look smart in your uniform," the blond youth remarked. "And that saber looks mighty sharp. It's no match against a rifle, though, is it?"

Alexei swung his sword at the man closest to him, who wielded an axe. There was a momentary clash of steel, and then the elegant weapon went sailing overhead, landing with a clatter on the foyer tiles. Alexei backed away, disarmed and helpless.

"Give me your sword," he cried to his friend, but the other man was already engaged in a fight with a red-haired man brandishing a cutlass. The blond youth leaned against the banister, watching with interest. He seemed in no rush to fire his rifle and waste bullets.

Valentina watched in horror as the redheaded peasant slashed at the officer, cutting him nearly in half. His innards spilled through the hole in his coat, his face going gray and his eyes glazing in death as he fell to the floor. Alexei backed away, but there was no escape. He was surrounded.

"Valya, get away. Go to France," he cried. "Save yourself."

The bayonet pierced Alexei through, the tip emerging on the other side, dripping blood. His eyes grew round with pain and shock. He fell to his knees, his gaze on the man who'd speared him like a fish. The man looked momentarily stunned, but then his lips drew back in a satisfied smile.

"Nighty night," he said with a vicious laugh as he pulled out the bloodied bayonet and Alexei fell forward, sprawling on the floor.

"Alyosha!" Valentina screamed, but he couldn't have heard her. He'd never hear her again. He was gone, just like her father. The two men she loved and trusted most in the world were gone, their blood obscenely red against the shiny tiles. She was now on her own, with no one to help her through the worst hour of her life.

It was much later, after the men had left and after Nyanushka and Petr had removed Ivan's and Alexei's bodies from the foyer, that Valentina was finally able to cajole her mother into having a shot of vodka and lying down in the back parlor. She couldn't sleep, but at least she'd stopped screaming and lay quietly like a corpse. Tanya and Kolya huddled in the corner, mute with horror.

They left in the morning, shrouded in the thick mist of an autumn dawn. Tanya and Kolya carried their valises. Valentina supported her mother as they ambled silently toward the station. Valentina had no idea where they were going or how they'd get there, but they had to get out, today. Many others had the same idea. A crowd of grim-faced, frightened people gathered at the station. Most had only a small bag with them, just large enough to carry a change of clothes and some food.

Valentina had invited Olga Alexandrovna and Nyanushka to come with them, but the women had refused. They were members of the working class, so they had nothing to fear from the rebels. There was nothing for them in exile, and they had no desire to look after a family who could no longer pay their wages. Even Petr had declined to help when Valentina asked him to drive them to the station.

"You'd best go on foot," he'd replied. He hadn't bothered to give a reason for his refusal, and Valentina hadn't asked. What did it matter? They were on their own.

Valentina had intended to go to France. Alexei was gone, but perhaps his family would meet them in Paris, and there was the aunt, who might help, but Elena dug in her heels, refusing to go to France.

"We must go to London," she insisted. "I have a cousin in London—Dmitri Pavlovich Ostrov. We grew up together. He lives in London and he will help us. I know he will. We were like brother and sister when we were small."

"Mama, you haven't seen him in years," Valentina protested. She'd never heard of this Dmitri Pavlovich before, but her mother was adamant.

"And I have never seen Alexei's aunt. What makes you think she'll help us? And the Petrovs will not flee, not with Alexei dead. They'll wish to bury him."

Like we buried Papa, Valentina thought bitterly. She'd extracted a promise from Olga Alexandrovna that Ivan Kalinin would get a proper burial. There'd be no service, given the circumstances, but at least he'd be interred at Volkovskoe Cemetery next to his parents. Elena wished to remain until after the funeral, but Valentina wouldn't hear of it.

"Mama, we have to go now. Today. Papa and Alexei are dead. We could be next. You have your children to think of."

"My children?" Elena asked, confused. "Who'd want to hurt my children?"

Valentina didn't bother to reply. She had no idea what would happen in the days to come, but she couldn't see anything worth staying for. Their house was no longer safe. The people they'd known all their lives were in danger, and the future of Russia was uncertain. There was no reason to remain and risk their lives.

She was right, of course. Elena retreated into a shell of her own misery once they left Petrograd, but Valentina talked to other refugees as they spent countless hours waiting for connections and traveling on overcrowded trains. People's homes had been broken into, their possessions stolen, their lives threatened. Some were wise enough not to resist, but many had chosen to fight back, and now their bereft families recalled their bravery and prayed for the eternal souls of their loved ones.

The journey to London took nearly a month. With the war still raging and many others like them trying to escape, everything took twice as long. There was no direct route, so they traveled through Finland, into Sweden and Norway, and then by boat to Great Britain. London had seemed grim and gray when they arrived, a city scarred by war. There were mounds of rubble where bombs had fallen and numerous ambulances racing toward hospitals with their precious cargo. But the people seemed surprisingly cheerful, and defiant. They hadn't been brought to their knees, and Valentina found their bravery inspiring. She wouldn't be brought to her knees either, she had vowed.

And now, two months after the fateful events that changed all their lives, they were installed in Whitechapel, a slum if ever there was one. Valentina had sold off some of her mother's jewelry to finance their journey and rented the mean little room on the first floor of a crumbling building that smelled of urine and decay. She could have found something better, but she was terrified to spend their money too fast, and positive that she'd been grossly cheated by the pawn broker who purchased the jewels. Surely it was worth more, but she knew nothing of the value of the British pound, nor did she have an inkling of what one pound could buy versus one ruble. They still had some money, but if they didn't find a way to support themselves soon, the money would run out, and they would be destitute.

"Oh, Dmitri Palvovich, where are you?" Valentina whispered into the frigid air. "Why have you not replied to Mama's letters?"

"Valya, are you talking to yourself?" Tanya asked as she woke. "God, I need to pee." She slid out of bed and pulled the chamber pot from beneath the bed. "Ah," Tanya said as she squatted over it, completely unashamed. They'd let go of all their pretensions, living like the lowest orders of society.

"Tanya, today is Christmas Eve," Valentina whispered.

"Don't remind me. It's too painful to even contemplate."

"I think we should do something special," Valentina suggested.

"Really, like what? Should we dress the tree, have a magnificent meal, and sing around the piano? Oh, and then we should open presents," Tanya added sarcastically.

"We don't have money for decorations or presents, but we should get something nice for supper. A little treat. What do you say?"

"I don't know, Valya. It's up to you. Sure, I'd love something besides boiled potatoes, cabbage soup, and brown bread with butter, but I'd rather eat that than find myself homeless next month."

"You have a point there. We must find employment."

"What kind of employment?" Tanya moaned.

"Any kind. Mama refuses to leave the room, so it's up to you and me to find a way to support us."

"Mama is in shock. I don't think she'll ever recover. Just look at her."

Valentina didn't need to look at her mother to know what Tanya was referring to. Elena had grown skeletally thin and her skin, which had been supple and creamy, was now gray and papery. Her eyes were often unfocused and she seemed to forget what happened for long stretches of time, forcing her daughters to repeatedly explain to her what they were doing in the dingy room and how they had come to be there. Her cousin's ongoing silence did nothing to aid their mother's mental state, and the girls were growing desperate with worry. They couldn't remain in this room forever, nor could they neglect Kolya's education. He'd turned eight in November but hadn't had any formal lessons since October, when he'd last studied with Olga Alexandrovna. This was their new reality and they had to find a way to move forward, rather than survive from day to day and wait for a miracle.

TWENTY-FIVE
JANUARY 1918

London, England

Valentina looked at her hands. What she wouldn't give for her fur muff and the creamy lotion she'd used back at home during the coldest months. Washing their clothes in cold water with smelly lye soap irritated her skin and left her hands red and chapped. She was hungry too, nearly all the time. Not only did she not get enough sustenance, but she missed variety and taste. The food they ate had no flavor. Her mouth watered when she recalled the Christmas feast. She'd decided to splurge after all. Nothing major, just something to lift their sagging spirits. After much consideration, Valentina had purchased four meat pies, four oranges, and four mince pies. They had eaten the mince pies on Christmas Eve and enjoyed the meat pies and oranges on Christmas Day. They hadn't found a Russian Orthodox Church they could attend, so they held their own service, during which they commended the souls of Ivan Kalinin and Alexei Petrov to Christ.

Their Christmas had been sad and lonely, but now that the New Year had begun, they had more pressing matters. The money was going fast, mostly due to their need for coal. Elena was always cold, huddling on the bed beneath her fur coat, and Kolya fell ill just after Christmas and still had a chesty cough and a runny nose. They also spent too much on tea and sugar, and their one luxury, a meaty bone from the butcher once a fortnight to make stew.

Valentina wrung out the laundry and strung it up to dry on a string suspended from one end of the room to the other. Everything took days to dry because of the infernal damp, but at least their clothes were relatively clean, although growing threadbare from so much use. Valentina made herself a cup of tea and sat down by the window. Elena was asleep, and Tanya had taken Kolya for a walk. He was still coughing, but he needed fresh air and exercise or he might get worse.

Valentina rested her chin in her hands and considered their situation. They had to find work. They'd picked up some English over the past few months, but not enough to work in a shop or with children. They had no useful skills, so the only employment they could aspire to would be as char women or laundresses. Tanya was handy with a needle, so perhaps they might try to get her a position with a seamstress. She might not be permitted to do anything fancy, but it didn't take great creativity to take up hems and sew on buttons. Valentina had considered looking for a position as a scullion, since that was unskilled grunt work, but even for that, she needed to understand enough English to know what was being asked of her and she'd have to live on the premises. She couldn't leave Tanya and Kolya. They needed her, so whatever she did had to be done during the day so she could return home in the evenings.

Valentina finished her tea and sighed. She'd never imagined things would be so hard. At this time last year, she'd been dreaming of her engagement and wedding, and of the home she'd share with Alexei, filled with beautiful things and capable servants. And now she was here, in London, with no one to turn to for help and no one to ask for advice. Her hand closed around the little blue egg Alexei had given her. She would never part with it. Ever. No matter what. It was her only link to that other life, and to the man she'd loved.

Oh, Alyosha, how I miss you, my darling. I wish you were here. You'd make everything all right.

It took nearly two weeks, but eventually, Valentina found Tanya a position with a local seamstress. Tanya was to work from eight in the morning until six in the evening, with only a half hour for dinner at noon. Tanya hated the tedious work and disliked her employer, but she dutifully went off every morning, while Valentina took on some cleaning jobs. They paid a pittance, but it was enough to buy bread and butter, some cheese, and a weekly bucket of coal. It wasn't nearly enough, but they used the coal sparingly, and only in the evenings. Valentina greatly looked forward to a break in the weather when they might cut back on heating.

Life went on, if you could call it living. Elena wasted away, Kolya spent his days playing with other boys in the street, and Valentina and Tanya worked to support the family. Valentina came home first and had to immediately start preparing supper, since Elena did nothing during the day but sleep and stare out the window. She wouldn't even eat if her daughters didn't set a plate in front of her. They helped her bathe on Saturdays and brushed her hair, since she showed no desire to take care of herself.

It was at the beginning of March that they received their first and only visitor. As it was late afternoon, they were seated around the scarred wooden table, having tea and bread, meant to tide them over until suppertime, when there was a loud knock on the door. Valentina and Tanya exchanged glances. Valentina thought it might be their landlord, but he never came for the rent on Sundays. She pushed her chair away from the table and went to answer the door. Outside, she found a man of about forty. He had dark soulful eyes, thick sandy-colored hair, and a short beard. The sable collar on his coat and the silver-tipped walking stick in his gloved hand looked out of place in the dingy corridor.

"Valentina Ivanovna, I presume?" he asked, smiling at her kindly. "I'm Dmitri Pavlovich Ostrov, your mother's cousin. May I come in?"

"Of course." Valentina stepped aside and invited him into the room. She inwardly cringed as he took in the two iron bedsteads, the laundry hanging beneath the ceiling and the grimy, narrow window. They didn't have an extra chair to offer him, so Valentina offered him her own. "May I pour you some tea?"

"Thank you. That would be wonderful."

Valentina quickly rinsed out her own cup, since they only had four, while Dmitri Pavlovich removed his coat, hat, and gloves. He looked about, unsure what to do with the items, until Tanya jumped to her feet and reached out to take them. She stowed everything on the bed, for lack of a coat hanger. Dmitri's eyes focused on Elena, who stared at him woodenly, confusion marring her brow as she studied his features. They hadn't seen each other in nearly twenty years, and no doubt found each other much changed.

"Dima, is that really you?" Elena breathed.

"It is, Lenochka. I'm so sorry I haven't come sooner. I was away on business, you see, and only arrived back a few days ago. That was when I saw your letters."

"What's type of business are you in?" Valentina asked.

"I have various commercial interests. You wouldn't be interested." Dmitri waved his hand in a dismissive manner. "Tell me about you. How long have you been in London? How've you managed to live?"

Valentina and Tanya gave him an abridged version of events. They simply couldn't muster the emotion to go over it all again, especially the cruel deaths of their father and Alexei. Dmitri surmised for himself that Ivan was gone, and Valentina saw no reason to bring up Alexei. Her pain was private, and she wasn't ready to share it with a man she'd just met. Perhaps she'd tell him about Alexei in time, if given the opportunity to further their acquaintance.

"Merciful Father, how you have suffered. You did right to come to London, my dears. I'm back now, and I will look after you."

Valentina watched Dmitri discreetly. She knew nothing of the man, but he seemed genuinely distressed by their plight and eager to help. She wouldn't ask him for anything, though. She'd wait to see what he proposed, and proceed from there.

Dmitri took a sip of tea and set his cup down with the look of a man who'd made a decision. "You are coming to live with me."

"Are you married, Dmitri Pavlovich?" Tanya asked. Valentina hadn't thought to inquire, but Dmitri's wife might have something to say about four people she'd never heard of taking up residence in her home.

"I was. Alas, my wife died several years ago. We weren't blessed with children."

"How did you come to live in London?" Kolya asked. "I don't like London."

"Many years ago, when I was a young man, I met an English lady who stole my heart," Dmitri said, his explanation dripping with romanticism meant to appeal to a young boy. "She worked as a governess for a family I knew well. She'd been engaged to teach the children English and Italian. She was lovely, my Emily. My parents were extremely angry when I married her, and cast me out, so we returned to the land of her birth to make a life for ourselves here."

"Where do you live?" Kolya asked.

"I have a house in Belgravia. It's not overly large, but it's comfortable, and has enough bedrooms to accommodate you all. Shall we go there now? My carriage is just around the corner."

Valentina gazed at Dmitri in some surprise. She didn't know much about London yet, but she knew that Belgravia was a very prestigious area, not the type of place where a cast-out nobleman and a former governess would reside. Dmitri had obviously done very well for himself over the past twenty years.

"Come now," Dmitri said as he rose to his feet and looked around the room. "Is there anything I can help with?"

"Just give us a moment," Valentina said.

"Bring only your clothes and personal items. You won't have

any need of domestic implements." He looked with distaste at the chipped china and blackened pans hanging by the hearth.

It took all of ten minutes to gather their belongings. Valentina looked around the bare, cheerless room. She hoped they wouldn't have to come back, but until she saw their accommodations and verified the terms of Dmitri's assistance, she wouldn't give up their home or their employment. They would just have to take an omnibus to work tomorrow, since it was likely too far to walk.

Dmitri supported Elena gently as he escorted her toward the carriage. Her fur coat hung on her thin frame, making her look frail and shrunken, and her hat obscured most of her face. She didn't bother to look around, just stared straight ahead, uninterested in the place they'd lived for several months. The carriage wasn't grand, but large enough to fit them all comfortably. Dmitri used his walking stick to tap on the roof once they were settled, and the vehicle moved smoothly away from the curb.

"Will I have my own room?" Kolya asked, earning himself a sharp look from Valentina.

"Of course you will. For the time being."

"For the time being?" Kolya asked. He looked frightened and Valentina laid a hand on his arm to comfort him.

"My dear boy, we will have to find you a good school. You need an education, and in England, boys your age go to boarding school. You will come home for summers and holidays, but you will live at the school along with the other students."

"But I don't want to go away."

"We'll discuss it later. Once your mama has had time to settle in. It's nearly the end of the school term, so let's not worry about it now. All right?" Dmitri asked smoothly.

"What about my job?" Tanya asked softly. "I'm due at work at eight tomorrow morning."

"Dearest Tanya, of course, you must give up your job. You have no need of it any longer. I will look after you from now on. You must write to your employer and advise him of your changed circumstances. I'll have my boot boy deliver the message."

"What happens now?" Valentina asked. She wasn't sure how to ask precisely what she wanted to know. Would Dmitri see to all their needs? Would he give them some sort of an allowance for personal expenses? Would he expect something in return?

"The first thing we'll do is bring in a reputable seamstress to make you some new clothes. You've lived in these rags long enough. You'll need morning dresses, day dresses, evening gowns for when we visit the theater, and of course, new undergarments. I'll take Kolya to my own tailor. He'll make him several suits and a number of new shirts. That will tide him over until he'll need a school wardrobe. And you'll need new shoes, hats, stockings, and gloves. You'll have much to do in the coming days."

Dmitri smiled kindly at Valentina. "I realize you're worried, Valentina. You don't know me, and your mama can hardly vouch for me, not having seen me in twenty years. You've been looking after your family and doing an admirable job, but you no longer have to carry this burden all by yourself. I must admit that it will be a joy to have a family again. I've been alone far too long, and I look forward to getting to know you all."

"You're very kind," Valentina replied, touched by his generosity and relieved that he understood her reservations.

"Kindness has nothing to do with it. I'm a selfish, lonely man who's thrilled to be of service to someone who genuinely needs me. Now, have you ever had hot chocolate?" he asked, looking directly at Kolya.

"Yes, but not since the Revo—not since we came here," Kolya replied.

"I will ask Mrs. Stern—that's my housekeeper—to make you a pot of hot chocolate when we get home. I wager you'd like that. And then you can all have a rest before supper. Mutton chops and potatoes today, with peas and carrots, and apple cake for dessert. How does that sound?"

"That sounds heavenly," Tanya exclaimed. "We've been eating nothing but potatoes and porridge for months. I'd sell my soul for a chop."

"And speaking of souls, have you been to church?"

"We didn't know where to find a Russian Orthodox Church," Elena said quietly, finally roused from her stupor. "Is there one?"

"There is a lovely little church in Welbeck Street. The St. Sophia. That's in Marylebone. Have you been there?"

"No, we've hardly left Whitechapel. We don't speak English very well," Valentina explained.

"Well, we must rectify that as soon as possible. I'll find you a reputable tutor who will work with you for several hours each day. You must learn English before you can go out into society."

"Go out into society?" Tanya asked, her voice filled with wonder. "Really?"

"Of course. You will have to marry one day, my dear girl, and you can't do that without meeting suitable gentlemen."

"Perhaps once I master the language, I could find myself a position as a governess or a teacher, so I wouldn't be a burden to you, Dmitri Pavlovich," Valentina said. She couldn't even begin to think of marriage. Loving anyone but Alexei seemed unimaginably wrong, but she wouldn't want to depend on Dmitri for longer than was strictly necessary. She'd have to make her own way eventually, once she'd had a little time to get her bearings and learn something of this new world she'd landed in.

"There's no need to decide anything right now. You've been through a lot, so it's only natural that you're not eager for more changes. Ah, here we are," Dmitri said as the carriage drew up to a modest red-brick building. It was set back from the road and the hedges flanking the front garden gave the house an aura of privacy. "Come inside."

The door was opened by a plump, gray-haired woman who reminded Valentina of Nyanushka. The woman looked momentarily abashed but quickly hid her dismay and invited them in.

"Mrs. Stern, I'd like you to meet my dear cousin, Countess Elena Kalinina. We were very close growing up. And these are her children: Valentina, Tatiana, and last, but not least, Nikolai. They've come to stay."

"A warm welcome to you all." Mrs. Stern bowed and lowered her eyes, as if greeting royalty.

"Please make us a pot of hot chocolate," Dmitri requested as he led them into a comfortable parlor. The beautifully appointed room was such a contrast to the dwelling they'd just left that Elena burst into tears as she sat down on a damask-upholstered settee. She dabbed at her eyes but then quickly pushed her handkerchief up her sleeve to hide how discolored and frayed it had become from frequent washing in harsh soap.

"Wherever did you find a Russian housekeeper, Cousin Dmitri?" Tanya asked as she took the seat closest to the fire.

"Mrs. Stern is Jewish. She and her family fled the pogroms in the Ukraine and came to England about five years ago, around the time my wife died. I was lucky to find her. She cooks me all the wonderful dishes I so missed when we had a stodgy English cook. All boiled mutton and stewed fish." Dmitri rolled his eyes in horror, making them all laugh.

"So, what does the wonderful Mrs. Stern make for you?" Elena asked, clearly curious about what to expect. This was the most interest she'd shown in anything in the past few months, and her sudden curiosity gave Valentina renewed hope for the future.

"She makes meat dumplings, potato pierogis, rich beef stews with egg noodles that she makes from scratch, and of course borsht and uha."

"Uha?" Kolya asked. "What's that?"

"What's that? Have you seriously never had uha? It's a fish soup that fishermen make with fresh catch. It has fish, potatoes, onions, and is flavored with bay leaf. Delicious."

"I'll take your word for it," Kolya replied rudely.

"Do you know what else Mrs. Stern makes?" Dmitri asked Kolya. "She makes raisin cake that's rich and sweet and dusted with confectioner's sugar, and homemade poppy seed roll. Do you like that?"

"I like pryaniki."

"She doesn't make those from scratch, but I know a place that sells them, believe it or not. I will make sure to buy some tomorrow, and we can have them with our tea."

"Can we have our tea with lemon?" Tanya asked. "We haven't had lemon since leaving home. And I don't like milk in my tea. It tastes strange."

"We can have lemon, if that's what you'd like. I must admit I've become accustomed to taking my tea the English way."

Mrs. Stern came in bearing a tray with a lovely porcelain pot, several cups, and a plate of peculiar biscuits that looked like elongated yellow bricks.

"Shall I pour, Dima?" Elena asked, taking on the role of hostess.

"By all means."

"What are those?" Kolya asked.

"Those biscuits are called shortbread. They are buttery and delicious. Have one."

Kolya reached for a biscuit and took an experimental bite. "Not bad," he said, "but I like sugar cookies better."

"Maybe Mrs. Stern came bake some for you." Dmitri accepted a cup of chocolate and turned to the housekeeper, who stood awaiting instructions. "Mrs. Stern, kindly prepare rooms for my honored guests. I think the yellow bedroom for the countess. It's the loveliest."

"Yes, sir." Mrs. Stern departed, leaving them to enjoy their hot chocolate.

"Dmitri, I will pray for you today and every day," Elena said tearfully. "You truly are our savior."

"There's only one Savior, Elena, but I'm happy to help."

TWENTY-SIX
APRIL 1918

London, England

Valentina closed her eyes and allowed the soothing notes of the sung prayer to wash over her. It felt good to be in a church again. She'd questioned her faith and the very existence of God during the dark days of their winter in exile, but spring had come eventually and renewed her spirits. Cousin Dmitri was indeed a godsend. He'd taken them in and made them his family. Even Elena had blossomed under his tender care. The first week had been awkward for all of them, but once they'd settled into a routine, it was as if they'd always lived in the house in Belgravia. Dmitri had been true to his word and saw to all the little details that made the transition easier. Now, a month later, they looked much as they had before the revolution, a well-turned-out, prosperous family, except that instead of Ivan Kalinin, her mother's arm rested on that of Dmitri Ostrov.

Tanya and Kolya stood next to their mother, Tanya in a high-necked pale blue dress with a lace collar and Kolya in a tweed suit and crisp white shirt. Elena wore a new dress in a muted shade of purple. Cousin Dmitri had talked her out of widow's black and assured her that purple and lavender were acceptable mourning colors in England. She'd gained a little weight over the past month, and her skin had lost that papery quality, partially due to better nutrition and partially with the help of the creams Cousin Dmitri had ordered for her. Elena's hair was beautifully dressed beneath her black lace headscarf, which she wore to church.

The service came to an end and everyone began to collect their belongings and make their way toward the door. The church wasn't as large as the one they had attended in Petrograd, but it was beautiful, in a cozy sort of way, and nearly full. Valentina was surprised to see so many Russian expats in London. There were many families with young children and several young women her age. There were also a number of young men, and Valentina noted shy looks and coy smiles between some of the young ladies and the eligible bachelors. She caught a few curious stares but didn't acknowledge them. She'd meet other people in time, but today, she wasn't ready to talk of her experiences and share her pain.

Once outside, Valentina was surprised to see that a folding table had been erected to the left of the door. A young man dressed in a shabby tweed suit and flat cap stood by the table, his gaze watchful. Newspapers were piled on one side of the table with a tin cup next to them. Nearly every man who exited the church helped himself to a paper and dropped payment into the cup. The opposite side of the table was covered with books. Several ladies drifted over and examined the offerings, while several more seemed to be selling their books to the young man. Valentina walked over to the table, eager to look at the books. There was no rush, as Cousin Dmitri seemed to be introducing Elena to some of his acquaintances and Tanya was chatting happily to a girl she'd just met.

"I didn't realize there was a Russian language newspaper in London," Valentina remarked to the young man. He reminded her of some of the Gypsies she'd seen back in Russia, with his dark coloring and coal-black eyes, but his pallor revealed that he didn't spend much time outdoors.

"There isn't. My brother and I print the paper ourselves."

"Really? You have a printing press?"

"We work for a printer. He allows us to use the press to print the paper as long as we reimburse him for the cost of paper and ink. We had to invest in Cyrillic typeset, of course," the young man added.

"Where do you get your news?"

"We still have contacts in Russia, and we also translate some of the articles from the London papers. Most of these people don't have a solid enough grasp of the English language to read the papers for themselves. And, of course, people are desperate for books since no Russian language books are sold in the shops."

"That's very clever of you," Valentina said. "Very enterprising."

The young man smiled, revealing straight white teeth. "Capitalism at its best."

"I'm Valentina Kalinina, by the way." Valentina held out her hand and the young man took it shyly.

"Stanislav Bistritzky."

"Will you be back here next week? I didn't bring my reticule with me, but I would like to buy a book."

"You can just take it and pay me later. Or, if you have any books you're finished with, you can bring me a book in exchange."

"That's very kind. I'll take this one." Valentina helped herself to a book of poems by Yesenin. Her mother would enjoy the poems, and perhaps Valentina would read them as well. She hadn't thought to pack any books into her valise, and the lack of reading material had been difficult to deal with at a time when any distraction would have been welcome.

"Enjoy it. I love poetry. I tried writing some myself, but it's rather maudlin, I must admit."

"Perhaps you should publish it, since you have the means."

"No, they are private. I'd be mortified if someone actually read them."

"I've never written poetry, but I tried my hand at writing

stories when I was younger," Valentina confessed. "My parents liked them," she added wistfully.

"You should try writing again. It helps deal with loss."

"How do you know I've suffered a loss?" Valentina asked, surprised by his astute observation.

"Everyone who's here has suffered loss, but I can also see the sadness in your eyes."

"I lost my father and my fiancé," Valentina said. She had no idea why she was telling this stranger, but something about him invited confidences.

"I'm sorry."

"Thank you."

Valentina walked away from the table when she saw Cousin Dmitri watching her. "I bought a book for Mama," she explained. "Look, Mama, it's poems by Yesenin."

"Thank you, my darling. That was very thoughtful of you. I shall enjoy reading them, although I'm sure they'll bring back some bittersweet memories."

"What were you talking to him about?" Dmitri demanded as they walked to his motorcar.

"About his newspaper and where he gets his information."

"The man is a charlatan," Dmitri growled as he started the engine.

"Why do you say that?"

"He's using the pain and suffering of others to line his own pockets."

"I think he's providing a valuable service," Valentina replied.

"Is he? Then he should give out the books and papers for free."

"Why? Other newspapers are not handed out for free. Everyone has a right to make a living, and he's supplying an obvious demand. There wasn't a single paper left by the time I left."

"Yes, he and his brother have certainly found a convenient place to sell their wares. By the church, of all places."

"Well, that's where the émigrés congregate, isn't it?" Valentina wasn't sure why she was defending the young man, but she couldn't understand why Dmitri was so incensed.

"He has no respect. He wouldn't, being a Jew."

"What does being a Jew have to do with it?" Valentina asked.

"They always find a way to make a profit off others, in any circumstances. It's disgraceful, but I wouldn't expect anything better from the likes of him."

"Dmitri, Valentina, please, let's talk of something else. Surely this young man is not worth such anger."

"I'm sorry, my dear. I didn't mean to upset you," Dmitri replied, his tone now gentle. "Of course, you are correct. The young man is providing a useful service."

"Indeed, he is. I very much look forward to reading these poems."

"Perhaps you can read them to us out loud after supper," Dmitri suggested.

"It would be my pleasure," Elena replied as she laid a soothing hand on Dmitri's arm. "I do like riding around in a motorcar. This is a new experience for all of us, isn't it?"

"It's grand," Kolya said. "When I grow up, I'll have a motorcar of my own. Maybe two."

"So will I," Tanya piped in. "And I will drive it myself. I've no need of a man."

"Tanya!" Elena cried.

"Women drive, Mother. Women do many things in this country."

"So they do," Elena replied bleakly. "So they do."

"Valya, you must show Dmitri respect," Elena said once they were alone in the parlor. Dmitri had gone out to run an errand, and Elena had called for tea.

"I did nothing wrong."

"You antagonized him."

"I had no idea he was such an anti-Semite."

"He's perfectly nice to Mrs. Stern."

"Because she serves a purpose. Isn't he benefitting from her family's hardship? So, why is it wrong for Stanislav Bistritzky to sell his newspaper?"

"It isn't, but you don't need to argue with Dmitri about it. He's entitled to his opinions, and given that we're living on his generous bounty, you will control your tongue in the future."

"Yes, Mama. I'm sorry."

"Have some tea."

Valentina accepted a cup of tea. She was grateful to Dmitri for all he'd done for them, and was still going to do, but she hated feeling beholden and having to hold her tongue for fear of offending their benefactor. Perhaps, in time, she could find some sort of employment, so that she'd at least have some of her own money and not feel entirely dependent on him.

London, England

Quinn set aside the necklace and padded into the kitchen to make a cup of tea. She'd never had tea with lemon and sugar but had a mind to try it as soon as she purchased lemons, because that was how Valentina's family always took it. She smiled to herself as she dunked a teabag in her mug and added a splash of milk. How fortunate for the Kalinins that Cousin Dmitri had finally received their letter. He couldn't have been kinder or more helpful. Elena had been right in choosing to go to England instead of trying her luck in France, where they'd have to beg assistance from Alexei's elderly aunt. Things must have turned out well, since Quinn knew for a fact that Valentina had eventually married and had children.

She dismissed the argument she'd witnessed between Valentina and Dmitri. It wasn't unnatural for people to have a difference of opinion, and it wasn't surprising that Dmitri wasn't fond of the Jews. The Russians and the Jews had never coexisted peacefully in Russia, and still didn't. Many Russian Jews had fled to England after the Revolution, and many more arrived after World War II. Despite his years in England, Dmitri appeared to be deeply rooted in his Russian ways, and probably would remain so for the rest of his days.

Quinn carried her tea through to the bedroom where Alex was beginning to wake up from his mid-morning nap, like clockwork. She changed his nappy and fed him, then went to the window to take a peek outside. The day was overcast, but it wasn't snowing or pissing down with rain, which was always a bonus. Perhaps a brief walk. She liked to leave the house at least once a day, to remind herself that she wasn't a hermit, and to make sure Alex got some fresh air. She was just about to dress the baby in a warm jumper when the doorbell buzzed.

I hope it's not Sylvia again, Quinn thought as she went to see who was at the door. She backed away in surprise when she saw Jude on the screen, waiting patiently to be allowed to come up. He looked nervous, stepping from foot to foot, as if he needed the loo.

"Hello," he said shyly when Quinn opened the door to him. She stepped aside and allowed him into the flat. Even in his winter gear—a navy-blue parka, a striped scarf, and a knitted cap—he looked trendy and artistic.

"What are you doing here, Jude?" Quinn asked. Jude never visited or rang her voluntarily, and they hadn't spoken since the day of Emma's birthday party.

"I came to bring this, and to apologize." Jude thrust a gift bag at Quinn. It contained a sweet brown teddy bear. "It's for Alex. I thought he might like a cuddly toy. Maybe it will even become his favorite, like Emma's Mr. Rabbit."

"Mr. Rabbit has been demoted," Quinn announced. "She has a new favorite toy now. But thank you. It's adorable."

Jude shrugged off his coat, as if he meant to stay for a while. "Look, Quinn, I'm really sorry about what happened at Emma's party. I never meant to hurt her. You must know that."

"You might not have meant to, but it would have happened just the same had Emma ingested the heroin you so carelessly dropped."

"I know, and I have to live with that knowledge every single day. It's realizing what might have happened that finally got me into rehab."

"And are you clean?"

Jude nodded. He actually looked healthier, if somewhat heavier. Without heroin, his metabolism was likely working at a slower rate, or maybe he had a better appetite now that he wasn't strung out.

"So, what are you plans?" Quinn asked as she walked into the bedroom, where Alex was still lying on the bed. Jude followed.

"Oh, he's sweet," Jude said as he leaned forward to take a better look. "May I hold him?"

Everything inside Quinn wanted to refuse, but it seemed churlish, so she nodded. "All right, but only for a minute. We're going out for a walk."

"It's not too bad outside," Jude replied as he lifted the baby into his arms and smiled down at him. "He looks—"

"Like Gabe. Yes, I know," Quinn snapped.

"Okay, sorry. Right. You asked me about my plans. I've actually broken things off with Bridget and moved back in with Mum."

"I thought things were going well between you and Bridget."

"I can't remain clean if I stay with her. She's an enabler."

"I see."

"I've quit my band too."

"So what will you do?" Quinn asked. Jude was obviously serious about his recovery, but he seemed to be purging all the things that normally made him happy.

"Logan got me a job at the hospital, as a porter."

"And what about your music? Will you give that up as well?" Quinn asked. She'd seen several of Jude's YouTube videos and he was truly talented.

"I want to focus on writing original music. I don't know how well I can do that without the aid of heroin, but I mean to try."

"Did it help you to compose?" Quinn asked.

"Quinn, have you ever been high?" Jude asked as he lowered the baby back to the bed.

"No. I smoked marijuana once, but I didn't care for it much. It only made me hungry."

"Life can be so colorless, so gray," Jude replied. His eyes filled with anguish as he tried to explain to her what he was feeling. "When you're high, everything is bright, bold, and pulsating with life. The simplest things become beautiful and unique. Some of the greatest songs in the history of music were written while under the influence. The drugs blow open that door in your mind that leads to a hidden chamber where all your creativity, passion, and individuality are stored. Once you've hit those highs, the lows become so much lower, and reality so much bleaker. I really want to stay clean, Quinn, but the pull is so strong. Even sex is boring when you're not high."

Quinn glanced over at Jude, whose scarf had shifted while he was holding the baby. He had those bruises on his neck again, just like the ones she'd seen before and assumed were caused by his studded leather collar.

"Jude, are those bruises from a belt?"

Jude paled but didn't look away. "Yes."

"You know that what you're doing is dangerous, right?" Quinn demanded. Erotic asphyxiation was not something to trifle with. She could think of at least three famous people off the top of her head who'd died because the game had gone too far.

"Do you believe some people are self-destructive by nature?" Jude asked.

"Are you saying you're one of those people?"

Jude nodded. "I suppose I am, or maybe I'm just an adrenaline junkie. Logan told me about Quentin, but the way," he said, deftly changing the subject. "Any news?"

"Are you interested in meeting her?"

"Of course I am. Just look at what fun it's been meeting you."

Quinn wasn't sure if he was mocking her but let the comment pass. "Nothing new. Drew Camden is trying to find out what happened to her once she arrived in London."

"What if he doesn't find her?"

"I refuse to even entertain that possibility. She's out there somewhere, and with today's technology it's hard to imagine that someone can elude you for long."

"Well, I hope he tracks her down for your sake. Anyway, gotta dash. I have a shift in a half hour. Thanks for talking to me. And give my love to Emma. But not to Gabe," he added.

"I will. Thanks for coming by. And thanks for the bear. I'm sure Alex will love him."

"I had one just like that when I was little."

"Where is it now?"

"Mum threw it away," Jude said sadly.

"Why?"

"Because I made a hole in it and stashed my heroin inside him."

Since there was no appropriate reply to that statement, Quinn simply wished Jude a good day and shut the door behind him. She was glad he wanted to stay in contact with her, but a relationship with Jude wouldn't be easy. As Quinn got Alex ready for their walk, she wondered if all families went through so much turmoil. Was it always this hard?

TWENTY-EIGHT

AUGUST 1918

London, England

As the summer of 1918 drew to a close, the tightly coiled self-control Valentina had imposed on herself since the deaths of her father and Alexei began to loosen. Cousin Dmitri was as good as his word and made sure they didn't need to worry about a thing. They enjoyed outings to the numerous parks London had to offer, attended several plays, and forged new friendships with some of the other Russian exiles. They no longer felt like outcasts, but they were still a long way from considering England their home.

Elena's health, mental and physical, slowly improved, but she took several drops of laudanum every night before going to bed to help her sleep through the nightmares that still haunted her. Dmitri was her dearest companion, and they spent hours sitting in the garden, or in the parlor on inclement days, reminiscing about people and events Elena's children knew nothing about. Valentina often thought of home, but Tanya and Kolya didn't like to speak of Petrograd. They grew restless and irritable whenever the "good old days" came up and made an excuse to leave the room. Valentina supposed it was their way of coping with the loss and fear they'd suffered.

With the help of Clive Brenner, the English tutor, their command of the language improved daily, and the children now felt confident enough to speak in public. Elena, however, made excuse after excuse, avoiding the daily lessons like the proverbial plague.

"Mama, you need to learn," Valentina reprimanded her repeatedly. "You can barely string two words together."

"And why do I need to string words together?" Elena demanded. "I can speak to you and Cousin Dmitri, and the other Russian émigrés at church. What do I want with English people? They will never understand me, no matter how well I speak their language."

"But, Mama, surely you don't want to feel like an outcast for the rest of your life."

"I have no intention of being an outcast. I will return to Russia as soon as it's safe and things have settled down. The party of thugs that's holding Russia hostage will lose. They will be defeated by the White Army and executed, one and all. 'The Red Army' they call themselves." She scoffed. "Red is a good description, since the streets will run red with their Bolshevik blood. The Civil War will come to an end, and things will go back to the way they were. The royal family will return from Siberia, and we will all do our best to forget this horrid episode in our lives."

"Mama, things might never be the same again," Valentina reminded her gently.

"Of course I know they won't be the same, you silly girl. Your dear papa is gone, and Alexei, God rest his soul, will never be your husband now, but Russia will rise again. The monarchy will be restored, and we will be able to return and reclaim what's rightfully ours."

"Let her dream, Valya," Cousin Dmitri said as they strolled down a lane in St. James' Park. "She needs to believe in something, so let her. Reality will set in soon enough; it always does. She's doing so much better, your mama, and if clinging to the old ways allows her to believe that she has some semblance of control over her life then it can't be a bad thing. Only time will tell what will happen in Russia. Perhaps she's right and the Reds will be defeated."

Elena's dream came to an abrupt end one Sunday in August when Father Mikhail held a memorial service for the royal family. The details were still unknown, but news had leaked out of Russia that Emperor Nikolai II, his wife, Empress Alexandra, and their children had been executed at Yipatiev House, the manor in the Siberian city of Yekaterinburg where they'd been kept under house arrest.

"Animals! Cretins! Bloodthirsty beasts!" Elena screamed, as soon as they got home and she could vent her emotions. "How could they? How could they lay their filthy hands on those defenseless, God-fearing souls? They've martyred them, is what they did. Nikolai and Alexandra were scions of divinity, God's children on Earth. They might as well have slaughtered God himself," she raged.

"They have, actually," Valentina pointed out unhelpfully. "The Soviet government has outlawed religion. They believe faith to be the opium of the masses—that's a quote from Karl Marx—and they intend to abolish the Church and forge ahead with a secular society."

"Wha-a-at?" Elena sputtered. "Abolish the Church? Why, they are paving the road to hell, those scythe-wielding heathens. I hope they roast over the pyres of hell, tormented for eternity by never-ending agony the likes of which they could never have imagined in their inferior peasant brains."

Elena collapsed into a chair, sobbing as she buried her face in her hands. Tanya and Kolya remained quiet. They were all shocked to the core by the notion that someone could shoot help-less young women and an ailing boy in cold blood. Valentina remained by her mother's side, but Tanya and Kolya retreated to their rooms, eager to get away from the gloomy atmosphere of the parlor and find distraction in a book or a game.

"Are you as devastated as Mama is?" Valentina asked Cousin

Dmitri later, once Elena had retired to bed, having taken a double dose of laudanum.

"I think killing the royal family is an act of barbarism, to be sure, but I never really believed they would be allowed to live, not after the Bolsheviks executed Grand Duke Michael, the Emperor's brother. You see, Valya, as long as the royal family was alive, the Whites had something to fight for. With their deaths, the restoration of the monarchy is nothing more than a pipe dream."

"There are other Romanovs."

"Yes, and they are in exile, terrified and impoverished. Perhaps if the White Army wins the Civil War, the next in line might be invited to take the throne, but the way things stand now, I wouldn't get too hopeful."

"And what of you, Cousin Dmitri? Had you ever planned to go back?" Valentina asked. She still knew precious little about her mother's cousin. Dmitri enjoyed talking about his youth in Russia but changed the subject as soon as questions were raised about his marriage to Emily and his arrival in England. Now that Valentina knew a little more of British society, she found it odd that Emily had worked as a governess in Russia when her family clearly had money and could not only have easily supported their daughter but provided her with a handsome dowry. The house in Belgravia had been a part of her inheritance. Valentina might have imagined that Emily's father disinherited her for marrying Dmitri, but Emily had already been in Russia, earning a living, when she met their cousin.

"My life is here, Valya. As is my livelihood."

"What exactly do you do, Cousin Dmitri?" she asked. She'd asked her mother, but Elena had no idea where Dmitri's money came from. She found the subject of money vulgar and gladly accepted his financial support without asking impertinent questions.

Dmitri looked as if he were about to dismiss Valentina's question, but something changed his mind, and he replied. "I own several textile factories up north. Over the past few years I've been under contract with the British Army to supply them with wool for uniforms. It's been a very lucrative proposition, I must admit."

"So, you benefit from the war?" Valentina asked. It seemed wrong to grow rich off the deaths of millions, and Dmitri's comments about Stanislav Bistritzky now seemed even more unfair.

"Someone has to dress the army, Valya. They need uniforms, boots, belts, caps, and socks. I made a profit, yes, but I have also provided an invaluable service. I've kept our boys warm and dry."

"It still seems wrong somehow," Valentina replied.

"And that, my dear, is why women are not suited for business. They don't have the mental wherewithal to comprehend the intricacies of commerce."

"And do you think women should be able to vote?" Valentina asked. She was of two minds on the subject, but being a woman, she felt instantly defensive when someone belittled the suffragette movement. She'd read about it in the papers and greatly admired the women who not only quietly supported the idea but actually put themselves out there on the front lines of the conflict, and risked their reputations, personal safety, and even imprisonment to fight for the right to vote.

"God preserve us, Valya. Don't tell me you fancy yourself a suffragette." Cousin Dmitri laughed, as if she'd said something highly amusing. "Women voting. What a ridiculous notion. In order to vote, you must understand the issues and form an intelligent opinion on how they should be best addressed. Women are not capable of such advanced thought. My dear, don't let all this tomfoolery go to your head. Men and women have their roles to play, and your role is no less important. You are meant to be a wife and mother, a companion, a caretaker, and an object of admiration and desire. Why would you want to take on the burden that we men have to carry? You should be grateful we spare you the necessity to familiarize yourselves with the tedious issues involved in every election. Besides, you're not a British citizen, so the subject is moot."

"Are you a British citizen?"

"Yes. I renounced my Russian citizenship when I married my Emily, God rest her soul."

"You still miss her, don't you?"

"Every day. I always put flowers on her grave on her birthday. She loved birthdays."

"I used to love birthdays too," Valentina said with a sigh. "Well, I think I'll go to bed now. I want to put this awful day behind me."

"Good night."

Valentina retired to her room, but she wasn't ready to sleep. She was deeply disturbed by the events in Russia but was equally upset about Dmitri's comments. He thought it wrong for a man to make a living by reporting news because he was a Jew, but saw no issue with selling wool to the British army and making a hefty profit. He also thought her, and her sex in general, to be too feeble-minded to understand anything beyond current fashions and the managing of a household. Even a year ago, Valentina had aspired to nothing more than marriage and family, but having been practically on her own and having seen what it took to survive, she now had somewhat different ideas. She didn't want to be wholly dependent on a man, not even if he was her husband. She wanted to have an income of her own, one that would give her some freedom and a say in her future.

Tomorrow, she'd go speak to Stanislav Bistritzky, but tonight, she needed a distraction. She reached for her book. Clive Brenner had recommended *The Woman in White* by Wilkie Collins when she'd said she wanted to read something absorbing. Of course, the language was beyond her and she struggled to understand the story, but she gleaned enough to remain interested. She found a Russian-English dictionary in Cousin Dmitri's study and looked up every word she didn't know. She started a notebook in which she copied out the words and their meanings. The process of writing the words down helped her remember them for next time, and she discovered that after a few weeks her comprehension of the story seemed to improve. She was still only halfway through, but at least now she began to understand the complexities of the plot.

After plowing through a chapter, Valentina was tired enough to attempt sleep. She closed her book, put away her notebook, and turned out the lamp. She closed her hand around the egg pendant of her necklace and whispered, "Good night, Alyosha," as she did every night.

TWENTY-NINE

Valentina took the omnibus to Fleet Street and then walked the rest of the way. McGovern's Print Shop was tucked away on a side street, its front window less than clean and the dark green sign faded and peeling. She hoped Stanislav wouldn't be angry with her for coming, but she had no other way to contact him and had no wish to speak to him in front of Cousin Dmitri on Sunday. Stanislav had told her where he worked during one of their conversations, and said that he and his brother took their dinner break at noon.

The bell above the door chimed, summoning a portly, balding gentleman who wore a pair of grimy specs and a leather apron. "How can I help, miss?"

"I'd like to see Mr. Bistritzky, please."

"Which one?"

"Stanislav."

"Stan!" the man hollered. "A charming young lady is here to see you." He winked at Valentina and left her to wait. She looked around, taking in various pamphlets, books, and leaflets.

Stanislav appeared through a door at the back of the shop. His hands were stained with ink and he wore an apron to protect his clothes.

"Miss Kalinina, what a surprise. Were you in the neighborhood?"

"No, I came to see you. I hope that's all right."

"Of course. I have my break coming up in a few minutes. Would you care to join me for a cup of tea? There's a little place Max and I go to just around the corner. The proprietor allows us to eat our sandwiches as long as we order a pot of tea."

"Yes, tea would be great."

Stanislav retreated back behind the door and reappeared a few minutes later, sans apron and with semi-clean hands. "Max will have his dinner here today. He has something he wishes to finish."

Valentina walked with Stanislav to the tea shop, acutely conscious of the awkward silence between them. She'd never called on a man before, and he'd probably never had anyone seek him out at work. He held the door for her and they entered the tiny shop. Stanislav nodded to the man who came to greet them and asked for a table for two and a pot of tea.

"Would you like some scones?" he asked.

"Why not? But please allow me to treat you. I'm the one who came to see you, and I'd like to recompense you for your time."

"There's really no need, Miss Kalinina. Seeing you is a pleasure, and I would have come here anyway."

"All right," Valentina conceded.

They settled at a table by the window and Stanislav shyly took out his lunch. "Would you like half?"

"No, thank you. Enjoy your lunch. What is that?" She couldn't quite make out what was spread between the bread of the sandwich.

"It's shkvarki," Stanislav replied, coloring slightly. "It's basically just onions fried in chicken fat and allowed to congeal," he explained when Valentina looked blank. "It's poor-people food," he added bitterly.

"I didn't mean to imply…"

"I know you didn't. My mother is very frugal. Max and I give her a portion of our salaries so she can buy food, but she scrimps and only makes a decent meal on the Sabbath. Then, we have brisket or roasted chicken. We look forward to it all week."

Valentina poured tea for both of them and helped herself to a scone and some clotted cream. She wasn't a huge fan of the stuff, but the tearoom didn't offer any jam or even butter. "The reason I came to see you today is that I want to make you a proposition."

"Oh?"

"These past few months I've lived off my cousin's bounty. He's been very good to us, but I would like to earn money of my own—without his knowledge."

"And how can I help?" Stanislav asked.

"I noticed that only men purchase your newspaper."

"I expect they convey the news to their womenfolk," Stanislav said as he reached for a scone, having finished his sad excuse for a sandwich.

"Well, what if there was a newspaper for women?"

"For women?"

"Yes. Like *Ladies' Journal* or some such."

"And who would print this paper?"

"You would. And I would contribute articles and back matter."

"What back matter?" Stanislav had stopped chewing and was watching her intently.

"I would think that some of these Russian families are always on the lookout for Russian-speaking maids, nannies, cooks, and even tutors. And it's usually the women who see to hiring staff. Perhaps the back page could be used for advertisements, for which we could charge a fee. There could also be write-ups of current fashion trends, maybe some society gossip. These women might not speak English, but they are very well aware of who is who, all the same."

"What type of articles would you write?"

"Well, for one, I would like to keep a running commentary on the suffragette movement. I know that many of the older ladies are staunchly opposed to women voting, but the younger ones are intrigued and would like to know more. I thought I might also do a monthly feature on some extraordinary woman, like Florence Nightingale. I read an article about her recently and thought that writing about her might inspire some young women to go into nursing."

"You've really thought this through, haven't you?"

"I've been thinking for a long while that I need to find a way to earn some money, and once I saw what you were doing, I thought it was rather brilliant. I have a little bit put away, so I could reimburse you for your expenses. We could put out several issues and see how it goes. Perhaps a pamphlet at first, and after a time, an actual newspaper. What do you think?"

"I think it's a very interesting idea. Let me consult Max. I can't agree to anything without his approval. We're in this together. We have plans of starting our own publishing house one day, so we can't afford to take any unnecessary risks."

"I completely understand. Do let me know your thoughts, but be discreet. I wouldn't want Dmitri Pavlovich to know what I'm up to."

"Would your articles be anonymous?"

"No, I'd take a pen name."

"Have you already thought of one?" Stanislav grinned at her. He understood her better than she'd expected.

"Yes. Vera Vechnaya."

"Oh, clever play on words. Eternal Faith. I like it. Very optimistic sounding."

"Truthfully, I couldn't think of anything else. I thought the religious overtone of the name might appeal to the matrons, while the notion of eternal optimism might strike a note with the younger generation."

"I think it's brilliant, Miss Kalinina."

"Please call me Valentina."

"Only if you call me Stan."

"Deal." They laughed as they shook hands. "If we're to be partners, we can dispense with the formalities."

"I can't promise you a partnership, but I will certainly try to convince Max. I think it's a good idea. Innovative."

"I've never thought of myself as innovative."

"No one does until suddenly they're not happy with the status quo and want to do something to change it. You're a woman of the twentieth century, and I have a feeling that you're all on the verge of something truly amazing."

"I hope you're right."

"Women are fighting for their rights for the first time in history. That's truly amazing already. If they don't give up, which I don't think they will, real, legal changes will come to pass, changes that will affect future generations. Women will become a power to be reckoned with."

"Would you want to marry a woman who challenges your ideas and wishes?" Valentina asked, impressed by Stanislav's take on the women's movement.

"My mama wouldn't be too pleased, but I want a partner when I marry, not a servant who has no opinions of her own. To be honest, I'm tired of my mother's matchmaking attempts. Some of these girls have been in England for years, but in their minds, they still live in some nameless shtetl."

"What's a shtetl? I've never heard that word."

"A shtetl is a small Jewish settlement."

"Did you grow up in a shtetl?"

"No, I grew up in Petrograd, like you. Only our paths would never have crossed, even if we had both remained."

"No, I don't suppose they would. Well, I'm glad our paths crossed now. This is a new world, and a new life, and I, for one, am planning to embrace it."

"I must get back to work, Valentina. I'm so glad you came to see me. Feel free to visit me again, even if you don't have any innovative business propositions. Just being seen with a pretty girl is doing wonders for my reputation." Stanislav held the door for her and they stepped out into the street.

Valentina smiled. She hadn't realized until that moment that Stan was actually quite attractive. Being seen with him might harm her reputation, but she didn't care. She was done doing things the old-fashioned way. She was a woman of the twentieth century.

THIRTY

Valentina waited anxiously for Sunday, eager to hear what Stan had to say about her proposal. He seemed interested, but she'd never met Max and had no idea what he might be like. Max might think wasting resources to attract female customers to be a pointless idea, one destined to lose money and waste time. At least the day was sunny and bright, so Cousin Dmitri wouldn't rush them to the car after the service. On fine days, he liked to linger outside the church, talking to other parishioners and making social plans that always included Elena. He seemed determined to help her assimilate and adjust to her new life. Valentina found his efforts endearing. He seemed to genuinely care, and Elena was slowly letting go of her grief.

The service was exactly the same length as every other church service they'd attended, but this one seemed to go on forever. Valentina turned toward the door as soon as the priest wished the congregation a good day, eager to be the first one outside. Stan was rearranging books on his table when she approached him.

"Good morning, Valentina." He kept his voice low for fear that someone might hear him using her Christian name and misinterpret his intentions. One complaint against him and many would stop purchasing his paper.

"Good morning, Mr. Bistritzky," Valentina replied as worshippers began to exit the church. "Fine day."

"It certainly is."

Valentina stepped to the far side of the table and pretended to leaf through a book while numerous men helped themselves to a paper and dropped money in the tin. "Have you spoken to Max?"

"I have. He thinks it's a risky idea, given that most women tend to echo the views of their husbands and fathers, but he thinks it's worth a try. We'll start with a leaflet and give out the first issue to the ladies for free. If they're interested enough to start paying, you'll get a fifty percent cut of the profits after we subtract the cost of paper and ink. Deal?"

"That sounds very generous."

Stan smiled. "Don't get too excited. Fifty percent of practically nothing is practically nothing."

"When do you want me to begin writing?"

Stan reached into his pocket and extracted a small card with a handwritten address. "Write an article about whatever you think would entice the ladies and post it to this address no later than Wednesday. I wouldn't start with votes for women. Too inflammatory. Something that might appeal to women who have been displaced and are forced to live in reduced circumstances. My sister, Sarah, is going to write a fashion column. She works as a seamstress for the House of Forsythe, and she's mad for fashions, even though our father doesn't permit her to wear anything even remotely stylish."

"I've heard of the House of Forsythe. Their label is very prestigious."

"Sarah's only allowed in the workshop and does grunt work, but she does see the designs and has strong opinions on what works and what doesn't. She heard us talking and wouldn't desist until we promised her a column. Father will have an apoplexy if he discovers that his daughter is writing for the public."

"Why?"

"Because he wants her to give up her job and marry a man of his choice. Sarah is holding out."

"My father wanted me to marry the man of his choice," Valentina said wistfully. "I loved him with all my heart."

"Well, this situation is a little different. My father has his sights set on a recently widowed brewer who has three children under the age of six. Not a future Sarah sees for herself. She's a headstrong girl, and Max and I support her all the way. No one should have to waste their life on someone they don't care for."

Valentina reached into her reticule and pulled out a coin, which she handed to Stan as one of the other ladies approached the table. "Thank you, Mr. Bistritzky."

"I hope you enjoy the book, Miss Kalinina."

Valentina stowed the card in her reticule and walked away from the table, her mind already on the article she would write. Perhaps she was just desperately searching for something to give her purpose and occupy her mind, but she was excited at the prospect of writing her first piece. She glanced back and was surprised to see Stan looking after her, an unreadable expression on his pale face.

THIRTY-ONE
DECEMBER 2014

London, England

Quinn had just taken a roast chicken out of the oven when she heard Gabe's key in the lock. He was late, which was unusual.

Emma exploded into the kitchen, looking disgruntled. "Dad was late picking me up," she complained. "I'm hungry. What's for dinner?"

"Roasted chicken, potatoes, and peas."

Emma made a face but didn't complain. She was about to pluck a roasted potato from a bowl when Quinn smacked her hand lightly. "Wash your hands first. And where's Dad?"

"Right here," Gabe said as he walked into the kitchen, as if on cue, and plopped into a chair. He looked tired and annoyed, and yanked irritably at his tie until he pulled it off and tossed it on the table.

"Bad day?"

"You could say that. I couldn't leave until the police showed up," he said by way of explaining his lateness.

"Why were the police called?"

Gabe shook his head in dismay. "Two more complaints were

filed against Luke. He called Monty a 'poof' and made a lewd comment to a student."

"What did he say?"

"Something about giving her a private tutorial on the nature of Roman orgies."

"Good God."

Gabe reached for the bowl and popped a potato into his mouth. "I'm starving."

"I'm starving more," Emma stated as she returned to the kitchen. "I don't want any peas."

"Well, you're getting some anyway," Quinn replied. "They're good for you."

"Fine," Emma said again, oozing attitude. She sat down next to Gabe and looked at him expectantly. "So why did the police come?"

"Yes, I was wondering the same thing myself," Quinn said, pinning Gabe with an inquisitive stare.

"I had no choice but to terminate his employment. Four complaints in two weeks are more than the board is willing to tolerate, especially since he never really denied the offenses. Luke grew belligerent and refused to leave. Jane called the police when she heard him threatening me."

"He threatened you?" Quinn gasped. In all her years with Luke, she'd never known him to be violent or crass. This was completely out of character, but then again, it seemed she didn't know him as well as she'd thought.

"He said some things. Now's not the time to repeat them," Gabe said, his gaze sliding toward Emma.

"You can say it in front of me. I know lots of bad words," Emma said, smiling proudly.

"Do you now?" Gabe asked, gazing down at her with interest. "And has this newfound knowledge anything to do with Aidan?"

"He says his mum swears all the time, mostly at his dad. She calls him a wank—"

"That's quite enough," Quinn said as she set a plate before Emma. "Eat your dinner."

Emma gave Quinn a sullen look but didn't comment. Instead, she turned toward Gabe. "Did they put him in handcuffs, Daddy?"

"No, they gave him a warning and escorted him off the premises. I hope he's not foolish enough to return. As is, he's just about committed career suicide."

"What's a suicide?" Emma asked, her mouth full of potato.

"It's when someone doesn't value something and allows themselves to lose it," Quinn replied. She wasn't about to explain taking one's own life to a five-year-old.

"You mean like if I lost Mr. Rabbit?"

"Exactly," Gabe said and dug into his meal. They couldn't continue the conversation in front of Emma, so they spoke about the upcoming holiday and their trip north, skillfully redirecting Emma's attention to her upcoming reunion with Buster.

It was only after Emma had finished her meal and returned to her room to play with Emme that Quinn was able to return to her earlier train of thought.

"Did something happen to set Luke off? I've never known him to behave so erratically. And he's always been deadly serious about his career."

"He's angry, Quinn. His girlfriend dumped him for another man, his contract in the U.S. wasn't renewed, and he returned to London to find that no one had particularly missed him. And he's been rejected for several grants. He was hoping to go off on a dig for a few months in the spring and reestablish his status as a rockstar archeologist, but instead, he'll spend the next few months searching for a new job."

"I know he's disappointed, but a few setbacks don't normally prompt a grown man to act out in this way."

Gabe's gaze slid away from Quinn. "I could do with a beer."

"What are you not telling me?" Quinn demanded.

Gabe shrugged.

"Gabe?" She was about to press him further when realization dawned. "It has something to do with me, doesn't it?"

"Leave it."

"I can't. I need to know."

Gabe sighed and met her gaze. "He's frustrated and upset and he's lashing out. He thought he could sweet-talk you into taking him back, but once Alex was born, he realized he's lost you for good."

"How do you know this?"

"He told me. Or more accurately, he accused me of stealing you from him and taking advantage of your vulnerability to rush you into making a commitment and having a baby, all in an effort to bind you to me."

Quinn was about to dismiss this foolish assertion when she saw the doubt in Gabe's eyes. Luke had hit a nerve, exactly as he'd intended to. She came around the table, sat down in Gabe's lap and wrapped her arms around his neck. "Do you really doubt me?" she asked softly.

"No," Gabe whispered into her hair. "Never. But Luke is right. I did swoop in when you were vulnerable and I did rush you into an engagement, and then I was careless enough to get you pregnant. Perhaps my motives were selfish."

"Gabe, I know my own mind. Had I not been ready, I would have said no, to both marriage and baby. I am exactly where I want to be, so can we please put Luke out of our minds once and for all? I don't want to hear his name ever again."

"I'm sorry," Gabe said. "It's been a strange day."

"It's been a strange and wonderful year." Quinn brushed her lips against Gabe's, gratified at his body's instant response. "Should we leave the dishes for tomorrow?"

"Hmm, I think we might have to."

Quinn giggled as Gabe lifted her up and carried her to the bedroom, kicking the door shut behind him.

THIRTY-TWO

The dishes could wait, but Quinn had to feed Alex before he went to sleep or he'd wake up during the night. He was finally beginning to sleep through until morning, and she was grateful for the uninterrupted sleep. Quinn was too spent to get up after their impromptu lovemaking, so Gabe lifted a drowsy Alex out of his crib and brought him to bed. He settled himself next to Quinn, watching as Alex sucked hungrily, his eyes closed in concentration.

"Have you learned anything new about who the man in the tub might be?" Gabe asked.

"I'm beginning to think he might have nothing whatsoever to do with Valentina," Quinn said as she stroked Alex's downy head. "Everyone in Valentina's life seems to be fairly amiable and helpful."

"What about Stanislav? Do you think he might be our victim?"

"He's too young. And honestly, I don't think he'd hurt a fly."

"Maybe not physically, but he was an aspiring journalist. Perhaps he wrote something damaging and needed to be silenced."

Quinn shook her head. "No, I don't think it's him."

"So, what do you know for a fact?" Gabe asked, ever the academic. Since Gabe served as a freelance consultant on *Echoes from the Past*, it was nice to be able to share her findings with him and exchange ideas. Gabe always had his own unique perspective, which often helped Quinn spin a credible story around the few facts she managed to discover in relation to the subjects of the program.

"I know that a middle-aged man died in the house where Valentina and her family lived with Dmitri Ostrov. It had to have happened while they were still in residence, given the timeframe. I also know that even if he died of natural causes, which is unlikely, someone went to great lengths to erase his identity and hide his remains."

"Perhaps Valentina knew nothing of what happened," Gabe suggested. "The skeleton was found in what would have been Dmitri's bathroom. Stands to reason that he's the one who murdered someone and hid their remains."

Quinn shook her head. "That doesn't make sense. Why would Dmitri want to hide a dead body in his bathroom? Surely his housekeeper would discover what he'd done as soon as she went in there to clean."

"But the wardrobe had been moved to block the door, so she wouldn't have."

"And you think she wouldn't question the reason the bathroom had been suddenly blocked off?"

"She might have questioned it, but if she valued her job, she would accept whatever explanation she was given and get on with it."

"Yes, I suppose that's possible. I think I need to find an object that belonged to Dmitri. It's his memories that are the key to this puzzle."

"Was there anything at the house?" Gabe asked as he carefully took the sleeping baby and went to lay him in his cot.

"The room had been stripped bare, as had the bathroom. Perhaps there's something of Dmitri's in storage, or in the attic."

Gabe came back to bed and lay down on his side, propping his head on his hand so he could look down at Quinn. "I still think Valentina had to have known something. Melissa Glover said that Valentina lived in that house until her death, so she must have inherited it from Dmitri. It's hard to imagine that in all those years she never discovered the hidden bathroom. People move furniture all the time. She knew," Gabe reiterated.

"Perhaps."

"You said Dmitri was very protective and solicitous of Elena and they'd shared a close relationship when they were children. They were of approximately the same age, were they not?"

"Yes. They were both in their late thirties at the time they were reunited."

"Could it be possible that the reason Valentina got the house was because Dmitri married Elena?"

Quinn mulled this over. Dmitri did seem to fawn over Elena and was determined to help her overcome her grief and find some happiness in her new life. They were second cousins, but it wasn't unheard of for cousins to marry, especially if procreation wasn't the goal. At her age, Elena would have been considered well past child-bearing age, so Dmitri and Elena's familial relationship wouldn't matter much if it evolved into something more. Perhaps it was time to start searching for some facts now that she knew the names of the key players. She might find something to help her fill in the glaring blanks omitted Valentina's memories.

"I need to find records, but where do I start?" Quinn asked.

"I would start with the Russian Orthodox Church here in London. The church they went to might no longer exist, but the parish register, if there was one, would not have been destroyed. It would have been passed on to the diocese, if that's the right term. Also, the local registry office might be able to help."

"They don't keep records that far back."

"No, but they might tell you where the records have been archived."

"I'll start making enquiries tomorrow," Quinn said. The Orthodox Church celebrated Christmas on January 7, so the end of December wouldn't be their busiest time. Hopefully, whoever she spoke to would be willing to help. "I'll go check on Emma and help her get ready for bed," Quinn said as she made to rise

"I'll do it. You look like you're very comfortable exactly where you are," Gabe replied and kissed her lightly. "Good night, love."

"Good night," Quinn replied, grateful to have an early night.

THIRTY-THREE

Quinn took advantage of the next day being Saturday to leave Alex with Gabe and go off on her own. It was a filthy day, with cold rain coming down in sheets and clouds so thick as to seem impenetrable. She didn't mind a bit of rain, but the pervading gloom soured her mood. Visions of sandy beaches and azure waves danced in her mind. It'd been a long time since she'd had a holiday. Perhaps they could make plans to visit her parents in Marbella over Easter break. Alex was too young to enjoy the beach, but Emma would have a ball. Her idea of going to the beach consisted of skipping around on a rocky shore in her wellies beneath a leaden sky and scooping up buckets of icy water from the North Sea to build a sand castle. Splashing around in warm water and lying on soft white sand would be an eye-opener for her.

Getting off at Gunnersbury tube station, Quinn hurried toward the Cathedral of the Dormition on Harvard Road. The white building, adorned with an onion-shaped cupola in cerulean blue and decorated with gold stars, looked incongruous against the angry-looking clouds that virtually swallowed the Orthodox cross displayed at the top. The building itself wasn't very impressive from the outside, but the colorful frescos and magnificent icons that covered every surface took Quinn's breath away when she stepped inside. She stood still for a moment, taking in the splendid images. The light reflecting off the gold leaf background of the icons cast a golden glow, giving the impression of sunshine streaming through the windows. There were no pews, just an open space at the center where the worshippers gathered for services.

"Dobro pozhalovat," a young priest greeted Quinn. He appeared to be in his late twenties and wore a long black cassock and rubber-soled shoes that made no sound on the tiled floor. The somber black of the priest's attire was relieved only by a large gold cross that came down nearly to his waist. "Welcome," he amended when Quinn didn't immediately respond to the greeting. "I'm Father Grigori. Have you come to worship with us? We have a simultaneous translation of the service for our English-speaking brothers and sisters. It's tomorrow at ten, and you're most welcome."

"Thank you. Actually, I was hoping to ask you a few questions. My name is Dr. Quinn Allenby. I host an archeological program called *Echoes from the Past*, and I'm currently researching a case that involves a Russian family that lived in London approximately one hundred years ago."

"Ooh, how fascinating. Is it something like *Time Team*? I love that program," the priest said, his eyes sparkling with enthusiasm.

"Yes, it's similar, but each episode focuses on a particular person or family rather than an archeological site. I'm interested in any existing information, such as births, deaths, and marriages. The family I'm investigating worshipped at the Church of St. Sophia in Welbeck Street. I was wondering if there was any way to take a look at the parish registers from that period. Would you know where they might be kept?"

Father Grigori shook his head. "Sorry. Wish I could help, but I haven't a clue. Perhaps Father Evgeni might know." The young priest extracted an iPhone from the pocket of his cassock and made a call. "Evgeni, would you mind coming out here for a moment? There's a lady here who's after some genealogical information. She's something of a celebrity," he confided to the person on the other end and winked at Quinn. "He'll be right out. He is making tea. Would you care for a cup? I bet you've never had tea from a samovar. We keep a small one in the sacristy."

"No, I haven't, and yes, I'd love some."

Father Grigori fired off a text, stowed away his mobile, then clasped his hands behind his back. "I'd invite you to sit down, but here we worship standing up. Keeps people awake during the service," he quipped, smiling.

A few minutes later, an elderly priest emerged from the back. He had a long gray beard, thick bushy eyebrows, and blue eyes that glowed with warmth. His egg-shaped head was entirely bald, the scalp as pink as that of a newborn baby. He smiled warmly as he carefully handed Quinn a mug of steaming tea. She was pleased to see a thin slice of lemon floating at the top. Getting to try Russian-style tea was a bonus.

"I added sugar. I hope you don't mind. It's too bitter without it," the old man explained. "I'm Father Evgeni. I'm an archpriest here. How can I help?"

Quinn repeated her request, then took a sip of the sweet, tangy tea. It tasted like an entirely different beverage, which probably took some getting used to, but she'd persevere. She took another sip and waited for Father Evgeni to reply.

"The Church of St. Sophia was destroyed during the Blitz. Took a direct hit. I believe it's an office building now. As a matter of fact, my parents were one of the last couples to be married at the old church." Father Evgeni shook his head sadly. "All the records were lost in the blaze."

"Were there no duplicate registers?" Quinn asked, deeply disappointed. Normally, churches kept a second set of registers that were stored at a separate location, usually the offices of the diocese.

"I'm afraid not. At that time, there were few Russian immigrants in London. Too few to warrant having a local bishop. The two functioning churches were under the jurisdiction of the patriarchy in Moscow, but I can't imagine they sent copies of their registers to Moscow for safekeeping. The Orthodox Church was on the verge of extinction after the Russian Revolution, so outpost churches, like the ones here in London, weren't actively monitored."

"Do you think a couple who was married in the church would also marry at a registry office?" Quinn asked.

Father Evgeni shook his head. "I wouldn't think so. My parents didn't. Getting married in church was legal and binding. What's the name of the family you're trying to trace? Believe it or not, everyone knows everyone in the Russian community, so I might be able to provide you with some unofficial information."

"Kalinina and Ostrov."

Father Evgeni stared into space for a moment as he tried to place the name. "Yes, the names are familiar, but I'm afraid I don't recall anything specific. I can tell you with certainty that there are no living descendants currently worshiping with us, which is not to say that there aren't any. Many scions of the old families married British citizens and left the Church, finding it easier to settle in their new lives as followers of the Church of England."

"Valentina Kalinina became Tina Swift after her marriage," Quinn supplied.

"That certainly isn't a Russian name. She must have married outside the community and left the Church. I'm sorry I couldn't be of more help, Dr. Allenby."

"You've been very helpful, Father. Thank you. And thank you for the tea."

"You didn't like it," Father Evgeni observed, an amused smile tugging at his lips. "You prefer your tea with milk."

"Perhaps it would have tasted better with a pryanik," Quinn replied, making the old priest laugh.

"I wish I had some to offer you. They're a particular weakness of mine. I still remember the pryaniki my grandmother used to make. Delicious. A taste of childhood." Father Evgeni sighed dramatically as he accepted Quinn's cup. "I wish you luck in your search, Dr. Allenby. Perhaps you'll stumble across some unexpected source of information."

"Perhaps I will."

Quinn thanked Fathers Evgeni and Grigori, said her goodbyes, and took her leave. She hadn't had high hopes when she set out that morning, but was still disappointed to have encountered another dead end. The rain had let up somewhat, but it was still dreary and cold, so she hurried toward the tube station, eager to get home.

How did you get into that tub? Quinn mentally asked the skeleton as she stared at the dark tunnel outside the train car. *And what had you done to anger someone enough to erase your identity and deny you a proper burial?*

THIRTY-FOUR

OCTOBER 1918

London, England

A golden September gave way to a cool, rainy October. The house was quiet and melancholy. Elena saw no reason to get up early, Tanya liked spending her mornings with Mrs. Stern, learning how to cook, and Valentina usually curled up in a wing chair by the hearth with a book. Kolya had gone off to school at the end of August, a day that was exciting for him and emotional for the rest of them. Kolya was well and having a good time, if his letters were to be believed, but their family had grown smaller once again and it was unsettling to find themselves so reduced.

The only thing that brought Valentina any sort of personal satisfaction was writing the articles for the paper. It was still nothing more than a leaflet, but over the past few weeks, Stanislav had reported several repeat customers. They claimed to be interested in the *Lady's Paper*, as it came to be called, because they were in need of household help or a new tutor for their children, but Valentina heard two women whispering behind her in church, discussing one of the articles she'd written and complimenting the writer on her insight. She wanted nothing more than to write about current issues, but Stanislav had been shrewd in warning her to take things slow. Valentina's first column was about loss, and given that everyone in that church had lost someone either to the war or the Revolution, the article had been well received. The following week she wrote about the bewilderment of having to start over in a new country, especially with school-aged children who, like Kolya, had to adjust quicker than the rest of the family if they were to keep up with their studies. Written from a female perspective, the article spoke to many women in the congregation, and by the following week, sales had increased almost twofold. It would be some time before Valentina received any compensation for her efforts, but she suddenly had a voice, and that was compensation enough.

At the end of October, the Kalinins marked the one-year anniversary of Ivan's and Alexei's deaths with a small supper and hours spent reminiscing about the men they'd loved. It was just the three of them, since Cousin Dmitri had gone up north for a few days and returned grumpy and sick on the first of November. He sneezed incessantly and took to his bed for two days. On the third day, when Valentina brought him a cup of tea, he dabbed at his nose and gave her a watery smile. "Valya, I wonder if I might impose on you to do me a favor. An associate of mine, a Mr. Timothy Mayhew, will be in London today. I promised I'd spend an evening with him, but I'm really not fit for company. Would you mind terribly joining him for an evening at the theater? He'll take you out to supper afterward. He's a charming man."

Valentina inwardly cringed. She had no desire to spend an evening with a total stranger, and without a chaperone. She also worried about her English. It was good enough to communicate, but to carry on a conversation all evening was a daunting prospect. But Cousin Dmitri looked so forlorn, she could hardly refuse. "Of course. I'd be happy to."

"Oh, thank you. You're a lifesaver. Make sure to wear something pretty," he added as he slid back down onto the pillows. "And ask Mrs. Stern to make some chicken soup. With dumplings."

"I will. Feel better."

. . .

Mr. Mayhew proved to be a charming companion. He was in his late thirties, or possibly even forty, with wavy dark hair and light blue eyes that glowed with good humor. He wore a neatly trimmed moustache and a short beard that was oddly becoming. After a few uncomfortable minutes, Valentina forgot all about her accent and began to enjoy herself. First, they saw a performance in Covent Garden, and then Mr. Mayhew took her to an out-of-the-way little restaurant that was both intimate and charming. He told her about his life in Yorkshire and regaled her with amusing anecdotes about Dmitri.

"How did you two meet?" Valentina asked.

"Through a mutual friend, who is sadly no longer with us."

"I'm sorry to hear that."

Mr. Mayhew inclined his head. "We live in unpredictable times. Dmitri told me something of your plight. You were very brave, Miss Kalinina. Very brave indeed."

"There's no valor in running away."

"There you are wrong. It's very brave to know when it's time to cut your losses and retreat. Many lives would be saved if more people were wise enough to admit to a lost cause."

"I suppose."

"But we're getting too maudlin, aren't we? Let's talk about something amusing. What do you like to do when there isn't a war on? Do you enjoy dancing, opera, shopping?"

"I like to read."

"As do I. What are you reading at the moment?"

"*The Woman in White*. It's slow going."

"One of my favorites. Don't give up. The ending is well worth it. Are you finding it dull?"

"Not at all, but I'm struggling with the language."

"I think you're doing very well, and your accent is charming. I find it utterly enchanting."

Valentina blushed, and Mr. Mayhew instantly drew back in his seat and assumed the air of a man having tea with his mother. "I'm sorry. I didn't mean to make you uncomfortable. I only wished to reassure you that your efforts at studying English are paying off with dividends."

"Thank you."

Valentina glanced at the clock on the far wall. It was nearly midnight, and she was tired. She rarely stayed out this late. "Perhaps it's time we were going, Mr. Mayhew."

"Of course. Let me get the check."

Mr. Mayhew paid and they left the restaurant. "I'll get you a cab."

Valentina allowed herself to be handed into a cab. She was wary of getting into a motorcar with a complete stranger, but Mr. Mayhew thought it perfectly safe, so she stopped fretting and settled into the back seat. She was glad he wasn't coming with her. To sit so close to him in such an intimate setting wouldn't be proper.

"I didn't mean to keep you out so late. It's just that I was having such a nice time. Perhaps we can see each other again someday," Mr. Mayhew said before closing the door and allowing her to be on her way.

"I'll look forward to it," Valentina replied, glad he hadn't tried to make any definite plans.

Mr. Mayhew tapped his hand on the roof, alerting the cabbie that he could start driving.

Valentina subconsciously fondled her necklace. It had been a pleasant evening, and she felt awfully grown-up going to the theater and dining with a man who wasn't a relative. This had been a new experience, and she hadn't found it to be as intimidating as she'd imagined, but the thought of seeing Timothy Mayhew again held little appeal. Once was more than enough.

THIRTY-FIVE
NOVEMBER 1918

London, England

Valentina didn't give Timothy Mayhew another thought until Cousin Dmitri called her into his study a few weeks later. Her mother and Tanya had already retired and Dmitri was enjoying his nightly snifter of cognac. He sat behind his desk, looking stern as he glanced over a ledger.

"Close the door, Valya," Dmitri said as he shut the ledger and returned it to a drawer.

"Is something wrong?"

"Timothy Mayhew will be in London again this Friday and he'd like to see you," Dmitri said without preamble. His eyes bored into her in an odd way. Perhaps this wasn't his first snifter of the evening.

"Mr. Mayhew is a nice man, but I have no interest in marriage, Cousin Dmitri. Besides, surely he's too old for me."

Dmitri leaned back in his chair and stared at Valentina across the desk. Something was different about him, but she couldn't quite figure out what it was—and then it hit her. Dmitri usually smiled when he saw her, but tonight his gaze was grim, almost predatory. She'd never seen him look this way before. "Mr. Mayhew is not interested in marriage either. He'd like you to come to his hotel room."

"Pardon me?"

"Mr. Mayhew is married, Valentina, but his wife has had some lingering health issues since the birth of their twins ten years ago. She hasn't been a proper wife to him."

"What's that to do with me?" Valentina demanded. An angry heat bloomed in her cheeks. Was Dmitri really suggesting that she go to Mr. Mayhew's bed? He couldn't be. She must have misunderstood. Cousin Dmitri would never condone such a thing, least of all suggest it. This was some ruse, surely.

"Mr. Mayhew liked you and would like to further your acquaintance. He's ready for the next step."

"The next step?" Valentina echoed, outraged by the euphemism. "What are you saying?"

"I'm saying that on Friday I will deliver you to Mr. Mayhew's hotel where you will service his needs. Afterward, I will take you home and we will speak no more about it."

"Are you mad?" Valentina cried, now truly frightened. If this was a joke, it had gone too far.

"No, Valentina, I'm not mad. But it is time you began to repay some of your debt to me."

"What debt?" she sputtered.

"Do you have any idea how much I've spent on you all since March? Thousands. Dresses, shoes, hats, gloves, parasols, tutors, outings, and now Kolya's school, the expenses for which I will have to shoulder for the next ten years. The war is over, so the milk from that particular cash cow has already begun to dry up. There's money to be made off sex, and there are plenty of men who don't fancy going to a whore. They want a clean, well-bred young lady who will make them feel like they are courting rather than indulging in some tawdry tryst. That's where you come in. I have several associates who are interested in just that kind of an arrangement. A weekly meeting, pleasant and discreet. And they are willing to pay handsomely for it."

"And what makes you think I would agree to such a thing?" Valentina demanded through clenched teeth. Her anger bubbled up like lava, threatening to explode and singe everything in its path.

"You certainly don't have to agree to anything. I won't force you. But if you refuse, tomorrow, I will put your mother and sister out of my house. I will stop paying the school fees, and you will go right back to where you started, living in squalor and scrubbing floors to earn your keep. And you will have to explain to your family why I had to ask you to leave. They won't believe you, of course, and think that you've done something unspeakable to offend me. They'll blame you. Your mother will end her days in poverty, your sister will never have a chance at a good marriage, and your brother will be nothing more than a soldier or a common laborer without the benefit of a good education. The choice is yours, Valya."

"You're a monster," Valentina hissed.

"I'm a businessman. I need to see some return on my investment."

"And what other return might you expect?"

"It's your brother I want. I never had children of my own, and I would like Kolya to take over my business once I'm gone. He'll be my heir. Isn't that magnanimous of me? Just think, your brother, who will now never take his rightful place among Russian nobility, will be a wealthy, well-respected gentleman."

"At the expense of his sister's virtue."

"You just said you have no interest in marriage. So why save yourself? For whom? You might as well use what you've got. You might enjoy it, you know. I think you have the makings of a sensual woman, Valya. Once you've overcome your silly bourgeois objections, you will come to like the pleasures of the boudoir. Besides, it's not as if I were asking you to open your legs for some filthy, crass johns. The men I have in mind are attractive, clean, and well-bred. They don't get what they need from their wives and would like to recapture something of their youth when passion with a beautiful woman was something they could still look forward to."

"You're despicable."

"Perhaps. I will give you twenty-four hours to think it over. You can either agree to my terms or go out first thing tomorrow and start looking for lodgings you can afford. Oh, wait, you can't afford anything because you don't have a tuppence to your name. Good night, dear. Sweet dreams."

Valentina stumbled from Dmitri's study and rushed to her room, nearly colliding with a wall in her haste. Her heart was beating wildly and her extremities were ice-cold from shock. She locked her door and threw herself on the bed. She didn't cry. She simply hugged her pillow and drew up her knees, making herself as small as possible. How could this have happened? How could she have underestimated Dmitri so thoroughly? He'd waited until they'd settled into his home and become accustomed to a life of comfort, and then sprung his trap. How could she tell her mother, who was finally beginning to regain something of her former vitality, and her overly romantic sister that they'd have to scrounge for a living?

They still had Valentina's pearl choker, but Dmitri had offered to store the necklace in his safe, and she had handed it over without a second thought, trusting him implicitly. Even if he agreed to return it, the money wouldn't last long—maybe a few months, and then what? And it wasn't as if he even needed the money. Valentina had seen him open the safe. There were stacks of money in there. It was his security fund, Dmitri had joked, in case the banks floundered during the war. He was a wealthy man. How much money could he make by pimping her out? Surely not enough to make a difference. Was this some sick game, or were there others he was already exploiting? The thought had never occurred to her before this moment, but now she began to wonder. Could he be running some sort of discreet enterprise, using well-

"Can we go shopping after the film?"

"We certainly can."

"Then Daddy can mind Alex. They can have a boys' day in. Won't that be nice, Daddy?" Emma asked coyly.

"It'll be amazing. Alex and I will go to the pub for a pint and play a couple games of snooker."

"Daddy!"

"All right. We'll stay at home, enjoy some breast milk—that's Alex, not me—and then hopefully have a long nap."

"Alex will like that," Emma said, oozing approval. "And I think Mum needs a night out. You really should take her on a date," she added.

"And how did you come up with that wise notion?" Gabe asked.

"Aidan said his parents have date night once a month, and if they don't have a blazing row during dinner, they usually wind up sha—"

"Right. I get the picture."

"She's right, you know. I could use a night out," Quinn piped in. "We haven't had a date since August."

Gabe stared at her. "Really? Has it been that long?"

"It has. I demand to be taken out for a nice meal, and maybe even a film, but not one about penguins."

"I'll call Brenda and see if she'd be open to minding the children for a few hours."

"If Brenda can't, then I'll ask Jill. She's offered in the past."

"Why can't we stay with Grandma Sylvia? I want to see Jude," Emma said. "I miss him."

Gabe and Quinn exchanged glances. Sylvia would have enjoyed spending a few hours with the children, but given recent events, it was safer not to try that experiment again. "Maybe next time. Grandma Sylvia has a touch of a cold," Quinn said.

"Are you lying to me again?" Emma demanded. "I can always tell, you know."

"Can you?"

"You always pause and take a breath before you tell me something that's not quite true," she said, pinning Quinn with her dark blue gaze.

"Do I?"

"Yes, you do. I'm going to go to my room now and let you discuss this amongst yourselves."

"Do I do that?" Quinn asked Gabe as soon as Emma departed in a huff.

"You sure do."

"My God, Gabe, she's only five. How can she be so perceptive?"

"She can't help it; it's in her genes."

"Should we tell her the truth about Sylvia and Jude then?"

"No. She's too young to understand the complexities of some relationships, and even though she's astute enough to realize that something is being withheld from her, we, as her parents, will be the ones to decide when and what to tell her, at least for now."

"How did you get so smart? Have you been talking to Aidan?" Quinn joked.

"No, but I think I will. Maybe I can book weekly sessions."

They burst out laughing and promptly woke up the baby, who'd dozed off.

THIRTY-SEVEN

Once Emma left the room, Quinn was able to finish telling Gabe about her vision, but saying the words out loud didn't make what she'd seen any less shocking. "The man was despicable. I would have never foreseen this turn of events."

"Yes, what he did was diabolical," Gabe agreed. "He came to their aid, gave them time to grow comfortable and secure in their new life, and then sprang the trap. Did Valentina agree to his terms?"

"I don't know yet. I can't bear to find out. Everything inside me is screaming for her to get away from this man, but I suspect she gave in for the sake of her family. Her mother was emotionally fragile and unsuited to any type of work, and her little brother would have no future without a proper education. Tanya was only fifteen at the time, but given the societal norms of the day, her only future security lay in marriage, the prospect of which would also be snatched away should they be reduced to a life of penury. Valentina wouldn't be the first woman to trade her dignity for security for her family."

"No, she wouldn't be, but she would despise the man who orchestrated her downfall."

"I wouldn't call it her downfall," Quinn protested. "We know that Valentina married twice, had two children, and was financially sound for most of her life. Something must have happened to turn things around for her. Rhys would like to arrange an interview with her daughter, Natalia, but I think I'll hold off a bit longer before speaking to her. I'd like to find out what happened first."

"Rhys will wait until you're ready. He has great respect for your process and is completely in awe of your ability."

Quinn chuckled. "My ability can be compared to a besieged castle. Everyone on the outside wants to get in and everyone on the inside wants to get out. Rhys would give up a vital organ to be able to see what I see, but I would gladly give up this curse once and for all."

"Would you really?" Gabe asked, smiling at her in that way that suggested he knew better. "All you have to do is wear latex gloves when handling objects, and you'll never see anything. Yet you choose to get involved with the victims. You feel compelled to tell their stories."

"Very few people throughout history were important enough to remember. Most were born, lived—some longer than others—and died. But when you delve into the past, you see that their lives were not nearly as ordinary or uneventful as historians would have us believe. The common view is that most women's lives could be summed up by three events. They were christened, married, and buried, leaving virtually no mark. For every Elizabeth Tudor, Mary Stewart and Margaret of Anjou, there are millions of women who've been completely forgotten. I feel obligated to give them back their voice and to applaud their bravery in fighting for a better life and the right to be happy in times when men held all the cards and a woman could do nothing more than cope with whatever was done to her."

"So you wouldn't give it up?" Gabe asked, still grinning as if he'd just proved his point without saying a word.

"I don't think I can."

"Then tell their stories and allow Rhys to be your tool. He

might not be able to see what you see, but he gives you free rein. This is your show, Quinn. This is your platform."

"You're right, as usual. God, that's annoying." Quinn laughed. She felt lighter after talking to Gabe, and ready to face whatever had happened to Valentina. The women she saw were long gone, so the events could no longer hurt them, but it was important to vindicate them in the eyes of history, and she was the only one who could do that.

THIRTY-EIGHT

NOVEMBER 1918

London, England

The day had been dreary and wet, the type of day when all one wanted to do was stay at home, close to the fire, and read or talk quietly before retiring for the night. And that was exactly what they had done. Valentina read, while Dmitri and Elena played several hands of whist. Dmitri had taught Elena how to play, and she'd fallen in love with the game, always ready for a rematch. Tanya sat quietly, just staring into space, a small smile playing about her lips. She was a dreamer, preferring to indulge in her own fantasy rather than the product of someone else's imagination, like Valentina.

"Are you still reading that book?" Tanya finally asked.

"It's very long, and very difficult for me to understand," Valentina complained. "There are so many words I still don't know. I can only get through a few pages a day since I'm reading so slowly. I try not to move on until I fully understand what's happening."

"Must be some story," Tanya said as she yawned. "Well, I'm off to bed. This weather is perfect for sleeping."

"Good night," Valentina replied wistfully. She wished she

could go to bed and forget the despair that had been gnawing at her for the past few days. Dmitri looked relaxed and happy, his demeanor betraying nothing of what went on beneath the surface. Valentina had taken his good nature at face value, assuming he was sincere in his regard for her family, but now she knew better. Dmitri had known all along that Valentina would agree, and had bet on it, in fact. And now that the day was upon them, he was solicitous and kind, treating her as if she were precious to him. She supposed she must be, if he was going to make as much money off her as he hoped.

Valentina lowered her head so her mother wouldn't see the panic in her eyes. She knew what would happen tonight, but it still seemed surreal. Would Dmitri really force her to go through with it? Would he allow her to change her mind if it came to that? Probably not. The arrangements had been made, and tonight money would change hands, money so filthy, she didn't know how it wouldn't soil Dmitri's hands when he touched it.

What kind of man forced a young woman to debase herself to prevent her family's ruin? There were many such men, she realized with bitter clarity, ranging from fathers who sold their daughters into advantageous marriages to pimps who preyed on defenseless women and took a large chunk of their earnings to "protect" them from violence, which they themselves would readily inflict should the women refuse to cooperate. She wouldn't be the first, nor would she be the last, to suffer at the hands of a ruthless and greedy man. She should have demanded a percentage of her earnings, but she knew what Dmitri would say. She had a debt to pay, a debt that accrued with every passing day. Only yesterday Dmitri had taken Elena to collect her new winter coat from the fashion salon. It was made of fine blue-gray wool and adorned with the sumptuous fur of black fox at the collar and cuffs. It hadn't been cheap, but Dmitri had encouraged her to order whatever she liked, reassuring her that nothing would give him greater pleasure than to make her happy.

"Do you need a new coat, Valya?" Dmitri had asked back in

September, his eyes brimming with concern for her well-being. "It promises to be a cold winter."

"My coat should last for another year or two," she had replied. She'd never ask Dmitri for anything ever again. She couldn't bear to.

Valentina's innards tightened into intricate knots as the evening wore on. A part of her wanted to stall forever, but another part wanted to get the deed over with. All she wanted was to lock her door, climb into her bed, and lose herself in deep sleep. She'd borrowed a few drops of laudanum from her mother and mixed them into a glass of water she'd left by her bed. She planned to drink it when she got home and slip away into opium-induced oblivion. She knew she wouldn't be able to get to sleep on her own and would lie awake for hours, reliving the awful minutes spent in Timothy Mayhew's company. She hoped it would be minutes and not hours. She simply couldn't bear the thought of having to keep up the façade for longer than was strictly necessary.

At last, Elena wished them a good night and went to bed. Dmitri turned to Valentina, the smile slipping and his eyes boring into her in a way that warned her not to try any delaying tactics. "Are you ready to go?"

She nodded, too terrified to speak. Her mouth had gone dry and her heart hammered in her chest, her panic forcing her to recall the night her father and Alexei had died. She hadn't thought she'd ever be so scared again, but here she was, in a warm, comfortable house in Belgravia, deceptively safe in a civilized, cosmopolitan city, about to become the victim of a man she'd trusted and even loved.

She donned her coat and hat and followed Dmitri into the rainy night, to the motorcar he'd left parked around the corner from the house so the noise of the engine wouldn't wake Elena. She would know nothing of her daughter's plight. Nor would Tanya. This sordid secret was between Dmitri and Valentina.

"Wipe that look of abject misery off your face," Dmitri said as he pulled away from the curb, his eyes on the foggy road. "No man can possibly enjoy making love to a woman who looks as if she's about to vomit."

"I'm frightened," Valentina admitted, immediately sorry that she'd shown him her weakness.

"There's nothing to fear. Timothy is a gentleman. He won't hurt you, nor will he treat you with disrespect. Could be a lot worse."

How would you know? Valentina thought angrily. She huddled deeper into the fur collar of her coat and stared straight ahead, bracing herself for what was to come.

The drive wasn't long. Valentina wasn't sure what she'd expected, but the building they pulled up in front of wasn't a posh hotel in the center of London, but a small, nondescript establishment. It was called the Falmouth Arms Hotel, and its name was probably the grandest thing about it. Valentina briefly wondered if Mr. Mayhew had paid the concierge to turn a blind eye to a young woman going up to a man's room, something a finer establishment wouldn't allow. The foyer was small and cozy, with a trio of sofas arranged around a low table stacked with newspapers and magazines. The reception desk was to the left of the door and manned by a middle-aged man who instantly perked up when they walked in.

"Good evening, Mr. Ostrov," the concierge said.

"Evening, Mr. Block."

Valentina glanced at Dmitri in surprise. How often did he come here?

"I own this hotel." Valentina detected a note of pride in his voice despite his stony expression.

"Are there others like me?" she asked as she followed Dmitri up the stairs.

He stopped and turned to look at her. "You're not as naïve as I first imagined."

"Is that a yes?"

"That doesn't concern you. Come."

Dmitri knocked on a door at the end of the passage, and a

familiar voice from within bid them to enter. Timothy Mayhew was sitting in a wing chair by the fire, reading. He was in his shirtsleeves but wore a tie and a pair of crisply pressed trousers. He set aside his book, sprang to his feet, and came forward to greet them, behaving as naturally as if they'd come for tea.

"Good evening, Valentina. It's a pleasure to see you again. Dmitri," he said, shaking her cousin's hand.

"I'll be downstairs in the parlor, Tim. Just send her down when you've finished. There's a good man."

Dmitri departed without further ado, leaving Valentina with Timothy Mayhew, who locked the door and invited her to sit down. "Would you care for a drink? There's sherry, and brandy if you require something stronger."

Valentina wanted to rage at him, to kick him in the shins or scratch his eyes out, but she mutely accepted a glass of sherry, her gaze pinned to the tips of her shoes. There was no point in making things more difficult. She'd only find herself back here another night, possibly with another man. At least Mr. Mayhew was courteous and respectful. She hoped he would continue to be. She took a sip of sherry and wondered what she was meant to do next.

"Valentina, I'll have you know I've never done this before. I am married and have four children. My youngest are ten-year-old twin girls. My wife never recovered properly after their birth, and we haven't lived as husband and wife since. I'm very lonely, you see. The lack of intimacy does something to a marriage. It chips away at the core day by day, leaving nothing but an empty shell behind after a decade of skirting around the issue and covering one's true feelings with pleasantries," he added, clearly hoping she'd pity him. But there was no pity in her heart, only resentment. It wasn't her fault his wife didn't share his bed, nor was it her responsibility to assuage his loneliness. She was heartbroken and lonely for Alexei, but she kept her grief to herself and didn't cause anyone pain to make herself feel better.

"Let's get this over with, shall we?" she said. "What would you have me do?"

"I'd like to watch you undress," he said softly. "I'll help you with any hooks or buttons, if you require."

"I can manage, Mr. Mayhew. Thank you."

"Won't you call me Tim?"

"No, I don't think I will."

She knew she was being unnecessarily rude, but she couldn't bring herself to call him by his Christian name. That would make the situation more intimate and she needed to keep a barrier between herself and the man who was about to violate her. She would not fight him, or accuse him of rape, but it was rape all the same in her estimation. He knew full well that she'd never have agreed to this meeting had she not been coerced, and he didn't care. Dmitri might have been the orchestrator, but Timothy Mayhew was a willing and eager participant.

Valentina undressed down to her corset and underwear. She was still wearing her stockings, but she didn't think that would matter.

"Let down your hair. It's so lovely. So golden," Mr. Mayhew said, his voice dreamy. He was still fully dressed, sitting by the fire, legs crossed. He didn't have the appearance of a man who hadn't done this before. He was relaxed and in control, enjoying every moment.

Valentina obediently took out the pins, allowing her hair to cascade over her shoulders. Mr. Mayhew smiled. "You are very beautiful."

She remained silent. What was there to say? Thank you? You're very kind? She hoped he wouldn't kiss her. She couldn't bear that. The only man who'd ever kissed her was Alexei, and she wanted to hold on to that memory and not have it besmirched by this pervert whose trousers were bulging obscenely as he gazed upon her.

He finally got to his feet and came toward her, but instead of facing her, he came up behind her. Valentina stiffened, not sure what to expect. Timothy Mayhew wrapped one arm around her waist and pulled her against him. He slid his other hand into her corset, cupping her breast and rubbing his thumb against her nipple. Valentina shuddered with revulsion, but her reaction seemed to please Mr. Mayhew. Perhaps he thought she was trembling with desire. He brushed his lips against the curve of her neck, then began to kiss her in earnest, forging a trail of feathery kisses down her neck and across her bare shoulder.

The arm that held her against his chest moved downward as Mr. Mayhew deftly pushed down her knickers and allowed them to fall to the floor around her ankles. Valentina's heart nearly leapt out of her chest, but she did nothing to stop him. His hand slid between her legs, stroking and probing in a way meant to arouse her while his engorged manhood ground against her buttocks. She wanted to scream, but the sound died in her throat. Instead, she allowed her mind to float free, imagining that the fingers belonged to Alexei and it was their wedding night. The fantasy made it easier to bear, and she relaxed slightly, leaning back against Mr. Mayhew in a way that seemed to please him immensely.

"There now. I knew you'd like it," he whispered. "Lie down on the bed."

She lay down and watched with surprising detachment as Mr. Mayhew quickly undressed and reached for a square packet that rested atop the bedside table. He ripped into it and extracted something that looked like a rubber circle.

"What's that?" she asked, alarmed.

"It's a French letter."

"A what?"

"A condom. A contraceptive. It's to protect you from pregnancy and disease. Dmitri's condition," Mr. Mayhew explained. "Now, please stop talking. There's a good girl."

She knew she should look away, but she couldn't. She watched as Mr. Mayhew rolled the sheer tube from the tip of his throbbing cock down to the base with practiced fingers. She was glad there were no sharp objects within her reach. She might have stabbed him had there been anything resembling a weapon. At that moment, she hated him with every fiber of her being, and wished she could slice off his manhood and feed it to the dogs. No amount of fantasy could turn him into Alexei, and no amount of detachment could keep the resentment at bay.

"Stop staring at me," Mr. Mayhew said as he got onto the bed and rolled on top of her.

Valentina closed her eyes. She wished he'd turned out the light, but the room was bright enough for Mr. Mayhew to watch her reaction as he guided himself inside and forced his way into her unwilling body. He was stretching her, violating her, and laying claim to something he had no right to. Her eyes flew open when she felt a sharp pain, but she gritted her teeth to keep from crying out. She wouldn't give him the satisfaction of making any sounds. He wanted her to, she could tell by the way he was watching her, his gaze hungry and triumphant at the same time.

"Relax, Valentina. I can give you pleasure," he said as he began to move inside her. Valentina lay perfectly still, her gaze fixed on a damp spot on the ceiling. Mr. Mayhew panted and grimaced as if he were in pain until he let out a final gasp and rested his forehead against hers, clearly satisfied. She felt him grow soft inside her, and she was grateful the ordeal was finally over. He rolled off her and slid off the French letter, tying it off and tossing it on the bedside table with a flick of the wrist.

"Thank you, my dear. That was lovely," Mr. Mayhew said as he turned his back to her and began to pull on his clothes. He turned and looked at her, having clearly expected some sort of response.

Lovely. Taking her virginity, ruining any possible future she might have, making her wish she were dead, had all been summarized in one word. *Lovely.*

"You'll learn to enjoy it," he promised. "It's always a bit uncomfortable the first time. I'm in London once a month on business, so that will be our standing arrangement."

"May I ask you a question, Mr. Mayhew?"

"Of course. What would you like to know?"

"How much did you pay for tonight?"

Timothy Mayhew cringed at the unexpected question, but he pulled himself up, puffed out his chest, and replied proudly, "Twenty-five quid."

Twenty-five quid was a lot of money. A great deal of money. It could feed a poor family for months, if not a whole year. Apparently, money was no object, or Timothy Mayhew would have shopped around for a better deal. He'd wanted her, and he'd had her.

"But that's only because you were, eh... intact. Next time will be much less, of course."

"Of course," she echoed. She was used goods now. Despoiled, deflowered, and destroyed.

"I do hope the weather improves," Timothy Mayhew said as he began to button his shirt. "I can't abide all this rain. Perhaps we'll have snow for Christmas this year."

Valentina sprang out of bed and began to dress, desperate to get away. She couldn't bear to look at Mr. Mayhew any longer, nor could she bring herself to talk about the weather as if nothing had happened. He prattled on, telling her that his children would enjoy a white Christmas, as if she could possibly be interested in anything he had to say. Valentina pushed her feet into her shoes, jammed her hat on her head, grabbed her coat, and fled down the stairs until she almost reached the bottom.

Then she stopped. She leaned against the wall and closed her eyes. She felt sick with shame and disgust. She'd enjoy it more next time, he'd said. How many times would there be? Every month for... years? How long would it take him to tire of her, and would there be others she'd have to service? Surely, Dmitri wouldn't be satisfied with just one client.

Dear God, she wished she were dead. How easy it would be to throw herself under a train, like Anna Karenina. She wasn't supposed to have read the book. Her mother had forbidden it. But she'd snuck it out of their library when she was sixteen and read it in one night, desperate to find out what all the fuss was about. After she finished the book, she'd spent weeks thinking about it, unable to comprehend the depth of Anna's despair. How could someone willingly end their life in such a violent, horrific manner, especially when they had a small child to think of? Suicide was a sin against God, but more than that, it took great courage to take such a drastic step. Valentina tried to imagine herself standing on a platform as a great locomotive, belching black smoke, roared into the station. To throw yourself beneath those massive wheels, knowing your body would be crushed and broken, and death might not be immediate, would take a lot more strength than she had.

No, she could never do it, not even if the manner of death were peaceful and painless. No matter how degraded and hopeless she felt, she couldn't bring herself to end it all. As long as she was alive, there was still hope for the future. No matter how wretched she felt, no matter how dead inside, she had to go on. She would find a way out of this predicament. She wouldn't allow it to break her.

Valentina took several calming breaths and descended the stairs. Dmitri was in the foyer, reading the paper as if he didn't have a care in the world. She supposed he didn't. He'd just earned enough money to pay Mrs. Stern and her daughter for a full year. This had been a very profitable evening for him, with more opportunities to turn a profit still to come.

"Ah, my dear. There you are," he said, folding the paper and setting is aside. "I trust all went well. How pretty you look. Flushed with pleasure."

Valentina had a momentary desire to grab the poker from the fireplace and skewer Dmitri right there in the foyer. How pretty he'd look with his guts hanging out as he breathed his last. "Shall we go?" she asked instead.

"Of course. You must be tired." He escorted her out to the car and held the door for her, ever the gentleman. "Not a word of this to anyone. Understand?" he said as he started the engine.

Who'd believe me? Valentina thought as she nodded obediently. And so, her career as a courtesan had begun.

THIRTY-NINE
JANUARY 1919

London, England

Timothy Mayhew had been the first, but he certainly wasn't the last. Over the holidays, two more clients had been added to the roster: John Gleason and Ian Murdoch. Valentina wasn't sure if these were their real names, nor did she care. She was determined to keep a distance between herself and these men who used her body. Mr. Gleason was in his thirties, a thin, balding man who wore wire-rimmed spectacles and looked like an undertaker. He seemed to be intimidated by her and asked her to get undressed and under the covers before he came to her. He always turned out the light and finished very quickly, thanking her profusely after each time and asking after her comfort. He left the room as soon as he put on his clothes, allowing Valentina a few moments to freshen up and compose herself.

Mr. Murdoch was a whole other matter. He was in his early forties—tall, broad, and very blond. His sparsely lashed light blue eyes missed little, and narrowed dangerously when he was displeased. He had the ruddy complexion of an outdoorsman and was fit and strong, where Mr. Mayhew and Mr. Gleason were as soft as white bread. He proudly informed her that he went to a boxing club every day, where he spent two hours pummeling younger men into submission. He had iron-hard muscles, a taut, flat stomach, and powerful thighs. Mr. Murdoch could have probably killed her with one hand if he chose to, and he had a fiery temper as well.

Their first meeting, just after Christmas, had been a rude awakening. Valentina hated Mr. Mayhew and Mr. Gleason, but they treated her with respect and never did anything to cause her discomfort. They were ordinary men who were happy to pay for an hour of intimate female company, secure in the knowledge that the outcome was assured. Ian Murdoch wanted much more. Not only did he expect her to participate, but he had no interest in straight sex. Valentina shook with fear every time she was meant to see him, which was unfortunately once a fortnight. She learned very quickly that denying him what he wanted would only make things more difficult for her and tried to refrain from provoking him.

The first time they met, Mr. Murdoch left her in no doubt that their meetings would not be quick and routine. He ordered her to undress fully and bend face down over the bed. He then explored her body in a way neither of the other two ever dared. The most they did was slide their hand between her legs before copulation or kiss her breast, but Ian Murdock probed and tasted her every orifice, making her inwardly cringe with embarrassment, especially when he paid undue attention to her anus after spending at least a quarter of an hour on his knees, his tongue exploring her more delicate parts intimately. But he seemed to enjoy it immensely. Unfortunately, he expected her to return the favor.

"Get on your knees," he ordered and forced his engorged shaft into her mouth the second time they met. "Suck."

He slapped her when she refused. Not hard, but enough to get his point across. He would have what he came for, and if she refused, he would make things very unpleasant for her. Valentina nearly gagged but eventually learned to perform the task to his satisfaction. She thought that'd be the worst of it, but that same night, he ordered her to bend over. She assumed he wished to fondle her again, but this time he slid his cock into her rectum, making her cry out in pain. He ignored her whimpering and continued, thrusting into her until she thought he'd never finish. He ordered her to turn around for round two, and lasted even longer, leaving her trembling and sore.

"You really are a delight," he said as he began to dress unhurriedly. "You will learn to enjoy the things I do to you."

"I doubt it," she replied.

Ian Murdoch smiled at her, a warm, radiant smile that transformed his face. "You'll see. Missionary sex is so boring. It's for people who have no imagination. Give it a few months, and you'll be aching to see me."

"If you say so."

He kissed the tip of her nose and smiled into her eyes. "I guarantee it. See you next time." He walked out, leaving Valentina blessedly alone. She curled into the fetal position and pressed her legs tightly together to stop the throbbing. Suddenly, Mr. Mayhew and Mr. Gleason didn't seem so bad.

To calm herself, she began mentally writing her next column for the ladies' paper. This time she would write about the suffragette movement and what winning the vote would mean for future generations. Never before had she realized how desperately women needed equal rights to men. Had she been a man, no one would dare use her this way. She'd have real career choices, more than the genteel occupations of governess or domestic servant that were open to her as a woman. And she'd earn enough money to support herself and her family, not the pittance that was paid to women who were desperate enough to need to work.

Her writing was the only bright spot in her life at the moment, and last week Stanislav had actually paid her seventy pence. It wasn't much, but it was a start. It was the first money she'd earned as a journalist. Perhaps, if demand for the paper increased, she'd begin to earn more, and maybe in time, try submitting her work to an English-speaking paper.

Valentina was about to get up when the door opened and Dmitri walked in. "What's wrong? Murdoch left some time ago."

"Get out. I'm not dressed."

"So get dressed. I'm not going anywhere."

There was no bathroom in the room, or even a screen behind which she could dress. She was forced to get out of bed and dress in front of Dmitri, who sat in the wing chair, his eyes glued to her naked form. "You really are lovely," he said, licking his lips.

Valentina stared at him in horror. He'd never touched her, but there was nothing to stop him from forcing her to service him as well.

"Don't worry, Valya. I won't push you that far," he said, responding to her obvious fear. "I'm more interested in your commercial value. Ian is very pleased with you. He might increase his visits to once a week. Won't that be nice?" Dmitri asked, his eyes crinkling at the corners. He knew what Murdoch liked, of that she was sure, and he was enjoying her misery. "Come now. I don't have all night. I'm tired."

Valentina finished dressing and followed Dmitri out the door. She froze when she saw a woman she knew from church emerge from one of the other rooms. The woman was married, with two small children. She lowered her eyes and tried to back into the room, but Dmitri hailed her.

"Good evening, Anna Mihailovna. Do give my regards to your husband."

The woman paled but only nodded in response.

"I lent her ne'er-do-well husband a large sum last year," Dmitri explained, his tone conversational. "He managed to repay half but couldn't come up with the rest. He was quite willing to whore his wife out in return for me forgetting the debt."

"How do you sleep at night?" Valentina asked through clenched teeth.

"Very well, thank you. Everything in life is a choice, Valya."

"Is it?" Valentina challenged him. "I don't think Anna Mihailovna would agree."

"Nothing in life is free. When someone does you a kindness, you must repay it. It's only fair. If you can't repay it in a way that was agreed upon, you must offer something else of equal value to offset the debt. Igor Lazarev could have found a way to raise the money, but he took the easy way out and used his wife as collateral. It was his choice, not mine."

"What you're making me do was never agreed upon," Valentina snapped.

"I'm not forcing you to do anything. I offered you a choice, and you chose the most practical solution because you know as well as anyone that self-respect doesn't pay the rent or put food on the table. You could have chosen to leave, found lodgings, jobs for yourself and Tanya, and made a life for yourself, but instead, you traded your so-called 'virtue' for a life of comfort. So, spare me your righteous indignation, Valya. It has no merit."

"And how long do you plan to hold me hostage to your demands?"

"That largely depends on how much your dear mama spends per annum and what it costs me to support your sister and pay for your brother's education. Kolya's got at least ten years of schooling ahead of him."

"I despise you," Valentina snarled as he handed her into the motorcar.

Dmitri smiled and shrugged. "I can't say that bothers me overmuch."

Valentina remained silent all the way home, her mind working furiously. She was looking at a minimum of ten years of sexual slavery. Ten years. She had to find a way to earn a living so she could start paying him back, but no matter how much she earned, she couldn't begin to hope to offset the amount of money Dmitri spent on her family. Elena had spent modestly at first, but her appetite for clothes and trinkets was growing, and Tanya still had years at home until she hopefully married.

Valentina swallowed back a wave of nausea. Now that she knew the real Dmitri and what he was capable of, the frightening reality of the next few years loomed before her like a death sentence. She was condemned, and there would be no last-minute pardon.

FORTY

Perhaps, in time, Valentina would have found a way to reconcile herself to the situation, as many women in her position have had to do in order to survive, but things rarely stay the same, and they almost never get easier. At the beginning of April, Mrs. Stern gave her notice. Her daughter was getting married and moving to Leeds, and Mrs. Stern was going with her. Rachel was the only family Mrs. Stern had, and she wasn't about to be parted from her girl. A new housekeeper and chambermaid would need to be found, and Dmitri overcame his dislike of Stanislav Bistritzky long enough to put an advertisement in the paper in the hope of finding suitable Russian candidates.

"Mrs. Stern has agreed to stay until Tanya's birthday," he announced over breakfast one day. "She will make a delicious supper and we will have a little party. After all, it's not every day a young lady turns sixteen. Tanya, you should invite those two girls you've grown friendly with and their families. It's been too long since this house has seen any kind of celebration. What say you, Tanya?"

Tanya's mouth opened in a charming "O" of delight. "Oh, yes. Thank you, Cousin Dmitri. That's very kind. I'd love to invite

Natalya and Larissa. They've both had me over for tea, but I have yet to return the favor. I'm sure they'll come."

"That's very generous of you, Dmitri," Elena said, smiling at him adoringly. "The girls' families are not titled, but in the circumstances we must take our friends where we can find them. Perhaps I'll invite their mamas to tea sometime in June to further our acquaintance."

"Absolutely, my dear. It's good for a woman to have female companionship. A good gossip over tea and cakes can do wonders for the spirit. You should try to make some friends, Valya. It would do you good. The only person you seem to talk to is that annoying Jew. I can't imagine what you two could possibly have in common." When Valentina ignored Dmitri's barbed comment, he turned back to Tanya. "And what would you like for your birthday, Tanya? Name it, and it's yours."

Oh, dear God, please don't ask for anything too expensive, Valentina thought desperately. She could already see Dmitri adding the sum to the ever-growing bill of expenses.

Tanya blushed prettily. "I would like to go to the seaside. I've never seen the sea, and it should be lovely the first week of May."

"Splendid idea! We will go to the seaside the day after your party. Bournemouth, perhaps. We'll drive there in the motorcar and enjoy the sights and sounds of the country. Won't that be grand?"

"I wish Kolya could come along," Tanya said. "He would so enjoy it."

"I'll tell you what. We'll take Kolya out of school for a few days. The headmaster is an acquaintance of mine, so he won't object. Kolya will just make up the work when he returns. The little chap deserves a treat. We all do."

Cousin Dmitri sounded so jovial, Valentina could hardly believe this was the man who'd forced her into prostitution and threatened her family. When she was around Dmitri at home, it was as if she'd imagined the whole thing, her mind conjuring up a sordid nightmare out of thin air. But then once Elena and Tanya retired to bed, the mask slipped, and the real Dmitri emerged: ruthless, greedy, and utterly devoid of compassion.

"Sixteen is a wonderful age," Dmitri said. "That's when young ladies truly begin to bloom into womanhood. The perfect age to start courting, don't you think, Elena?"

"I wouldn't say no if a suitable young man took an interest in our Tanya," Elena replied, giving Valentina a reproachful sidelong glance. They'd had several arguments about her lack of interest in finding a husband, and Valentina knew her mother wasn't about to give up. Marriage was the ultimate goal for any well-bred Russian female, and in Elena's estimation, becoming a spinster was a fate worse than death. Valentina could now argue that there were worse things but ignored her mother's loaded gaze and turned to Dmitri instead.

It was fleeting, but Valentina didn't miss the speculative gleam in his eyes. Did he hope Tanya would find a beau and marry? She wasn't exactly sure how things worked in England when it came to marriage. Only two couples married since they'd joined the church, and they didn't know the families well enough to ask such indelicate questions. Would Tanya need a dowry? Would Dmitri provide one? Would he pay for a wedding? Valentina could only assume that she would have to work off any expense incurred, so Dmitri could afford to be generous.

Elena and Tanya threw themselves into planning a menu for the birthday supper and discussing the arrangements for the trip to the sea immediately after breakfast. Dmitri promised to find a charming little hotel where they could spend a few nights, so they could fully enjoy their holiday.

"Dmitri, we wouldn't want to put you to such an expense," Elena protested. "A day at the seaside should be enough."

He took Elena by the shoulders and smiled into her eyes. "No expense is too great for my girls, Lenochka. We will go for three days at least, and we will have a marvelous time. Agreed?"

"Agreed," Elena said, her resistance having melted away under Dmitri's warm gaze.

The man really is a consummate actor, Valentina thought as she watched Dmitri's performance.

"Valya, stop looking so glum. We'll have a ball," Tanya said, smiling happily. "Help me write out the invitations. You have beautiful penmanship, much nicer than my chicken scratch. Is there anyone you'd like to invite? I'd be happy to include them."

"No, Tanya. This is your birthday. Don't worry about me." Valentina plastered a smile onto her face and followed Tanya to the desk where the stationery was kept. Perhaps helping Tanya with party planning would keep her mind off her upcoming assignation with Ian Murdoch.

"Tanya really is lovely," Dmitri said as they drove to the hotel that evening. "A real beauty. You must have been stunning at sixteen."

"I was pretty enough."

She wasn't pretty anymore. Not in her own eyes. She looked haunted and traumatized, but no one seemed to notice. People simply assumed she still mourned her fiancé. Elena had confided to the ladies at church that although the marriage had been arranged, the young people had been genuinely fond of each other and it would take some time for Valentina to get over her loss. Of course, this was cleverly designed to explain away Valya's reluctance to socialize with any of the young men who tried to approach her and to assure their eager mamas that their sons shouldn't stop trying, since it was only a matter of time until her daughter was ready to love again.

"I'm torn, you know," Dmitri continued. For some reason, he loved sharing his thoughts and plans with Valentina while they drove to and from the hotel. She couldn't decide whether he needed someone to talk to or just enjoyed toying with her. "A part of me wants to see Tanya well married, but a part of me is loath to pass up this once-in-a-lifetime opportunity. You girls cost a fortune, and now this little holiday will set me back a few quid."

"You are the one who offered to stay at a hotel," Valentina replied sharply.

"Well, what's the sense of driving all that way only to start back a few hours later? I'm only trying to be practical."

"Are you?"

"I'm nothing if not practical," Dmitri replied. "Which is why I can't help seeing the potential for profit in your sister."

"If you hurt Tanya, I'll kill you," Valentina snarled. "She's still a child."

"Oh, I beg to differ. She's a child no longer. I see how the young men look at her. She's a woman, Valya, and a beautiful one at that. Murdoch would pay a fortune to lay his hands on her. He likes them young."

"You heard me, Dmitri."

Dmitri patted her knee, making her want to slap his hand away. "You're adorable when you're angry. Don't worry, Tanya is safe."

Valentina let out the breath she'd been holding and slumped into the leather seat of the car. Tanya was safe—*but for how long?* she wondered, as she studied Dmitri's shadowed profile. For how long?

FORTY-ONE
DECEMBER 2014

London, England

Soft snow fell outside, the snowflakes twirling lazily against a pale winter sky. The London skyline was hazy, the pearly light of day slowly giving way to the dusky lavender of twilight.

Rhys leaned back in his chair and stared at Quinn, his eyes wide with disbelief. "He sold her virtue for twenty-five quid? Her own cousin? I'm not at all sure how our viewers will react to such a supposition, given that we have no physical proof it actually happened. It's a rather sordid tale."

"Do you really think Valentina was the first woman to be blackmailed into prostitution? And don't think twenty-five quid is a paltry sum. Today, that would be in the vicinity of one thousand pounds. He didn't sell her cheaply, if that's what you're implying. Timothy Mayhew must have wanted her pretty badly to pay that kind of money, and I'm sure he wasn't the only one. Dmitri likely put feelers out to see who'd pay the highest price for Valentina's virginity."

"That's unspeakable," Rhys muttered, shaking his head in dismay. "I know what you're telling me is true, but I find it hard to believe that anyone could be that depraved."

"He wouldn't be the first or the last to make a profit off a girl's virginity. The practice is old and widespread. Have you ever heard of Mizuage?"

"And what's that, when it's at home?"

"It was a practice of selling a geisha's virginity to a patron, for a very sizeable sum. They called it a rite of passage, when in fact it was nothing more than a way to make a profit. Mizuage was outlawed as recently as 1959. And of course, many bawdy houses in Victorian England made a big production of auctioning off the virginity of their youngest girls. The madams would parade the new girl before their patrons, whetting their appetites, then ask them to submit written bids. The highest bidder got the girl, and the house got a healthy infusion of coin."

"I've heard of these things, of course, but I never realized how barbaric and demeaning these acts were. I suppose everything takes on a new meaning when you have a daughter of your own."

"Are you having a girl?" Quinn asked, smiling at Rhys's sheepish expression. He obviously hadn't meant to give the secret away, but now that he had, he was beaming with paternal pride.

"I saw her on the scan. Oh, Quinn, she's perfect. She looks just like Haley."

"Have you got a name picked out?"

Rhys chuckled. "If Haley has her way, she'll name her something outlandish, like Heavenly Starlight, or Rainbow Twinkle Posey. I think Ambrosia is also in the running."

"And what's your preference?"

"I'm partial to Sophie Elizabeth," Rhys admitted shyly. "Sophie means *wisdom* in Greek, and I have great admiration for Elizabeth I and II. Inspiring women: courageous, intelligent, and selfless."

"Perhaps you'll prevail."

"I highly doubt it. Haley is so hormonally volatile just now, I'll agree to anything to keep her from bursting into tears."

"How is she feeling otherwise?"

"She's well. She's actually extremely disciplined," Rhys

replied. "She does antenatal yoga every morning. She's joined a walking group for expectant mums, and she watches her diet religiously. All baking ingredients have been consigned to the rubbish bin and I'm not allowed to even think about anything that might be high in carbohydrates and sugar. There are certain words I'm not allowed to utter."

"Such as?"

"Butter, for one."

"Surely, in moderation, butter is good for the baby."

"She prefers healthful fats, like olive oil and avocado. Butter is the devil."

Quinn studied Rhys's blissed-out expression and smiled. "I'm glad to see you happy, Rhys. You'll make a wonderful dad. When is the baby actually due?"

"Mid-April. I can't wait. I suggested we start decorating the nursery, but Haley seems reluctant."

"Maybe she's superstitious. Some women are. They think naming the baby before it's born or preparing a nursery will somehow anger the gods."

"I haven't noticed that Haley is particularly superstitious, but she performs evasive maneuvers every time I try to discuss the future with her. She's been awfully skittish lately, so I try not to upset her."

"Could it be that she doubts your commitment?" Quinn asked. Rhys was not known for having a good relationship track record, and at nearly fifty, had never been married.

"I've assured her time and again that I'm not going anywhere. I'd marry her tomorrow if she didn't mind getting hitched while pregnant. But Haley is an actress, and she wants to look her best on her wedding day."

Quinn grinned, reminding Rhys that she had, in fact, got married while pregnant. She'd wanted to marry Gabe so desperately she hadn't cared if she were in labor during the ceremony. She simply couldn't bear to wait any longer, especially after what had happened in New Orleans. Looking svelte in her wedding photos had been the least of her concerns, and she was happy she hadn't insisted on waiting. She and Gabe had shared a warm and loving relationship before they got married, but making things official had actually made their commitment stronger, and their love for each other had grown and matured. She hoped the same would be true for Haley and Rhys.

"There's no longer a stigma about being unmarried and pregnant. I suppose I can understand her desire to wait. Just be patient with her."

"I am. I won't be dragging her to church to stand up in front of a priest. This is the twenty-first century, after all. Whenever she is ready. You know," Rhys mused, "if we were having this conversation a few hundred years ago, we might have decided to betroth our children. Of course, I'd need Gabe's approval for the scheme. Your opinion would be completely irrelevant."

"Gabe wouldn't agree to an engagement at this time, but he might be open to a play date, perhaps in 2016. I have to get going. My opinion might be irrelevant, but my breasts aren't. Alex is due for a feeding soon."

"I'm trying to talk Haley into nursing. She's not in favor," Rhys confessed. "She can't wait to get her body back."

"I know how she feels."

"Quinn, I'd like to do a formal interview with Valentina's daughter, Natalia. Perhaps she can tell us something of Valentina's early years in England. She might know all about Dmitri's dealings with her, so her account would lend legitimacy to the program."

"That sounds like a good idea."

"I'll get it on the calendar and get back to you. And, Quinn, I'd like to get this wrapped up before Christmas."

"I'll do my best."

"I know you will. Cheers."

FORTY-TWO

MAY 1919

London, England

Valentina set the delicate china cups on a tray and added the teapot, the sugar bowl, and a saucer of lemon slices. Dmitri had asked her to take on the household duties for a few days, to bridge the gap between Mrs. Stern and Rachel's departure and the arrival of the new housekeeper. Once she started in a few days, she would be arriving in time to organize breakfast and then leave after clearing away after supper. Now that Valentina knew Dmitri better, she understood only too well why he no longer wanted live-in help. He liked to keep his affairs private, and with someone constantly in the house, there was always a chance of his secrets being discovered.

Hands splayed on the kitchen table, Valentina closed her eyes and bowed her head. She'd been with Ian Murdoch last night, and she felt battered, both emotionally and physically. She feared the man. There was a suppressed violence in him that could easily erupt at any moment if provoked. He worked out his aggression at the boxing club, but she was in no doubt that he would pummel someone to death if the situation called for it. She needed to know more about the man in order to protect herself, but he never spoke of his real life. He wore no wedding ring, but that didn't mean he wasn't married. He might even have children, like her other clients. Daughters who might be close in age to Valentina. Or Tanya.

Valentina trembled with fear when she thought of Tanya. Murdoch had asked about her last night. "I hear you have a sister," he'd said as he watched her undress. "Quite a beauty, Dmitri tells me. Does she look like you?"

"A bit," Valentina had squeezed out through clenched teeth.

"Now, there's a plum that's ripe for the picking," he'd said, watching her through narrowed eyes.

She knew he'd been toying with her, tormenting her, but his words had hit their mark. Would Dmitri agree if Murdoch offered him enough money for Tanya? Would he go back on his word?

"Valya, where is that tea?" Elena called out. "We're parched."

"Coming."

Valentina made a herculean effort to get hold of herself and sailed into the parlor, tea tray in front of her. She set in on the low table in front of Elena, who reached for the teapot and began to pour out. She saw herself as the mistress of the house, and no one challenged her view. She was, after all, the closest thing to one, and Dmitri treated her as a beloved sister.

He accepted his cup and took a long sip, sighing with pleasure. "Perfect. Mrs. Stern's tea was always too weak for my liking."

"Tanya, would you be a dear and bring some milk? I actually prefer my tea the English way now. Less acidic," Elena explained.

"Of course, Mama."

"You're awfully quiet, Valya," Elena remarked. "Is everything all right?"

"Of course. Just a bit tired."

"You have been looking rather wan lately. I know just the thing to put roses in those cheeks."

"If this is going to be another lecture on how I need to find a husband, let's pretend we already had it and move on to the next topic."

Elena glared at her but didn't persist. "So, what topic would you like to discuss, given that you're now censoring my efforts at conversation?"

Talking about the weather is always safe, Valentina thought. She stirred in some sugar and added a slice of lemon to her tea. She didn't want to talk. She just wanted to drink her tea and pretend that everything was normal, but she saw Dmitri watching her from beneath hooded lids. He watched her all the time, as though fearful that she would give something away and upset the delicate balance they'd managed to maintain in front of the others. Spending three days under his watchful gaze in Bournemouth had been sheer hell, the only bright spot being Kolya, who'd been overjoyed to have been pulled out of school for the impromptu holiday. Thinking of Kolya brought tears to Valentina's eyes, and she quickly blinked them away before anyone noticed.

Kolya put on a brave front, but she'd seen the fear in his eyes and the bruises on his still-childish body. He wasn't having an easy time adjusting to life in a school where he was only one of two non-English-born children. The other boy was Indian and probably got bullied as well, just for being different. Kolya never complained and returned to school bravely when the time came, but it'd pained Valentina to see him go. Perhaps hiring a tutor and keeping him at home would have been the kinder option. She'd locked herself in her room and wrote an impassioned column about the impact of boarding schools on the children of immigrants and their emotional welfare. Stanislav had been pleased, since many women at church were faced with the decision whether to send their children off for a "proper" education, as their husbands called it, or keep them at home until they were a little older and less vulnerable.

"I'm afraid I must go away for a few days," Dmitri announced, saving Valentina from having to come up with a suitable topic of conversation. "I must visit my factory. Now that the war is behind us, changes must be made, and corners need to be cut. The golden goose has stopped laying eggs," he added with a bitter chuckle. "But there are always other opportunities, if one knows where to look," he added, his eyes sliding to Tanya, who was delicately sipping her tea and nibbling on a biscuit.

"Will you be taking the motorcar?" Elena asked. "It's a long journey, is it not?"

"I'll take the train tomorrow morning," Dmitri replied. "Someone from the factory will collect me at the station. I'm in no mood to drive all that way, although it is a pretty drive."

"Maybe we can all go one day," Tanya suggested.

"My dear, we just spent three days in Bournemouth," Elena admonished her. "Don't be an ungrateful brat."

"Didn't you enjoy the seaside?" Dmitri asked, looking amused.

"I loved it. I've never seen anything so beautiful in my life," Tanya gushed. "Which is why I want to take more trips. The countryside is lovely this time of year, isn't it, Cousin Dmitri? So green and fresh. I'd like to have a picnic on a hillside, so I can enjoy the view while I eat. There's something very romantic about being able to see for miles in all directions. Perhaps we can take a drive once Kolya is home for the summer holidays."

"That sounds like a splendid idea. We will find a charming little spot and spend a few days there. The Cotswolds, perhaps, or Cornwall. Perhaps we can have a picnic on a clifftop. We can ask the innkeeper to pack us a basket of goodies," Dmitri promised. His gaze never left Tanya as he spoke, nor did his jovial smile reach his eyes. "Valya, dear, can you make sure there are clean towels in my bathroom? I'll have a bath tonight. The accommodations near the factory are practically medieval. You can almost see some poor serf lugging up buckets of hot water to the master's chamber."

"You have such an imagination, Dima," Elena said, smiling at him.

"You have no idea," Dmitri drawled, making Elena giggle.

Valentina wasn't quite sure when the idea had first presented itself or at what point doubt had changed to certainty. She only knew that what was about to happen was inevitable, and had been since the day Dmitri called her into his study all those months ago. She moved about as if in a dream, going about her business as if nothing in the world were amiss. She served a simple supper of cold fowl and salad at seven, then cleared up with Tanya's help, stowed away the leftovers, and washed the dishes. She then put two fresh towels in Dmitri's private bathroom.

No other bedroom had its own bath, but Dmitri had converted a small, windowless dressing room he had no use for into a fully functioning bathroom. He'd installed a claw-footed tub, a sink with a mirror for shaving, and a flushable commode. A small table next to the tub was stocked with a decanter of cognac and cigars, which Dmitri liked to smoke in the bath. The decanter was nearly empty. Normally, Valentina would make a note to top it up, but today, it served her purpose. She added a dozen drops of Elena's laudanum to the cognac and gave it a vigorous swirl. She hoped it would suffice.

Valentina returned to the parlor and remained there, reading a book, until Elena and Tanya went upstairs and Dmitri finally said good night. She periodically turned the page, but none of the words made sense, nor did she expect them to. The book was just a convenient prop that enabled her to keep her eyes downcast and her hands occupied. It also forestalled conversation with others, a tactic that was vital when she could barely remember her own name or verbalize a coherent thought. She would have gladly gone upstairs to her room, but it was imperative to keep an eye on Dmitri to make sure things went according to plan.

She was simultaneously terrified and amazed, unable to believe what she'd set in motion. A few times she nearly closed the book and went upstairs to pour the cognac down the drain and replace it with a fresh supply, but she remained in place, completely relaxed and composed, at least on the outside. Having had to keep a part of herself separate from the men she serviced came in handy, since she'd been forced to learn to hide her feelings and school her face to appear expressionless and calm. She might have found that ironic, were she not inwardly shaking like a leaf, knowing that the time of reckoning was upon her now that Dmitri had gone up to take a bath.

After enough time had elapsed, Valentina made her way upstairs and slipped into Dmitri's bedroom. The door to the bathroom was slightly ajar, and she could clearly see his profile, peaceful in repose. The empty snifter stood on the table and a half-smoked cigar was suspended between Dmitri's fingers, ashes falling to the tile floor as it smoldered.

"Dmitri," Valentina called as she advanced into the bathroom and shut the door behind her. "Dmitri."

There was no response. Dmitri appeared to be in a deep sleep. His head lolled to the side, resting against the back of the tub, his mouth was slack, and his dark lashes fanned against his flushed cheeks. Steam rose from the bathwater, filling the air with stifling heat and fogging the mirror. No wonder Dmitri preferred to leave the door slightly ajar when he bathed. Valentina leaned against the door and considered her options. Pushing him under might prove too difficult. He could wake up and struggle. She needed to render him helpless in order to make her task easier.

Valentina walked to the other side of the tub and stared down at Dmitri's naked form. Would he feel vulnerable if he knew she was looking at him, or would he enjoy the experience and find a way to make her feel uncomfortable instead? She thought the latter. Dmitri was in good shape for a man his age. His waist was still trim, his arms were well defined, and his legs were long and well-muscled. He went to a boxing club three times a week. Perhaps that was where he'd met Ian Murdoch. Valentina wrinkled her nose in distaste at the sight of his penis, flaccid and wrinkled in the warm water. How many women had there been, and had they been forced to submit to him as payment of some debt? A year ago, she would not have believed Dmitri capable of such malice, but now she knew better.

Valentina shook her head in annoyance. She had to focus, not speculate about Dmitri's secret life. The laudanum was at work, but Dmitri was a big man, and the dose, diluted by the cognac, might begin to wear off sooner rather than later. It was time to act.

Dmitri's legs were stretched out, crossed at the ankles, his elegant feet rising above the water, since the tub wasn't long enough to accommodate him. Most people would have bent their legs at the knees, but he hadn't. Perhaps this would make it easier for her to do what had to be done. Valentina grabbed Dmitri by the ankles and pulled upward as hard as she could. His upper body jerked as he began to slide beneath the water. It took only a few seconds for his head to dip below the surface. Dmitri's hair floated around his head, moving gently like seaweed in the ocean. It was an unsettling sight.

Valentina let out a frightened squeak and nearly let go of his ankles when Dmitri's eyes flew open. They appeared larger than normal, magnified by the water, and his brown stare was blank with confusion and then dawning panic. He began to struggle, trying to grab the sides of the tub, but his hands were wet and couldn't get a firm hold on the smooth porcelain. Valentina's arms trembled with effort as Dmitri thrashed, but his senses were dulled by the laudanum and his reflexes too slow. Air bubbles rushed to the surface in furious succession as Dmitri's mouth opened in a silent scream. He fought to get his head above the water, but no matter how hard he tried, he couldn't break the surface to gulp a lifesaving breath of air. He almost managed to yank his slippery ankles from Valentina's grasp, but she held on for dear life, knowing that if he survived, all was lost.

Dmitri flapped like a landed fish deprived of oxygen, his eyes growing huge with terror as soapy water filled his lungs. Water splashed over the sides of the tub and pooled on the tiled floor, but thankfully, the spot where Valentina stood remained dry, allowing her to put all her weight on her feet without losing purchase as she continued to grasp Dmitri's ankles. It felt like an hour had elapsed since she'd entered the bathroom, but it had probably been no more than ten minutes.

Eventually, Dmitri stopped struggling and went quiet and still. His eyes were still open, but they stared straight up at the white-painted ceiling, and his arms dropped to his sides, the hands relaxing once they stopped clawing at the tub.

Valentina held on for another few minutes, terrified that Dmitri would somehow rally and rise from the tub like some other-worldly leviathan, very much alive and intent on punishing her for what she'd tried to do. At last, she let go of his ankles and rested her hands on the rim of the tub, desperate for support. She was trembling and the muscles in her arms and legs ached and throbbed, unaccustomed to such strain. She gulped in mouthfuls of air until her heart rate began to slow down and the queasiness that made her stomach feel as if it had been turned inside out finally passed.

Valentina eventually relinquished her grip on the tub and inched toward Dmitri's torso. He looked like some mythical merman as his hair continued to float around his head. Valentina gingerly reached into the tub and grabbed hold of his wrist. There was no pulse, no sign of life. He was gone, really and truly gone.

She sank to the floor and leaned her forehead against the cold porcelain of the tub. Her skirt and stockings soaked up the water that had spilled to the floor, but she hardly noticed. Now that the deed was done, she felt as if every ounce of energy had seeped from her body. A crushing heaviness settled on her chest, making it difficult to breathe. She wished she could have some cognac to fortify her but remembered that it was laced with laudanum. A glass of water would have been nice, but fetching one would require getting to her feet and she simply couldn't find the strength to rise.

She'd thought once Dmitri was dead she'd feel a sense of euphoria. She'd be free of him at last, but the only thing Valentina felt was an overwhelming dread that seeped into her bones along with the damp from the cooling water. Initially, she'd planned to tell the authorities that Dmitri's death was an accident. Surely a person could drown in the bath if they were intoxicated, but in order to report the death to the police she'd have to erase any trace of laudanum and signs of struggle. She wasn't well versed in British law, but she knew that in cases of suspicious death, an inquest was held, and sometimes there was a postmortem. Dmitri had read to them from the paper when there was an interesting case a few months back. Ground glass had been discovered in the stomach of the victim, who'd bled to death internally, compliments of his long-suffering wife. The woman was hanged.

If a postmortem were performed, would traces of laudanum be discovered? How long did it remain in the body? No one in their right mind would take laudanum before a bath, especially a person who didn't use it on a regular basis. Dmitri had been in good health, anyone would attest to that, especially his doctor, who'd prescribed the laudanum for Elena's nerves and would know exactly where it'd come from. Perhaps the authorities would even uncover signs of a struggle. To Valentina, the only thing out of place was the spilled bathwater, but an experienced policeman might notice something that wasn't obvious to her. What could she do to hide her crime?

She looked around wildly. Her body had been nearly inert a few moments ago but now once again thrummed with tension. There was no way she could dispose of Dmitri's body. He was too heavy, and even if she managed to get him out of the house, which was a very big if, what then? She could hardly bury him in the back garden. The motorcar was parked in front of the house, but she didn't know how to drive, and dragging a grown man's body from the house to the car would surely attract attention, even in the middle of the night. Besides, where would she take him if she could figure out how to drive? Dump him in the Thames and watch him get carried away by the current? *Corpses float*, she thought grimly. His body would be discovered and an inquest would still be held. She'd be implicated one way or another, having been the last person to see him alive. No, the body had to remain in the house, at least for now.

She had to stop panicking and think. What she did in the next few minutes could mean the difference between life and death for her. Valentina used all her resolve to pull herself up off the floor and began to wipe the wet floor with the towels so the moisture wouldn't seep between the tiles and stain the ceiling of the room below.

At least she didn't have to worry about Mrs. Stern, who would have discovered Dmitri's corpse as soon as she arrived in the morning and came up to bring him his cup of tea. The new housekeeper wasn't due to start for two days, so no one would enter Dmitri's room until then.

Valentina finished cleaning the floor, hung up the towels on hooks, and let herself out of the bathroom, locking the bedroom door with Mrs. Stern's keys. She retreated to her bedroom, stripped off her wet garments and hung them up on the back of a chair. They'd be dry by morning. She then changed into her nightgown, sat on her bed, and wrapped her arms about her legs, resting her chin on her knees. She was exhausted but wouldn't be able to sleep anyway. She had to come up with a plan.

Tomorrow morning, her mother and Tanya would assume that Dmitri had left for his trip just as he'd said he would. But what would happen when he didn't show up at the factory? Would someone ring to inquire about his absence? Would they involve the police? They'd find him in a matter of minutes if they came to the house, and then Valentina's life would be forfeit. She'd hang. She began to tremble violently, her teeth chattering with fear. She didn't want to die. She wasn't a cold-blooded murderess; she was a young woman who'd been pushed past the point of endurance.

Prisons are full of people who've been pushed past the point of endurance, her mind replied. *They are called murderers.* And even if by some miracle the authorities believed Dmitri's death had been an accident, what then? How would her family live? How would they support themselves in the days to come? They had no claim on his fortune, no claim to the house. They'd have to leave, move to the cheapest lodgings they could find, pull Kolya out of school, and find work. In the end, she might end up having to sell her body just to survive. Now that the men had returned from the front, they wanted their jobs back. The demand for female labor had dropped, and the only type of work women could find was laundering, cleaning, sewing, or minding children. No respectable English family would hire her to mind their children. People were wary of foreigners, especially ones without references of past employment.

Why hire an immigrant with nothing to recommend her when they could find a good, respectable Englishwoman?

And what would happen to Dmitri's estate? Whom would it go to? He'd mentioned making Kolya his heir, but she had no idea if he'd ever made out a will or changed an existing one. As far as Valentina knew, Dmitri had no living family except for the Kalinins, but that didn't mean his property would automatically revert to them. Dmitri kept a tidy sum in the safe, along with Valentina's jewels, but she didn't know the combination, so they would be starting out with nothing, not even the items that lawfully belonged to her.

Valentina angrily wiped her cheeks with the back of her hand. What was the use in crying? She should have thought this through. She should have asked herself all these questions ahead of time. She'd acted on impulse, terrified she'd be too late to save Tanya, and possibly herself. She could still find her way back to some sort of respectability, given the chance, but a few more years of prostitution and she'd be nothing more than an empty husk, used up and broken, her self-respect and self-worth permanently eradicated. She'd been drowning and grabbed onto the first bit of flotsam she could see, not realizing that this chunk of wood might carry her further out to sea.

The clock in the corridor struck midnight. In approximately six hours, the sun would rise on a new day, and it'd be too late to do anything. She had to decide what to do. She could either summon the authorities in the morning and claim the drowning had been an accident, or come up with a plan that would ensure her freedom and some sort of financial restitution for what Dmitri had done. He owed her that much. Valentina pushed her palms into her eyes. She was so tired. She wished she could go to sleep and never wake up. It'd be easier for everyone. Well, not her mother, sister, and brother. They'd be lost without her. Elena was useless at making any sort of decisions or earning a living, Tanya was young and unskilled, and Kolya was just a child.

Valentina's gaze fell on her bedside table. *The Woman in*

White was there, a bookmark sticking out of one of the last chapters of the book. She'd almost finished it. It had been an amazing story, a fantastical one, but what an imagination the author had. She had the utmost respect for him. This wasn't a tale of a woman throwing herself under a train; this was a story of good triumphing over evil, of determination and faith righting a wrong.

"Dear God," Valentina breathed. "That's it." The answer was right there in front of her. One of the characters in the book, Sir Percival Glyde, had tampered with the parish register to record a marriage that had never taken place, therefore erasing his bastard status and legitimizing his claim to the baronetcy and his father's estate. He'd managed to get away with it too, for many years, until his secret was discovered by someone driven by love and a desire for justice.

Valentina sat up and bit her lip as she considered this idea. How difficult would it be to add a line to the church register? Would anyone notice? Father Mikhail was new to the Church of St. Sophia, having replaced Father Khariton, who'd died of pneumonia six weeks ago. He'd just assume the marriage had been performed by the old priest and have no reason to suspect foul play unless someone specifically questioned it. But would they, and how difficult would it be to tamper with the register? In a bigger church, the register would most likely be kept locked in the vestry, but St. Sophia was small, having until 1917 served a much smaller community, and the register was displayed in full view of the congregation.

There likely wouldn't be any empty spaces between entries, but at the bottom of a page there was bound to be room. The trick was not to add the false marriage to the current page, so as not to draw attention to it. All she'd need was a few minutes alone in the church, which shouldn't be too difficult to orchestrate given that the female parishioners of St. Sophia loved to gossip. It was practically a Russian national pastime, and no one escaped their notice. Valentina rarely paid attention and chose to exchange a few words with Stanislav after the service, but she knew the goings on at the church through Elena, who liked to keep abreast of everything that went on in their small community.

Unlike Father Khariton, who'd been elderly and kept the church open only during certain hours, Father Mikhail was in attendance from eight in the morning till eight at night, locking the doors only when he left for the day to protect the priceless icons and solid gold cross that graced the altar. He made himself available to his parishioners, whether they simply wanted to come in and pray, ask for guidance, or unburden themselves. The only time Father Mikhail left the church was when he went out to visit the sick or to perform a graveside funeral service. The church grounds weren't very extensive, so the parishioners who died were buried in a small Orthodox cemetery on the outskirts of London.

On the occasions when Father Mikhail left the church, an elderly caretaker called Kirill looked after the building, but he rarely remained inside. He tended the patch of garden around the church, swept the walkway, or enjoyed a cup of tea while sitting on a bench outside. Kirill's wife cleaned the church every Saturday morning. All Valentina had to do was wait for the next funeral, which would be held in three days' time, on Wednesday. At the Sunday service, Father Mikhail had prayed for the soul of Agraphena Petrovna, who had died just that morning. He'd recited the first *Panikhida*, which he'd also said over the body of the deceased at her bedside. The body would be laid out on the dining table, covered in a shroud with its head positioned beneath the icon corner for three days, until the funeral. Valentina wouldn't go to the house to pay her respects, but no one would think it strange if she attended the church service.

Valentina sighed loudly and propped up her chin with her hand, deep in thought. She still had to decide what to do about Dmitri's body. Leaving things as they were was too dangerous, even for one day. Someone might call from the factory when Dmitri failed to arrive, or even initiate a missing person's report with the police, which could bring someone to their door as soon as tomorrow. And the new housekeeper would be starting in a few days. She would ask for the household keys and go into every room, including Dmitri's bedroom. Valentina couldn't take the chance of her walking into the bathroom and coming face-to-face with a bloated corpse.

Valentina jumped off the bed and tiptoed outside. She had to ensure the body would never be found, and there was only one way to do that. She had to make sure no one ever set foot in Dmitri's private bathroom. The only people who'd ever gone into Dmitri's bedroom were Mrs. Stern and Rachel, but they were long gone. The new housekeeper had yet to familiarize herself with the house, so if she never learned of the bathroom, she'd never think to ask about it. There was another, larger bath just down the corridor from Valentina's room, and the housekeeper would simply assume that Dmitri had used that bathroom.

The only real problem would be the smell, and Valentina had a notion of how to deal with that. Alexei had been mad for military history and often shared what he'd learned with her, going on and on in his excitement and failing to notice her eyes glaze over with terminal boredom. She'd hated hearing about famous battles and military strategy but tried to feign interest for Alexei's sake. After all, he'd often listened to her prattle on about the ballet. Valentina thought it magical, while Alexei simply couldn't comprehend the point of telling a story without the use of words. Spending several hours sitting still while men in tights performed unnatural jumps and women in tutus flapped their arms and grimaced to convey emotion had been the stuff of nightmares for poor Alexei. He'd said that even the opera was better, since someone usually died at the end, if after a very long aria, and there were better costumes.

Valentina must have absorbed something of what Alexei talked about because she recalled that lye was often used in mass graves to accelerate decomposition and prevent the spread of infection. There was lye in the kitchen. Mrs. Stern had used it to make soap, dissolve grease, and even in certain recipes, but only in miniscule quantities. Valentina wasn't sure how much lye was required, but she'd use all of it.

She fetched the tub of lye from the kitchen, along with an oilcloth and a ball of string, and took them upstairs to Dmitri's bedroom. It took all her resolve to unlock the door and face what she'd done, but it was too late to be squeamish or suffer pangs of remorse. She set the tub of lye on the floor and, hands on hips, stared at Dmitri's remains. Mrs. Stern had mixed the lye with water, but it would probably be more effective in concentrated form. Valentina pulled the plug and allowed the water to drain out of the tub. She then folded Dmitri's legs, grateful that they weren't yet stiff with rigor mortis, and pushed them into the tub. She opened the container of lye and liberally spread the contents over the body, making sure to douse every part. She then used the oilcloth to cover the tub completely and wound a length of string around, securing it down firmly, so that no odors would escape. If any liquids oozed out of the body during decomposition, they'd simply drain away.

Valentina smiled grimly as she finished her work. It served Dmitri right not to have a proper funeral, and to be left to rot like an animal carcass with no signs of respect or prayers for his soul. He'd been a horrible man, a ruthless predator, and he deserved no sympathy from her. She collected Dmitri's clothes and the nearly empty decanter, along with the lye tub and the string, and left the bathroom, closing the door behind her. Now all she had to do was move the massive wardrobe in front of the door to the bathroom, and no one would ever suspect there'd been a room there.

She set down the decanter and tossed the clothes on the bed, then tried to move the wardrobe. It wouldn't budge. It was way too heavy for one person to move. She tried again and again, but couldn't move it.

Frantically, Valentina began to take everything out of the wardrobe. There were suits, shirts, coats, and hats. The items weren't heavy in themselves, but taking them all out made a differ-ence. After nearly an hour of inching the wardrobe along, she finally managed to push it in front of the door. The floor got a little scuffed, but if she shifted the rug, no one would notice. She quickly replaced all the clothes in the wardrobe, except for a few season-appropriate items, which she tossed into a valise Dmitri used when travelling. She added his wallet, which she emptied, and his passport to the contents and took the valise to her room. In the morning, she would weigh the valise with a few stones and dump it in the river. It would never be found, but even if it was, it'd be proof that Dmitri had been set upon by hooligans, who'd disposed of the evidence after taking what they wanted.

By the time Elena and Tanya came down to breakfast just before nine a.m., Valentina was already in the kitchen, boiling eggs and making tea. She should have been exhausted, but the terror she'd experienced had kept her wide awake long enough to see to every detail of her plan. She went about her day, keeping up a pretense of normalcy for as long as she could. Just before dinner, she claimed a terrible headache and retreated to her room, where she collapsed onto the bed without undressing and fell into a dreamless sleep.

FORTY-THREE

For the next few days, Valentina lived in abject terror. She imagined that every motorcar driving down the street belonged to the police, who were coming to arrest her. Every footfall was that of someone heading to Dmitri's room. Every time the telephone rang, which thankfully didn't happen often, she feared it was the factory manager calling to inquire after Dmitri's whereabouts. She walked past Dmitri's room first thing every morning, sniffing experimentally. She couldn't smell a thing but opened all the windows nonetheless, claiming that it was a good time to air out the house. The weather was glorious, so no one questioned her desire for fresh air.

Valentina desperately tried to maintain a façade of normalcy, but she felt queasy throughout the day and could barely manage to keep any food down. Her hands shook when she attempted to prepare the meals and she nearly sliced off her finger while peeling potatoes for supper. Any unexpected noise sent her into a mindless panic, and her head throbbed, the pain blurring her vision and making her irritable.

"Goodness gracious! What is the matter with you, Valya?" Elena asked when she walked into the kitchen to find Valentina trying to bandage her bleeding finger.

"I just don't feel well," Valentina mumbled. It was no use pretending everything was well, especially when her voice sounded as tearful as that of a little girl who'd fallen and scraped her knee.

"It's that time of the month, isn't it?" Elena laid a sympathetic hand on her shoulder. "Why don't you let me do that?"

Valentina held out her hand and Elena bound her finger and skillfully tied the ends of the gauze.

"I hope you cleaned it first."

"Of course, Mama."

"Go lie down for a little while. Tanya and I will take care of supper."

Valentina scoffed. Elena had never cooked anything in her life, much less an entire meal.

"I'm not as useless as you think, Valya. I can manage to boil a few potatoes. And since you've already prepared the chicken and set it to roast, all I have to do is keep an eye on it. I think I can be trusted not to burn it to cinders."

"Of course you can, Mama."

Elena leaned down and kissed Valentina's forehead. "Go on."

Valentina nodded and sprang to her feet. She knew she wouldn't be able to sleep, but an hour alone in her room, where she could give vent to her fears and maybe even have a good cry, would be a welcome reprieve from having to put on an act and pretend nothing was amiss. The strain was getting to her, and if she wasn't careful, she'd give herself away.

Valentina closed the door behind her and stretched out on the cool sheets. The window was partially open and a pleasant breeze cooled her flushed cheeks. The funeral was tomorrow. The mere thought of forging an entry in the register nearly made her sick, but she forced herself to close her eyes and breathe deeply until she was in control once again. The rest of her life, assuming there would still be a life left to live, hinged on tomorrow. She'd committed murder and hidden the body. Forgery and fraud would be a walk in the park compared to what she'd already had to endure.

FORTY-FOUR

DECEMBER 2014

London, England

Pale winter sunlight streamed through the windows of the small Italian bakery. The air was thick with the heavenly smell of roasting coffee and freshly baked pastries. A plump, dark-eyed young woman maneuvered between the closely packed tables, deftly carrying a tray loaded with Quinn's decaffeinated cappuccino, Rhys's espresso, and a plate of almond biscotti. She beamed at Rhys as she set the espresso in front of him, but ignored Quinn.

"No cheesecake today, Mr. Morgan?" the waitress purred.

Rhys shook his head. "Not today, Giovanna."

"Mama made it fresh this morning," she replied, giving Rhys a winsome smile.

"I'm sure it's to die for, but I don't think I can fully appreciate it today. I'll have it next time. Promise."

"I'll hold you to that." Giovanna tossed her abundant hair playfully and walked away, swaying her ample hips in a way that would have made Sophia Loren nod with approval.

"I think you have an admirer," Quinn joked as she reached for a biscotto. Rhys had taken her to this little bakery the first time they met, and the cheesecake, which he'd insisted she try, truly was to die for. "Why no cheesecake today? You love the way they make it here."

"I feel a bit queasy, to be honest."

Rhys did look pale, now that she studied him more closely, and there were dark smudges beneath his eyes, as if he hadn't slept. "Should you be having espresso? It might make you feel worse."

Rhys took a sip of his espresso and sighed. "I'm desperate for caffeine."

"Is everything all right?"

"Haley and I had an argument last night," Rhys confessed. "She's obsessed with staying in shape and not gaining any more weight. She's not eating enough, and her exercise routine is too strenuous for a woman in her second trimester. She gets angry anytime I say anything and refuses to discuss my concerns, but I'm worried."

"What does her doctor say?"

"He's concerned by her lack of weight gain. She's only gained four pounds, and she's more than twenty weeks along."

"I see. Are you two speaking?"

"Not as of this morning. I tried talking to her before I left for work, but she ignored me and rushed off to a Pilates class. Without having any breakfast," Rhys added. "Anyway, enough about my problems. Update me on your progress with this case." His expression underwent a remarkable change, from naked vulnerability to stoic professionalism. "Have you been able to discover anything we can verify?"

"I think I have. Valentina killed Dmitri Ostrov in May of 1919. She mixed laudanum into his cognac and then drowned him in the tub. Now that I have a date and the name of the victim, I can begin to search for information in earnest."

"She clearly got away with it," Rhys replied as he reached for a biscotto and took a bite. "In 1919, the penalty for murder was death by hanging, so it stands to reason that either Valentina was never arrested on suspicion of murder or wasn't convicted during her trial. See if you can find any evidence relating to the crime. Otherwise, we might have to rethink the entire storyline. We can't very well accuse a woman of murder, especially while she has living descendants who might sue us for slander."

"Give me a few days."

"You are scheduled to interview Natalia Swift on Thursday. Push her as hard as you need to. We must have something concrete to go on."

"Yes, boss," Quinn replied, smiling at him. Rhys might be tired and upset, but his instincts were as sharp as ever. He'd tell this story his way, seamlessly blending romance, drama, and suspense. Knowing Rhys, he'd also make sure to dot all the i's and cross all the t's, making sure the story was told in a way that left no grounds for legal action from Valentina Swift's descendants.

"Any news on the other situation?" Rhys asked.

"You mean Quentin?" Quinn shook her head. "Nothing yet. I'm very frustrated with the lack of progress. Gabe tells me to be patient, but that's easier said than done. I really thought Drew Camden would have something for us by now."

"Quinn, this is real life, not an hour-long segment about searching for long-lost relations, where the happy reunion is shown within the final five minutes of the program and everyone wipes away tears of joy as they reflect on the miracle of modern-day technology that made it all possible. These things take time. Gabe is right—be patient." Rhys tossed some money on the table and pushed to his feet. "I have to get back to the office. I have a meeting in a half hour. Keep me updated."

"I will," Quinn replied.

She buttoned her coat, grabbed her bag, and followed Rhys out into the street. Despite the sunshine, the day was windy and cold and she wished she'd worn a warmer jumper. Rhys gave her a peck on the cheek and rushed off, leaving her alone on the pavement. Quinn considered going to the library to troll through newspaper articles from May of 1919 on microfiche but changed her mind.

She needed to know what had happened before she began searching for hard evidence. Jill had offered to take Alex for a few hours so Quinn could immerse herself in Valentina's life without constant interruptions. She huddled deeper into her coat and began to walk in the direction of the nearest tube station, eager to get home.

FORTY-FIVE

MAY 1919

London, England

On the day of the funeral, Valentina came down early. She planned to leave the house before her mother and Tanya woke, so as to avoid any awkward questions. Elena had no plans to attend the funeral, which suited Valentina just fine. She put on the navy dress she'd brought from Russia. It was the most somber garment she owned, since there hadn't been time to order mourning clothes after her father and Alexei died, and she paired it with a navy hat she wore during the winter months. She stared at her pale reflection in the mirror. The dress brought back poignant memories of a time when the men she loved had still been very much alive and talk of escape from her homeland had been nothing more than a wild idea, never meant to become reality. She'd been so young then, and so naïve. How quickly life could change.

Normally, Dmitri drove them to church, but this morning Valentina had to take an omnibus and make two changes before she finally arrived at her destination. The service was about to begin, so she stood off to the side, not wishing to intrude on the family. There were about two dozen people in total, all dressed in black, heads bowed. The open casket stood at the center.

Agraphena Petrovna lay inside, her hands folded over her chest, a gold cross carefully inserted between her stiff fingers. Her folded shroud lay on her stomach, to be used after the service when Father Mikhail would cover the corpse, and a white paper headband had been placed on her forehead. It read HOLY GOD, HOLY MIGHTY, HOLY IMMORTAL, HAVE MERCY ON US.

Father Mikhail began to sing and Valentina bowed her head in respect, but her eyes strayed to the church register, displayed on a small table beneath the high window just to Valentina's right. The ledger was open to the current page, the last entry a bit darker than the rest, since the ink was still drying. The priest must have recorded the death just before taking his place next to the coffin, ready to begin the service.

After the prayers were finally over, family members and close friends came up to the coffin to prostrate themselves. They kissed the cross and the headband, then crossed themselves before finally stepping aside to allow Father Mikhail to cover the deceased with the shroud and sprinkle some holy oil into the coffin before closing the lid in preparation for burial.

Four pallbearers lifted the coffin and followed Father Mikhail out the door, chanting "Holy God" as they went. The rest of the mourners followed. They would make their way to the cemetery and meet at the graveside for the burial, then go to Agraphena Petrovna's house for a final vodka-soaked sendoff. Valentina wouldn't go to the cemetery, nor would she go to the house for the *pominki*.

She hung back, letting the mourners file out the door. A few moments later, the church was blessedly empty and strangely silent after all the singing and weeping. She waited until she heard the sound of engines being started, then inched toward the register. For convenience, a pen and a closed bottle of ink were stored inside the small drawer beneath the register, and Valentina took them out and unscrewed the cap on the ink. She stared down at the register. She thought she'd have to go back several pages, but the previous page went all the way to the start of 1919. In such a small congregation, months went by without any births, deaths, or weddings. There were only five entries since the start of the year, and only because one couple had married on January 1, 1919, and another had welcomed twins at the beginning of February, accounting for three of the entries. The other two entries were the death of Father Khariton on March 2 and the death of Agraphena Petrovna on May 11.

Valentina flipped back one more page and scanned the contents. There was only one obvious place. An empty line had been left at the bottom of the previous page since two events were recorded for the same family on the same date. She supposed Father Khariton had wished to keep the events grouped together for consistency. A death and a birth were listed on December 17, 1918. Anastasia Andreeva had been born, and her mother, Yulia Andreeva, had died bringing her into the world. These were the last entries made by Father Khariton before his death.

Valentina said a quick prayer for the old priest before carefully adding a line at the bottom of the page, recording the date of her fictitious marriage to Dmitri as December 21. She remembered the day well. Dmitri had asked her to help him pick out a present for Elena's birthday, which was on December 27. They'd spent several hours shopping in Oxford Street. Once the news of the marriage came out, her mother and Tanya would both recall that Valentina and Dmitri had been conspicuously absent from the house that day, and realize that they'd snuck out to get married.

The fresh ink looked alarmingly dark against the creamy beige page, but it would fade in time. Valentina's handwriting wouldn't draw any attention to the entry. Russian children were taught penmanship as a matter of course, so everyone's handwriting looked very similar, since individuality was not encouraged. The entry blended right in. The only way she would get found out was if Father Mikhail had familiarized himself with all the entries upon starting his tenure as priest at the Church of St. Sophia. She could only pray that he hadn't.

Valentina closed the register, put away the pen and ink, and slowly walked toward the door. A few stragglers were still at the curb, getting into a motorcar. An elderly woman was already installed in the front seat and a tall, gaunt gentleman with a pencil moustache was holding the door open for his wife, who was about to get in.

She looked at Valentina with interest. "We thought you'd gone to the cemetery with the others," the woman said. Valentina knew the family, but her mind suddenly went blank and she couldn't recall their surname.

"I, eh, had to go to the lavatory," Valentina stammered. "There isn't one at the cemetery."

"Indeed there isn't. Would you like a lift?" the man asked solicitously. "We have room for one more."

"I would be most grateful," Valentina replied. She hadn't planned on going to the cemetery for the burial, but this opportunity was too good to miss. There was something she needed to check and a trip to the cemetery by omnibus would take up most of her day.

Valentina got into the car and settled in next to the woman, whose name she was finally able to recall. Angela Vitalyevna Danilova.

"How is your dear mama?" Angela Vitalyevna asked. "I do so hope to further our acquaintance."

"She's well. Thank you."

"Do you think she'd accept my invitation if I asked her to tea?"

Valentina hated to be put on the spot. Elena didn't like Angela Danilova. She thought her common and ill-mannered, but Valentina could hardly be rude. "I am sure she would," she replied, hoping the woman wouldn't get around to issuing the invitation.

"I'll send her a note today, after we return from the pominki. I do hope they have some decent food. I'm starving. I overslept and had no time for breakfast," she complained.

"I'm sure Agraphena's daughter will have a good spread," Angela's mother-in-law replied from the front. "They have an excellent cook."

"I hope they'll have blini with caviar," Angela said wistfully. "We don't often have such delicacies anymore. The blini we can manage, but caviar is so dear. It's worth its weight in gold."

"Really, Angela," her husband said, sounding extremely annoyed. "One would think you only came to the funeral for the food."

Angela Vitalyevna smiled guiltily. "I came to pay my respects to a woman I liked and admired. And I will eat my fill and drink to her memory along with everyone else." She turned away from Valentina and looked sulkily out the window. "I hope it doesn't rain," she mumbled.

The rest of the ride passed in silence, which was just fine with Valentina. Perhaps she would go to the *pominki* after all. Now that the terrifying task of having to tamper with the register was behind her, she was suddenly ravenously hungry. She could use a shot of vodka as well, to calm her nerves. What she did today would either save her or point a finger in her direction once Dmitri's disappearance became public knowledge. She leaned back against the seat and closed her eyes, desperate for a few moments to compose herself.

FORTY-SIX

"Where in the world is Dmitri?" Elena asked as they sat down to supper one night at the end of May. "He said he'd be gone a few days, but it's been nearly a fortnight. Several gentlemen have called for him on the telephone. It seems he missed his appointments with them. A Mr. Murdoch called several times, demanding to know where Dmitri is. Oh, I do hope he's all right."

"I'm sure he is, Mama," Tanya replied as she helped herself to some fricassee. "I do wish he'd hurry back. Kolya will need to be collected from school soon, and then we can go on our little jaunt to the country. I can't wait."

Valentina tried to hide her shock. She'd forgotten all about Kolya. The school year was nearly at an end. She'd have to take the train and bring him back to London for the summer, along with his trunk. In the past, Dmitri had taken the motorcar, but now it was up to her to fetch him back.

"Valya, you should learn to drive," Tanya said.

"I couldn't."

"Why ever not? There are female motorists. I read that a woman named Alice Ramsey drove across the United States in 1909. That was a decade ago."

"A respectable woman shouldn't drive. Such pursuits are for men," Elena said sharply.

"Why? Is a male appendage required to drive a car?" Valentina asked, suddenly irritated with her mother. It was nearly 1920. The world was changing, and they had to change with it. She was through being told what to do and being treated like a commodity. If she survived long enough to have a future, she would make her own choices and be her own woman.

"Don't be vulgar, dear. It simply isn't ladylike. And anyway, Valentina, you should really focus your energies on getting married. You are going to be twenty-one next year. You've had plenty of time to grieve for Alexei. A woman needs a husband, and you mustn't miss your chance. There's nothing worse than being a spinster."

"Isn't there?" Valentina asked, trying to hide her sarcasm. Being sodomized by a man you despised and then forced to suck his cock until his seed erupted in a warm stream into your mouth was infinitely worse, in her opinion. She'd take being a spinster any day.

"No, there isn't. As a spinster, you are nothing, no one. You need a husband to protect you, give you respectability. And children. Having children makes many things bearable."

"Such as?" Valentina asked.

"Widowhood. I would never have survived without you. I would have simply curled up and died after your father was murdered. I'd have had no reason to go on."

"Have you ever thought of remarrying, Mama?" Valentina asked. She caught Tanya's shocked gaze, but persisted. "If I'm to stop mourning, so should you."

"You loved Alyosha, I know that, but you weren't his wife. You never shared his bed, or carried his children. You mourn the promise of a life. I mourn a life I actually had."

"I know, Mama, and I'm not comparing our grief, but you're still a young woman. You're only forty. There are several men at church who find you attractive."

Elena smiled coyly. She was well aware of the admiring looks she received from the widowers in the congregation. "To be honest, I see no reason to marry again. Dmitri takes such good care of us. It's like having a husband without having to tolerate his moods and needs."

"Dmitri might wish to marry again," Tanya said. "He's not that old."

Elena's face fell. She'd clearly never considered the possibility, but if she had, perhaps she'd thought he'd marry her. They were second cousins. No one would stop them marrying if they wished to, and they'd known each other since they were children. They had a bond, an understanding. Perhaps that was what her mother had been hoping for. She loved Dmitri. Maybe not as she had loved their father, but she loved him nonetheless, and marriage would be a natural next step. But Dmitri would never have married her. If they'd married, the sword of poverty and homelessness he'd held over Valentina's head would disappear. As his wife, Elena would want for nothing, and he'd be obligated to provide for her children. Valentina would be free of him, as would Tanya. And that hadn't been part of his plan.

Had he always meant to recoup his investment? Valentina wondered as she prepared for bed that night. When he came to see them in Whitechapel, had he been sizing her up and making plans for her future? Or had he genuinely wished to help and only hit on a means of making money off her later? Had they cost him so much more than he'd anticipated? Surely, he could have helped Valentina find a suitable position if that had been the case. She could have started paying him back from her wages. She'd have paid him for the rest of her life, if that was what it took. Or did he enjoy humiliating her and wielding power over her life? Did he get pleasure from knowing he could break her? Perhaps he'd even watched her humiliation. Several times she'd heard movement in the next room, despite the fact that Dmitri had said it was vacant. Had it aroused him to see her on her knees, naked and defenseless?

Not for the first time, Valentina wondered about Emily,

Dmitri's late wife. Had he truly loved her as he'd claimed, or had he ruined her life as well? What had their relationship been like? He'd always spoken of her with longing and regret. Of course, it could be that he'd simply missed the woman he'd loved, but what if there was more to that story? Dmitri seemed to have done very well for himself since coming to England. Had Emily's family been responsible for his swift change in fortune? Emily had been an only child, as far as Valentina knew. Had Dmitri married her so he could inherit when her father died? Emily had worked as a governess in Russia when she met Dmitri, but he'd once mentioned that her family had been quite well-to-do. Valentina supposed she'd never find the answers to her questions, but now that she knew what Dmitri had been capable of, she couldn't help questioning everything he'd told her.

Valentina had snuck into Dmitri's study several times since the night he died. She needed to open the safe, but she didn't know the combination. Money set aside for household expenses was running out, and Mrs. Nemirovsky, who'd started her job as a housekeeper two weeks ago, had hinted once already that her wages were due. Valentina had tried Dmitri's birthday and the date of his name day. She'd even tried Emily's birthday after memorizing the dates on her gravestone the day of Agraphena Petrovna's funeral, but the safe wouldn't open. She had to try again. She waited until everyone went to bed, then tiptoed to Dmitri's study.

She closed the door behind her and stood in front of the safe, thinking, then began to turn the knob. The date of Emily's death. If that didn't work, she had no other ideas. She couldn't quite believe her luck when she heard the lock click and pulled open the steel door. Why would anyone wish to use the day of someone's death? But as she already knew, Dmitri had his secrets, and perhaps this was one of them. Whatever might have happened to his wife didn't matter anymore. What mattered was that her family now had enough money to sustain them for months, if not years.

In the meantime, she had to start working on implementing the next phase of her plan. Dmitri had been gone for more than two weeks. It was time to act. First, she would ring the factory and inquire about Dmitri's whereabouts, then alert the police to his disappearance. That out of the way, she'd need to find a solicitor who would help her legalize her claim to Dmitri's assets. If he asked for a marriage certificate, she would go see Father Mikhail and pray that the priest would simply leaf through the register, find the marriage, and issue a legal document. Once she was over that hurdle, she'd be one step closer to financial freedom. Of course, it would take years to have Dmitri declared legally dead, but at least she'd have the house, the car, access to his bank account, and the run of the businesses.

If it all went smoothly, she'd then tell her mother and Tanya about the marriage. Elena would feel shocked and betrayed by the news, possibly even a little resentful that Dmitri had chosen her daughter over her. Tanya would be surprised and hurt that Valentina hadn't trusted her enough to share the news with her, and Kolya likely wouldn't care one way or the other. Ultimately, everyone would accept her secret marriage to Dmitri and be grateful for their newfound wealth. As long as Dmitri's body never turned up, Valentina would remain safe.

FORTY-SEVEN

Valentina alighted from the omnibus and walked toward Stanislav Bistrizky's place of work. She'd been so preoccupied with her problems that she'd forgotten to mail in her weekly column. If she sent it by post today, it wouldn't get to Stanislav in time, so she'd decided to deliver it in person. It also gave her something to do and a reason to leave the house. She'd spoken to the factory foreman yesterday morning, and when he'd predictably said that Dmitri had never arrived at the factory nor sent any word, Valentina had gone to the police. She'd considered asking Elena to come along but had changed her mind. Her mother's nervous disposition wouldn't help matters, and since Valentina planned to make it known that she was Dmitri's wife, it was only natural that she should be the one to sound the alarm.

The police station had been surprisingly quiet, and a detective had been immediately summoned to take her statement. The policeman's name was Detective Sergeant Cooper, and he was a lot more pleasant than Valentina had expected. She'd imagined being interrogated by a gruff, middle-aged civil servant with a drooping moustache and pomaded hair. Detective Cooper was no older than thirty, and surprisingly attractive. He invited her to his office and had one of the junior officers make her a cup of tea before taking her statement. Valentina did her best to keep calm as she summarized the facts, but her hands trembled and her voice broke several times before she finished her account.

"Please don't worry, madam. We will begin searching for your husband immediately and inform you of any developments in our investigation. I assure you that most missing persons turn up safe and sound."

"Where will you look for him, Detective Cooper?" Valentina asked. "He could be anywhere."

The detective met her gaze without flinching, but there was a hint of sympathy in his warm brown eyes. "We will check with all the hospitals and mortuaries first. If we find no trace of him, then we will check with customs to determine if Mr. Ostrov might have left the country."

"You think he's run off?" Valentina gasped, her eyes wide with pretend shock.

"I don't think anything, Mrs. Ostrov. Not yet."

Valentina nodded. "I'm sorry. Of course you don't."

"Nothing to be sorry about. Naturally, you're very worried about your husband and desperate for answers. We will get in contact with you as soon as we learn anything."

"Thank you, Detective."

"Please let us know if there are any developments," Detective Cooper said as he escorted Valentina out of his office and toward the door.

"What sort of developments?"

"Such as your husband coming home, or any odd telephone calls or letters you might receive. Perhaps you should take a look at his personal papers. You might find something that could give us a clue. Might there have been financial difficulties?"

"Not that I know of."

He nodded and held the door open for her. "Try to keep calm, Mrs. Ostrov. Good day."

"Good day."

Valentina had gone for a long walk after her visit to the police station. She'd needed to calm her nerves and practice her speech before returning home. It was time she told her mother and Tanya about the marriage, since the detective might ring and ask for Mrs. Ostrov, or show up at their door. Their reaction had been one of shock and dismay, but Valentina had been prepared for that. She'd have been angry too, had Elena suddenly announced that she'd been secretly married for months. They would get over the betrayal in time, but at the moment, neither was speaking to her.

The silence actually made things easier, since she didn't have to answer countless questions or put on a pretense of sorrow. Instead, she retreated to her room where she wrote several columns for the paper. Writing calmed her and allowed her to marshal her thoughts. After her conversation with the detective, Valentina had decided to write a column about the importance of keeping abreast of family finances. Most women had no clue what their husbands did when they went to work, nor what their financial situation was. The lucky ones never had to worry, but there were plenty of women who lost their possessions and their homes when their husbands died unexpectedly and didn't leave their families provided for.

"Valentina, what are you doing here?" Stanislav asked when he came out from behind the counter to greet her. He wore his leather apron and there was a smudge of ink on his cheek.

"I'm sorry to show up like this. I forgot to mail my column." She handed Stanislav the folded pages she'd extracted from her reticule.

Stanislav unfolded the pages and scanned the neatly written paragraphs. "Are you all right?" he asked.

"Of course. Why do you ask?"

"Last week you wrote about funerals, and today, it's about unexpected loss and how to protect yourself against a life of penury."

"I think women need to be more aware of what's going on right in front of their noses."

"And what is going on in front of their noses?" Stanislav asked, his eyes dancing with amusement.

Valentina blushed. "I just think too many women would rather remain ignorant than know the truth of their situations."

"What truth are you referring to?"

"Things are not always what they seem. Are they?"

"No, they certainly aren't. And you're right, most wives would rather not know about an affair or worry about possible financial ruin. Instead, they focus on trivialities and hope the unpleasantness will simply go away."

"It rarely does," Valentina replied. She hadn't meant to be so frank, but there was something about Stanislav that made her feel safe. She wished she could tell him the truth of her situation and ask for his help. He was clever and resourceful, and he was her only real friend in a city of millions.

Stanislav smiled ruefully. "Unfortunately, I have my own unpleasantness to deal with at the moment."

"What's happened?"

Stanislav shrugged and hung his head, like a little boy who'd been caught doing something he shouldn't have been. "A shidduch has been arranged for me."

"What's a shidduch?"

"A match. She's a nice girl from a good family, and my parents are over the moon."

"What about you?"

"I have no desire to marry her, but if I don't marry, my brother cannot marry, and neither can Sarah. I'm the oldest. I must marry first."

"Will they find you another shidduch if you refuse this one?"

"Yes. They will keep parading eligible girls in front of me until I pick one, but if I refuse to marry Esther, her reputation will suffer. People might think she has some hidden flaw that put me off her. Max quite likes her. I wish he could marry her instead."

"This is the twentieth century, Slava. Why are we still slaves to the expectations of others?" Valentina exclaimed. She hadn't meant to use the intimate version of Stanislav's name, but it just slipped out, surprising them both. His eyes widened and a sad smile tugged at the corners of his mouth.

"Because as much as the world changes, it stays the same, Valya," he replied. "People want to hold on to their customs because the old ways make them feel grounded and secure. To do away with centuries of tradition would bring on chaos, in their minds. This way of doing things has worked for them and their parents, and they assume it will work for this generation as well. Fighting against it only causes sorrow and pain to all involved."

"Does this mean you're going to marry this girl?"

Stanislav sighed. "Not yet. But I must give my answer soon."

"I must go," Valentina said. "I wish you happiness, Slava, whatever you decide to do."

"I don't think happiness is in the cards for me, because I can't be with the girl I love."

"I suppose people like you and I must make the best of a bad situation. Mustn't we?"

Stanislav nodded. "Or fight to change it." He stuffed the pages she'd given him into the pocket of his apron and turned to go. "See you on Sunday," he called over his shoulder.

"See you," Valentina replied, but he was already gone.

FORTY-EIGHT

JUNE 1919

London, England

Valentina felt as if she'd aged ten years by the time the search for Dimitri was finally called off after a month. The police came and went. Detective Sergeant Cooper interviewed everyone several times, and even contacted Mrs. Stern and Rachel in Leeds. The only fact they could establish with any certainty was that Dmitri Ostrov hadn't been seen since May 6th. None of the agents at the train station could remember him purchasing a ticket that morning. The conductor, who'd been on the train Dmitri had planned to take, could not recall a man matching Dmitri's description, and no one from the factory had heard from him since May 5. A car had been sent to collect Dmitri from the station, but he'd never arrived. None of Dmitri's business associates could shed any light, and thankfully, Mayhew, Gleason, and Murdoch had gone to ground, clearly having no desire to have the police look into their affairs, since their activities were less than savory.

The police searched the house for clues to Dmitri's whereabouts. They turned his study upside down but found nothing but ledgers, correspondence, and a diary, the pages of which made no mention of assignations at the Falmouth Arms Hotel. Valentina sat in the parlor, shaking with fright, as the police searched the upstairs. They spent an hour in Dmitri's bedroom but found nothing out of the ordinary. The stench of decomposition had been obliterated by the lye and contained by the tightly wrapped oilcloth.

"Mrs. Ostrov, I am very sorry, but there is nothing more we can do. Unless some clue to your husband's whereabouts presents itself, there's no place else to look. His trail has gone cold." Detective Cooper's brow was creased with tension, his eyes full of regret as he spoke the words Valentina had been praying to hear. He had been very thorough and left no stone unturned, but she'd been cleverer than the police. She'd committed the perfect crime.

"What do I do now, Detective?" Valentina asked, her eyes shimmering with unshed tears.

"You try to get on with your life as best you can. If, after seven years, there's no evidence that your husband is alive, he will be legally declared deceased. Until then, I'm afraid you're in limbo."

"Do you think he's gone abroad?" Valentina asked. "He's taken his passport."

The detective shook his head. "We've found no evidence to suggest that he left the country. Might he have returned to Russia under a different name?"

"I suppose," Valentina replied. "But I can't see why he wouldn't have told me. We were newly married, Detective. We were happy." She sighed dramatically.

"I'm sorry, Mrs. Ostrov, but I have absolutely nothing to go on, and I don't like to speculate. I hope, for your sake, that he'll turn up alive, but in some of these cold cases, the wives pray we find the body, so they can at least be spared the uncertainty and get on with their lives. Do ring us if you discover anything. Anything at all. No matter how insignificant it may seem."

"I will. And thank you, Detective."

"I wish I could have done more."

"So do I."

Valentina walked Detective Cooper to the door and watched him walk down the path toward the gate. It was only when he got into his motorcar and drove away that she exhaled the breath she hadn't realized she'd been holding.

London, England

Quinn was surprised to find Rhys in attendance when she arrived to interview Natalia Swift, Valentina's daughter, at her flat in Fulham. Normally, Rhys allowed her do all the leg work on her own after the initial evaluation of the case, but today he hovered at Darren's shoulder as the cameraman set up his equipment and kept offering helpful hints, driving the poor man crazy.

Natalia Swift was standing by the window. When contacted by Rhys, she'd readily invited them into her home. The polar opposite of her mother's frozen-in-time abode, Natalia's flat was modern, comfortable, and filled with light. Natalia had to be in her mid-seventies, but could easily have passed for a sprightly sixty-year-old. She wore her gray hair curly and long and was dressed in a colorful tunic paired with black leggings and suede boots. An oversized silver-and-turquoise necklace accessorized the tunic and several silver bracelets jangled when she moved her hands. Her makeup was skillfully applied and her large blue eyes sparkled with excitement as she settled in a wing chair, facing the camera.

"Good afternoon, Mrs. Swift," Quinn began once she settled in the other chair and adjusted her microphone.

"Oh no, dear, it's just plain old Miss, and please call me Natalia. No need for such formality."

"Okay, Natalia, as you know, human remains have been found at your parents' home in Belgravia. We've yet to identify the victim, but thanks to forensic analysis we know that the deceased would have been born toward the end of the nineteenth century. He was in his late thirties when he died, which would have been around 1920. Any ideas who he might be?"

Natalia smiled happily. "Not a clue. He must have been there from before my mother's time. It was her house, you know, not my father's. Mother was very attached to it. Said the house gave her visibility."

"In what way?"

"As an immigrant, she believed herself to be invisible. She said that until she became a British citizen, she felt like she had no voice, no rights. She was a person unseen."

"Do you know much of your mother's history?" Quinn asked carefully. If Natalia could confirm what Quinn had already seen, it would make it much easier to bring Valentina's story to the screen.

"Mum led a charmed life until she was eighteen. She was a Russian countess, you know. She was born in St. Petersburg, as it's called now, and brought up in luxury and comfort in a house on the bank of the Neva River. She was engaged to marry the scion of another titled, wealthy family. She'd have had a very different life had the Revolution not destroyed everything she held dear. The night Petrograd fell to the revolutionaries, my mother lost both her father and her fiancé, as well as her mother, in a way. My grandmother never quite recovered from the terror and uncertainty of those events. She withdrew, leaving my mum to become the head of the family."

"Why did your mother choose to immigrate to England when most Russian émigrés were flocking to France?"

"My grandmother had a cousin here, someone she'd been close to when she was a girl. The house in Belgravia actually belonged to him, and to his wife's family before that. Grandmother said that

Dmitri saved them from utter ruin. He was her guardian angel," Natalia recalled with a warm smile.

"In what way?"

"Well, when they finally arrived in England after months of travelling, they were frightened and bedraggled. There was nothing and no one waiting for them here. They spoke practically no English, and had no possessions beyond what they could carry. My mother's fiancé, Count Alexei Petrov his name was, had advised her to sew some valuables into her garments, and it was the money from the sale of those valuables that sustained them during the initial months. Mum got cheated blind, of course, when she tried to sell the jewels, but she got enough to pay for lodgings and food. They were running low on funds when Cousin Dmitri finally found them. He took them in."

"And what happened to Cousin Dmitri?" Quinn asked, all innocence.

"He went missing, actually. Left the house early one morning and vanished into thin air."

Quinn patiently waited for the penny to drop. She could almost hear Rhys's glee as he stood next to Darren, watching the interview.

"It must be him that you found, mustn't it?" Natalia asked, her eyes wide with shock. "Golly. How did he wind up there?"

"That's what we're trying to find out. Do you think your mother knew about the secret room behind the wardrobe?"

"I can't imagine that she did. She would have never left him to rot in that bathtub had she known," Natalia replied, squaring her shoulders and staring angrily into the camera. It was time to take a step back, so Quinn changed tack.

"What was your mother like, Natalia? What type of person was she?"

Natalia shrugged, still a bit defensive. "Mum was quite forward-thinking for her time, but at home she was very proper. Everything had to be just so. Once I got older, we were constantly at odds. Mum's refusal to let go of the old ways drove me mad. It was a new world, a new life, but she clung to her Russian roots, and the morals of the previous century, despite being an advocate for women's rights. I swear, if she could have had me chaperoned every time I left the house, she would have. I don't think Mum ever did an improper thing in her life. It was difficult to imagine her ever acting on impulse or doing anything racy."

"She was married twice. Was she not?"

"Yes. Her first husband was Cousin Dmitri. She said they fell in love once they moved into his house, but she was afraid my grandmother would disapprove, so they married in secret. Mum mourned him for a long time. She married my father after Dmitri was declared legally dead. It took seven years. My dad was Stanley Swift, of Swift Publishing. Mum met him while working as a reporter."

"What do you think happened to Dmitri?"

Natalia giggled like a schoolgirl, her earlier pique forgotten. "How would I know? If the remains are really those of Dmitri Ostrov, well, that just raises a million questions, doesn't it? He didn't seal himself in that bathroom, so someone had to know something."

"Can you conceive of your mother having had anything to do with Dmitri's death?" Quinn asked, keeping her voice soft and neutral.

"No, absolutely not." Natalia shook her head stubbornly. "Mum was the least devious person I've ever known. She just didn't have it in her to hurt anyone."

"How would you feel if you discovered your mother was responsible for her husband's death?" Quinn asked. She had no desire to shatter Natalia's view of her mother, especially without tangible proof, but the story would have to be told, and Valentina would be implicated regardless. The world believed her to be Dmitri's wife, and his remains had been discovered in the house. It wasn't very likely, even without definitive forensic evidence to support the facts, that Valentina would not have known her husband was still in the house, especially since the bathroom had been sealed from the outside.

"Let me tell you something, Dr. Allenby. If my sweet, guileless mother killed her first husband and hid his remains from the world, all I can do is applaud her because if that man drove her to such depths of despair, he deserved whatever he got. My mother and I didn't get on, and I'd be lying if I said we ever understood each other, but there's one thing I can say with certainty. My mother was a woman of great strength and impeccable character. If she was driven to murder, then she must have been dreadfully wronged and most likely abused. I'm sad to say that now I'll never know, since I can no longer ask her, but I would like to see Mum vindicated."

"Do you think Dmitri could have been capable of causing such irreparable damage?" Quinn asked, hoping for family gossip.

"I couldn't say with any certainty, but my aunt Tanya did say there was something off about him. She said he was too smooth, too nice almost, as if there were someone quite different lurking just beneath the surface."

"Were you close with your aunt?"

"She died twelve years ago. Lived to a ripe old age, Tanya did. She was a pistol. Unfortunately, I didn't see her often after I went off to uni. She and her husband lived in the south of France. Mum used to send me and my brother there for the summer when we were kids. Those were enchanted days."

"Your mother never went with you?"

"She only came for a week at the end of August. She had a job and couldn't get the whole summer off."

"She became a journalist, you said?"

"After her husband went missing, she went to school. She wished to become a journalist, but her English wasn't good enough to write for any reputable paper. It took her about five years to get her first piece published, but once she did, she began to make a name for herself. She changed her name to Tina Swift after she married my dad. She said Valentina sounded too foreign."

"And your Uncle Nikolai, what became of him?"

"Uncle Kolya was killed during the Blitz. Didn't get to a shelter in time."

"Was he married? Did he have children?" Quinn asked, seeing that sweet eight-year-old boy in her mind's eye.

"He married and had two sons. His widow eventually remarried and moved to New Zealand. She's gone now, of course, but I keep in contact with my cousins."

"Natalia, do you have any photos or mementoes of your mother we can show on the program? Any letters?"

"I'll have a rummage. I have a box of photos somewhere. Mum wasn't big on writing letters. She had no one to write to, and unlike many women of her time, she wasn't fond of journal keeping. Said nothing worth writing about ever happened to her."

"It would have been wonderful to hear her voice through her letters," Quinn mused as she wrapped up the interview.

"Yes, it would. Knowing what I know now certainly puts a new perspective on Mum's life. I wish I knew what really happened between her and Dmitri."

"So you believe she killed him?"

"He didn't hide his own corpse and block the door to the bathroom, so either he committed suicide and Mum wanted to keep that from the world, or she did away with him and cleverly hid the body. If she did, she committed the perfect crime."

"She certainly did. Do we have your permission to tell her story as it unfolds?"

"Absolutely. And do let me know when the program's going to air. I can't wait," Natalia squealed. "I've always wanted to be on the telly."

"It'll be a while yet. Probably next autumn."

Natalia looked momentarily disappointed but then perked up. "I can wait. I'm just glad to be a part of it. I saw the first episode and it was heartbreaking. What a story."

"Sorry, but I actually have one more question I'd like to ask you," Quinn said.

"Fire away."

"Did your parents have a happy marriage? If you don't mind me asking."

"Oh yes. It was them two against the world. You see, neither family was pleased with the marriage. My father's parents didn't approve of him marrying a Russian, and my grandmother wasn't thrilled with my mother's choice of husband either. She thought Dad was beneath her. But they were both widowed early in life and refused to listen to anyone's opinion. Mum was heartbroken when Dad died. He was only sixty-seven, so she outlived him by quite a few years. She never stopped talking about him. He'd been her best friend, and she was lost without him. I suppose that's why I never married. I never found anyone who could give me what my parents had, and I wasn't willing to settle for less. I had a number of relationships and got to experience motherhood, but I never found anyone I loved enough to spend my life with."

"I appreciate your honesty."

An hour later, Natalia walked them to the door and watched as Quinn and Rhys got into the lift. Darren decided to take the stairs.

"Are you all right?" Quinn asked, turning to face Rhys. He'd been unusually quiet after they wrapped up the interview and accepted Natalia's invitation to stay for tea and scones. Normally, he would have peppered the conversation with questions and observations, drawing Natalia out without her realizing it, and would have extracted a few interesting tidbits to throw into the script, but he'd just sat there, sipping his tea, his plate empty. The Rhys she knew would never pass up a fresh scone.

"I'm fine."

"Are you sure? Have you and Haley made up?"

"Leave it, Quinn," Rhys snapped.

"All right. I'll speak to you later then," Quinn said as they exited into the street. Rhys turned on his heel and strode away without saying goodbye.

FIFTY

Quinn was about to walk into her building when someone called her name. She turned around, startled out of her reverie, to find Drew Camden striding toward her. He looked rather dour and his limp was more pronounced than before, possibly because he'd been rushing to catch up with her.

"Good afternoon," Drew said as he stopped next to Quinn. "Did you not hear me calling you?" he asked irritably.

"Sorry, I was a million miles away. I didn't know you were coming today."

"I was in the neighborhood and thought I'd stop by to give you an update in person."

"Have you got something?" Quinn asked, breathless with anticipation. "Have you found Quentin?"

Drew shook his head. "I haven't. I have a good mate in Border Protection. He ran Quentin's information from the year she left Jesse Holt through the system. She left the U.K. that summer. The next entry for her came up three years later. She flew into London from Paris. After that, the trail goes cold."

"So, what now? How do we find her?"

"I have an idea, but I have to wait and see if it works before telling you about it. I don't want to get your hopes up."

"Drew, how can a person just disappear in this day and age? Would there be no record of her changing her name?"

"Change of name records are not public domain. You wouldn't find it online."

Quinn stared down at the tips of her shoes. She hadn't meant to cry in front of Drew, but bitter tears of disappointment slid down her cheeks. Her sister's absence pained her like a phantom limb. She'd been desperate to find her parents, but that quest had never felt as important or urgent as this need to find her sister.

"Drew, please. I need to find her," she whispered.

Drew placed a sympathetic hand on her shoulder. "Quinn, I'm pursuing every possible lead, but they don't seem to go anywhere. As a private investigator, my resources are limited. My buddies on the force were able to look into Quentin's passport control record, but I can't ask them to do more than that. That would be unlawful use of resources. There's one more thing I'd like to try before admitting failure. Shall I give it a go?"

Quinn nodded. "Yes. Try anything you can think of. I'm not giving up, Drew. I'm not."

"I'll ring you in a few days."

Quinn watched Drew walk away. She felt angry and deflated. Without the cooperation of Quentin's solicitor or her siblings, Drew had hit a dead end in his investigation without getting much further than Quinn and Logan had.

She fished out her mobile and dialed Logan before walking into the building. Logan answered on the first ring. "Hey, Quinny. Any news?"

"The only news is that there's no news. Drew has exhausted his resources, Logan." Quinn sniffed loudly.

"Are you crying?" Logan asked, his voice softening.

"A little," she admitted.

"Look, sis, it seems to me that Quentin doesn't want to be found. Maybe we should respect her wishes and back off. Surely she's heard of our existence by now, either from her solicitor or from her siblings. It's been months, and still we've had no word.

Sometimes you have to let things go, no matter how much it hurts to admit defeat."

"I can't, Logan," Quinn whimpered. "She's our sister—my twin. If she doesn't want to have anything to do with me once we've found her, I will walk away and never bother her again, but I want to see her and speak to her. If only just once. I'll never feel whole until I do."

"I understand," Logan replied. "And I'm here to help in whatever way I can."

Quinn ended the call and walked slowly toward the door of her flat, her shoulders slumped and her head bowed.

FIFTY-ONE

JUNE 1919

London, England

A gentle sun glowed in a cloudless sky, bathing the garden in golden light. It was the kind of day that made a person believe that anything was possible and that nothing terrible would ever happen again. Of course, that was just an illusion, but as Valentina sat back in a lounge chair and turned her face up to the sun, she truly wanted to believe it. After months of oppression, anxiety, and fear for the future, she felt free as a bird. She still couldn't quite believe her mad idea had worked. No one had questioned her marriage to Dmitri Ostrov. In fact, everyone had offered their condolences on the loss of her husband, even Father Mikhail, who'd been only too happy to provide a marriage certificate for her solicitor, Mr. Gravelle.

In the past two weeks, Mr. Gravelle had initiated an application for citizenship, since, as the wife of a British subject, Valentina could now apply, and had been able to obtain access to Dmitri's bank accounts, through which he'd been able to track Dmitri's business activities. Mr. Gravelle had contacted the managers of the textile factory in Lancashire, the warehouse Dmitri owned at Victoria Dock, the Falmouth Arms Hotel, and the boxing club

Dmitri frequented to advise them of Dmitri's disappearance and his wife's new role as acting director. Valentina had had no idea Dmitri had his fingers in so many pots, and the knowledge that he hadn't exactly been strapped for cash made her blood boil. Perhaps he'd simply enjoyed exercising his power over helpless women, and she strongly suspected that his wife Emily had been one of them. The paperwork stored in the safe showed that all the holdings except the boxing club had passed to Dmitri from Emily's father upon his death.

Valentina couldn't sell any of the businesses without Dmitri's signature or a valid death certificate, but she could take up the reins until his death was legalized. She had much to learn, but she had all the time in the world, and she would hire a competent man to help her manage all of Dmitri's holdings.

Valentina closed her eyes and sank deeper into the chair. What utter bliss. Especially since the house was quiet. Elena, Tanya, and Kolya had gone off to the zoological garden, per Kolya's request, but Valentina had pleaded a headache and remained at home. She needed a little time alone to gather her thoughts and try to make peace with her new reality. Deep down, she still couldn't believe she'd taken a man's life, but the night Dmitri had died had taken on the quality of a fragmented dream that one recalled upon waking, grateful that the warm light of day had come to chase away the shadows of the nightmare. Now that the "truth" was out, everyone treated her as if she were a fragile glass ornament that might break from excessive handling. Forced to play the part of the grieving widow, she was starting to believe it herself and enjoy the role. It was easier than dealing with the hideous truth of what she'd done and asking herself over and over if there was something she might have done to avoid the disastrous events that had led her to murder.

Valentina must have drifted off in the warm sunshine, but woke with a start when a shadow loomed over her.

"Sorry to wake you, Mrs. Ostrov, but there's a gentleman to see you," Mrs. Nemirovsky announced in gentle tones. "He's most insistent."

"Show him into the parlor. I'll be right in."

Valentina took a moment to collect herself. She wasn't expecting anyone, but she wasn't overly worried. Mrs. Nemirovsky had met Detective Cooper and his associates. If the caller was from the police, she would have said so. This had to be a social call, perhaps another acquaintance come to offer condolences. Dmitri had been well-known in the quickly growing Russian community, and well-liked, at least by those he hadn't victimized.

Valentina smoothed back her hair and walked slowly toward the parlor. She'd get rid of the visitor quickly and go back out to the garden. She was no longer sleepy, but an hour of peaceful reading before the rest of the family came home would be most welcome. Perhaps she'd even have tea *al fresco*, all by herself. She was the mistress of the house now; she could do what she pleased.

The man stood with his back to her, gazing out the window into the street, his hands clasped behind his back. Valentina saw the tension in his posture, the rigid set of his shoulders, feet set apart, as if to maintain a better balance. There was something familiar about the set of his head and his defiant stance.

"Good afternoon," she said softly, so as not to startle him.

He turned around and the world stopped. Their gazes met across the room, his eyes full of uncertainty and longing. He took a step forward, then stopped, as though unsure what to do. Reeling with shock and disbelief, she grabbed onto the back of a settee for support. And then she was rushing toward him and his arms encircled her waist as she buried her face in his shoulder, quaking with violent sobs.

"Oh, dear God, Alyosha, how is this possible?"

"Valya, my love, I've been searching for you for over a year," he whispered into her hair. "I thought I'd lost you for good."

"How are you alive? I saw that bayonet go right through you. Nyanushka said you were dead," Valentina sobbed. "I would have never left Petrograd had I known you were still alive."

She finally let go of Alexei and stood back, drinking him in. He looked the same, but completely different. He'd matured, aged even. Strands of gray silvered his blond hair and there were fine lines around his eyes. They were still warm and filled with good humor, but now there was also pain. He'd suffered. He'd lost.

"What of your family, Alyosha?"

"My mother died on the way to France. She suffered a heart attack. My father and sister are all right. They made it to my aunt's house and remained there until I was able to join them."

"Alyosha, how? How did you survive?"

Valentina led him to the settee. He sat down and reached for her hands, as if loath to let go of her.

"I was very lucky, Valya. The bayonet pierced my lung but missed my heart. A tiny bit to the left and I would have died that day. My lung had collapsed and I lost a lot of blood. I was in and out of consciousness that night, and for most of the following day."

"But Nyanushka told us you died," Valentina cried. "Why did she lie?"

"Because I asked her to, Valya. I begged her to lie. Had she told you I was still alive, you would have remained in Petrograd to nurse me, and your family wouldn't have left without you. After I saw what happened to your father, I couldn't detain you. You were in terrible danger, as were my parents and sister. If I died of my wounds, they'd already be in mourning for me, and if I lived, I'd come and find you all. It took me several months to recover. Nyanushka called for a doctor after you left and he remained by my side for three days. He saved me. Nyanushka did the rest. She looked after me while I convalesced. She nursed me back to health. I wrote to my aunt as soon as I was able to, so my father and sister found out I was alive as soon as they arrived in Paris. They inquired after you every time a new Russian émigré arrived in Paris. No one knew what had become of you."

"Alyosha, how did you find me?" Valentina asked. Her heart was thudding in her chest, her head throbbing with a sudden headache. The joy and tranquility of a few moments ago was gone. She could barely breathe.

"An acquaintance received a letter from a cousin in London,

who wrote that a wealthy Russian industrialist had gone missing. She mentioned your mother's name. Valya, why didn't you go to my aunt like we discussed? Why did you come here to London?" Alexei exclaimed.

"I thought you were gone. There was no longer any point in going to your aunt's house to wait for you, was there? My mother wished to come here, to her cousin. He took us in and cared for us. We might have perished without him."

"And now he's gone missing?"

Valentina nodded miserably. "We don't know what's happened to him." She hated lying to Alexei, but she could hardly tell him the truth of what had happened. The lie had taken on a life of its own and would have to run its natural course.

"I'm so sorry, Valya. It must be a difficult time for you all, especially for your mother. To think that a man who'd been so kind to you just vanished. Have the police found nothing?"

"Not a trace."

Alexei shook his head. "I wish I'd had a chance to meet him, to thank him for looking after you all." He lifted her face with his finger and gazed deep into her eyes. "We can be married now, Valya. We can finally begin our life together."

Tears of heartbreak slid down Valentina's cheeks. "Alyosha, I'm already married. I married Dmitri six months ago."

"No!" Alexei shook his head. "No."

"I thought you were dead," she exclaimed.

"Did you love him?" Alexei whispered urgently. "Did you truly love him?"

"No, of course not, but I cared for him. I respected him. I felt indebted to him," she replied, inwardly cringing at her lies. "He offered security for me and my family."

"He's gone now, Valya. We can still make a life together."

"Alyosha, Dmitri may still come back, and even if he doesn't, it will take seven years for the court to declare him legally deceased. I will remain his wife until then."

"I'll wait. I'll wait forever if I have to."

Alexei's lips captured hers and she gave herself up to the kiss, desperate to feel something other than shame and disgust. Alexei pulled her close. He felt so solid, so strong. All she wanted was to be with him, now, today, forever. She wanted him more than she'd ever wanted anything in her life. She grabbed his hand and pulled him to his feet. Her gaze was full of purpose as she moved toward the door of the parlor, fully intending to take him upstairs, when there was an ear-piercing shriek.

Tanya had just walked in through the front door. Her hand was pressed to her mouth in shock, her eyes glowing with joy. She tossed her hat onto the console table and rushed forward, nearly knocking Alexei off his feet as she wrapped her arms around his waist.

"Oh, God, Alyosha. You're alive. You're alive!" she cried. "Mama, come see who's here. Kolya, hurry!"

Alexei's eyes sought Valentina's over Tanya's head. He'd understood only too well what she'd intended, and his soul reached out to her, pleading with her not to change her mind.

"Where are you staying, Alyosha?" Valentina asked once Elena and Tanya finally calmed down long enough to go upstairs to change. Kolya remained by Alexei's side, gazing up at him adoringly.

"I don't know yet. I came straight here after I was given your address at the church."

"Go to the Falmouth Arms Hotel. I'll give you the address. I own it. I'll ring the manager and tell him to prepare a room for you."

"Will you come?" Alexei whispered.

"Yes."

FIFTY-TWO

Valentina thought she'd spend the rest of the day in an agony of indecision, but there was nothing to decide. Alexei was alive. He was in London. He had found her, and she'd be damned if she'd deny herself the joy of loving him. Tomorrow, she'd think about the consequences of her actions and start to doubt the wisdom of what she'd done, but tonight was hers, and she would take full advantage of her hard-won freedom.

The evening wore on, the long hours an eternity of breathless anticipation. It seemed that Elena and the children would never retire, but they went up at last, tired after a day filled with excitement. Valentina didn't bother to change. She couldn't bear to waste another moment on mindless ritual. Instead, she grabbed her bag and slipped out the door into the balmy night. The moon was nearly full in a cloudless sky that was a study in violet and lavender. The air was heavy with the smell of honeysuckle and roses, which grew in wild profusion at the front of the house. Valentina hailed a taxi and got in, ignoring the curious stare of the driver, who probably didn't see too many well-bred young ladies going out on their own after dark.

The ride seemed eternal. Valentina made a pretense of looking out the window, but all she saw was Alexei's beloved face, and her heart hammered a joyful melody as she drew closer to the hotel. That place was associated with such awful memories. She'd faced degradation, humiliation, and indifference within its walls, but everything was about to change. Alexei's presence would wipe out the past and usher in a new beginning. She'd not only been spared the noose but given a new lease on life, a new hope for the future. God had forgiven her, and it was a heady feeling. It was as if an unbearable weight had been lifted off her shoulders and suddenly she could stand up straight again, and look the world in the eye without being weighed down by crippling shame and regret.

She paid the taxi driver and was out the door before he could even offer to give her change. She ignored the raised eyebrows of the night clerk and asked for Alexei's room.

"Madam, you can't go up," the clerk said, shocked by her brazen behavior. He was new. He had no idea. The night concierge who'd witnessed her degradation had been dismissed with a glowing reference and a full month's severance pay.

"I can and I will. I own this hotel," Valentina replied and turned on her heel. She took the stairs two at a time, a terribly unladylike thing to do, she reflected, as she patted her hair into place before knocking on the door. Thankfully, it wasn't one of the rooms she'd been in before. She'd asked the manager to give Alexei the best room, not one of the smaller, dingier rooms reserved for Dmitri's less savory activities. The knock sounded unnaturally loud in the silence of the corridor. And then she heard his footsteps, walking briskly toward the door.

Alexei opened the door and smiled, his relief evident. "I wasn't sure you'd come."

"I was," she replied, and then she was in his arms, kissing him and tearing at the buttons of his waistcoat, desperate to touch the hot skin beneath his starched shirt. Alexei pulled at his tie as she threw her hat on the bureau. The years of loneliness fell away, but not the experience they'd gained during their time of separation. They were adults now, and neither bothered to pretend there'd been no others. Their kisses weren't shy and gentle; they were hungry, demanding, and filled with purpose. Alexei's fingers flew over the buttons of her dress, and it fell to the floor, pooling around her ankles, quickly followed by her corset and bloomers. Valentina yanked at Alexei's belt buckle with trembling hands, for once eager to get to the business at hand. She undid the buttons of his fly and pushed his trousers down over his hips, desperate to remove the final barriers between them.

Alexei's gaze clouded with desire as he drank her in. She'd never seen a man look at her that way. There'd been lust, and need, but never love, never this speechless reverence. He stood in front of her, naked and ready. Valentina took him by the hand and pulled him toward the bed, silently letting him know that she knew what she was about and wouldn't change her mind.

He pushed her down, and she spread her legs willingly, guiding him inside with an urgency she hadn't known she was capable of. She cried out as their bodies finally came together after years of longing, the past few months falling away like the dead skin of a snake as it shed. The men she'd been forced to service had disappeared, the memory of them erased as Alexei moved deep inside her, bringing her to heights of pleasure she hadn't thought were possible. She moved her hips against him, calling out his name as he taught her the meaning of love and brought her to her first orgasm.

She clung to him long after their desire was sated, needing to feel his solid presence. He wasn't a dream, a delusion caused by her loneliness and fear. He was real. He was back. And he still loved her. Valentina traced the jagged outline of the scar on his chest. It had healed, but there was still a ropey mark left by the sharp blade of the bayonet.

"You're alive," she whispered, filled with wonder. "You're really alive."

"I'm alive and I'm here," Alexei replied. He took her hand away from the scar and kissed her fingers, one by one, then moved to her wrist. The skin was so sensitive, she gasped when his lips brushed across it. "I'll never leave you again, Valya."

Valentina touched his cheek. His skin was flushed and his eyes were heavy with fatigue. "When did you last sleep, Alyosha?"

"Not for a while," he replied.

"Then go to sleep. I'll be here when you wake up."

"Will you really?" Alexei asked, smiling into her eyes. "I dreamed of waking up next to you so many times, and then I awoke to find myself alone, and it was like losing you all over again."

"I'll be here," she replied.

"Won't you be missed?"

"I'll leave early in the morning and get home before the housekeeper arrives. I won't give up this night with you."

Alexei pulled Valentina close and she rested her cheek against his chest and slid her leg between his. They fit perfectly together, like two pieces of a puzzle finally clicking into place. *So this is what it's like to share a bed with someone you love*, she mused as she began to drift off to sleep. To her, falling asleep in the arms of a man was the ultimate act of trust. Knowing that she was safe and cherished and had nothing to fear was more intimate than any lovemaking could ever be.

Morning came all too soon and Valentina disentangled herself from Alexei and got up. Her hair tumbled down her back and her skin was flushed from the warmth of his body. She was naked, but she felt no shame as she stood before the bed, smiling down at him.

"You are so beautiful," Alexei whispered.

"So are you."

"Come back here."

She had to get dressed and get home before Mrs. Nemirovsky realized she'd been gone all night, but couldn't find the strength to leave. She pulled back the covers and admired Alexei's body, so strong and lean, and pulsing with life. She straddled him, taking him into her body with one sure stroke. He cupped her breasts as she leaned down to kiss him, all the while moving against him in a rhythm as old as time. Alexei's hands slid down her body and grabbed her hips as he took control and thrust deep into her body. Valentina collapsed on top of him, her insides still quivering as she began to spiral back to Earth and reality.

"I have to go," she whispered. It was fully light out now, and the sound of morning traffic had begun to replace the peaceful silence of the night. "Come for lunch."

"When can we tell your family about our plans?" Alexei asked as he watched her dress.

"What *are* our plans?" Valentina asked as she did up the buttons of her dress with practiced fingers. She hadn't thought beyond last night, but now that the harsh glare of a new day filtered through the net curtains, she was suddenly overcome with uncertainty.

"To be together," Alexei replied.

"Alyosha, I can't openly be with you. I'm a married woman. My husband might still turn up, and if he doesn't, I must observe a period of mourning." She tried not to cringe as she uttered the words. Her "husband" was rotting in his bathtub, his body being slowly devoured by lye. She hated Dmitri with every fiber of her being and rejoiced in his death, but she was now bound to him more securely than if she'd actually married him. She could never leave his house. The truth could still be discovered at any time and she had to safeguard her secret, never, ever allowing the mask to slip for fear of giving herself away.

"Come back to Paris with me."

Valentina shook her head. "I must remain here in case Dmitri returns."

"You sound as if you're hoping for that," Alexei snapped. His eyes brimmed with pain as he studied her face. "You did love him."

Valentina shook her head. "Alyosha, I can't pretend he never existed and erase him from my past," she argued, knowing full well that was exactly what she'd done. "I must wait until a year has passed, at the very least."

"Then we'll wait together."

"Yes. We will wait."

FIFTY-THREE
DECEMBER 2014

London, England

With shaking hands, Quinn set aside the Fabergé necklace and wiped her damp cheeks. Alexei coming back from the dead was a development she hadn't anticipated, and witnessing the tender reunion between Valentina and her love had utterly demolished the fragile emotional barriers Quinn had erected to keep Valentina's feelings separate from her own. Valentina had murdered a man in cold blood, but Quinn couldn't find it in her heart to condemn her, and secretly rooted for Valentina to get away with murder and find happiness. But interviewing Natalia had generated more questions than answers. She'd never mentioned Alexei's return, and Valentina's marriage to Stanley Swift had taken place seven years after Dmitri's death, according to the copy of the marriage certificate Quinn had been able to obtain over the weekend, along with newspaper clippings describing his disappearance and reporting on the fruitless investigation. So, what in the world had happened between Alexei's arrival in London and Valentina's marriage to Swift? And who was her son's father?

Quinn was jerked out of her reverie by the ringing of her

mobile. Rhys's office number appeared on the screen. She picked up the phone. "Hi, Rhys."

"Dr. Allenby, it's Rhiannan Makely, Mr. Morgan's PA. I was wondering if he might be with you." Rhiannan sounded nervous and apologetic, but there was something else in her tone—a hint of panic.

"No, he isn't. I haven't seen him or spoken to him since Thursday. Is something wrong, Rhiannan?"

"I don't know. Mr. Morgan had several meetings scheduled for this morning, but I can't raise him on his mobile, and he's not responding to texts or emails. He's never just not shown up, Dr. Allenby. It's not like him."

"Have you tried Haley? He's probably with her."

Rhiannan's anxiety was almost palpable. "Her phone is switched off. I'm worried something's happened."

"I'll go to his house and see if he's all right."

"Oh, would you? I'd be most grateful. I can't leave the office, the phone is ringing off the hook today. It's probably nothing and I'm just being silly," Rhiannan said. "I do tend to overreact. He's just normally so punctual. I bet he'll stroll in any minute with a tin of freshly baked muffins and chastise me for bothering you," she added tearfully. "He always brings me treats. He's so considerate."

Oh, Rhys, you muffin bandit! Quinn's lips twitched with a smile of amusement. She hadn't realized until that moment that Rhiannan had a crush on Rhys, her feelings unwittingly encouraged with a few freshly baked scones and Rhys's dazzling smile. Quinn often forgot just how handsome Rhys was, and how charming he could be. Blond, blue-eyed, and at least fifteen years his junior, Rhiannan was a lovely woman whose sweet manner and adoring looks weren't lost on Rhys. He'd never been as charming or solicitous to his previous PA, Denise, who'd been grumpy and middle-aged. Rhys had always treated Denise with the utmost respect, but hadn't shed any tears when she'd decided she'd had enough of his artistic temperament and asked for a transfer to another department.

"You're not being silly, and I'm glad you called me. I'll ring you as soon as I know anything."

"Thank you, Dr. Allenby. You're very kind."

Quinn disconnected the call and went into the kitchen. Gabe was seated at the table, his eyes glued to the screen of his laptop. Gabe was already off for Christmas break, and they would be leaving for Berwick on Saturday, once Emma's school let out for the holidays on December 22.

"What are you doing?" Quinn asked.

"Just going over the roster for next term. With Luke gone, I'm one professor short, so someone will have to pick up some additional classes until I can find a replacement."

"Gabe, I need to step out for an hour. There's milk for Alex in the fridge."

"Everything all right?"

"Rhys's PA just called. She's worried. Rhys missed his meetings this morning and isn't answering his mobile."

"That's not like him," Gabe replied, looking concerned. "Shall I come with you?"

"There's no need. I should be back in time for lunch."

"All right. Regards to Rhys," Gabe said, his gaze already sliding back to the screen.

A taxi deposited Quinn in front of Rhys's address a short while later. He occupied the two top floors of a terrace house in Mayfair. There was a sitting tenant downstairs who had come with the house when Rhys purchased it about a year ago. Mary Kent, whom Quinn had met when Rhys invited her and Gabe for dinner one night, was an elderly lady who'd lived in the flat for over forty years. She treated Rhys as if he were her long-lost son, which exasperated him at times. He was a private person and didn't like anyone meddling in his affairs, but the widowed Mrs. Kent reminded him of his own mother, so he bit his tongue and allowed her to fuss over him.

Quinn walked up to the door and rang the bell. There was no answer. She knocked, using the old-fashioned knocker that had come with the house. The sound reverberated through the empty foyer, but didn't raise anyone. Quinn pulled out her mobile and selected Rhys's mobile number. The phone rang somewhere inside the house, the distinctly audible ringtone suggesting that the mobile had been left close to an open window. Rhys never left the house without his phone, so he had to be at home. Something wasn't right. Quinn knocked again. Perhaps he was asleep and couldn't hear the knocking, but Rhys had mentioned more than once that he was a light sleeper. All this banging would have woken him by now.

Quinn descended the stairs and rang Mrs. Kent's bell. The woman answered the door a few moments later. "Can I help you?"

"Mrs. Kent, I'm sorry to bother you, but I think something is wrong. Rhys missed several meetings this morning and he's not answering his mobile. I can hear it ringing inside, but he's not answering the door. I think he might be ill. Would you know if he keeps a spare key somewhere?"

Mrs. Kent looked at Quinn thoughtfully, appearing torn between concern and wariness. She clearly didn't recall meeting Quinn.

"Mrs. Kent, we've met before. I'm Dr. Quinn Allenby. I work with Rhys."

Mrs. Kent suddenly brightened. "Are you the Dr. Allenby from the telly? *Echoes from the Past*? Rhys is so proud of that program. He told me all about it when he invited me in for tea. And Haley was wonderful in the first episode, playing Elise. That's how they got together, you know, Rhys and Haley. He auditioned her for the part," Mrs. Kent added, lowering her voice as if the information were confidential.

"Mrs. Kent, does Rhys keep a spare key somewhere?" Quinn asked again, her anxiety mounting.

"I have a spare. He gave it to me before Haley moved in. He locked himself out after he first moved in, poor dear, and had to call a locksmith. They charge a fortune, those scoundrels. A hundred pounds to open a door. Can you imagine? Highway robbery is what that is. So Rhys gave me a key. He knows I hardly go out, so I'm here if he needs me. Here, let me fetch it."

Mrs. Kent produced a key and handed it to Quinn. "You bring it right back. You hear? He entrusted it to me, and I want it back."

"Would you like to come with me?"

"No, you go ahead. I don't feel right traipsing through his flat when he's not there. And he's not there; I'm sure of it. I haven't heard footsteps since last night. He always comes down around seven and puts the kettle on. Creature of habit, he is."

"I'll bring this right back," Quinn replied and made for the stairs. She let herself into the house and called out Rhys's name. Her voice echoed through the house, but there was no response. She looked around. The place was a mess. The kitchen cupboards were open, there were dirty dishes in the sink, and there was broken glass on the floor, the shards lying in a puddle of amber-colored liquid. Quinn peeked into the front room, but it was deserted. She slowly made her way upstairs. "Rhys!" she called out. "Rhys, it's Quinn."

All she heard was silence. The upper floor contained a bath, two bedrooms, and Rhys's study. His mobile lay on his desk, next to his laptop. His keys were next to the phone, so he was definitely at home. The door to the master bedroom was closed. Quinn knocked loudly. "Rhys, it's Quinn. I'm coming in."

There was no answer, so she slowly pushed the door open. Sunlight streamed through the net curtains, casting slanted rays onto the walls, which were hung with black-and-white prints. The room was minimalist and masculine, decorated in shades of gray and blue. The focal point was the low platform bed, on which Rhys lay sprawled on his back, his eyes closed and his hair tousled. Thick auburn stubble shadowed his face, which was turned away from the door. He wore flannel pajama bottoms and a navy blue T-shirt. His bare feet hung off the bed.

Quinn came closer. At first glance, Rhys appeared to be asleep, but his skin looked gray, the unnatural color accentuated by the crisp whiteness of the sheets. His right arm lay across the bed, an empty bottle of Scotch next to his hand, as if it had slipped from his grasp when he dozed off. His other arm was folded across his stomach. There was an open bottle of sleeping pills on the bedside table.

"Rhys!" Quinn cried. "Rhys, wake up."

She gently slapped his face in an effort to rouse him, but she knew he wouldn't come to even as she called out to him. His skin was cold to the touch and his face was perfectly still, and lifeless. She grabbed his wrist and felt for a pulse. It was faint, but it was still there. Quinn fumbled for her mobile and rang for an ambulance.

"Please hurry," she pleaded with the dispatcher.

"Is Rhys all right?" Mrs. Kent asked as she shuffled into the room, out of breath from climbing the stairs. "Good God!" she exclaimed when she saw Rhys's still form on the bed. "Is he...?"

"He's alive. Emergency Services are on their way." Quinn needed to stay strong for Rhys, but her voice shook and her eyes swam with tears. She thought her legs might give out, so she sat down on a padded leather bench at the foot of the bed. She leaned in and clasped Rhys's outstretched hand. "Hold on. Please," she whispered.

"What's driven him to this?" Mrs. Kent cried as she wrung her hands in anguish. "He was so happy, so excited about the coming baby. Where's Haley?" she asked, looking around. Quinn followed her gaze to the open wardrobe. Empty hangers filled half the space. There were no feminine items on the bureau, not even a hairbrush or face cream. Haley was gone. She'd left.

"Oh, Rhys," Quinn whispered. His fingers were icy against her warm palm. "Hold on," she begged. Hot, salty tears slid down her cheeks and into her mouth. She wiped them away with her sleeve, not caring if she ruined her coat. She cared for this man, cared a lot. He'd said once that he wished she'd been his daughter, and to some degree she'd wished he'd been her father. They had a connection, an understanding that had come naturally and unexpectedly and had surprised them both. "Rhys, I love you," Quinn whispered. "Don't leave me."

Mrs. Kent glared at her, as though assuming there was something sexual between Rhys and Quinn. *So that's why Haley left,* her accusing stare seemed to say. *This is your fault.*

Quinn was about to explain when she heard the paramedics downstairs. "Up here," she called out as she rushed toward the door. She wished Mrs. Kent would leave. She didn't want her to see Rhys helpless and broken. Quinn pressed the key into the woman's hand and turned away, her undivided attention on Rhys.

"Step aside, please," the paramedics ordered as they entered the room. "Are you his wife?"

"No, I'm his friend," Quinn replied. "I think he's taken sleeping tablets and Scotch."

"Has he done anything like this before?"

"Not that I know of."

"Was he depressed?"

"Possibly," Quinn said, unsure what had happened with Haley.

"Is this a suicide attempt?" the female paramedic asked as she began to check Rhys's vital signs.

"I don't know."

Quinn watched the paramedics work on Rhys. They hooked him up to an IV and placed an oxygen mask over his face before moving him onto a stretcher. Rhys was like a rag doll, his limbs limp and lifeless, his face a death mask. "I'm coming with him to the hospital."

"All right, love," the male paramedic said with a nod. "Let's go."

Quinn followed the paramedics as they carried Rhys down the stairs. Mrs. Kent brought up the rear, sniffling loudly as she went. "Where are you taking him? Which hospital?" she asked. "I'll call for an update."

"University College Hospital," the woman replied briskly. "They won't give you any information unless you're a relative."

"I'll ring you, Mrs. Kent," Quinn promised. "Does Rhys have your number in his contacts?"

"Yes, he does."

Quinn raced back upstairs and grabbed Rhys's phone and keys. He'd need them when he was released. *If* he was released. She shut down the awful thought and followed the paramedics to the waiting ambulance.

"Is it all right if I hold his hand?" Quinn asked as she sat down next to Rhys.

"Of course. Let him know you're here," the male paramedic said. "They always know, even when they're unconscious. The mind is a marvelous thing."

"Yes, it is." Quinn reached for Rhys's hand and enveloped it in her own. "Rhys, I'm here," she whispered as she leaned close to him. "I'm going to stay with you until you're all better, and then I'm going to kick you into the middle of next week, you thoughtless moron," she said, borrowing an expression from Seth. It was easier to be angry than frightened, and she was frightened. Rhys hadn't stirred since she'd found him, and his breathing was ragged and shallow, even with the oxygen mask.

The woman gave Quinn a filthy look, but she didn't care. She was on a roll. "How could you do such a thing?" she raged. "How could you?" Tears were streaming down her face again, and she angrily wiped them away. "You're not going anywhere. You hear me?"

Quinn felt some measure of relief when she felt the life-affirming pressure of Rhys's fingers around her own and saw his lips twitch. He'd heard her.

FIFTY-FOUR

"You look like hell," Quinn said as she pulled a chair closer to Rhys's bed.

"I feel like hell. They pumped my stomach." Even though Rhys's voice was hoarse from having a tube down his throat, he still managed to sound peevish. He really did look awful. His skin was a unique shade of gray-green, and his eyes were bloodshot and puffy. He was still hooked up to an IV and the polka-dot hospital gown wasn't doing him any favors.

"Rhys, how could you?" Quinn asked gently. "If I hadn't found you..."

"I wasn't trying to top myself, if that's what you're thinking," Rhys protested. "Please tell me you didn't tell Rhiannan. I don't want anyone at the office to know."

"I told her you're ill and will ring her tomorrow."

Rhys nodded his thanks.

"How about a little juice?" Quinn held up a box of apple juice to Rhys's lips, and he obediently took a long pull. "Rhys, where's Haley?"

"Gone."

Quinn didn't persist. If he wanted to tell her what had happened, he would.

Rhys let out a painful breath and sat up a little, his gaze fixed on the window behind Quinn. If he was trying to regain his composure, he failed utterly. Silent tears slid down his cheeks and he pressed the heels of his palms to his eyes, rubbing them angrily.

"Rhys," Quinn began, but he shook his head, not ready to talk.

They remained like that for a few minutes, a silent tableau of a grieving man and an anxious woman. Rhys finally sniffed and removed the hands from his face. He looked miserable, but at least he was no longer crying.

"I'm sorry," he mumbled.

"You have nothing to be sorry for."

"I don't normally go to pieces in front of people."

"No, you don't."

Rhys used the back of his hand to wipe his moist cheeks. "Haley miscarried on Friday. She was jogging when she began to bleed, and then the pains came. A kind passerby called an ambulance, so she got to the hospital quickly, but it was too late. By the time I got there the baby was gone. Incinerated."

"Incinerated?"

"That's what Haley decided. She didn't want to name her or even bury her. She wanted her incinerated, like a piece of rubbish."

"Oh, Rhys."

Rhys rubbed his eyes again. He looked so heartbroken, Quinn wanted to gather him into her arms and hold him, but thought the gesture might embarrass him. "When we returned home from the hospital, she said she was leaving."

"Rhys, she was in shock. She wasn't thinking clearly. She'll come back. You can try again, in time."

Rhys shook his head and sniffled loudly. "She's not coming back, Quinn. She said she was glad the baby was gone. She'd realized she wasn't ready to be a mother, and she certainly didn't want me for her child's father. She said I'm old-fashioned and controlling and all I wanted was a millennial version of my own mother, who'd put all her dreams on hold to wipe snotty noses and change nappies."

"She was just lashing out," Quinn replied.

Rhys bowed his head, staring at his IV needle as if it might have all the answers. "She said she wasn't even sure the baby was mine," he confessed. He tried to sound matter-of-fact but couldn't mask the unbearable pain behind the words. He looked like he was about to cry again. "She thought I'd give the child a better life than the other guy, who's a bartender or some such. She never loved me, Quinn."

"Rhys..."

"Please don't say anything. I've heard it all from my mother and my brother. And even from Rhiannan, who tried to warn me about Haley."

"Rhys, the only thing I'm going to say is that I'm here for you. Whatever you need, all you have to do is ask."

Rhys reached out and took Quinn's hand. "I couldn't sleep. My mind kept going over everything, searching for signs I'd missed. Imagining what life would have been like had it all turned out differently. I was only trying to get some sleep."

Quinn nodded. "I understand."

"I never meant to..."

"I know."

"I'd never felt so alone. There was no one I could confide in, no one I could call," Rhys confessed. "I didn't want to upset my mum, and Owain would have said, 'I told you so.' He's good at that. Got to love older brothers."

"You could have called me." Quinn moved from the chair to Rhys's bed and wedged herself in next to him. She wrapped her arm around him, and he rested his head on her shoulder. She didn't say anything, but just held him for a long time, allowing him to grieve.

"She was supposed to come home with me for Christmas, to meet my family," Rhys finally said.

"Come to Berwick with us. We'll have a lovely, peaceful Christmas. I won't allow you to be on your own."

Rhys shook his head. "Thank you, but I already told my mum

I'm coming home. She's expecting me. Don't worry; she'll set me to rights. She'll lock me in the kitchen and make me bake mince pies for the whole town. And if that doesn't do it, after spending a week with my nieces and nephews, I'll remember that kids are annoying brats and I've had a lucky escape."

"I can always lend you a squalling infant for a few hours."

Rhys smiled. "I knew I could count on you."

"Always."

"Quinn, thank you."

"For what?"

"For caring. Now, go home to your children. I'll be all right."

"Is there anyone you'd like me to call?"

Rhys shook his head. "I'd rather keep this little episode to myself, if it's all the same to you."

"Just text Rhiannan and tell her you're on the mend. That poor woman is utterly besotted with you."

"She can't help herself, I suppose. I'm quite the catch," he added with a sad little grin. "I do like her. Too bad it's no longer acceptable to shag one's secretary."

"Political correctness is a bitch," Quinn agreed, getting a chuckle out of Rhys. This was the old Rhys, the one she knew and loved. She gave him a motherly kiss on the forehead. "I'll see you later. Ring me if you need anything."

"Will do."

FIFTY-FIVE

JULY 1919

London, England

The clock in the corridor struck the midnight hour, but sleep wouldn't come. That clock taunted her every night, reminding her that no amount of time would erase the past. Valentina curled into a ball and hugged her knees to her chest. The euphoria of being with Alexei had worn off, leaving behind crushing guilt and crippling doubt. How could she build a life with him after everything that had happened? She was a harlot and a murderess, not to mention a liar and a fraud. She was no longer the girl Alexei had fallen in love with, nor was she the woman he believed her to be. What if the truth came out? Alexei would be crushed, but his inbred sense of honor would prevent him from leaving her.

He'd remain by her side and make her his wife when the time came, but how would he really feel about her? Would he still respect and cherish her, or would he cringe with shame every time she walked into the room? Would he still desire her, or be forever repelled by the knowledge of those who'd come before him? She could never completely erase the memory of those men, no matter how hard she tried. Had they been men chosen and loved by her, she might have been able to justify her immoral deeds, but having been repeatedly violated and used regardless of her needs or feelings, she was forever tainted and forever broken by what she'd been driven to do to save herself and Tanya.

Perhaps he'll forgive me if I tell him the truth, Valentina thought but instantly rejected the idea. She could never bring herself to tell Alexei she'd whored for Dmitri, then killed him in cold blood, doused his corpse with lye, and hidden it in his own house. And if that wasn't bad enough, she'd lied to the police and desecrated a church register, adding a fraudulent marriage in order to claim Dmitri's assets. Put like that, she fit the profile of some criminal mastermind, conjured up by the likes of Arthur Conan Doyle. If the truth ever came out, she'd be branded a madwoman. The newspapers would paint her as someone degenerate and deranged, a natural born sinner whose debt to society could only be paid by her gruesome death. Valentina's hand automatically went to her neck. She could almost feel the rough hemp of the rope. No, she could never tell Alexei the truth, nor could she take the chance of him finding out.

Bitter tears of heartbreak slid down her cheeks. She could never marry Alexei, not even after Dmitri was declared legally dead. Nor could she ever leave this house. She'd have to spend the rest of her days protecting her secret and keeping her neck out of the noose. As long as Mayhew, Murdoch, and Gleason were out there, there was someone who could expose her. If the police found out about the prostitution, they'd have grounds to dig deeper, and then her whole story would unravel. Granted, the men had nothing to gain by coming forward, especially since they were all married, with children, but they had the power to hurt her, and they knew it.

You have the power to hurt them as well, Valentina thought.

But who will believe you? a tiny voice responded. *They are respectable businessmen, British citizens, beloved husbands and fathers. You are nothing, no one. You are a refugee. A foreigner. Someone who's viewed with suspicion and doubt. You are despised at worst, invisible at best.*

Valentina wiped the tears away again and again, but they kept coming, sliding down her cheeks as her heart caught up to her mind. Her decision was made. She would tell Alexei she couldn't marry him and that he should return to Paris. There were countless Russian émigrés in Paris—young, beautiful, pure young women who'd like nothing more than to give him their love and respect. She loved him too much to ruin his life and bring disgrace onto what was left of his family. And she was too fragile to risk him finding out the truth and steeling his heart against her, living with her in shame and regret because divorce wasn't an option. Valentina covered her head with her arms and made herself as small as humanly possible, wishing she could simply disappear. What she'd done was a stain that could never be erased, a land mine that would explode if she stepped off it.

FIFTY-SIX
DECEMBER 2014

London, England

Rhys turned in surprise when Quinn entered his hospital room. He was already dressed in his own clothes, ready to be discharged. He still looked pale and sick, but there was no longer any reason to keep him. Mrs. Kent had informed Quinn that she'd brought him some clothes and shoes, since he could hardly go home barefoot, wearing nothing but pajama bottoms and a T-shirt, but she couldn't visit him today since she had a doctor's appointment.

"What are you doing here?" Rhys asked. He tried to sound nonchalant, but Quinn could see he was pleased to see her.

"I'm taking you home."

"I'm all right, really."

"I know, but I am still taking you home. I will make you dinner and keep you company until it's time for bed."

"Will you read me a bedtime story?" Rhys asked, unable to keep the sarcasm out of his voice. "I feel like a toddler."

"Can't you just graciously accept?"

"I'm not very good at accepting sympathy."

"Don't I know it. How about accepting company?"

"That I can do. Can we have some wine with dinner?" Rhys asked, blessing her with a wry smile.

"Absolutely not. You can have something starchy to soak up the bile in your stomach and a cup of sweet black tea."

"So no sticky toffee pudding then?"

"You're not going to make this easy, are you?"

"Nope. Aren't you off to Berwick on Saturday?" Rhys asked as he followed Quinn out the door, carrying the plastic bag filled with his possessions.

"Yes, we're leaving first thing Saturday morning."

"Quinn, really, go home. You have much to do, and I'll be all right on my own. I'll have some tea and toast and put myself to bed."

"Keep walking, mister," Quinn said. She hailed a cab and held the door open for Rhys. He tried to pretend he was well, but he was still weak and unsteady on his feet.

"Please don't tell Mrs. Kent I've been released. Not yet," Rhys pleaded as they alighted from the taxi in front of his house. "If the pills and booze don't kill me, she will."

"Don't be uncharitable. She worries about you."

"I know, but I already have a mother, and she gave me such an earful, I kind of wish I'd died."

Mrs. Kent poked her head out the door. "Rhys, how are you, love? I've been looking out for you since I came back from the doctor. Shall I come up? I made some soup."

"Thank you, Mrs. Kent. Perhaps tomorrow," Rhys replied, pasting on a fake smile. "Dr. Allenby has a fun-filled evening planned for me."

Mrs. Kent threw Quinn a suspicious look but got the message and retreated back to her flat.

Rhys tossed his coat on a chair and sat heavily on the sofa, leaning his head against the back and closing his eyes. Despite putting on a brave face, he still looked like death warmed over.

"Toast and egg or pasta?"

"Can't I have some meat?" Rhys complained. "I've had nothing but broth and mashed potatoes for two days."

"No, you can't. You've just had your stomach pumped."

"Fine. Toast and egg then. Will you make me some soldiers?" Rhys asked, clearly trying to annoy her since she wouldn't relent.

"Only if you really want me to."

Quinn put on the kettle, and went to work on Rhys's bland supper. He came into the kitchen, sat down at the table, and propped his head with his hands. He looked miserable.

Quinn placed a mug of tea before him. "When are you off to Wales?"

"I'll leave tomorrow."

"Are you sure you feel up to it?"

"I'll be all right. I just need to get out of London for a few days. My mum will feed and coddle me until I'm ready to scream. Coming back will be a treat."

Quinn placed a plate in front of Rhys and took a seat across from him. She wrapped her hands around her own mug of tea. "Eat."

Rhys nodded, but didn't pick up his fork. He paled when he looked at the egg. "I don't think I can."

"Have a bit of toast then."

Rhys picked up a piece of toast and bit into it experimentally. He washed it down with a gulp of tea. "It's too sweet. I don't usually take sugar."

"Sweet tea is good for settling the stomach."

He took another sip, his expression pained. "Want some?" he asked as he pushed his plate toward Quinn.

She accepted a piece of toast and munched on it silently. She wasn't at all sure what to say to him. Rhys didn't want her pity. He'd carry the scars of what had happened for the rest of his life, but no one would ever see the cracks in the façade. He would return to work after Christmas, refreshed, restored, and brusque as ever. Haley would become a thing of the past, as would the baby he'd so longed for.

Quinn's mobile rang, and she pulled it out, thinking it might be Gabe, but it was Drew Camden.

"Hi, Drew," she said warily. She no longer held out any hope that Drew would find Quentin. He seemed to have exhausted all his resources, both personal and professional, since his mates on the force couldn't do anything more for him. "Any news?"

There was a sigh on the other end. "No, but I do have a Christmas treat for you."

"Oh?"

"I received a packet from Jesse Holt today. He sent me some photos he found. I thought you might like to see what your sister looked like."

Quinn's breath caught in her throat. She still had no idea what Quentin looked like. "Text me a photo. Right now."

"You got it. I'll drop the rest by your flat after Christmas."

"Yes. Thanks, Drew. Happy Christmas."

"You too, Quinn. And don't despair. 2015 is the year we find Quentin."

Quinn ended the call and stared at her phone, drumming her fingers on the table in her impatience. The phone buzzed when a new text popped up. With shaking hands, Quinn picked up the mobile and opened the image Drew had forwarded. There she was —Quentin. She looked to be about twenty in the photo. She had dark wavy hair and large dark eyes, so like Seth's. She was smiling shyly, looking as if she'd been deep in thought when someone called her name.

Quinn's vision blurred as she gently touched the screen with her finger. "Hey there, sister."

"Let me see," Rhys said. "Does she look like you?"

"A bit. She looks more like Seth, I think. I look like Sylvia."

Rhys held out his hand for the phone and stared at the image, his brow furrowing in concentration. "Quinn, I know her."

"What?"

"I know her. I've met her several times, in fact. She's a photographer."

"Are you sure?"

"Yes, I am. She's a bit thinner now, and has shorter hair, but it's definitely the same woman."

"Name! Give me a name," Quinn cried. Now that she was so close to finding her sister, she couldn't wait another second.

"Jo Turing."

"What? Like Alan Turing?"

"Yes. I thought she might have been distantly related, since he was gay and never had children of his own. Her company is called Enigma Enterprises."

"Jesse Holt said she was mad for history. Of course she would take a name that'd mean something to her. She called herself after the man who changed the course of the war when he invented the Enigma machine. My God, Rhys, couldn't you have said something sooner?"

Rhys gaped at her. "How could I have known Jo Turing was Quentin Crawford? There is a resemblance between you two, but not enough to make your relationship obvious. She's very different from you."

"In what way?"

"She's all sharp angles, where you're gentle curves."

Quinn gave Rhys the gimlet stare. "Rhys?"

"No. I didn't sleep with her, if that's what you're asking. We chatted several times and butted heads, but that's all."

"So what was she like?"

"Intelligent, funny, sarcastic," he added with a smirk. "Sounds just like someone else I know."

"Oh God, Rhys. I must speak to her. Now. Today."

"My computer is in my study. There's no password. Go to it."

Quinn raced up the stairs and turned on the computer. It seemed to take forever to boot up. At last, the home screen came up and she googled Jo Turing. Hundreds of entries popped up. Jo had taken several award-winning photos, and there were snaps from various parties and press events. One photo in particular caught

Quinn's eye. It was of Quentin, just staring into the camera, much as she had when she was twenty, her gaze earnest, a small smile playing about her lips. She held a professional-looking Nikon in her hands as if she'd just taken a photo and lowered the camera. Quinn looked into her sister's face and felt as if she'd known her all her life.

"Aha, Enigma Enterprises," Quinn muttered under her breath as she clicked on the website. There was no phone number for Quentin—or Jo, as she had to think of her now—only an email address, a Facebook page, and a Twitter account. Quinn had no desire to send a message and be left in limbo to await a response. She wanted to contact Jo directly, and there was a telephone number for her agent. Quinn grabbed the phone and dialed. It was after five p.m. on a Thursday before Christmas. There'd probably be no answer, but she had to try.

A man answered on the third ring. "Charles Sutcliffe."

"Mr. Sutcliffe, my name is Quinn Russell. You might know me as Dr. Quinn Allenby," she added. The man was in the entertainment industry, so he might have heard of her, and that would give her credibility in his eyes.

"The archeologist?" His tone warmed considerably. "I'm a fan of your new program."

"Mr. Sutcliffe, I'm looking for Quent—Jo Turing. I must speak to her urgently."

"Do you know Jo?"

"No, but I will. I must. I'm her twin sister. I've only just recently found out," Quinn prattled on. She was so nervous, her hands were shaking. She was so close. So close.

"Dr. Allenby, I haven't heard from Jo in several months. She's been off the grid."

"What do you mean, 'off the grid'?"

"Jo goes to dangerous places. She's not someone who takes snaps of flowers and puppies, or adorable children. She goes into war zones and photographs human tragedy—life, death, and suffering. She takes risks."

"Where was she the last time you heard from her? And when was it?"

"Kabul. September."

Quinn sank into Rhys's chair. There had been two deadly suicide bombings in Kabul just that month. "Oh God," she moaned.

"Look, there's no reason to suspect the worst. She's done this before. She just goes off sometimes. She always comes back."

"Has she ever been gone this long without checking in?"

"No," Charles Sutcliffe admitted. "The longest was two months."

"So she's been out there for three months without contacting anyone?"

"Yes, I'm afraid so."

"Have you alerted the authorities?"

"I've spoken to someone at the British Embassy in Kabul. They're keeping an eye out for her."

"An eye?" Quinn exclaimed.

"Look, Dr. Allenby, there's no reason to panic. She'll turn up. She always does."

"Thank you, Mr. Sutcliff. Happy Christmas," Quinn said and hung up.

"Well?" Rhys asked when she came back into the kitchen.

"She hasn't been heard from in three months. Her last known location was Kabul," Quinn replied as she slid back into her chair. Standing was too much of an effort when her legs felt like jelly.

"Right."

"Rhys, I think she's missing."

"You don't know that."

"She hasn't been in contact in months. No wonder she never responded to my letter. She probably never received it. Rhys, who, in today's day and age, goes silent for three months?"

"Perhaps she has no access to the internet or a telephone."

"Exactly."

Rhys stared at her. "Quinn, what are you saying?"

"I'm saying that something has happened to her. I can feel it. It's like there's a void in my gut that's telling me something's wrong."

"Quinn, Jo Turing is a professional. She knows what she's doing, and I'm sure that if anything happened to her, we'd have heard about it by now. There are reporters from all over the world stationed in the Middle East. Her disappearance would have made headlines."

"What if no one's realized?"

"Someone would have. Stop fretting. She will return, and then you two will have a long-overdue reunion. I know you're desperate to finally meet her, but you must be patient. It will happen."

Quinn nodded. "I know. I just feel so helpless."

"Quinn, you now know who she is and how to contact her. That's tremendous progress. And I'm sure her agent will tell her you rang as soon as Jo checks in with him. Go to Berwick and have a wonderful Christmas with your family. You will meet Jo in the New Year. It's a certainty."

"I have to tell Logan. And Seth."

"Go on, then. Honestly, I'm ready for bed anyway. I'm exhausted."

"You've barely eaten."

"I'll be all right. I promise. I just need a little time to grieve my loss."

Quinn walked around the table, put her arms around Rhys, and pressed her cheek to his temple. Rhys leaned against her. There was no need to say any more.

FIFTY-SEVEN
JULY 1919

London, England

A reluctant sun emerged from behind the clouds and shone lazily on the park, dispelling the gauzy mist of the early hours. Valentina strode along, her gait that of an elderly lady out for her morning stroll. She felt heavy, inside and out, her limbs dragging like a plow behind a horse. She'd asked Alexei to meet her in St. James Park since she didn't trust herself to talk to him at the hotel and trying to have a conversation at the house was virtually impossible. Elena, Tanya, and Kolya were so giddy at the sight of him, they didn't give him and Valentina a moment's privacy, much less a chance to have an uninterrupted conversation. Elena assumed that now that Alexei had found them, he'd remain in England and make a life with her daughter. She was swept along on Alexei's enthusiasm, making plans for a future that could never be.

Tanya, who'd loved Alexei since she was a child, was now shy around him, her eyes following him about the room like those of a devoted puppy. She blushed whenever he spoke to her and had nearly fainted when Alexei caught her up in a bear hug and kissed her the first time they saw each other again. Tanya was happy for her sister, but Valentina could see that the seeds of envy planted years ago had grown into sturdy, green shoots of jealousy.

Valentina stopped for a second and stared out over the pond, where ducks floated along merrily, quacking to their hearts' content. It was such a peaceful scene, it nearly made her cry. Why couldn't Alexei have found them nine months ago? Everything would have been so different then. She'd have never learned the truth of Dmitri's plans for her and would have married Alexei without delay.

Valentina shook her head, tired of the never-ending internal argument. Had she gone off with Alexei, Dmitri would have used Tanya and ruined her life instead. At least Tanya still had a chance at happiness and freedom from shame. If Valentina had accomplished anything of value in her life, it was that she'd saved her sister from ruin. And she'd do it again. The only thing she might have done differently was kill Dmitri before he had a chance to force her into prostitution. But then again, she'd never have been able to bring herself to commit murder had her soul not been torn to shreds by Dmitri's depravity and her own humiliation. No, things couldn't have happened any other way, and there was no point in giving in to regret.

Valentina smiled sadly when she saw Alexei striding toward her. For just a moment, as the sun peeked from behind a passing cloud and shone in her eyes, she imagined he was wearing his cavalry uniform, his sabre at his side and his cap perched on his blond hair at a rakish angle, but Alexei was wearing civilian clothes. The brim of his hat shaded his eyes and his gray suit looked commonplace among the well-dressed passersby who were free to go for a walk during business hours.

"Valya," Alexei exclaimed. "You look radiant."

Hardly, Valentina thought bitterly. *Devastated, miserable, devoid of all hope for the future, but surely not radiant.*

"I'm glad you wanted to meet at the park. I love your family, but they barely let me draw breath without asking if I'm all right or if I urgently require a cup of tea."

"They're so happy you're all right."

"I know. Seeing them again has been..."

"Bittersweet," Valentina finished for him.

"Yes."

Alexei gave her his arm and they strolled along, listening to the soothing sounds of nature. The quacking of ducks, the trilling of birds, the rustle of leaves overhead were all so pleasant on this summer morning that for a moment Valentina wondered if she might give in to the beauty around her and allow herself to hope, but then she felt a wave of dizziness followed by the telltale nausea that had plagued her for the past few weeks, and steeled her resolve.

"Alyosha, we must talk." She'd put off this conversation for several weeks, alternating between unshakable resolve and desperate hope that she might find another solution to her dilemma. She'd been unable to deny herself the joy of spending time with him, and loving him in a way a wife loved her husband, but now she no longer had a choice. Circumstances were forcing her to act.

Alexei smiled serenely at her. "Isn't that what we are doing? Do you think we could escape the city for a few days and go to the seaside? The weather is so lovely."

"Alyosha, please, let me talk."

"Go on, then." He stopped walking and turned to face her, his eyes growing serious and the easy smile sliding off his face.

"You must return to France."

"Why?"

"Because there can be no future for us, and the longer you remain in London, the more tongues will wag."

"Wag about what?"

"I can't marry you, Alyosha."

"I know. I understand. I told you I'd wait, and I haven't changed my mind. I will have to go to France to see to my affairs, but then I will return. I might even convince Papa and Sveta to come with me. We'll make a life here—all of us."

Valentina shook her head like a stubborn donkey. "You don't understand. You must leave for good. There's no future for us, Alyosha. Things have changed."

"Have they changed so much that we can't move past them?"

"Yes."

"In what way?"

"I'm married," Valentina exclaimed. Oh, why was he making this so difficult?

"Valya, your husband has been missing for two months. It's highly unlikely he's coming back. Now, I realize you're consumed with worry for him, but all the evidence points to the fact that he's no longer with us. I know you need time to grieve, and I won't rush you into anything. I promise."

"Alyosha, I cannot move forward from this. Not yet. Maybe not ever."

"Why?" Alexei exclaimed. "Surely, in a year's time..."

"No. You must not ask me again."

Alexei's eyes widened with sudden understanding. "You really loved him, despite what you said before. You're hoping he'll return, aren't you? When we made love, you weren't welcoming me into your life, you were saying goodbye. You were seeking closure to something that could never be. It was an odd way of going about it. I never expected you to toy with me so cruelly."

"I wasn't toying with you."

"Weren't you? What kind of woman goes to bed with a man and then rejects him when he wants nothing more than to make a life with her, honestly and openly, in a relationship sanctioned by God?"

"It wouldn't be a relationship sanctioned by God though, would it? I'm married to another man and will remain so for another seven years. Are you prepared to wait that long, and court me in a chaste and respectful fashion?"

"Chaste? After what we've already done, more than once?"

"Alyosha, I was overjoyed to see you. I wasn't thinking straight. I was lonely, frightened, and emotionally overwrought. Seeing you was like breaking the surface and gulping lifesaving air when you think you're drowning and can feel yourself sinking to the bottom. But I can't continue to sleep with you. That's adultery."

"You don't love me," Alexei whispered. His eyes shone with tears. "You don't love me anymore. Maybe you never did. You were a young, impressionable girl, influenced by the wishes of your parents. You'd never known anyone but me, but you've been on your own for nearly two years. You've matured, grown into a woman, and you realized that I was nothing more than a childhood dream. Perhaps you've even learned what you like in bed, and I wasn't able to give that to you, something you realized when you compared me to your husband."

"I never meant to hurt you."

"I know that. You thought I was dead and moved on with your life. Perhaps I should have moved on with mine, but I spent every day longing for you and dreaming of the day I'd finally find you. I never imagined I'd make such a fool of myself."

"Alyosha, please. I want to offer you something in recompense."

"What can you possibly offer me?"

Valentina took a deep breath and plunged in. "Tanya."

"What?"

"I want you to marry Tanya."

"Are you mad? She's a child."

"She's a child who's in love with you. Always has been. She'll be able to give you the kind of pure, innocent love I am no longer capable of. She'll make you happy."

Alexei stared at her, as if seeing her for the first time. "Are you seriously doing this?"

"Yes. Please, think about it."

"Valya, I will return to the hotel, pack my belongings, and go back to France, where I will make a future for myself. I won't spend my life pining for someone who doesn't want me. I ask you again. Are you sure about this? Is your decision final?"

"Yes, it is. I know you need time to come to terms with your disappointment, but please don't turn your back on Tanya. She loves you, Alyosha. Probably more than I ever did," Valentina added, twisting the knife a little deeper to make sure he let go of her.

"Goodbye, Valya. I hope you find peace and happiness. I won't trouble you again."

Alexei leaned in and kissed her cheek, then turned on his heel and walked away, his back ramrod straight, his shoulders stiff. He never looked back. He wouldn't allow himself that moment of weakness. He was a soldier; he'd been taught to hide his pain.

Valentina found a bench and sat down. She wanted to howl with grief, to run after Alexei and beg for his forgiveness, to disappear off the face of the earth, but she no longer had that option. She had to live, and she had to put on a brave face and look to the future. There was a tiny life growing inside her, and in the eyes of the world, that life was the result of her brief marriage. Her child would be accepted as the son or daughter of Dmitri Ostrov, his legacy. She couldn't allow her baby to be tainted with scandal, whispered about and called a bastard. She couldn't allow her child to believe that its mother had fallen into bed with another man weeks after the disappearance of her husband and got pregnant. No, the future was no longer about her. It was about the little person who'd suddenly given her a reason to go on. She would remain where she was, have her baby, and look after her family. That was her role now, her purpose.

Valentina got to her feet and began to walk, her back ramrod straight, her shoulders stiff. She was a soldier too, and she'd learned to hide her pain.

FIFTY-EIGHT
DECEMBER 2014

Berwick-Upon-Tweed, Northumberland

Christmas morning dawned bitterly cold. The old casement windows were decorated with a lacy pattern of frost and the radiator made pitiful sounds as it worked overtime to heat the drafty old house. It was still early, but Emma would wake soon. She rarely slept in, but today of all days she'd be eager to rise and open her presents. Quinn checked on Alex, who was sleeping peacefully in the portable cot they'd brought from London. Gabe was asleep as well, his face peaceful and relaxed.

Quinn considered waking him but changed her mind. She'd let him sleep a little longer while she saw to Emma's present. She got out of bed, pulled on her warm dressing gown, and quietly made her way downstairs and into the mudroom. The puppy was wide awake. It yapped eagerly and wagged its tail, hoping for a treat. "There you are," Quinn said as she set a bowl of dog food in front of it and made sure it had enough water. "Enjoy. I'm sure Grandma Phoebe will have a lovely treat for you after Christmas dinner, but for now, this will have to do."

She petted the dog affectionately as it began to eat. "I'll be back for you later," she promised.

Quinn closed the door behind her and padded into the front room, where a beautiful Christmas tree stood in pride of place. This was a bittersweet Christmas in so many ways. It was her first as a wife and mother, the first without Graeme, and the last in this house. It was also the first time Quinn felt a gaping hole where her sister should be. She'd shared her concerns about Jo's well-being with Gabe, but like Rhys, he'd dismissed them and attributed her anxiety to her desperate desire to finally meet Jo. She didn't persist. Having a blazing row with Gabe on Christmas Eve would accomplish little, and given his track record, he was probably right in his belief that Jo would come back after the New Year and contact Quinn.

Quinn smiled brightly as Emma came skipping down the stairs, with Gabe behind her, Alex in his arms. The baby was wide awake, his round blue eyes peering around with great interest, especially when he saw the shiny baubles on the tree. Quinn reached out and Gabe handed him over, his gaze meeting hers over Emma's head.

"Where are my presents?" Emma demanded.

"Under the tree. Don't you want to wait for Grandma Phoebe?" Gabe asked.

"I'm here. I wouldn't dare keep my granddaughter waiting," Phoebe said as she appeared at the top of the stairs in her paisley dressing gown.

Emma raced toward the tree and began to rummage through the pile of gifts, looking for the packages with her name on them. She ripped into them, oohing over a bedroom set for her American Girl doll, sent by Seth, flipping through the lovely picture books from Phoebe, and smiling gleefully at the children's laptop Quinn and Gabe bought to help with her reading and sums. She'd also be able to play games and listen to music. Of course, being only five, she assumed the gifts were from Father Christmas.

"Do you like your presents?" Gabe asked innocently.

"Yes, thank you." Emma dutifully kissed each of them in turn. "They are wonderful." Quinn tried to hide her smile as she heard the quiver of disappointment in Emma's voice. "Grandma Phoebe, maybe you can read me a story later?"

"Of course, darling, but I think you might be busy later."

"With what?" Emma asked, her shoulders drooping in dejection.

"With this." Gabe had melted away and reappeared, holding the sweet little spaniel in his arms. Its dark eyes glowed with curiosity, and it let out a woof of joy when it saw the tree.

Emma's mouth dropped open as her eyes filled with tears of happiness. "Is he for me?" she whispered.

"Yes, he is. He's two months old, but he doesn't have a proper name yet. We thought you'd like to name him," Gabe said as he set the puppy on the floor. It made a dash toward the tree, barking happily at the strips of torn wrapping paper. Buster growled and bared his teeth, but Phoebe instantly distracted him by calling out, "Buster, walkies."

Buster ran toward the door, eager to get outside. Phoebe opened the front door and let him out to do his business. He'd run around for a while and come back when he got hungry.

"Oh, he's gorgeous, Dad. And Mum," Emma added, realizing she'd left out Quinn. "I love him." She was already on her knees, trying to scoop up the overexcited puppy. "Come here, Rufus."

"Rufus?" Quinn and Gabe asked in unison.

"Yes. What's wrong with Rufus?" Emma demanded.

"Absolutely nothing," Gabe replied. "Rufus Russell it is. I have something for you too," he said softly to Quinn, his eyes glowing. "Come back upstairs."

"Gabe, this is hardly the time."

"Just come up." Gabe chuckled as he sprinted up the stairs.

"I'll get breakfast started," Phoebe said to Quinn's retreating back.

Gabe was sitting on the bed when Quinn came into the bedroom. He was smiling happily, a small, beautifully wrapped box in his hands. Quinn set Alex down on the bed and accepted the package, ready to love whatever Gabe got her. She didn't really need any jewelry, but men always thought it was the best gift, and she wasn't about to argue. Quinn tore off the festive paper and took off the lid. Inside was a shiny new key.

"What does this open?" she asked, turning the key over in her hands.

"Our house."

"You bought a house? Without consulting me?" Quinn gasped.

"I didn't need to consult you," Gabe replied smugly. "You told me you loved it."

"Did I?"

"We walked past this house, and you stopped and said that you'd love to live in a house just like that one. You said it was perfect."

"You mean that lovely Georgian terrace house we saw in South Kensington? The one with the red door?"

"That's the one."

"Oh, Gabe!" she squealed. "I can't believe it."

"There's a virtual tour online. You can see all the rooms. I put down a deposit, but if you don't like it anymore, I can still back out. I told the estate agent I needed until Boxing Day. I just really wanted to surprise you." Gabe was glowing like a Christmas candle, proud of himself for pulling off this feat.

"I love it. And I love you. But where did you get the money for a down payment?"

"Someone made an offer on my parents' house. They are willing to pay the asking price, which is unheard of in the current market. Mum and I discussed it and accepted the offer. The buyer has offered a sizeable down payment. I used it to secure the house in Kensington."

"That's brilliant. I can't wait. Now we have to put my chapel on the market." Quinn had been putting off listing her lovely chapel with an estate agent.

"There's no need. I know how much you love it, and the money from the sale of this house will be enough to pay the death duties, set my mum up in a retirement cottage, and cover the down payment on the Kensington house."

"Really?"

"Really. You can still use the chapel as a retreat."

Quinn walked into Gabe's arms and lowered her head to kiss him. She hadn't expected such a lovely surprise this Christmas, especially given her current mood.

"2015 will be a wonderful year," Gabe whispered as he captured her mouth in a sweet kiss. "Only good things will come our way."

"Only good things," Quinn echoed, and at that moment she totally believed it.

"Why don't you put Alex in his cot for a few minutes?" Gabe suggested, giving her a seductive look.

"Mum, Dad, where are you?" Emma cried as she burst into the room. "Can I go play outside with Rufus? Grandma Phoebe says I need to put him on a leash or he might run off."

"Later," Gabe said, giving Quinn a meaningful look.

"Not later. Now!" Emma exclaimed, misunderstanding Gabe's promise. "I want to go NOW!"

"All right, Miss Bossy Boots. Let's go get that leash," Gabe said as he grabbed his jumper and followed Emma out the door.

Quinn sank into the mattress and closed her eyes. Despite her worry for Jo, she felt happy and at peace. Their own house. She couldn't wait. How wonderful it would be not to feel cramped anymore. Alex would have his own room and wouldn't have to sleep in a cot in their bedroom anymore. Quinn thought about her beloved chapel. It had been a home and a refuge, but she was ready to let it go. She didn't need it anymore. She now had a family, and the chapel was really only big enough for two. It was a part of her past but would not fit into her future. It was time to let it go, since the next chapter was about to begin.

Quinn scooped up the baby and placed him on her chest, his face level with hers. "Happy Christmas, my little man," she cooed. The baby smiled and rested his nose against hers, his eyes an inch away from hers. Quinn laughed joyfully. "You are the best gift I could have asked for."

She kissed Alex on the tip of his nose and got up. "Come on. It's time to make breakfast and open the rest of the presents. I could be wrong, but I think there is something there for you, and you're going to like it. Well, you'll probably enjoy playing with the box more, but still," she joked.

The aroma of frying bacon and toast began to waft from the kitchen, and Quinn headed toward the heavenly smell, glad there was no longer a body beneath the black-and-white tiles. She saw Emma and Gabe running around outside, Rufus and Buster barking as they chased the ball Emma tossed to Gabe.

"I wish Graeme were here to see this," Phoebe said as she gazed out the window. "He'd be so happy."

Quinn put her arm around Phoebe, and they stood together, watching their family.

FIFTY-NINE
JANUARY 2015

London, England

Quinn accepted a cup of tea from Rhiannan and leaned back in her chair, waiting to hear what Rhys had to say. He'd sounded very mysterious on the phone, refusing to tell her why he wanted to see her in his office.

Rhys took a sip of his espresso and smiled at Quinn. He looked almost like his old self, so she didn't ask about his trip to Wales. It had obviously helped him deal with his loss, although the pain in his eyes was still there, barely hidden.

"So, what was so urgent?" Quinn asked.

"I have two wonderful surprises for you. You can thank me later," he added with a smug grin.

"The only wonderful surprise would be a month off between filming so I can pack up the flat and set up my new house. Oh, Rhys, it's gorgeous. I can't wait for you to see it."

"I'm very happy for you, but unfortunately a month off is not part of my gift just now." Rhys took a manila envelope out of the top drawer of his desk and slid it toward her.

"What's that?"

"Natalia Swift sent it to me. Take a look."

EPILOGUE
JUNE 1925

London, England

Valentina set aside the storybook and gently brushed a blond curl away from the child's forehead. He looked peaceful in sleep, his cheeks rosy with good health. He'd exhausted himself running in the park and fallen asleep before she even finished the story. The midafternoon light filtered through the curtains, casting a golden glow onto the sleeping boy. At five, he was intelligent, precocious, and surprisingly artistic. He could already pick out a melody on the piano in the parlor and had asked for music lessons.

Valentina's heart melted as she gazed at her son. For the first few years of his life, she'd obsessed about Michael's paternity, but by the time he turned three, she'd been no closer to figuring out who'd fathered him. He'd arrived in February of 1920, a healthy baby boy of average weight and height. He might have been a full-term baby, or he might have come a few weeks early.

Valentina had stared at the baby for hours, desperate to find some hint of Alexei in his round face and blue eyes, but she could never be sure. Ian Murdoch had been fair as well, with light blond hair and blue eyes, and she'd heard that French letters weren't one hundred percent effective against pregnancy. She'd never know the truth, so she'd given up trying to find it. Misha, which meant "little bear" in Russian, was hers and hers alone. He was her reason for being, her pride and joy, and she would love him enough for two parents and give him the security every child needed. She'd refused to hire a nanny and had taken care of him herself until he turned three, but then decided that Misha would be just fine with his aunt and grandmother while she took a couple of classes to better her knowledge of English. Reading novels wasn't enough.

She'd loved writing for the ladies' paper and had secret aspirations of becoming a freelance journalist once Misha was old enough to start school. She hadn't written anything since the summer of 1919 but had kept up with the paper for the first year after Dmitri's death. Tanya had always brought her a copy from church once Valentina got too heavily pregnant to attend, but by the time she began attending services again after Michael's birth, Stanislav had been gone. Perhaps he'd no longer had time to publish two newspapers once he married Esther, or had decided that the return wasn't worth the time he invested every week into translating and writing the articles, setting type, and printing numerous copies.

Valentina would have liked to see him again but didn't think it appropriate to seek him out at his workplace. Things had changed for them both, and even though she missed her friend, it was time to let go and focus on her new life. She had a child to raise and several businesses to run. Her days were full, but her nights were long and lonely. Several eligible bachelors had tried to spark her interest, but although they were all nice men, she simply couldn't bring herself to agree to a date. She wasn't ready to open her heart to anyone, or give her trust to someone who might not be worthy of it. She tried not to think about Alexei. She mostly succeeded during the day, but when she lay in bed at night, her love-starved body ached for his touch and she wondered if she'd done the right thing in driving him away.

But life had moved on for Alexei as it had for her. The summer after Misha's birth, Valentina had sent Tanya and Elena to Paris to visit with Alexei's family. She'd known Alexei would never return to England, but she hadn't given up hope of a match for Tanya. She knew them both well enough to believe they'd be happy together, once the ghosts of the past were finally laid to rest. She'd given Alexei sufficient time to grieve his loss, and Tanya was more woman than girl by the time she turned seventeen, and more than ready for the highs and lows of her first romantic relationship.

Valentina sighed. Tanya and Alexei were expecting their first child in September. She was happy for them, truly she was, but she was glad Tanya had gone to live with Alexei in Paris after their wedding because seeing them together on a regular basis would be more than she could bear. She'd barely survived the wedding and cried herself to sleep on their wedding night, tormented by the knowledge that while she tossed and turned in her lonely bed, Alexei was making love to his adoring new wife. She hadn't seen him since, but his face was burned into her memory, his voice still so familiar when she dreamed of him, and his touch so intimate as to make her cry out with longing. She was only twenty-five, but she felt like a woman of eighty who spent her days reminiscing about her youth and reliving past glories. She knew it was time to move on but simply couldn't find the strength to let go.

Valentina let herself out of Misha's room and walked quietly down the corridor, so as not to wake him. She'd go downstairs and have a cup of tea in the garden. Maybe read a while. She came face-to-face with Mrs. Nemirovsky just as she reached the bottom of the stairs. The housekeeper seemed to be waiting for her.

"There's a gentleman to see you, Mrs. Ostrov."

"I'm not expecting anyone. Who is it?"

The housekeeper handed her a card. "Stanley Swift, Swift Publishing," Valentina read. "I have no idea who he is."

"Shall I ask him to leave?"

"No. I'll see what he wants."

Valentina walked into the parlor. Her heart skipped a beat when she saw a man standing by the window, looking out, hands clasped behind his back. He looked just like Alexei had the day he walked back into her life. Except this man was dark, his curly hair neatly trimmed and his olive skin illuminated by the afternoon light streaming through the window. He turned around and Valentina's face broke into a joyful grin.

"Stanley Swift?" she asked, laughing as she came forward to take his outstretched hands.

"I anglicized the name to suit my new role as respected publisher. What do you think?" Stanislav asked, grinning.

"I think I like it, Mr. Swift. It suits you."

"How have you been, Valentina? How's your boy?"

"I'm well, and Misha is a delight."

"And the rest of your family?"

"My mother is well. She's resting at the moment. Tanya is married and living in France, and Kolya is still at school. He's thirteen now," Valentina added. "And you? How's your wife? Do you have any children?"

"Esther died two years ago, giving birth to our first child. The baby died with her. The cord had been wrapped around his neck and he suffocated during the birth." Stanislav spoke the words calmly, but Valentina saw the depth of his loss in his eyes. He was still grieving for his family, and trying to come to terms with the injustice life sometimes dished out.

"Oh, Slava, I'm so sorry. How awful."

"It was. I didn't love Esther when I married her, but I had grown to care for her and her death left me paralyzed with grief. The only thing that kept me going was the desire to start my own publishing house someday. Max and I are partners in our new venture."

"How is Max?"

"He's married, with two children, and Sarah is expecting her first. They are happy," Stanislav added, the desolation in his voice underlining the fact that he wasn't.

"Would you like some tea? We can have it in the garden."

"That would be lovely."

Stanislav followed Valentina out into the garden and took a seat across from her. They made small talk until Mrs. Nemirovsky brought out tea and a plate of freshly baked scones, accompanied by clotted cream and strawberry jam. A small jug of milk was next to the saucer of lemon slices on the tray.

Valentina reached for the milk and added some to her tea. "I'm embracing the English ways," she said in response to Stanislav's look of surprise.

"You'll never see me refuse a freshly baked scone," he said and helped himself to some jam. "Valentina, I'm very happy to see you, but this isn't purely a social call, although I've thought of coming by many times."

"Why didn't you?"

"You were grieving for your husband and coping with motherhood on your own. It didn't seem appropriate. Besides, I don't think Esther would have liked it. She was jealous of you."

"She had no reason to be."

Stanislav blushed and looked away. "She had every reason," he said softly.

Valentina bowed her head and smiled. She'd guessed at Slava's feelings for her but never gave them much thought. He came from a poor Jewish family and she was the daughter of a Russian count— not exactly an acceptable match in anyone's eyes. But now they were both widowed, and although she went to church regularly, she no longer had any faith in God. He'd let her down too many times, and she still hadn't forgiven him. It seemed that Stanislav hadn't fared much better in the faith department, since he was here on a Saturday afternoon when he would normally have been observing the Sabbath with his family.

"Valentina, I know you are busy running your late husband's businesses, but you really enjoyed writing your column and you were very good at it. You understood what was important to women, both young and old. I thought you might like to try your hand at journalism again. I've come to ask you to write for my new publication. It's a weekly magazine for women, only this time it's in

English, and it has much wider circulation. You can write under a pseudonym, if you like, to maintain your privacy."

"I'm through hiding, Slava. I would love to write for your publication, but I will do so under my own name. I might shorten it to Tina, though. Sounds more anglicized."

"I'm thrilled to hear it. I've hired a young woman who's recently returned from Paris to cover fashion, and a homosexual screenplay writer to spice up the society pages, but I'd like you to report on current events and their impact on women's lives. In the past, you did it with such insight and compassion."

"All right. I accept. When is my first assignment due?"

"How about next Saturday?" Stanislav asked. "Perhaps we can discuss it over dinner." They were talking about her article, but the hope in his hazel eyes betrayed him. He was asking her on a date. Stanislav set down his teacup, sat up straighter, and lifted his chin, as if preparing himself for the blow of rejection.

"Won't your family object to you having dinner with a shiksa?" Valentina asked, cautiously probing the situation. Where Stanislav came from, there was no worse fate for a mother than her son courting a gentile.

"Valya, I've done my duty to my family. I married a girl of their choice, I've supported my parents and looked after my siblings until they were ready to stand on their own two feet. But I'm thirty now. I'm widowed, and I finally have something to call my own. I will live my life on my own terms, and if my family cares for me, they will accept that. So, is that a yes to dinner?"

Valentina smiled into his eyes. She didn't think she'd ever feel at ease with anyone but Alexei, but she trusted this man, and she liked him. He had integrity, determination, and most of all, genuine warmth and compassion. Dinner didn't obligate either one of them to anything, but as they gazed at each other in that shady garden, they both knew it did. If she said yes, there'd be no going back for either of them.

"Yes," she said, her voice clear and firm. "Yes."

Slava's eyes lit up and his shoulders slumped with relief, and suddenly, Valentina knew with unwavering certainty that if she told him the truth of what had happened to her, he wouldn't condemn her, nor would he think any less of her. She'd never burden him with the knowledge of what she'd done, but knowing that she could made all the difference. And maybe in time...

A LETTER FROM THE AUTHOR

I hope you've enjoyed this installment of the Echoes from the Past series. If you want to join other readers in hearing all about my new releases and bonus content, you can sign up for my newsletter.

www.stormpublishing.co/irina-shapiro

The Unseen delves into the Russian Revolution and my own family's background. Sadly, I don't come from royalty or even nobility, but the character of Stanislav is based on my grandfather Naum, who was a very enterprising young man and published his own newspaper during his student days. He was the first writer in the family, and whatever creative talents I possess, I owe to him.

I would also like to thank Rhiannan Kristina and Mary Kent-Wade for allowing me to use their names as monikers for the characters in this story.

I love hearing your thoughts, so if you enjoyed this book and could spare a few moments to leave a review, that would be hugely appreciated. Even a short review can make all the difference in encouraging a reader to discover my books for the first time. Thank you so much.

And, as always, thank you for your support. I hope you'll stay in touch—I have so many more stories and ideas to entertain you with!

Irina

KEEP IN TOUCH WITH THE AUTHOR

irinashapiroauthor.com

facebook.com/IrinaShapiro2
x.com/IrinaShapiro2
instagram.com/irina_shapiro_author